RECKLESS DISREGARD

ALSO BY ROBERT ROTSTEIN

Corrupt Practices

RECKLESS DISREGARD

A Parker Stern Novel

ROBERT ROTSTEIN

SEVENTH STREET BOOKS®
AN IMPRINT OF PROMETHEUS BOOKS
59 JOHN GLENN DRIVE • AMHERST, NY 14228
www.seventhstreetbooks.com

Published 2014 by Seventh Street Books®, an imprint of Prometheus Books

Cover image © Tony Rowell/Corbis
Cover design by Jacqueline Nasso Cooke

Inquiries should be addressed to
Seventh Street Books
59 John Glenn Drive
Amherst, New York 14228
VOICE: 716–691–0133
FAX: 716–691–0137
WWW.SEVENTHSTREETBOOKS.COM
18 17 16 15 14   5 4 3 2 1

Library of Congress Cataloging-in-Publication Data

Rotstein, Robert, 1951-
    Reckless disregard : a Parker Stern novel / by Robert Rotstein.
        pages cm
    ISBN 978-1-61614-881-2 (pbk.) • ISBN 978-1-61614-882-9 (ebook)
    I. Title.

PS3618.O8688R43 2015
813'.6—dc23
                                                                    2013047665

Printed in the United States of America

To my mother

PROLOGUE

The intro drags on too long, but everything else about the game is perfect. The woman is sexy, especially to a ten-year-old boy like Brighton. There are 3D anime-style graphics and an awesome metal-rock soundtrack. It's another soon-to-be classic video game by the developer known as Poniard.

What Brighton especially loves about *Abduction!* is how hard it plays. No super-easy, easy, or intermediate stages. Just one mode, tagged *Unattainable.* Leave it to Poniard to disrespect his audience by branding them losers. And what better way to attract their attention? *Abduction!* has already gone viral. According to the gamer blogs, no one has beaten the game yet, though it's already been out for three days. That's a long time—usually the top experts crack a new game in a couple of hours. Some bloggers write that there's no solution even though Poniard has promised there is. Brighton doesn't really expect to beat the game, but why not try?

He dims the monitor and goes down the hall to check on his aunt, who's really his great-aunt. She's in the living room, still snoring away, asleep in her ratty armchair. A cooking show is on TV, the emcee loud and energetic. An empty bottle of sauvignon blanc teeters on the edge of an end table. Several times a month, Aunt Greta drinks too much wine, letting Brighton steal a few hours of freedom. Aunt Greta doesn't approve of computer games or much of anything else that's fun.

He goes back to his bedroom, powers on the monitor, and starts *Abduction!* from the beginning. The game, like all of Poniard's offerings, starts with a short burst of classical music. Brighton read online that this music is a goof on the major studios' old-fashioned fanfares. The game itself opens with a long shot on a neon sign that says *The Tell Tale*

Bar, the *B* flickering on and off. The scene quickly shifts to an empty bar, dark and dingy. There are footsteps, and the hot woman, visible from the neck down, struts in. She's wearing a green leather jumpsuit, the neckline plunging to just above the navel, exposing a lot of breast. Her back toward the screen, she sits down on a bar stool, swivels toward the camera, and with flair scissors her legs before crossing them. Her hair, the color of animated fire, is styled in dreadlocks that fall to mid-back. Her skin is fair and freckled. Around her neck, she wears a silver chain, to which a small cross is attached.

"I'm Felicity, and this is my story." Her voice is singsong, kind of like a canary. "It's a story of love and betrayal. And blood. My blood." With her head still facing the viewer, she turns her body sideways and rests her right forearm on the bar, her green eyes narrowing to sultry slits. "Did you ever get lost? So lost you can't find your way out of the darkness? I did. One day when . . ." She sits up with a start, places an index finger to her lower lip, and shakes her head vigorously, each computer-generated dreadlock swaying in perfect rhythm to her movements. Nobody but Poniard can make a game seem so real.

"That's *so* wrong," she says in her fluty voice. "That's what they want you to think. But it's a lie. I didn't get lost at all. I was taken. Abducted by William the Conqueror and his band of thugs. You see, in this game, you not only know what the crime was, you know who committed it. But this game's not over, it's just beginning. All *you* have to do is find out how it all happened. Easy, huh? Hardly. An unattainable goal, because you can't rescue me. But there's an answer to what happened to me, I assure you. Let me show you something."

She swivels to face the bar and raises an arm toward the wall. When she snaps her fingers, a big-screen television lights up, displaying a view of the same bar, this time crowded with patrons. The picture zooms in, and the images on the TV and the computer screen merge.

Brighton pauses the video and checks the time. A few minutes after eight. He listens. Another Food Network cooking show. Aunt Greta must still be asleep, because at eight on Mondays she always watches that show with the celebrity dancers. Safe for now, he rewinds the game to get another look at Felicity's boobs and then advances to the next cutscene.

Felicity sits in a booth alone, sipping a glass of amber liquid. Everything in the scene is old-fashioned. Felicity's hair, auburn now, is piled on top of her head. She wears a black jacket over a tight black dress. The scene starts with a classic rock song. *Money for Nothing*. He knows from an Internet search that the song, by a band called *Dire Straits*, came out in 1985. So the *Abduction!* story must have happened in the eighties, a clue. One of the things that make Poniard's games so hard to beat is that you often have to get outside knowledge to advance from level to level.

Felicity gulps down her drink and slams it on the table with a cartoonish clatter. Immediately, the bartender, a tiny man with a mullet, thin face, and rattish moustache, walks out from behind the bar and brings her another.

She continues to stare straight ahead. "Thanks, Dexter." She slurs the words.

"This has to be the last one, Felicity," the bartender says in a squeaky voice that clacks at the end of each sentence. "And I shouldn't say this, but Billy's not coming. He's too much the all-powerful pooh-bah to come into a place like this anymore."

She shrieks, her laugh all the more frightening because Poniard increases the decibel level for the sound effect. Brighton flinches every time he hears it.

"Oh, Billy will come," she says. "He knows if he doesn't, he'll regret it."

The bartender shakes his head and clears the empty glass. When he turns to the side, his overlong apron string resembles a rat's tail. Poniard is really playing the rodent card with this character. Over the next minute, a succession of men approach Felicity. Each time, she shakes her head and they leave.

Two goons in identical suits sit down on each side of the booth, one blocking Felicity from leaving. Slasher film music starts playing. Brighton knows this because he secretly watched *Saw* on TV one night when Aunt Greta fell asleep. The man who sits next to Felicity is tall and burly; the one who sits across from her is short and slim. Both men are white. They have the same exaggerated kinky hair—buzz cut on the sides and absurdly high and cylindrical on top.

"Well, if it isn't George and Lennie," Felicity says.

"You're coming with us, doll," the little one rasps. "Now!"

"If you think I'm going anywhere with you, you're dumber than I thought. Now get out of my way, Einstein." She makes a move to get up, but the hulk puts his hand on her shoulder and pushes her down again. Her scarlet lips open in a newborn scream, but then there's an old-fashioned iris-in like from a silent movie, the click of a switchblade, and a starburst gleam on metal. The big man touches the pointed blade just below her left breast. Her hardened nipples poke through her dress. Aunt Greta hates Poniard's video games because she says they have too much sex and violence.

"You won't get away with this," Felicity says. "I've left—"

"Shut up," the small man says.

They stand up, making their way through the crowd of tough guys and skanky girls. The bar is filled with cigarette smoke and the sounds of loud laughter and clinking dishes. The scene shifts outdoors, skid row at nighttime, the street empty except for a homeless man—drunk, asleep, or both—curled up in the alcove of a building. Then the scene cuts to the beach, where the men drag a struggling Felicity across the sand toward the black ocean. Halfway across the beach, she loses one of her gold high-heel shoes. They half-carry her down to a motorboat tied to a pylon on the pier. Her shoulders slump, and her body caves into itself. Literally. That's the beauty of animation—no live actor could do that.

Just as she's about to step into the boat, she turns and raises her hands. Her black-polished nails extend from her fingers, and she makes a catlike swipe at the big man's eyes, hitting the mark. Blood showers down from his face, a dark red. He bellows and falls to his knees, grabbing at her as he goes down. His fingers catch in her silver chain, which breaks and falls to the sand. She runs, but the small man catches up to her and pushes her against a slimy concrete pylon. Her head hits the pylon with a sickening thwack. The blood from her head spurts out like fiery streamers from a skyrocket. Her eyes widen and fade. The picture goes dark except for the fountain of scarlet droplets that continue to cascade down the screen.

"So gross," Brighton says aloud, though he's watched the cutscene twice before.

The screen lights up again. The earlier Felicity reappears, again dressed in green leather and sporting dreadlocks.

"I disappeared," she says. "And I haven't been seen since. Oh, a few reported sightings here and there, but nothing verified. Where am I? What happened? A puzzle. But I do promise that William the Conqueror won't get away with this." She points at the viewer. "Retribution is up to *you*." There's an extreme close-up on her face, and she lowers her voice as if speaking confidentially. "Here's a tip—don't start in the bar. That's the end of the journey, not the beginning. That's all I can tell you, now and forever." She smiles sadly. A single sparkly tear slides down her cheek. Then the screen shifts to gameplay mode: *Level One—Felicity's Appointment*.

There's a shatter of glass. Brighton has never heard that sound effect before, and he's about to click the rewind arrow until he realizes the sound came not from the computer but from the living room. He gets up and runs down the hall. Aunt Greta is still sleeping, still snoring, but it's not a snore that he's ever heard before. And her arm is extended, dangling over the end table where the bottle was. There's a snuffling, more animal than human. Afraid to touch her but knowing that he must, he takes a step forward. A shard of glass from the wine bottle pierces the ball of his foot. He yelps and then reaches down and pulls the sliver of glass out of his foot. The blood is nothing like that fake stuff in the video game.

He nudges her. "Aunt Greta. Aunt Greta. Wake up!"

She snorts, almost an oink. And then nothing. He fixates on her chest, willing her to breathe, willing himself to believe she's breathing. He grabs her shoulders and feebly shakes her, still hoping that she'll feel pain if he shakes too hard. Then he remembers her pulse. How do they do it on TV? The arm? The neck? Which side? He feels her wrist and probes at her neck with his fingers. Her skin is the texture of the raw chicken breast that he helped her prepare for dinner the night before. He tries to find her pulse, but he's forgotten what a pulse is.

Brighton is an intelligent boy. He knows he must dial 911, knows it will be futile. He understands now that actual death is ordinary, and for that reason more horrifying than anything he can ever see in a video game.

CHAPTER 1

Judicial Alternative Dispute Solutions employs three kinds of mediators. There are the retired judges—former jurists who are sick of government bureaucracy and civil servants' wages. They get the most lucrative cases. The title *Judge* and the salutation *Honorable* can make an imbecile seem credible. Then there are the idealists, mostly law professors and young lawyers with undergrad psychology degrees who naively believe that they can transform the legal system from adversarial to conciliatory. They do almost as well as the ex-judges—many cases need a touchy-feely facilitator who can convince even the most misguided litigants that their legal positions matter. On the bottom rung are the burnouts like me: the once-driven trial lawyers who can no longer cope with the stress of a courtroom, though I'm not yet forty and supposedly just hitting my prime. We get the dross—the slip and falls, the unlawful detainers, the Worker's Comp disputes. No matter. There are no winners or losers in mediation, so no pressure. If the case settles, fine. If not, let the judge and jury decide.

I recently became a JADS mediator so I wouldn't have to try cases anymore. I used to love trials. Everything changed three years ago, when my mentor Harmon Cherry died and our law firm Macklin & Cherry—my only family—broke up when the clients deserted us. Since then, every time I walk into a courtroom, I battle stage fright. I only got through that last trial because of passion-induced adrenaline, in its own way more destructive than the terror. So I began settling cases *before* they get to trial. Parker Stern, warrior turned pacifist.

JADS is housed in a brick and glass low-rise building adjacent to the Santa Monica Municipal Airport. My cubbyhole has a window with a partial view of the north runway, the walls and glass insulated so thickly that you can't hear the planes take off. I filled the particle-board shelves with books about famous lawyers. I can use the conference rooms so long as I reserve them forty-eight hours in advance. I can call on a case assistant to schedule mediations and manage my docket. I can drink all the tepid coffee I want. What JADS doesn't provide is a salary. Instead, I pay them thirty percent of all revenue I bring in from my mediations. The "eat what you kill" system, they call it.

Except for a computer, my Formica-top desk is empty. Until a few weeks ago, I attributed my lack of mediations to the summer lull. But Labor Day has come and gone, and the lawyers and judges and litigants have returned from vacations, ready to resume battle in their lawsuits. And yet, my workload hasn't picked up. So on this day, I take sips from my fourth cup of coffee, watch the Cessnas and the occasional Learjet take off, and listen to alternative rock music on my computer.

At 10:47 a.m., the synthesized message alert rings. Why do computer notifications always sound like church bells, door chimes, a child's xylophone? Do the tech companies want to convey innocence?

The chat is initiated by someone who uses the handle *Poniard*.

>*Mr. Stern, I'm looking for a top trial lawyer to represent me in a possible new lawsuit and you're number 1 on my list*

I pride myself on my ability to suss out online phishing schemes or mail spam or a virus-infected file. If the message had arrived in an e-mail, I would've deleted it immediately and blocked the sender from forwarding future e-mails. But this message has come in through the internal JADS chat program, so I assume that someone in the company has sent it. I don't know a Poniard working at JADS, but that doesn't mean anything, because it's a large company.

PStern
>*I'm free now. Your office or mine?*
Poniard:
>*Not that simple. I'm not with your company*

PStern
>Then how did you gain access to ResolutionChat?
Poniard:
>I'm good with computers
PStern
>You hacked into our system?
Poniard:
>Not saying yes to that . . . given my circumstances, I used the best method to get your attention

I reach for the telephone to call the head of Information Technology. Even if she can't trace the source of the hack, she can take immediate corrective measures to minimize the damage from the breach. But then:

Poniard:
>You must think this is bizarre. If I were you, I'd be calling IT and running around your office like Paul Revere before Lexington and Concord. But before you do that or shut down the chat program, PLEASE give me a chance. Check your e-mail and read the attachment. I PROMISE you no virus . . . no Trojan horse. Just a pdf image file I'm sure you'll be interested in . . . and you'll see I'm legit

Harmon Cherry always said that a good lawyer must have a relentless drive to uncover the truth. I embraced that advice, often to my great regret. I'm interested in the truth about this Poniard. And without work to do, I'm mightily bored. But there's something else. For the past six weeks, I've been caught in the throes of a low-grade despair that makes the days flatten out, makes the nights sere and empty. The woman I adore left me. Anyway, this silly chat with a hacker is the most amusing thing to happen in weeks, and I want to hold onto it for a while longer.

I switch to Microsoft Outlook. An e-mail from Poniard is at the top of my inbox. The message contains an attachment called *scan.pdf*. I click the icon. If *scan.pdf* contains a malicious virus, JADS will just have to deal with it.

As soon as the file launches, I recognize the gold-embossed letter-head: *The Louis Frantz Law Office.* Lou Frantz is a bully and a blow-hard. Also one of the top trial lawyers in the country, and someone who'll never forgive me for what I did to him in the case we tried against each other a couple of years ago. I'm sure that Frantz would welcome a rematch, but I have no intention of giving him one. I'm now a mediator.

September 12, 2013
Via e-mail
The Individual known as Poniard

Dear Poniard:
  This office represents William M. Bishop, Chairman and Chief Executive Officer of Parapet Media Corporation. We write to demand that you retract certain statements made against Mr. Bishop and that you immediately cease and desist from making false and defamatory state-ments of and concerning Mr. Bishop, to wit, that Mr. Bishop is responsible for the disappear-ance of an actress by the name of Paula Felicity McGrath. Such statements are made, and continue to be made, in a video game called Abduction! (the "Video Game.")
  More specifically, the Video Game depicts the circumstances of McGrath's disappearance in 1987, and then contains various levels and scenes that a reasonable person would understand as accusing Mr. Bishop of criminal activity. The language is false and defamatory and has been uttered with malice, i.e., with knowledge of its falsity or with reckless disregard for its truth, all to the grave damage to Mr. Bishop's reputation.
  Please acknowledge by September 19 before

the close of normal business hours that you will
refrain from all publication, distribution, or
other dissemination of the Video Game. Please
also make all efforts to retrieve all versions
of the game that you have distributed. If you
do not do so, Mr. Bishop will have no choice
but to file a lawsuit seeking tens of millions
of dollars in compensatory damages to his reputation, plus punitive damages. Please also be
aware that you will be subject to deposition and
other discovery and the obligation to testify in
court. The deposition will be recorded on video
and will become a matter of public record. Be
governed accordingly.

When I finish reading, I can barely steady my fingers to type into the keyboard. William Bishop is a billionaire, in control of a movie studio, a television network, seven newspapers, thirty radio stations, and a record company, among other businesses. And I certainly remember Felicity McGrath. She was an up-and-coming star, breaking out in 1983 in the role of a drug-addicted young housewife in *The Fragile Palace*. She got rave reviews, but after that she became typecast. By 1987 her once promising career was on the decline. And then she vanished.

> PStern
> >*Who are you?*
> Poniard:
> >*You read the letter?*
> PStern
> >*Yes. Who are you?*
> Poniard:
> >*So you don't play video games*
> PStern
> >*You're right about that.*
> Poniard:
> >*I'm simply Poniard, a video game developer of some renown among
>   some people*

PStern
>Legal name, address, telephone?
Poniard:
*>I exist here in cyberspace . . . no other address than the e-mail you
    already have, no other name but Poniard*

I should call security or maybe the cops. But I keep typing.

PStern
*>And yet you're real enough to accuse William Bishop of kidnapping
    Felicity McGrath? In a video game? And real enough to get a cease
    and desist letter from Lou Frantz?*
Poniard:
>True
PStern
>Why??!!
Poniard:
>Why what?
PStern
>Why did you accuse him?
Poniard:
>He's guilty
PStern
>You have proof?
Poniard:
>Some. I will share that info if you take on my case
PStern
>What motive would Bishop have to do such a heinous thing?
Poniard:
*>One theory . . . Bishop was a married man back then; still is to the
    same woman, an heiress. An affair with Felicity he wanted to keep
    quiet?*
PStern
*>Implausible. And even if I thought you could win I wouldn't take it
    on. I don't try cases anymore. I settle them.*

Poniard:
>You've won some high-profile cases recently
PStern
>I've retired.
Poniard:
*>You're only thirty-nine ... looked it up on the Web. Too young to
retire! In fact, in the prime of your career*

He's right that most trial lawyers don't begin to reach their prime until their mid-forties. They do their best work well into their late sixties and even past that. Lou Frantz, for example, is seventy-two. But I'm not one of those lawyers. Even when I'm performing well in court, the fear is like a dormant virus residing in my nerve cells ready to flare up at any time. As much as I love trying cases, I can't afford to stir up the virus.

PStern
>I can recommend some topnotch trial attorneys.
Poniard:
*>I want you! I did my research ... you know how to handle Frantz
better than any lawyer around. And that motherfucker William
the Conqueror Bishop killed Felicity. Truth is still a defense to
libel, right?*
PStern
*>Yes, if you can prove it, which you won't going up against those two.
My free advice to you is to retract immediately and make this go
away. Bishop and Frantz are letting you off easy.*
Poniard:
>Will not happen! Bishop has to answer for his crimes!!
PStern
>Why do you care about McGrath? What's your interest in this?
Poniard:
*>I want to see justice done ... that's what all my games are about, and
life is the ultimate video game*

This particular game has gone on long enough. It's never wise to engage vindictive madmen in conversation.

I switch back to Frantz's letter. I'm not sure why I read it again, why I look at it more closely the second time, but when I see what I've missed, I jerk back in my chair. My limbs thrill with a mixture of anger and excitement, an intoxicating brew. I return to the chat program. Poniard is still there, waiting. How did he know to wait?

> PStern
> >*Still there?*
> Poniard:
> >*Still*
> PStern
> >*I'm thinking of taking this case on after all if Frantz files*
> Poniard:
> >*Awesome!!! I have resources. I'll advance legal fees in any amount you
>   say*
> PStern
> >*Not necessary yet. Notify me immediately if you're sued. How do I
>   reach you?*
> Poniard:
> >*E-mail*

He signs off. Not even a *thank you.*

Harmon Cherry taught me that there are many legitimate reasons for an attorney to take on a lawsuit—to earn a legal fee, to gain experience, to get public exposure, sometimes even to serve justice. But he also said that a lawyer should never take on a case for personal reasons, because the results are more often than not disastrous for both attorney and client. My reasons for taking on Poniard's case are purely personal. Harmon said something else—don't waste time groping for what's been irretrievably lost. I'm not following that advice either.

CHAPTER 2

Before I can search the name *Poniard*, there's a knock at my door, though it's wide open. Brenda Sica, the case assistant I share with three other mediators, stands at the threshold. It's her job to schedule mediations, organize the case files, collect retainers in advance, do basic Internet research, and word process my official correspondence—more responsibility than a secretary but less than a paralegal. During the six weeks she's worked at JADS, we've merely exchange pleasantries, and yet she's cowering in my doorway as if she expects me to hurl a paperweight at her.

"Mr. Stern, I—"

"Call me Parker." I've told her this before.

"Yeah, sorry. P ... Parker." Her voice is tremulous, her shoulders slumped, her eyes downcast. Her anxiety clashes with her brassy appearance. In her mid- to late-twenties, she's small and voluptuous, with long black hair, creamy skin, dark brown eyes, and a long Greek nose. She's heavily made up, with ivory foundation, black eyeliner, and eyebrows plucked so thin that they look like tattoos. Maybe they are tattoos. She's dressed in a form-fitting white sweater and a black pleated skirt too short for an office full of staid lawyers and judges. The four-inch platform heels make her five-four. And then there's her perfume—drugstore-chain quality, licorice and vanilla and musk, over-applied.

"I'm wondering if you have any work you need me to do," she says, shrugging and not bothering to lower her shoulders.

"You know how slow I've been."

Instead of leaving, she leans back against the wall and shuts her eyes, like a child after a scolding. Her body seems to accordion into itself. I wait for her to leave, but she just stands there.

"Is everything OK?" I ask.

"No, sir, Mr. Stern. I need this job, and since I was hired I've only been working part time. They said I'd be working for four people, mostly you, but you're not busy and Judge Mitchell still keeps using Lucy as his assistant and Ms. Ross has been out on maternity leave, so it's only Judge Croninger, and she doesn't have enough work to keep me busy full time, so I think they're going to lay me off if I don't have more to do. I'm on probation still."

I'm to blame. If I brought in even half the mediations I should, I could keep her busy. I've been sitting in my office, waiting for the work to come to me rather than going out into the legal community and aggressively marketing. Yet, here I am, about to conduct research on a potential lawsuit. Nothing in my deal with JADS prevents me from taking on a case as a lawyer, but the company expects me to make mediation my first priority. My laziness and disinterest shouldn't affect Brenda Sica.

"Are you working on anything at all?" she asks.

"I have a possible matter as a lawyer, but it's not a JADS thing."

"I can help you out."

"I don't think it's fair to you or JADS to—"

"It's OK with me. At least I'll look busy." She puts her hands together, prayer style. A passive form of advocacy but an effective one. I can easily reimburse JADS for a few hours of her salary. I'm not here for the money anyway—I have other sources of income.

"How are you at Internet research?" I ask, though I don't expect much because JADS gives the new hires only three hours training on LexisNexis and Westlaw.

"Whatever you need, Mr. Stern."

"Just don't tell anyone what you're working on. I'll make it right with JADS."

She nods and crosses her heart like a child swearing an oath.

I tell her about Bishop's potential lawsuit against Poniard and describe the research I need. She keeps nodding her head and brushing away the same strand of hair that falls into her face every third nod.

When I finish, I ask if she has questions. She shakes her head and leaves. I suspect that she hasn't understood half of what I said.

I spend the next forty-five minutes reading a biography of Edward Bennett Williams, the famous DC trial lawyer who once owned the Washington Redskins. Williams said, "I will defend anyone as long as the client gives me total control of the case and pays up front." This Poniard character has offered to pay me up front; taking total control of the case will be the hard part.

There's a slight rustling in the doorway, fabric against skin. I start and then look up to see Brenda slouching against the doorjamb, arms folded, papers dangling from one hand. She has a look of repose, almost ennui, as if she's been watching me for a long time.

"What is it?" I ask, sounding more abrupt than I intend.

She straightens up suddenly, as if I startled her and not the other way around. "No. I finished the research."

"So fast?"

She shrugs apologetically. I gesture for her to come inside. She sits down in the client chair, crosses her legs, and tugs the hem of her skirt down hard.

"Can we start with Felicity?" she asks.

"However you want to do this, Brenda."

She takes a heavy breath. "OK. The best thing I found on her is from this website called *The Tommy Foundation*, named after a California boy who disappeared in 1961. It collects cold cases involving people who have disappeared. Here's a short summary of the vital statistics."

I skim the printout:

- **Name:** Paula Felicity McGrath
- **Missing since:** July 23, 1987
- **Classification:** Endangered missing
- **Age:** 28 years old
- **Distinguishing characteristics:** Caucasian female. Red hair (dyed auburn at the time of disappearance), blue eyes.

- **Medical condition:** McGrath was rumored to be three months pregnant at the time of her disappearance, but this has not been confirmed.

"I don't remember anything about her being pregnant," I say. "It's been a long time, but—"

"This is the only website that says it. I haven't done a full Lexis search, but most of the news articles I found don't mention pregnancy. I . . ." She puts a hand to her mouth. "Sorry, Mr. Stern . . . Parker."

"For what?"

"Because I interrupted you."

"It's OK. It's called conversation."

She fumbles with her printouts. "So, OK. On July 23, 1987, Felicity leaves her apartment in the Carthay Circle District of Los Angeles. At approximately 6:00 p.m., she tells her roommate Natalie Owen, a teller at a local bank, that she's going to meet a friend for dinner at the Farmer's Market on Third Street. She also says she's going to a nighttime film shoot afterwards."

Brenda has rarely said more than a few words to me. So I never noticed that her speech has a vaguely foreign lilt, a softening of the R's, a rising inflection at the end of sentences that sounds musical and child-like. And though from her name I assumed she's Latina, her speech doesn't sound like it came from a Hispanic country or the barrio. I can't place it. Or maybe she simply has a slight, endearing speech impediment.

"Natalie Owen filed a missing person's report after Felicity failed to return home the next day," she continues. "A city worker on the Santa Monica beach found a gold or yellow high-heel shoe belonging to McGrath on the sand not far from the pier. Later, a police search turned up a chain and cross that might have been Felicity's. The CSI people found blood on a concrete pylon, the blood type matching Felicity's. Of course, everybody knows the cops never found her body." She wraps her arms around her chest and shudders visibly.

"Pretty scary stuff," I say.

"Every girl's nightmare. Anyway, her purse was never found. Her brown seventy-eight Honda Civic was later found parked on Abbott Kinney in Venice." She takes three shallow breaths. "Anyway, the rumors and gossip were that Felicity was a skank, that she slept around with both men and women. Of course, there's no proof, but . . . this bartender in Venice told the police that at approximately 11:30 p.m. the evening she went missing, she left his bar with two men in their late thirties or early forties. One tall and one short. Both with dark curly hair. The cops thought she was hooking, that maybe she picked up the wrong johns, and they raped and murdered her and dumped . . . and dumped her body at sea. Their other theory is that she committed suicide because she was mentally disturbed, manic-depressive."

"They call it bipolar disease these days."

She looks up at the ceiling. "The cops couldn't find evidence that Felicity had an acting job that night."

"What about suspects?"

"There weren't any."

"William Bishop's relationship with her?"

"None that I can find yet. I checked the Internet Movie Database. McGrath worked on two films released by Bishop's studio—both bombs—but the company made twenty-three films during that time, so there's no reason to think that Bishop was involved in her movies. He's a corporate executive, right? You know he's in control of a ton of the media in the Western world? Movie studio, TV network, newspapers, Internet and cable companies. I can't believe I never heard of him before."

"William the Conqueror does have scary power."

"Why do they call him that?"

"You've never heard of—?"

She shakes her head.

"The original William the Conqueror was a Frenchman who invaded England, overwhelmed his opponents, and became king. They call Bishop "the Conqueror" because he'll do anything to defeat his opponents. Except, he does it in the corporate world rather than on the battlefield. He's a media mogul whose companies pry into other people's business, and yet he somehow manages to keep his private life private even in this Internet era."

She shuffles through her stack of papers. "I did find one weird thing that's not publicized. Did you know he was an actor?"

"You must have the wrong William Bishop."

"He acted in a movie in like, the nineteen seventies—*The Boatman.*" She hands me a printout, all in text. It's a stub article—the name of the movie, Bishop's name, but no information about the rest of the cast or company and crew or movie's plot. Even the date is vague—*197?*

"Where did you get this?"

"The Internet Movie Database. Well, not the website IMDb, but—"

"If the IMDb says Bishop is an actor, the whole world would know about it."

"No. I mean, it was posted before the IMDb was a website. It used to be what they call a newsgroup, rec.arts.movies. Obsolete. I looked in Wikipedia and . . ."

"How do you know it's the same guy?"

"I guess I don't, Mr. Stern. But why isn't *The Boatman* on today's IMDb? Every movie's on today's IMDb. Bollywood movies, Japanese movies, even porn."

"The IMDb is wrong a lot," I say.

"Yeah, but it wouldn't leave this out."

I'm not sure I buy her theory, but I certainly underestimated her. "Good job," I say.

I thought that would get a smile from her, or a thank you, but she just stares at me as if my compliment is a cruel joke.

"OK. What about Poniard?" I ask.

She hands me a printout from Wikipedia.

Poniard is a pseudonymous video game developer and political activist. His games include Bomb Rats, *the simulated government game* Macbeth in the White House, Eggheads and Skinheads, Reality Rogues, *and* Abduction! *His earlier games oppose imperialism, cap-*

italism, fascism, and the cult of celebrity. Some call him a nihilist. His most recent game Abduction! *allegedly accuses business magnate William Bishop of orchestrating the 1987 disappearance of actress Paula Felicity McGrath, though there has never been any evidence of Bishop's involvement. As always, Poniard released the game without fanfare. Speculation is that it first became available on the Internet sometime in June 2013 and took some weeks to catch on with the general game-playing population.*

Later in the article:

There have been numerous rumors and theories about Poniard's identity. Theories often suggested include a former Xerox PARC researcher, a teenager in Oslo, Norway, and a mysterious computer programmer named Vladimir Lazerev. There's one alleged photograph of Lazerev, taken at a 2010 video game conference in London. His whereabouts are unknown. Another theory is that Poniard is actually a collective of game developers rather than a single person. A "poniard" is a long, lightweight thrusting knife with a continuously tapering, acutely pointed blade.

"So, he's a mystery man," I say.

"Yeah, like Banksy."

"The English graffiti artist."

"His stuff is incredible. But nobody knows who he is."

"I saw his film *Exit Through the Gift Shop*. Good documentary, mediocre art."

She narrows her eyes and leans forward as if to protest, but sits back. I wish she had protested. But I was trained in law school to believe that you get to the truth by arguing. I often forget that most normal people don't believe that for a moment.

"The photo of Lazerev?"

She slides another sheet of paper over to me. "Sorry, I tried to blow it up, play with the printer but . . . no wonder they can't identify the guy."

The blurry, sepia-toned photo must've been taken from a balcony or an upper-floor window or a rooftop. A large crowd has gathered in a plaza, perhaps a party, perhaps a protest. There's an arrow—part of the graphic, not anything that Brenda has drawn in—pointing toward the head of a man wearing a hoodie. Only the left side of his face is visible.

He looks like a nerdy college student—beak nose, slightly receding chin, John Lennon eyeglasses. The only things that distinguish him are his height and a dark spot on his cheek, maybe a birthmark, maybe just a smudge in the photo.

She takes a deep breath, then another, wheezy, like an asthmatic. "So. This Poniard dude is real rich. He usually sells his video games for a premium, and people pay it. But he gave this *Abduction!* game away for free. The game's gone viral. And you should know that . . ." She averts her eyes, as if she's about to confess to a mortal sin. Her cheeks begin to flush.

"Are you OK?"

"Yeah, it's just . . . Poniard posted Louis Frantz's cease and desist letter on his blog. He wrote . . . he wrote that Bishop is 'too big a pussy to sue.' Sorry for the language." Her cheeks and neck splotch red. She uncrosses and recrosses her legs and pulls at her skirt again. What makes a woman dress revealingly and then spend all day trying to cover up?

"What about the video game?" I ask.

"I'm sorry, I . . . I didn't know that was part of the assignment. I'll go look it up now."

"You any good at video games?"

She squinches her nose as if smelling something putrid. "No, sir. I hate them. My last boyfriend was a gamer. Obsessed. Maybe if he would've spent as much time with me as he did playing *Call of Duty* . . ." She catches herself. "Sorry."

"I'll work on the video game angle."

"Really, I can—"

"No, it's OK. Again, great job."

"Thanks, Mr. . . . Parker." When she reaches the door, she turns back and smiles before leaving the office.

I go to the computer and find a wiki devoted specifically to *Abduction!*, which is described as a "survival horror" game—an adventure game that draws on horror fiction conventions. Survival horror games, I learn, involve a vulnerable player who must survive horrific forces through intelligence and evasion, not violence.

The article links to the online game. I'm not much of a player, but I launch it anyway and register using Brenda's name. At first, there's nothing to do but watch, because the game starts with a gory intro depicting Paula Felicity McGrath's kidnapping, after which she invites the player to fill in the details of William the Conqueror's crime. Poniard's libel of Bishop's good name couldn't be clearer—unless, of course, Bishop actually committed murder.

In this opening scene, the Felicity character comes across as a wisecracking bimbo who flashes a lot of skin. And yet, Poniard conveys more than that. I remember Felicity McGrath's work. In her films, she was a beautiful porcelain figurine—wonderful to look at, but cold and brittle. In the video game, Poniard has given her a pouting lower lip, large anime eyes, and fluttery hands. She bobs her head slightly when she speaks. These subtle touches make Video Game Felicity captivating in a way that Big Screen Felicity wasn't. Despite its cartoon façade, the video game shows Poniard's true artistry—that rare ability to invest the subject with more humanity than she seemed to have in life.

I launch Stage 1, *Felicity's Appointment*, supposedly the easiest level. The screen shows Felicity inside her apartment. This level seems like a puzzle game—I can use the mouse and the arrow keys to change point of view, to walk around the room, to turn door handles, to move objects around. But to what end? There's no sign of Natalie Owen, the roommate. Is she even a character in the game? There's a telephone, an old-fashioned landline—Felicity disappeared in 1987—but though I can grasp the receiver and get a dial tone, I can't press the buttons to dial out. I look for a *help* option but can't find one. I pause the game and search the Internet for cheats but find only complaints from frustrated gamers accusing Poniard of playing a cruel practical joke. There's an equal number of Poniard defenders who insist that the game is beatable simply because Poniard says it is.

I set the mouse aside and watch the screen. Felicity continues to move on her own volition. She puts on a slinky dress and flashy jewelry and sits down in front of her mirror and applies makeup. Her movements are precise, her mannerisms realistic. At this point, the game seems geared to little girls from nine to twelve. But when Felicity sits on the bed, rolls sheer fishnet nylons up her legs, and attaches them to a garter belt, the target demographic changes. The soundtrack begins to play a steamy trombone line, stripper music out of the nineteen fifties. I feel creepy, as if I'm peeping through a woman's bedroom window. Is that the point, to make the player feel grungy and strange?

Something else confuses me. In the video games I've played, the player assumes an on-screen persona—a medieval warrior, a Vietnam vet, a bellicose bird, a hyperactive mouse. I've even read about a Japanese game where the protagonist is an unfaithful boyfriend. With Poniard's game, I have no idea who I'm supposed to be. I'm not Felicity. Her actions seem beyond my power to control, independent of my manipulations with keyboard and mouse—oddly antagonistic to those manipulations, actually. So who am I? The chief police investigator? A hard-boiled private detective hired by the family à la Chandler's *The Big Sleep*? William the Conqueror, looking to commit the crime? Parker Stern, attorney for the artist known as Poniard? Is that one of the objects of the game—to discover who you really are?

I should be preparing for a mediation, a mini-geopolitical war disguised as a rent dispute between a Pakistani slumlord and his Indian tenant, but instead I'm sitting in my office playing *Abduction!* In the three days since my online chat with Poniard, I haven't advanced one level, can't get out of Felicity's room, can't even manage to open up a dresser drawer. Frustrated, I exit the game and check the blogs. The online buzz over *Abduction!* has become feverish. Poniard's critics call the game a cheesy pretext to smear Bishop. Some of the news sites—*Drudge*, *The Huffington Post*—have picked up the story, but even they tread lightly, careful to dismiss Poniard's allegations as a lunatic's rant. The largest media outlets don't report the story at all. Of course, Bishop controls so many of them.

I'm talking to my assistant Brenda about a research assignment when the chat program launches, the synthesized alert jarring, because the speaker volume is turned up high.

Poniard:
>*GAME ON!!*

Brenda cranes her neck toward the screen and covers her mouth with her hand. "Oh my god, Mr. Stern, is that him?"

"Yeah, it's . . . will you excuse me, Brenda? And please shut the door behind you."

Her neck immediately mottles pink. "I'm so sorry, Mr. Stern, I didn't mean to . . ."

"It's just that this particular client values confidentiality."

"Yeah, I get it, I shouldn't have . . ." She turns and tiptoes out of the office, as though I were sleeping, gingerly closing the door. I turn to the computer screen.

PStern
>*???*
Poniard:
>*Check your e-mail*

I find a message from Poniard with no subject line, no body text, and a single image file attachment, which I launch immediately. The file contains three documents. The first is a complaint in the newly filed lawsuit titled *William Maxfield Bishop v. The Individual Known as Poniard*. So here it is—every lawsuit's Fort Sumter, the opening salvo that triggers a supposedly bloodless civil action between the parties. Except that when you're dealing with plaintiffs like William Bishop, the action is never civil and the battles aren't always bloodless.

In the bombastic style typical of the Louis Frantz law offices, the complaint describes William Bishop as *a pillar of society, a successful entrepreneur, a devoted family man, a patron of the arts, a noted philanthropist, a man with a spotless reputation*. Lawyers revere clichés. Then the complaint attacks Poniard, calling him a hacker, a nihilist, a pornographer, a narcissist intent on garnering publicity at the expense of the truth. Not until page twenty-seven does the complaint charge that

Poniard has falsely accused Bishop of kidnapping and murdering Paula Felicity McGrath.

The second document is a court order permitting Frantz to serve the complaint on Poniard by e-mail rather than by personal service. It's not surprising—Poniard has no known address, so how can a process server use the old-fashioned method of catching him unaware and handing him the summons?

The third document is a surprise, though. Frantz is asking the court to force Poniard to attend a deposition within three days, claiming that my client has no respect for the law and might destroy evidence. It's a ploy, an attempt to flush Poniard out into the open, or worse, to have him fail to show up at the deposition and default, effectively ending the case.

I switch back to the chat program.

PStern
>Have you read the docs?
Poniard:
>Skimmed it. LMAO!
PStern
>There's nothing funny about it. They've demanded 25 million dollars.
Poniard:
>That's exactly what makes me laugh
PStern
>You must understand. Bishop really can recover 25 million from you. He can get punitive damages on top of that. If he wins, he will own you. And I know Frantz. Settlement is off the table once he files.
Poniard:
>Just what I'd hoped for. You can't beat the game if you don't vanquish the boogeyman
PStern
>This is not a game. This is your future.
Poniard:
>We're at Level 1 . . . everything is possible at Level 1

PStern
>They want to take your deposition this Friday. There's a hearing
    tomorrow. They call it an ex parte—an emergency motion.
Poniard:
>I'll be happy to answer all their questions in writing
PStern
>They want you in person at the courthouse. And they want to image
    all your computer hard drives for evidence.
Poniard:
>That violates my right of privacy
PStern
>You don't have that right in civil litigation. You can't withhold your
    identity from the other side.
Poniard:
>You WILL stop this, WILL get the judge to say I may answer in
    writing!
PStern
>Very unlikely
Poniard:
>You're a great trial lawyer. You'll defeat this

Harmon Cherry told us that every new client believes his lawyer
capable of working magic—until the client receives the first invoice.
But what worries me is that this client is glibly using video game
jargon to describe a lawsuit that has the very real potential to destroy
his life. I planned to find out what Poniard knows about Felicity
McGrath's disappearance and Bishop's involvement in it, but the next
words seem to spring not from any part of my brain but from my
fingertips.

PStern
>How old are you?
Poniard:
>???
PStern
>I want to know if you're a minor

Poniard:
>Ha!
PStern
>No, seriously. How old are you?
Poniard:
>You've seen ABDUCTION!—it's not something a kid could do

It doesn't seem so, until you consider the legion of adolescent savants, the pimply, pudgy-bellied introverts who can't look you in the eye or say two words without stammering and yet who can power up their MacBook Pros and create fantastical worlds so fraught and engaging and complex that you can, for a while, escape from a life that's anything but dreamlike. I suddenly fear that I'm dealing with a fourteen-year-old who's pulled a prank that's gotten out of control, who thrills at the attention without regard for the consequences. And if it turns out that Poniard is forty years old, so much the worse, because he's behaving like a child. So I write back:

PStern
>EVERY video game looks like a kid designed it. Now, how old are you?
Poniard:
>That's fucked up
PStern
>And that's a childish response.
Poniard:
>Many believe that Poniard is ageless
PStern
>I can't represent you under these circumstances. So stop playing games and tell me who you really are. I need a name, address, telephone number, driver's license, Dun & Bradstreet credit check. And we need to talk real time so I can hear your voice.
Poniard:
>It can't happen . . . but I'll immediately wire transfer my retainer to your client trust account—isn't that what you mouthpieces call it? Six figures is fine, whatever you need. Won't that show my bona fides, as you lawyers say?

PStern
>*I must have the information I request or I'll resign effective immediately after tomorrow's court hearing.*

Outside in the corridor, one of my more unscrupulous colleagues is bragging to another that he's extended a mediation over two full days when it should've lasted three hours—a major economic coup when you bill each side $750 per hour.

Poniard:
>*Wow. I thought if anyone would respect a person's right to keep their identity secret, it would be you, Parky G. I'm disappointed in you, my man*

I rest quivering fingers on the keyboard and tap out inarticulate clatter—words of protest, denial, feigned ignorance, righteous indignation. I even type out *who the hell ARE you?* before realizing how absurd that question is. All of which I delete before I can bring myself to hit *send*. There's only one positive—I've learned that Poniard is an adult. Children aren't such good blackmailers.

What Poniard has somehow discovered about me is this: while William the Conqueror Bishop's acting credits might not appear in the up-to-date version of the Internet Movie Database, mine do.

Parky Gerald, born July 16, 1974, in Los Angeles, California; active 1977–1987; a blond, rosy-cheeked waif who was a child star of the 1970s and 1980s, known for his wide eyes and piercing shriek of fear; appeared in 28 movie and TV productions, most notably Alien Parents (fourth top-grossing PG movie of 1983) and Alien Parents 2; dropped out of sight in late-eighties, current whereabouts unknown.

I've spent the last twenty-five years trying to keep this secret. My celebrity almost ruined me, and I don't want it back, not even a vestige of it. I'm a lawyer, not an actor. I closely guard the truth about my past and have kept it secret through luck and hard work—mostly luck. My career ended before the Internet era, so there was no instantaneous cyber-stalking. Hormones helped—once I hit puberty, I looked nothing like my onscreen self. I became an emancipated minor—divorced my mother, in other words—and so had control over my own affairs. I spent my teenage years hiding in Southern California's over-populated public schools—loners aren't much noticed—and after law school emerged as the newly minted Parker Stern, Attorney at Law. The few people who know about my childhood haven't revealed it, either because they care about me or because they have secrets of their own that they want me to keep. I thought that after my last trial, which garnered so much publicity, some reporter or blogger or fan would finally discover that I was Parky, but so far it hasn't happened. Maybe it's not that surprising—these days, Parky Gerald is far less prominent than Poniard, or that graffiti artist Banksy, or writers Cormac McCarthy and Thomas Pynchon, and they've all managed to keep secrets about themselves. There's a music group called The Residents that's been around since 1974 and whose members' identities are unknown. I cling to these examples in the hope that my background, too, can remain hidden.

> Poniard:
> >And it's just not the one thing you have to worry about becoming
>   public. Revelations beget revelations
> PStern
> >How biblical of you.
> Poniard:
> >Or if you prefer Greek Mythology, think Pandora's Box. That's why I
>   won't reveal even my age. But tell you what—I'll keep your secret
>   if you go to court and make sure I get to keep mine, OK? And
>   together we will nail Billy Bishop for what he did to Felicity

So now I have to win the court hearing to get Poniard to keep my secret? I'm tempted to tell him to go fuck himself, but I don't, and not because of the blackmail. I'm going to stay on the case for a different reason.

PStern

>*I'm in for now. But make no mistake . . . I won't continue to play your game forever.*

Poniard:

>*My game is as good as any other. Better, actually, from what I read. No reason to blow your cover to make a point. Another rule of game design—never lose sight of your objective*

PStern

>*Why me?*

Poniard:

>*I told you in our first chat—you're good. You're not intimidated by Frantz. You can keep a secret*

PStern

>*You'll do far better with another lawyer for so many reasons.*

Poniard:

>*We gamers have a saying: embrace the chaos. So, hey, Parky embrace the chaos. You'll find life more exciting*

This kind of excitement is the last thing I want. I type *fuck you* into the text box, punch the *send* key hard, and sign off. But I'm not about to leave this case, and somehow this Poniard senses it. From what I read, part of his genius is his ability to manipulate game players on a quest into believing that they can take alternative paths, when all the time they're unwittingly being funneled in one direction. The technique is called creating a *chokepoint*. How fitting.

CHAPTER 3

On the night that Brighton's great-aunt died, the paramedics called Social Services, which placed him in what on TV they call The System, and he thought he'd stay there for a long time. But then those two people marched on in and told him those unbelievable things. Now he lives with them in a large house. He's made up secret names for them. The man is Bugsy because he talks like an old-time TV gangster. The woman is Hoar Frost Queen—his fourth-grade class read this poem called *Hoar Frost* and of course everybody cracked up—because she's cold sometimes though not always, and because of what he's read about her on the Internet. In September, they force him to go to a rich kids' school, where of course he doesn't have any friends.

The one good thing is that they have a computer with a twenty-four-inch LED monitor, way bigger than the one he had at home. And they have a new Xbox One. As long as he cleans his room and does some chores—clearing the dinner table, loading the dishwasher, making his bed, finishing homework—Bugsy lets him play video games, though the HF Queen doesn't like it. The game he plays most is *Abduction!*

In the few months since the video game came out, Poniard's critics have accused him of scamming them, of releasing a game that doesn't have a solution. Brighton refuses to believe that Poniard would cheat his fans like that. And yet, he can't get past the beginning stage, in which Felicity sits in her bedroom getting ready for some kind of appointment. At first, this frustrates him, and if *Abduction!* were any other game, he would have given up long ago. But as he continues to play, he finds comfort in the way Felicity's voice sometimes quavers like a tragic violin. There's the way she sits at the mirror, gently brushing her red hair and gazing at her reflection. He finds himself getting protective of her. He's never wanted to protect anyone or anything before, not even a pet. Aunt Greta owned a cat, but it hissed and scratched if he tried to pet it.

Poniard has given Felicity a lot of dialogue, part of the game developer's genius. Brighton feels sometimes that Poniard has invented the game for him alone, that he and Felicity are having a real conversation. As he maneuvers the cursor across the screen, she'll talk about random things—the weather, how her roommate Natalie is a pain in the butt, how men treat her badly, how she has a hot date that night. She talks a lot about being an actress, how she got famous for starring in a movie called *The Fragile Palace,* but her favorite role was in the flop *Meadows of Deceit* because she didn't have to play a dumb, sexy girl in that one. Then there are her displays of flesh. When he first started playing, it turned him on, but now he gets embarrassed, as if he's accidentally walked in on his big sister while she's in her underwear. Sometimes it seems as if she can read his mind and answer his thought questions. He'll be thinking of a strategy—wondering if a series of keystrokes will open a drawer or if dragging the mouse in a certain way will unlock the front door—and she'll frown and shake her head before he even starts the move. Or he'll walk into his room and stare at the computer screen without even moving the mouse, and she'll look up at him and smile.

He works so hard to solve the puzzle that when he goes to bed at night and closes his eyes he can see Felicity's room on the inside of his eyelids—the mattress and box springs with the flower comforter and puffy pillows; the knotty pine wardrobe that goes from floor almost to ceiling, with its large and small drawers, all of which will rattle at a mouse click but none of which he can open; the black wood dresser where she keeps her perfume and makeup; the old-fashioned mirror with light bulbs all around it like you see in an old movie; the household accessories, which seem so real that when Brighton accidentally bumps the mouse with his elbow, a lamp falls off the nightstand and breaks into tiny pieces. Felicity gives him a dirty look, gets a broom and dustpan from a dark corner of the closet, and sweeps up the glass.

Once he accepts that he'll never get past Level One, that so long as he keeps playing the game he'll be trapped with Felicity in her bedroom forever, a funny thing happens—he begins to treat the aimless keystrokes as a sort of ritual—superstitious, maybe even religious. Each time he touches the keys, it seems as if he gets a bit closer, not to winning, but to earning a divine reward. The world of *Abduction!* becomes more familiar, far safer, than the world that Bugsy and Hoar Frost Queen rule. Not that he confuses the game with reality. Just the opposite—the game is so clearly imaginary that it begins to feel truer than his real life.

And then one warm September evening, while trying random combinations on the input devices, a hidden drawer in the wardrobe opens, spewing out hundreds of envelopes and letters that swirl in a paper tornado up and out of the screen.

CHAPTER 4

Kava, Celexa, Toprol, Argentum, Valerian—loyal soldiers all. Not in some massively multiplayer online role-playing game, but in my battle against stage fright. These are the names of the herbs and the beta-blockers and the anti-anxiety drugs that I mix and match and sometimes misuse to get through a court hearing without becoming awash in flop sweat or passing out on the courtroom floor. But these potions can't vanquish the rodent that will decide to hone its teeth on my lower thorax at the very moment I enter a courtroom. Which is one reason I gave up trial work to become a mediator.

I park in the Music Center lot and cross the street to the courthouse. By the time I reach the Grand Avenue entrance, my eyes are teary and my forehead is hemorrhaging sweat. It's the afternoon heat and the acrid smog, I reason, not rising fear. I pass through security— belt off, shoes off, smartphone in a plastic bin, flash your bar card so the bailiffs don't confiscate the phone, get dressed, and hurry down the windowless corridor. Though courthouses are supposed to reflect the power and solemnity of the judiciary, the Superior Court for the State of California, County of Los Angeles, is a dump. The air-conditioning system rattles and coughs and makes the air dry, so that if you spend more than an hour inside you develop this hacking cough that will last for hours. The third-floor cafeteria serves food whose freshness is measured by the color of the mold propagating on the surface. Every courtroom smells like a combination of caked-on floor wax, fusty law books, and the rank body odor of the inmates from the County Jail who've passed through for sentencing. I revere the place. Or, I did before the fear descended upon me.

I take the escalator up to the seventh floor, where the Honorable

T. Tedford Triggs presides in the courtroom designated Department 79. Most court business occurs in the morning, so in the afternoon the hallways are usually deserted except for a few harried trial lawyers conferring during a recess, anxious witnesses waiting their turn to take the stand, and a smattering of regulars flitting from courtroom to courtroom hoping to find the real-life equivalent of *Law & Order*. But on this afternoon, a large crowd has gathered outside Department 79. Lined up near the locked door are members of the media, many of whom I recognize—entertainment reporters, tabloid writers, and an earthworm named Brandon Placek who recently joined an online gossip website called The Tinseltown Zone. Bishop's publicity machine has undoubtedly alerted them to the hearing. A bailiff stands guard in front of the courtroom, which I know is locked because pieces of cardboard obscure the tiny windows in the doors.

On the opposite side of the hall, maybe half a dozen people are huddled in an alcove, each wearing a costume patterned after a character from one of Poniard's video games. There's a woman wearing a pink wig, with ribbons and a matching pink dress—Raggedy Ann Dohrn, a violent radical who led a revolution of dolls in Poniard's game *Eggheads and Skinheads*. There's a college-aged Goth Abe Lincoln with tattoos covering each arm, a tall man in his thirties dressed like a character at a Renaissance faire, a woman dressed like a combination druid and guerilla fighter—Sigourney Guevara, Poniard called the character in *Reality Rogues*—and a man dressed up as a Samurai Elvis Presley (sans sword, of course). And there's a woman dressed like Felicity McGrath—a replica not of the real person but of the caricatured Felicity from Poniard's video game. The bailiff glances over at them nervously. I'm sure he'd like to kick them out of the courthouse, but it's a government building, and under the First Amendment, they have a right to be here no matter how they're dressed. Way back in 1971, the Supreme Court held that a man named Paul Cohen had the right to wear in this very courthouse a jacket that bore the inscription "Fuck the Draft."

The Renaissance man approaches me, bows, and waves his right arm in a courtly swirl. "Banquo Nixon at your service, Mr. Stern." He has a full black beard that needs a trim, a long nose, and the dark, swampy eyes of a meth addict. It's clear from the name he's adopted that he's fanatical about Poniard's *Macbeth in the White House*, a role-playing game that conservative pundits, not without justification, have interpreted as advocating the violent overthrow of the United States government. He's carrying a laptop computer under his left arm, the cover scratched and dented. The thing is so antiquated, it must weigh fifteen pounds.

"Nice to meet you." I extend my hand, but he doesn't shake it. Instead, he moves closer to me, almost aggressively. He reeks, emitting an alliaceous body odor. He has the wan face of a transient, but how could a transient access a video game? Though I want to move back, I hold my ground because I don't want to offend the guy.

"Thanks for your support," I say.

"We're here for Poniard, not you," he says. "We don't know you. We're here to protest this vicious attack on Poniard's privacy, the attempt to silence one of the greatest minds of our era. We're here to defy the corporate oligarchs and their Führer, the murderer William the Conqueror." He speaks in a faux English accent, addressing not me but rather an invisible throng that must find his every word riveting. Then he meets my eyes and jabs an index finger at my chest. "It's *your* job to stop Bishop and his henchpeople."

The redhead dressed like Felicity McGrath comes over and loops her arm in Banquo's. "Is this the lawyer?" she asks.

"Parker Stern, Esquire," Banquo says.

"He's cute," she says. "Looks a little like Mercutio Clinton, don't you think?"

"I most certainly do not," Banquo says, pulling his arm away. "But Mr. Stern, if you need help—"

"Thank you, but my staff and I—"

"Even if it's just playing Poniard's video game. It's a difficult game, and that's what we do."

As I struggle to find a way to decline this man's offer of help without offending him and perhaps setting him off—who knows how stable he is?—there's a jangle of keys and the click of a lock. The members of the media push forward, but the bailiff, a somber man in his late forties, shouts, "Hold on. Only the attorneys. Are counsel for Mr. Bishop here?"

As I wend my way through the pack of grumbling media members, Brandon Placek pushes past me and says to the bailiff, "Haven't you people heard of freedom of the press? We have a First Amendment right of access to the courthouse. Our lawyers are standing by. If Judge Triggs thinks he can—"

"Nothing's going to happen without you," the bailiff says. "Logistics."

"Out of my way, Placek," I say, and he backs away when he hears my voice. We've clashed before. He's made the mistake of considering himself a legitimate reporter when he's nothing but a gossipmonger.

"What're you doing down here, Stern?" Placek asks.

"Unlike you, trying to do the right thing."

"You have court business, counselor?" the bailiff says.

"I'm representing the defendant in the Bishop ex parte," I say.

He twitches the side of his mouth upward in a kind of oral shrug. "All right, come on in. The judge didn't expect anyone to show up for the defendant."

Once I'm inside, he locks the door. I don't expect to see my adversaries. Lou Frantz and his protégés always come late, as if they're heavyweight-boxing champions who've earned the privilege of waiting for the right moment to enter the ring.

The thought of what's to come sends my heart careening. I list to the left and grab a chair-back to steady myself. I take some slow breaths and plead with my heart to decelerate. It doesn't, but it doesn't accelerate either. If it gets no worse than this, I can get through the hearing. I go to the defense side of the lawyers' table and sit down. To take my mind off the stage fright, I power on my laptop and use the court's Wi-Fi to search for Poniard and costumes. It turns out that many of Poniard's most rabid fans are into cosplay, short for costume play. Or maybe they're larpers—

live-action role players who act out fantasy adventures physically and in real time. It's common for rabid fans of comic books, anime, and video game fanatics to become cosplayers or larpers. Grownups playing dress-up, though some consider it performance art. There's a whole society built around it. They worship Poniard like he's a god. The thought makes me even queasier. I learned enough about fanaticism as a child to make me shun any charismatic leader or organized religion. That's probably why I became a lawyer. The law is a profession that encourages you to get your questions answered, and I have a lot of questions. Maybe believers do too, but they don't demand answers, because their faith or their prophet provides all the answers. As a matter of fact, that's why I'm in court on this day, Poniard's threat to expose my past aside. I hope to get an answer that has so far escaped me.

CHAPTER 5

The bailiff opens the courtroom door, and Bishop's attorney Lovely Diamond walks in. That's her real name. I've seen her driver's license.

"This is wild," she says. "The media and the Muppets. Anyway, please let Judge Triggs know I'm here. Our application is unopposed, so—"

"Not unopposed, Ms. Diamond," the bailiff says, tilting his head toward me.

Lovely stops halfway down the aisle.

"Good afternoon, counselor," I say, drawing on the remnants of my childhood acting skills to deep-freeze my voice. "Parker Stern appearing for the defendant." It's the most I can muster without my voice shattering, just as I shattered when she left me a few months ago without explanation. For nineteen months, three weeks, and four days, I played her leading man in a sublime romantic dream, only to wake with a start and find that I'd nodded off in the back row of a seedy movie theater. I even missed the end credits, the hilarious outtakes, the fade to black, and now there's only malign diffuse light and a future as blank as the screen. I shouldn't have been surprised. After the excruciating pain dulled down into a cruel, incessant ache, I once again embraced a central fact of my life—the people I love always leave. Why had I expected her to be any different?

What does puzzle me, though, is what happened after we split. She was a rising star in the US Attorney's office, a prodigy with an illimitable future, and yet suddenly she left her dream job to go back to work as a drudge for Louis Frantz, her former mentor. The same Lou Frantz who'd turned on her when she became involved with me. I agreed to take Poniard's case because her name appeared as a cc recipient on Frantz's cease and desist letter.

Her eyes widen and then shut for a moment, as if she's trying to stave off a migraine. "Seriously?" She walks down the aisle and sets her briefcase on the table. I inhale, expecting the scent of orange blossoms and ginger, but now all I smell is soap. It occurs to me that she's washed me out of her life, and now she smells sanitized. It seems as if she's about to reach out and touch my arm, but she only set her hands on the table and leans forward.

"Did you take this case because you found out I'm working on it?" she says. "Because you shouldn't have."

There are few things more pathetic than a spurned lover's futile hope. I've seen therapists and doctors and even a hypnotist for my glossophobia—the technical name for my stage fright. None of them helped. Only Lovely did. I wanted her to be proud of me, and she infused me with a quiet strength. And so for her I fought the fear and refused to fail in the courtroom. Now she helps rid me of the fear in a different way—she makes me angry. Anger sops up all other emotions, including terror, though only for a short while. Anger also makes you lie.

"I took this case because your client is trying to run roughshod over the First Amendment," I say. "I took it because I want another chance to litigate against your arrogant boss. I guess he sent in the second team today."

I want her to blanch at the insult, to quiver in regret, to storm away in rage, to show any form of emotion that will serve as a connection between us, however frayed. She doesn't react, not even an arrhythmic blink.

"Are you filing opposition papers?" she asks in a tone colder than dry ice.

I hand her a set of my papers and give another copy to the clerk, an Asian woman with short dark hair and half-moon reading glasses already perched on her nose. The bailiff unlocks the main door, and the spectators file in, the reporters taking seats in the back so they can quickly exit the courtroom to report breaking news. Poniard's groupies fill the rows immediately behind me. I wish they hadn't. Harmon Cherry warned us that the judge or jury will draw inferences about you from the appearance of people who sit on your side of the room. Some courtroom regulars and several bemused lawyers who obviously have afternoon appearances find the remaining seats.

"All rise and come to order, this court is now in session," the bailiff says.

Out of a hidden door emerges a hulking black man with a Beat poet's goatee and a malevolent glare. Judge T. Tedford Triggs, former All-American offensive tackle and Rhodes scholar before going to law school. At the moment, in his billowing black robe, he resembles one of Poniard's video game characters. Not just any character, but a treacherous level boss whom you have to defeat to advance to the next stage of the game. Triggs has a reputation for trying to do justice, though sometimes he uses his own definition of the term. "*Bishop v. Poniard,*" he says. "Counsel, state your appearances."

"Lovely Diamond of the Louis Frantz Law Firm appearing for the plaintiff William Bishop."

A woman giggles behind me. I twist in my chair and see the Felicity impersonator sitting in the second row and trying to stifle a laugh. I shake my head slightly at her—whether I like it or not, she and her cohort of crazies have become my responsibility. When she sees me, she shuts her eyes, as if that will stop the giggling and snorting, which only gets worse. Banquo, who's sitting next to her, catches my eye. He wraps his arm around her shoulders, puts his hand on the side of her head, and forcefully draws her to him, so that her face and mouth are buried in his broad chest. He seems to be holding her so tightly that for a moment I worry that he's smothering her, that the heaving in her shoulders is a struggle for breath. He whispers something to her, and the heaving subsides. When he lets go, she sits back, holding a fist to her mouth and biting down on her knuckles.

"Counsel for Defendant," the judge says. "Are you going to state your appearance? I haven't got all day."

I have to enter an appearance for my client and myself, a simple task for everyone but me. As soon I stand, I experience that familiar rush of heat and light-headedness that has become a sine qua non of a Parker Stern court appearance. I fight the imminent syncope by gripping the edge of the table with both hands.

"Parker Stern for the Defendant." My voice is raspy. Better that than no voice at all.

The judge lowers his head slightly, which turns his stare into a glower. "I've looked at the papers. Who wants to go first?"

I taught Lovely that a lawyer should always try to get to the lectern first. Now she hurries to the podium as if elbowing her way onto a crowded New York subway. I don't move. Whatever happened between us, I will not push her out of the way.

The judge leans forward and strokes his goatee, his eyes fixed on her, almost a leer. She draws that kind of look wherever she goes. No matter that she spares the makeup, conceals the curves, cuts her hair. I've seen lawyers in a courtroom look at her that way, elderly judges, even women. But once she starts speaking, she has an uncanny ability to get even the most overheated admirer to focus on her words and forget the rest.

Without using notes, she briefly summarizes the case law giving a party the right to take early discovery and then says, "This person who calls himself *Poniard*, this so-called *man* who doesn't have the . . ." she pauses, letting everyone think she'll say *balls*, because in her short time as a lawyer Lovely Diamond has developed a reputation as someone who might say anything in a courtroom . . . "the *guts* to use his own name, has defamed Mr. Bishop. Instead of being brave and standing behind his words, he wants to hide. This *Poniard*"—she spits so hard on the *P* that a fine mist of saliva sprays into the air—"should be ordered to face his accuser, to face the man whose reputation he's trying to destroy. But Poniard says he'll submit to a deposition only in writing. How convenient, because that means we can never get a look at his face to see if he's a liar or a con man or just some smartass doing this for the publicity."

The judge shakes his head. "Ms. Diamond—"

"Apologies, Your Honor. I meant to say wiseass." There's laughter, but this time none of it comes from my side of the room. The worst part is that the judge laughs too.

"Let's say you're right about requiring the defendant to appear for deposition in person," the judge says. "Why so soon?"

"Because the man who hides behind the name Poniard has no respect for the law. Unless we can inspect his computer and take his deposition immediately, we'll have no chance of preserving evidence that will show that he targeted Mr. Bishop for political purposes. Poniard is a radical and a propagandist posing as some sort of artist. Here are his words: 'I design my video games to subvert, and I don't mean just laws or governments, but also the minds of the game players.' Remember that children and teenagers play his video games. He also says, 'The only laws I respect are the rules of my own games, because I create them. The rest is just flawed coding that needs to be deleted.'" She shakes her head disdainfully. "Poniard may have already destroyed evidence. But we won't know unless we have a chance to look, and the longer we have to wait, the longer he'll have to cover up. We have a right to question him and do a forensic analysis of his computers right away. Poniard should be ordered to appear in this courtroom in three days so that we can get a fair chance at discovery. Thank you, Your Honor."

She's left me an opening by focusing on rhetoric and not on the letter of the law, which is on my side. She's a gifted advocate. I was gifted once, but no longer. I'm still more experienced, though, and experience is one of the two antidotes to the venom that is talent, preparation being the other. So said Harmon Cherry.

Harmon wasn't always right.

I get to my feet slowly, so as to keep my balance. Like Lovely, I try rhetoric, taking a risk in quoting the controversial Ayn Rand: "Civilization is the progress toward a society of privacy." I cite the favorable legal precedent in great detail. It's all to no avail. An impatient Judge Triggs looks up at the ceiling. Stage fright is a peculiarly repellant form of narcissism, and now I begin to focus not on what I'm saying but on the sound of my own voice, which grates like feedback from a cheap guitar amp. Some of the media members have folded up their laptops. The Poniard freaks are as quiet and wrung-out as mourners at the end of a funeral.

I hear Tom Petty singing, "I Won't Back Down."

For a moment I think I'm hallucinating, suffering a new symptom of stage fright. Then the smartphone plays the chorus twice more before its owner locates the power button.

"Whose phone?" the judge says.

No response.

"The owner of the cell phone shall identify himself or herself!" A bellow this time.

Again, there are no volunteers. The judge looks at his bailiff and then at his clerk, who both shake their heads.

Silence—not empty but palpable, a whiff of sulfur before the bomb explodes. It's I who light the fuse.

"Your Honor, it's Brandon Placek's phone." I know because I've heard his ringtone before, an obvious symbol of what he must consider his journalistic iconoclasm in the face of the powers that be.

"Identify him," the judge says.

I point to Placek, who's smirking like an insubordinate teen whose life's goal is to flout his parents' values. He mouths the word *asshole*.

I've never been a stool pigeon. On the contrary, I keep far too many secrets. But Placek is in the business of tattling on others for profit and so deserves to suffer at least a pinprick's worth of retribution. Two years ago, he almost destroyed Lovely's career by revealing that as a young woman she performed in hardcore porn videos. They still call her names online—the Licentious Litigator, the "Solicitor" General, the Courthouse Whore, and terms uglier and far more graphic. I blame not only Placek but also Lou Frantz, who permitted his client to leak the information in an attempt to derail my trial. I can't begin to fathom why she's gone back to work for someone who'd do that to her.

Now she's looking down at the table, grinning slightly. She probably thinks I ratted Placek out on her account. Sadly, it's just the opposite.

"Stand up, sir," the judge says to Placek.

Placek stands.

"Give your cell phone to the bailiff," the judge says.

"I won't do that, Judge. I'm a news reporter and need my phone to do my job."

"Hand it over or I'll hold you in contempt and you'll spend the night in jail."

Placek puts the phone in his pocket and crosses his arms. "I'm a member of the news media. The Constitution guarantees freedom of the press. You can't confiscate my phone any more than you could have taken away a reporter's typewriter thirty years ago." Though I hate to admit it, he's right—Triggs is exceeding his authority. But sometimes a little judicial insanity is exactly what an underdog attorney needs. Placek has given me more ammunition than I hoped for.

"Your Honor," I say. "I give you the online media in all its arrogance. Brandon Placek is one of the people . . . no, one of the wolves . . . to whom William Bishop and his lawyers would throw my client. Placek calls himself a journalist but makes his living off of the next premature death of a big-breasted reality star, the next manufactured political scandal, the next accidentally-on-purpose celebrity sex tape."

The judge puts down his pen and sits back in his chair. He's listening.

"The desire for privacy is one of the things that makes us human, that separates us from beasts," I continue. "If we're lucky, the right of privacy lets us forget a difficult childhood, escape a troubled past. Privacy allows us to maintain our dignity.

"And then there's Poniard. He's a worldwide celebrity." I turn and gesture toward the cosplayers. "As you can tell, there are people who worship him and his video games. And despite all that, he's chosen to remain anonymous, to maintain a private life. That's refreshing in this era of Kardashians and New Jersey Housewives. And yet people like Brandon Placek would sacrifice Poniard's right of privacy in the guise of seeking truth. Your Honor, there's no good reason to order Poniard's deposition to go forward on Friday, and there's no reason to order him to ever appear in person. I implore that you not make Poniard choose between his right to privacy and his due process right to defend himself in this lawsuit."

Lovely is at the lectern before I sit down. "Mr. Stern likes to throw around quotes about privacy. How about this one from Judge Richard Posner? 'Privacy is greatly overrated because it means concealment. People conceal things in order to fool other people.'" And that's exactly what Mr. Stern is trying to do. His client leveled the most scurrilous charges against a good man and sent the libel out to billions of people on the Internet. And now we're supposed to feel sorry for poor Poniard. The hypocrisy of the argument is breathtaking. Poniard's problems are of his own making, and he shouldn't be able to hide behind—"

"I understand your point, Ms. Diamond," the judge says. "But not to put too technical a spin on it, two wrongs don't make—"

"Except there aren't two wrongs here, there's only one wrong, and that's Poniard's—"

"My point, counsel, is that—"

"—obvious libel of Mr. Bishop."

"One moment, Ms. Diamond, I—"

"If you'd only let me finish my sentence—"

"Ms. Diamond, stop talking now!"

Maybe Harmon *was* right about experience trumping talent.

Her jaw quivers and her lips move, and I think, Lovely, please don't say another word, because I don't want to win this way, and I don't want to see you screw up.

The judge shakes a finger at her. "Ms. Diamond, I've read about you. Given your checkered past, I would think that if you weren't advocating a case, you'd be the first one to agree that a person has the right to keep their private life private."

The spectators react with a mixture of gasps and titters, the media with frenzied keystrokes on laptops, because what can be more newsworthy than a judge's reference to a female attorney's porn past? I stand up to speak, though a lawyer should never stand up to speak when he's winning. "Your Honor, I want to state for the record that the defense rests on the merits. The defense does not agree with the reference to Ms. Diamond's past."

"I don't need Mr. Stern or anyone else to help me," Lovely says. "I'm not ashamed of my past, and I don't care what the media says about me. Unlike Poniard, I'm perfectly willing to live with the consequences of my choices. If you'd really done research on me, Judge Triggs, you'd know that. The only thing that Mr. Stern and I agree on, Your Honor, is that it's inappropriate for the Court to bring my personal life into a legal argument."

"I've heard enough," the judge says. "The application to take Poniard's deposition in three days is denied. You'll both follow the normal rules of procedure."

Lovely grabs the sides of the podium. "Your Honor, I haven't finished—"

"Yes, you have," the judge says. "Here's my order. Poniard doesn't have to appear in person for a deposition. The deposition will be taken telephonically or by other audio means. Ms. Diamond, when you do depose him, you and your colleagues may *not* ask him any questions about his identity, residence, whereabouts, or other identifying information. Mr. Stern, be forewarned that if you proceed this way, you are not permitted to call Poniard as a witness at trial. You're stuck with his audio deposition, and I'm sure you know that's a poor substitute for a live witness." He picks up a file folder, turns pages, puts it down, and whispers to his court clerk, who shrugs.

"Will this be a jury trial?"

"Defendant will not demand a jury," I say. No jury would trust someone who refuses to show up and defend himself. I like Judge Triggs. We'll have a better chance if he decides the case.

"Ms. Diamond, will the plaintiff demand a jury?" the judge asks.

"No, Your Honor," Lovely says, her displeasure with the answer evident in her abrupt tone. I'm sure that's what Frantz instructed her to say, that he's concerned that twelve ordinary people wouldn't relate to Bishop, a billionaire with a reputation for destroying anyone who stands in his way. Thanks to Brandon Placek's cell phone, I got the better of this one.

"All right then," Judge Triggs said. "A court trial. That'll expedite things." He abruptly gets up and lumbers back to his chambers before those in the courtroom can stand. It's surprising that such a big man can move so fast. He's evidently forgotten about jailing Brandon Placek.

Lovely leaves the courtroom immediately, pushing past the media. They begin shouting questions to me, all variations of "Who is Poniard?" Placek outlasts them all, taunting me about Lovely's adult film career, as if the stale story still means something to me. I sit down at counsel table with my back to him until he leaves. When I turn around, Poniard's cosplay fans are standing. They begin to clap. They don't realize that this most insignificant of victories has nothing to do with whether Poniard has libeled William Bishop or with what happened to Paula Felicity McGrath almost thirty years earlier.

CHAPTER 6

The Hoar Frost Queen and Bugsy are arguing—well, the HF Queen is arguing—about Brighton. She comes home and announces that he shouldn't be allowed to play *Abduction!*, says that the game is a lie and children shouldn't be exposed to lies. Now Bugsy says that she's being unfair, that television and movies and, yes, video games are lies, but they're supposed to be, and that Brighton is doing very well in school, so why not give the kid a break? The HF Queen starts ranting about her *fucked-up life*, and all the while Bugsy stands leaning against the wall, arms crossed and eyes half-closed, maybe listening to her, maybe not. When the HF Queen notices Brighton peeking out through the crack in the door of his room, she raises her hand and points, her fingernails a burnished maroon, and it seems as if she's about to issue an edict in that icy voice so cutting that it can lop off the head of an impudent subject, but instead she drops her arm wearily, goes into her bedroom, and closes the door. Brighton, figuring that it's safe to leave his own room, walks up to Bugsy and shrugs a question. Bugsy raises a hand palm forward, a gesture that can mean *leave me alone*, *leave her alone*, or *leave it to me*. This time it means all three. Bugsy turns and goes into the large room with the pool table and the big-screen TV that he calls his study.

It's true that Brighton is doing well in school—almost. When he first came to live in this house, he worried that the Archwood Community School of the Santa Monica Mountains—that's actually what they call the place—would be too difficult, that all the kids would be geniuses. But it's not hard at all, no harder than his old public school was, and while the kids are richer than his former classmates, they certainly aren't any smarter. In fact, they're dumber if you factor in their lack of street smarts. He's doing well in math (graphing, fractions, no problem) and Language Arts/Literature (they're reading *Peter and the Starcatchers*, a book about an orphan, how annoying). Social studies is the problem, although Bugsy and the HF Queen don't know it yet. He doesn't see the point of history, even when the teacher talks about being doomed to repeat the past. So what? No matter how bad the past was, how can anyone be sure that the future won't be worse? But what worries him is this new assignment. It's going to ruin his grade. He has to write a report on his family history, an assignment that will supposedly teach them about immigration in America but really is intended to get the students' grandparents to donate money for the new gymnasium. So said Bugsy. Which made the HF Queen mad. *Don't make the kid a cynic*, she said, as if Brighton weren't one already. Anyway, what family history does he have to write about? That his parents abandoned him when he was a baby, that his Aunt Greta took him in, that she died ten years later of cardiac arrest, and that Bugsy and the HF Queen showed up? He will *not* write about Bugsy and the HF Queen.

The bigger surprise at school is his popularity. Well, not popularity, really, because he knows deep down that they still think of him as a video-game geek from the OC. But he commands respect. After all, he's the only person they know who's beaten Level One of *Abduction!* In the last few days, others claim to have done it. And now suddenly, Felicity's letters from her nightstand are all over the web, and everyone wants to know what they mean.

Brighton starts toward his room but hesitates. Instead, he goes to the HF Queen's bedroom and raises his fist to knock, but his hand freezes when he hears rhythmic snuffling, a sorrowful sound, and he realizes that the HF Queen can cry.

CHAPTER 7

Most people complain about the traffic in Los Angeles, but not me. Maybe it's because I was so lonely as a child—perhaps other kid actors had friends, but I didn't. When my mother shuttled me from one audition to another, our old Ford Fairlane inevitably getting stuck in traffic, I'd look at the other cars and imagine that the burly man behind the wheel of the Plymouth Barracuda was the father I'd never known or that the giggling girl in the back seat of the BMW was my sister. While my mother would mouth profanities at the traffic gods, I'd silently pray that the red light wouldn't change to green, that the traffic would gridlock so we couldn't move a foot, that we would sit forever amidst the cars and the strangers and the sweet vehicular chaos that kept me out of the casting agent's office. I still find solace on the city streets, in the senseless sprawl, in the low-rise grit and glamour of Los Angeles. So it doesn't bother me that I arrive at work a little after ten in the morning.

As an employee of JADS, I'm supposed to be mediating lawsuits, not propagating them, and so I foolishly hope that despite the extensive news coverage of the previous day's court hearing, my JADS bosses won't notice that I'm defending Poniard in Bishop's lawsuit. Any possibility of that is dashed when I arrive at work to find Poniard's cosplayers, in full costume, milling around on the sidewalk in front of the JADS main entrance. When they see me approaching, they start applauding and shouting my name. I don't want to be anybody's hero, even on this small scale. I learned as a child that fame is a molecular bonding of other people's fantasies, absorbed into your own body like an intravenous drug that trades short-lived ecstasy for a life of constant peril.

I should ignore them, should push my way inside and have the receptionist call security, but when Banquo beckons me over, I stop. He raises his hand, and the others surround me in a ceremonial semicircle. The Felicity impersonator steps forward. She's wearing the same outfit that Felicity wears in the video game—the tight black dress, even the black jacket, though a late-September heat wave has set in—and like Felicity's, her red hair is still in dreadlocks. She curtsies and hands me a wilted gardenia that I'm sure she picked from the bush outside the JADS back entrance. Then she moves close, stands on her toes, and kisses me full on the mouth, thrusting her tongue between my lips. I jerk my head back in disgust, but not before I taste stale Cheetos and marijuana. I almost gag.

"Don't!" I say, backing away, but she skitters forward, pushing her chest against mine. She stands on tiptoes to kiss me again, but I reach out to push her away.

Banquo's Shakespearean voice resonates over the rush-hour traffic on Gateway Avenue. "Leave him alone, Courtney!"

She doesn't move an inch. Her green eyes shimmer with sexual challenge. "My name's *Felicity*," she says with a pout, and then runs back into the crowd, giggling.

"Apologies, Mr. Stern, Esquire," Banquo says. "She gets ... overly enthusiastic."

"Why are you here?" I ask.

He bows. "Your servants, sir, in service of your person and the truth, are here to guard your flank as you do battle against the darkling demon, William the Conqueror."

"Very kind, but I've got it covered."

"Don't patronize me, sir. We'll remain here until the boss William the Conqueror has been vanquished."

"What do you mean you'll remain here?"

"Just what I said. We will remain here until you win."

I study his expression for any sign that he's joking. "Look, if you're intending to camp out in the parking lot, there's no way that—"

The main door swings open, and Brenda Sica walks out. "Mr. Stern, come inside. It's urgent."

I go inside and follow her down the corridor.

"You shouldn't be talking to those people," she says.

"They're harmless."

"How do you know? What if they work for Bishop or Frantz?"

Though she might be a conspiracy theorist, she also might be right. The Felicity impersonator—Courtney—almost made a scene in court the other day that could've severely hurt our side. Maybe her behavior just now was a cover. While I don't think even Lou Frantz would stoop to such tactics, William Bishop would. A couple of years ago the managing editor of one of his Parapet Media newspapers was charged with illegally hacking into private computers looking for dirt on celebrities and politicians. Of course, Bishop let his editor take the fall. But if he could hack the computer of a member of Congress, he's certainly capable of dressing up some unemployed actors in costumes and having them disrupt my place of business.

Just before we reach my office door, Brenda grabs my sleeve and stops me. "There's a weird old guy in there. Real sweaty. I think he's crazy. He says he works for you, that he . . . should I call security?"

"Give me a minute." I hurry into my office. A stocky man in his mid-sixties is sitting in one of my client chairs. He's wearing a suit and a white cotton dress shirt that's tight around the collar and barrel chest. Though it's cool inside, his forehead and nose glisten with a thin layer of sweat, causing his rimless glasses to slip slightly down the bridge. His breathing is audible, as if he just climbed seven flights of stairs. He's nibbling on a blueberry scone. He's made my desk his table and a paper napkin his tablecloth. Some of the pastry has missed his mouth and is stuck to his face. Not unusual—perhaps his only downside is that he's a sloppy eater. It's all I can do not to reach over and wipe his face for him. But I wouldn't. Philip Paulsen is a proud man.

He cranes his neck toward me. "Hello, Parker." The voice is soft, almost breathless.

"Hey, Philip. I didn't think you'd come."

"Joyce didn't want me to," he says. "But I've been going stir-crazy these past few years. Besides, I've never had a fondness for William

Bishop. His television networks claim to be objective and churn out propaganda. His hypocrisy bothers me more than his politics. Consider me hired."

"Great. Welcome aboard."

He wipes his hands with the napkin, stands up and formally shakes my hand, and sits down again.

For ten years, Paulsen worked at my former law firm as the top paralegal. To his wife Joyce's displeasure, I've talked him out of retirement. He's intelligent, adept at using technology, a stickler for detail, and that unusual soul who revels in the mind-numbing job of organizing documents and researching arcana. He's an analytical thinker and someone who can keep his cool during the pressure of a trial. And no one is more tight-lipped. But Philip is different from most paralegals. While most are in their twenties and thirties, Paulsen is sixty-four. And before he earned his paralegal credential he was a Catholic priest, an expert in canon law. When one rather inebriated associate at a Macklin & Cherry cocktail party asked Paulsen why he'd left the priesthood, he replied, "Joyce and I fell in love and wanted to get married, and no, she wasn't a nun."

I call Brenda into my office and introduce Paulsen as our new paralegal. She nods without enthusiasm.

"I guess I'll see if Judge Croninger has something for me," she says.

"Nonsense," Philip says. "There's plenty of work on this case."

She gives a rare smile. Philip always makes others feel comfortable.

"So what do you make of the letters?" he says.

I look at Brenda, who shrugs.

He reaches under the chair, picks up his attaché case, retrieves some computer printouts, and hands them to me. The first document is copy of a handwritten letter.

Dear Scotty,
    As always, you worry too much. Bad vibrations. It's just make-believe, remember? And Big Bad Billy Bishop has our Backs (how's that for alliteration?) Anyway, my darling, he's my insur-

ance policy. Stop worrying. Free ticket out of purgatory. So relax
while I enjoy for once.
  Love ya,
  Felicity

"And you got this from where?" I ask.

"From the *Abduction!* game, of course."

"I don't understand."

He furrows his brow. "You mean your client didn't ... ? I just
assumed ... I only brought them with me because I wanted to impress
you with my skills as a gamer."

"You play video games?" Brenda says. "I mean you're ..."

"You're right, Brenda," he says. "I'm old."

Her face flushes. "I'm sorry, I didn't mean—"

"No one knows technology better than Philip," I say.

He waves his hand dismissively. "Read the others, Parker."

The second letter is typewritten.

May 12, 1987

Hey, hey Paula,
  You're treading over old ground and on a poisonous snake. I do not trust Wm. the Conqueror
as far as I can throw his budding corporate
conglomerate. He's not who he was in the old
days. This isn't some phase. He's one of them,
which means he's dangerous. And you are worried
or you'd be calling instead of writing. Afraid
that the phones are bugged, that they have video
cameras in your room? If that's true, be a good
girl and keep your panties on.
  Better yet, come home to us.
  Love,
  Scotty

And a last one, undated:

Dear Scotty,
　　Surprise! You're going to take that trip to Paris you've always dreamed about. The tickets have been reserved in your name. The flight leaves in three days. Au revoir, my sweet.
　　Love always,
　　Felicity.

"You said you got this from *Abduction!*?" I say.

"I beat the first level by opening a drawer in Felicity's bedroom, and out these papers flew. Mostly junk—rants about Bishop, historical facts about Felicity's career—but these three are important. They're screen captures."

"You can't seriously believe they're real."

"I can't say one way or another. You should ask your client. But if they are real, it proves that Paula Felicity McGrath and William Bishop knew each other and were involved in something."

Trying to control my anger, I ask them to leave and shut my door. I immediately ping Poniard. It takes five minutes to get a response.

Poniard:
>Good result yesterday, counselor—though I would've expected to hear from you directly instead of learning about it online
PStern
>I had more pressing things to do. Like reading my book and having a cup of fine Ethiopian blend.

It takes a long time to get a response. Has my snide remark angered him? I hope so. But finally:

Poniard:
>Rule of professional conduct 3-500: "A lawyer shall keep a client rea-sonably informed about significant developments relating to the employment or representation"
PStern
>You're the last person who should lecture me about ethics. But I want to know something. Are those letters from the video game genuine?

Poniard:
>*Ha! So you beat level 1. Not many have*
PStern
>*Are those letters genuine?*
Poniard:
>*Yep*
PStern
>*Why didn't you give them to me before?*
Poniard:
>*Not as much fun that way*
PStern
>*That's no answer.*
Poniard:
>*OK, then I did it my way so I could get Wm. the Conqueror to deny they are real and catch him in a lie. He doesn't know I have the originals. FYI, I set a classic "skill-based trap." Which means that the player has to have skill to avoid it, and Bishop doesn't have skill*
PStern
>*No skill? Bishop isn't nicknamed "The Conqueror" for nothing.*
Poniard:
>*He has no skill this time. My trap takes advantage of the fact that Bishop doesn't understand the mechanics of what's happening. But for a trap to work, you need a trigger. The game was a trigger, and the trap was sprung!! If I'd just given you the docs you would've produced them in the lawsuit and he would have thought up some excuse and we would not have trapped him in his lie. His press release is online*

I switch programs and search for "William Bishop *Abduction!*" Poniard is right—as soon as people started beating Level One of the game, Felicity's letters spread virally over the web. Bishop formally denied the letter's authenticity in a press release issued early this morning.

PStern
>*How did you get these docs?*

Poniard:
>*Cannot share that even with you. Someone could get hurt. So do not ask again*

PStern
>*Send me the originals immediately!*

Poniard:
>*OK then, I will send you the originals; but you must protect them with your life*

PStern
>*FedEx them for overnight delivery; I want them by tomorrow.*

Poniard:
>*No fedex. I'll get them to you in my own way*

PStern
>*Immediately. And I hope for your sake they're legit.*

Poniard:
>*Security measures?*

PStern
>*JADS has an office safe.*

Poniard:
>*NO!!! Somewhere only you know about*

He's right. Too many people have access to the safe in this office.

PStern
>*My personal safety deposit box, then.*

Poniard:
>*Where?*

PStern
>*Community Bank of Marina Del Rey. It's stable and reputable.*

I wait a long time for the response.

Poniard:
>*OK, better be secure*

PStern
>*I have another question. Who's Scotty?*

Poniard:
>Don't know

I don't believe him. But as Harmon Cherry would say, a good lawyer knows when to ask questions, but a great lawyer knows when to stop. I close the chat program. So, either Poniard is a forger or William Bishop is a liar.

I wait until my anger at Poniard cools and then pick up the phone and ask Brenda to bring Philip back to my office. She's at my door thirty seconds later, alone, carrying some papers.

"Where's Paulsen?" I ask.

"Gone," she says. "He doesn't think it appropriate for him to be working at the JADS offices." She walks over and hands me the documents. "He wanted to give you these, in case we don't have the information, which we don't, though I've been looking . . ." Flustered, she primps at her hair. "I thought I should've found this, but Mr. Paulsen says he has a special subscription to the St. Thomas More University archives, their entire library network, that he's a librarian, and. . . . He's so nice. Anyway, he says good things really do come in threes."

CHAPTER 8

Philip Paulsen has located three potential witnesses whom we haven't been able to find. The first, Natalie Owen, now Natalie Jones—no wonder we couldn't find her with that name—was Felicity McGrath's roommate at the time of McGrath's disappearance. She lives in Florida. In a phone call, she rebuffs my offer to fly to Tampa and meet with her, insists that she told everything she knows to the cops back in 1987. After some prodding from me, she says that she placed an ad for a roommate, was surprised when a famous actress like Felicity McGrath answered it, and then found herself chasing McGrath for the rent every month. They roomed together for only five months before McGrath disappeared. The women never became friends—Owen would return in the evening from her job as a bank teller, and McGrath would immediately leave, never saying where she was going and often not returning to the apartment until the next day. Or sometimes McGrath would stay in her bedroom for days at a time, as if depressed. Owen thinks that McGrath was out partying, sleeping around with men, drinking and doing drugs. McGrath was secretive, which made their last encounter odd—Felicity went out of her way to tell Owen that she was meeting with a friend and going on a movie shoot. I probe for more information, but Owen doesn't know anything else. Or maybe she doesn't want to get involved.

So Brenda and I get in my car—we have to dodge Banquo and his cosplayers—and drive to Century City, hoping to have better luck with Herman "Bud" Kreiss Jr., a former LAPD detective and current owner/operator of Kreiss Security & Protection Services, LLC. Kreiss's office is located on Santa Monica Boulevard, on the ground floor of a white stucco low-rise strip mall that also houses a dry cleaner, a Tarot card reader, and a "We'll Sell It for You on eBay" shop. This is the side of the street where the homeless are allowed to loiter and crash so as not to disturb the wealthy mall and restaurant patrons on the south side of the wide thoroughfare. Despite the rundown condition of his offices, Kreiss bills himself as *Protector of the Stars*. Hardly.

We walk up to Kreiss's address, a wrought iron fence that encloses a small, grimy concrete slab that passes for a patio. The gate is locked, so I press the intercom button. There's a loud buzz that makes Brenda flinch. I open the gate, and we walk across a patio that's bare of greenery except for an overgrown juniper hedge and a pathetic overwatered ficus. When we get to the actual entrance to Kreiss's office, there's another galvanized security gate, and we have to be buzzed in a second time.

A heavy-set fiftyish brunette sits behind the reception desk, her gray roots so uniform that they appear to have been dyed in under the brown rather than the other way around. She's looking down at the desk.

"Parker Stern and Brenda Sica to see—"

"He's waiting for you," she says, pinching her brows together and lifting her eyes into a glower.

I open the office door to find Kreiss standing behind a massive walnut desk, which has only a pen in a holder and an ink blotter on it. An obsolete PC and monitor sit on the credenza behind him. There isn't a single piece of paper on the desk. The walls are covered with black-and-white publicity-grade photos of Kreiss with people I surmise are his "celebrity" clients, mostly one-hit-wonder pop singers and small-time character actors, the names of whom only someone with a show business past will recognize. He motions for us to sit down and then sits behind his desk.

He has a wiry build for a man in his sixties. His face is so scored with wrinkles that it looks as if it once served as a restaurant chopping block. He's wearing a blue blazer with gold buttons, a solid red tie that isn't quite long enough, and khaki slacks. His gray hair is cropped short, and his moustache is neatly trimmed. He could be a mall security official.

As soon as Brenda and I introduce ourselves, he says in a cop-like monotone, "It appears that your client has some major obstacles to overcome."

"Not if you can help me prove that William Bishop is involved in Felicity McGrath's disappearance," I say.

"What makes you think I have information that relates to your case?"

It's a fair question. His name doesn't appear in the police report that Philip Paulsen located, or in the citywide newspapers of the era—the *Times* and the *Herald Examiner*—or in any of the tabloid articles that obsessively characterized Felicity McGrath's disappearance as a modern-day *Black Dahlia* crime. I hand him a printout.

"It's a story from the *Venice Beach Breeze* dated July 27, 1987," I say. "Four days after McGrath's disappearance. Written by a reporter for the Breeze named Dalila Hernandez. The article identifies Detective Sergeant Bud Kreiss, LAPD Venice substation, as the chief investigator. Quotes you as saying that you had a lead on a person of interest. We'd like to know who that person was."

He tosses the piece of paper back at me. "The *Venice Beach Breeze* was a throwaway rag devoted to the legalization of cannabis sativa and to following the career of that chainsaw juggler who performed on the boardwalk. There's no such person of interest."

"Why were you taken off the case, then?"

"That's not accurate, sir."

"Sure you were. We've done our research, Mr. Kreiss."

"I was based in the Pacific Area station and Ted Gorecki, my superior in Downtown Central, decided to take over the investigation. So I watched over the case for a few days at the beginning and then went on to other things. Nothing more sinister than that."

"Please take a look at this, sir," Brenda says, and hands him another printout from the *Venice Beach Breeze*. This time, his eyes deaden, and I'd bet my SAG residuals that if his skin weren't a weather-beaten bronze, I'd see the color leave his cheeks. This article reported that six weeks into the McGrath investigation, Kreiss was busted back down to patrolman, working the graveyard shift.

"So you were taken off the case," I say.

There's a loud creak from the outer office, and the receptionist appears at the office door. "Your eleven o'clock will be arriving shortly, Bud."

"Isla, stop."

"Please," she says.

"Isla's my wife and business partner," Kreiss says. "Also the Protector of the Stars's protector." He swivels his chair to the side and says to her, "Everything's OK."

She nods without conviction and leaves the room. Kreiss gets up and shuts the door.

"You were demoted because of the McGrath investigation," I say. "Why?"

"They said . . ." He clears his throat. He appears to be a man who rarely speaks haltingly, but now he has to force the words out. "The brass claimed I engaged in an inappropriate relationship with Dalila Hernandez. It was a damn lie. She and I were just friends." He gazes at me—past me, really—for a long time.

"What happened to Felicity?" I ask. "Because I think you truly believe that William Bishop kidnapped her." How odd my profession—I literally want to hear that Bishop, by all accounts a devoted family man, a renowned philanthropist, someone with no criminal record, has committed a heinous crime.

He leans forward, rests his chin in his hands, and waits for a long time. It's all I can do not to repeat the question, but I know I'll lose him if I do. Eventually, he sits up and inhales deeply.

"There's this wino who crashed on Venice Beach during the summer," he says. "Luther Frederickson. Boardwalk Freddy, they called him. A polite panhandler who'd always say *god bless you* even if you didn't give him a handout, even when the patrolmen were rousting him for loitering. He'd been an accountant in the late sixties who'd gotten into LSD. He quit his cushy desk job, deserted his wife and two kids, and moved up to Haight-Ashbury during the Summer of Love. By nineteen eighty-five, he was a Thunderbird lush living on the streets. The night McGrath disappeared, Freddy was sleeping one off in the alcove of the Pacific Avenue Hotel—it was a flophouse back then, trendy now. He told me he saw McGrath leaving the Windward Bar with two men, one tall and one short."

"So did ten other people," I say.

"What isn't in the police report is that Boardwalk Freddy saw a yellow Volkswagen Rabbit pull up," he says. "The two men put her in the VW, which sped away north toward the Santa Monica Pier. According to Freddy, thirty seconds later the two guys were picked up by a blue Mercedes Benz. The driver stepped out of the car and went into the backseat. The shorter man got behind the wheel. The tall guy got into the passenger seat. They drove away south down Pacific Avenue, the opposite direction from the VW." He speaks as if he were testifying at trial, the experienced police witness dispassionately recounting facts to a jury.

"They found her blood at the pier," Brenda says, visibly shuddering.

"Her blood *type*," Kreiss says. "AB positive. Doesn't mean it was hers."

"Yeah, but only three percent of the population has it," Brenda says.

Kreiss hesitates and then seems to gather courage again. "According to Boardwalk Freddy, the man in the Mercedes was William Bishop."

Brenda turns and taps me on the shoulder excitedly, but if she thinks I'm going to jump out of my chair in glee, she's mistaken.

Kreiss understands. "Mr. Stern's next question is why would I give any credence to the word of a drunk and an addict like Freddy."

"Especially a drunk sitting in an alcove in the dark of night who supposedly glimpses a man from fifty yards away and identifies him as Bishop," I say. "Who, by the way, wasn't nearly as famous in 1987 as he is now."

"That's what my superiors thought," Kreiss says. "But I already told you that Freddy was an accountant before he tuned in, turned on, and dropped out. A cost accountant for the movie industry. He knew very well who Bishop was."

"It's still pretty thin," I say.

"Maybe. But why did my superior order me not to follow up? And when I went over his head, why did they back him up and send me out on the streets? Maybe a witness like Freddy was reliable, maybe not. But a good cop follows up on all leads. My bosses didn't."

"And after that you just let it go?" Brenda says. "Just like that, you ignored what you knew and maybe let a killer go free?" It's a harsh indictment, all the more caustic because it comes from timid Brenda Sica.

He looks up at the ceiling, embarrassed.

"What happened to Luther Frederickson?" I ask.

"A week after Felicity disappeared, some regulars on the beach reported him missing. They found his Samsonite suitcase in an alley off Rose Avenue. He'd never have abandoned that suitcase. It contained everything he owned."

"Who else knows about Boardwalk Freddy?" I ask.

"Isla knows, of course. And my superior Gorecki and whoever was in the department back then who covered it up."

"Names?" I ask.

He shakes his head. "Only Gorecki. I don't think the Chief would. ... I hoped the demotion would be temporary, an object lesson, but when it became clear I'd never be a detective again, I quit the department."

"Do you truly believe that William Bishop kidnapped Felicity McGrath?" I ask. "That he was behind the disappearance of Luther Frederickson?"

He reaches back and massages his neck. "I found Boardwalk Freddy very credible. So, I'd have to say yes, Bishop was involved somehow. He should have been the prime suspect based on the eyewitness identification. But . . ." He gestures to the pictures on the wall. "I've made my living representing actors and singers, mostly. Protecting them against stalkers, deranged fans, vengeful ex-spouses. C- and D-List celebrities, sure, but they're targets of the crazies, too. Bishop controls Hollywood. If he wanted to put me out of business, he could have. One word from him, and no one walks through this door. I don't understand why he let me survive."

"Maybe it was a reward for your not talking," Brenda says.

"Maybe yes, maybe no," he says. "But there's something else—I could never think of a motive."

"Cheating on his wife?" Brenda says. "Felicity was going to expose their affair?"

He shrugs. "Bishop has the reputation of being a faithful husband. Remarkable in Hollywood if it's true. I never had evidence otherwise."

"Will you testify to what you know?" I ask.

He's silent.

"It's time to reveal the truth, Mr. Kreiss," Brenda says softly.

He glances at the office door as if checking on whether his wife is eavesdropping. "OK, yeah. It's past time. If you subpoena me and get me under oath, I'll tell the truth."

We thank Kreiss and leave his office. As we pass the front desk, I nod at Isla, whose eyes emit high-voltage anger.

Once outside, I swing the patio gate open. The corroded hinges squeal, and the sagging gate scrapes on the concrete, the dissonant sounds mimicking the proverbial fingernails on slate. But that's not what sends the arpeggio of needle pricks up my spine.

Banquo, Courtney, and the other Poniard cosplayers are gathered on the sidewalk, standing like some sort of church choir. Banquo bows and says, "We stand ready, willing, and able to serve the cause, Mr. Stern, Esquire. Please just let us know how we can help."

CHAPTER 9

Philip Paulsen's third possible witness is Nathan Ettinger, a professor in the Film and Theater Arts Department at Topanga College, a liberal arts college tucked in the hills above Malibu. Ettinger's scholarly book on 1980s cinema reveals some new details about Felicity McGrath. She was born in Springfield, Illinois, in 1959 and came to Hollywood in 1975 as a fifteen-year-old runaway, fleeing an alcoholic, impoverished mother and the mother's abusive boyfriends. She apparently used a fake ID to land some small roles in failed sitcoms and marginal direct-to-video movie productions. Though she never appeared in true pornography, her early roles were so sexual that when her true age was discovered after *The Fragile Palace* made her famous, authorities investigated the makers of her early films for putting an underage actress in sexual situations. He concludes with, "At the time of McGrath's disappearance, it was rumored that she'd been having an affair with an unidentified Hollywood studio executive."

William Bishop, of course, was a studio executive. He's been married to the same woman for decades, a fact he's long used as a PR talking point. Was Felicity going to ruin Bishop by exposing an affair?

I navigate to the end of the book, the *About the Author* section. Before becoming an educator, Ettinger was a film producer. Most of his credits are on movies I've never heard of. One credit catches my attention, though—"Nate" Ettinger was an associate producer on a movie called *Climbing Panda Hill*. As a nine-year-old, I starred in that movie, and if memory served, Ettinger was the same Nate who'd slept with my mother, a fact that might appear fortuitous except that, for males with production credits on my movies, sleeping with my mother was the rule rather than the exception.

Brenda can't seem to schedule a meeting with Ettinger, so one afternoon, about a week after our interview with Bud Kreiss, I tell her to grab her purse and come with me. The moment we get into the car, I crack my window a bit, discreetly I hope, because without air circulation Brenda's perfume will have my car smelling like a turn-of-the-last-century bordello. As we drive west to the coast, we're separated by that off-kilter silence that happens when two strangers who work together find themselves alone in close quarters. In an attempt to regain some equilibrium, I ask, "Are you from LA?"

"I'm kind of from nowhere. And everywhere. How would you say it, like a Navy brat? But not."

She doesn't want to talk about her past, and who am I to argue with that? As far as most people know, my life started when I was eighteen years old.

We take the 10 Freeway to PCH and drive up the coast to chaparral-covered Topanga Canyon, which lies in the hills above the Malibu coast. The Canyon has long served as the epicenter of LA's hippie, Bohemian, and New Age cultures. And six-year-old Topanga College, where Nate Ettinger taught cinema, gladly embraces that culture, lining the halls with photographs of former Topanga residents like Woody Guthrie, Humphrey Bogart, Carole Lombard, Shirley Temple, Will Geer, Jim Morrison, Neil Young, and Etta James. Brenda checked out the course catalog. Along with the usual liberal arts courses, the college curriculum includes classes on the Philosophy and Ethics of Veganism, and Religions of the New Age.

Ettinger's office is in the Humanities Building, a sparkling octagonal structure with three cantilevered stories, glass exterior walls, and a spacious common area on each floor. The college has some wealthy benefactors interested in promoting alternative higher education, whatever that means.

We go up to the second floor. We learned from his website that he holds office hours between two and four every Tuesday and Thursday. I just hope he's not with a student.

We find him at his desk, reading what looks like a movie script. His office is large compared to most university offices I've seen and boasts a view of the northern hills, lush because they're so close to the ocean. I knock on the open door.

"May I help . . . ?" He sits back in his chair and removes his reading glasses.

"I'm Parker Stern and this is Brenda Sica," I say. "We're representing someone named Poniard in—"

"I know who you are, Mr. Stern." He looks around, as if searching for an escape route.

"Apologies for dropping in unannounced, but it's very important that we speak with you," I say. "And we did try to make an appointment."

"You did. I've been . . . please come in." He has keen blue eyes, a long nose, salt-and-pepper hair, and a gray goatee. He is, indeed, the kind of man whom my mother would've fallen for. Whatever his Hollywood past, he's certainly embraced the stereotype of an academic. He's dressed in a herringbone tweed jacket with suede elbow patches, a white turtleneck, prewashed blue jeans, and brown Docksiders.

We sit. The bookcase behind his chair is filled with tomes on film production, screenwriting, and critical theory. Two of the shelves are overstuffed with movie scripts. "Let's cut to the chase," he says. "I have to prepare for a class I'm teaching in a half hour. You're here because of what I wrote in my book, about Felicity McGrath having an affair with a movie producer."

"I think your exact words are *studio executive*."

"Let me be candid. I'm certainly not going to tell you that it's William Bishop. I don't want to be the next person he sues for defamation."

"But it is Bishop?" Brenda says in a hopeful voice.

Ettinger gives her a sidelong glance and speaks to me. "Felicity McGrath reputedly had affairs with many men in Hollywood. As I say, I don't want to—"

"I could subpoena you," I say. "Maybe that'll work for you. There's something called the litigation privilege. It gives you absolute immunity from a defamation lawsuit no matter what you say."

"It's not only being *sued* by Bishop that concerns me." He tries so hard to maintain eye contact that his head quivers slightly.

Part of me is disgusted by Ettinger's fear, but I understand. Bud Kreiss, a former cop and someone who made a living facing physical danger, kept his information secret for decades.

"I assume you learned about Felicity's affair from your time in the movie business," I say.

"I was a producer," he says. "I started from the bottom, as a grip, a gaffer, a script reader, a camera operator and worked my way up until I got sick of the phoniness. And yes, Felicity's affairs were well known. But no one had the guts to name names. In nineteen eighty-one, eighty-two, Bishop's corporate raiders took over the studio where I had a housekeeping deal and killed everything that had any artistry to it, including a movie I had in development. In writing my book, I let my disgust for his hypocrisy get the better of me. In hindsight it was bad judgment on my part to mention the affair at all. And I'm not going to expand on what I wrote one iota."

I ask a series of questions about his work history, which he's happy to talk about. I stay away from one movie, of course—the one he and I worked on together. So far, he hasn't recognized me as Parky Gerald. But why draw a connection? Each time I try to turn the conversation back to a possible Bishop-McGrath relationship, he shuts down. Even Brenda's bashful attempts at drawing him out are fruitless.

I'm about to give up when I ask a question I hope will save the interview from being a total waste of time. "You're a film historian, Dr. Ettinger. Have you ever heard of a movie called *The Boatman*? William Bishop supposedly acted in it."

"Bishop an actor?" he says. "I can't even imagine it."

"My colleague Ms. Sica found evidence that he acted in at least one film."

He gets up and goes over to the far bookshelf. "*The Boatman*, it's called? What year?"

"Nineteen seventy-something," Brenda says.

He reaches for a thick book with a tattered cover. "Everyone thinks the Internet has all the information you need. It's not true. For old movies, there's nothing like the hardcover version of Magill's." As he thumbs through the volume, I let myself believe that maybe he'll find something. After reading for a few minutes, he shakes his head. "There's a nineteen eighty-five film from the Philippines called *Boatman*. Another with that exact title from Turkey dated nineteen ninety-three. But I doubt Bishop had anything to do with those. And anyway, they're too late."

Brenda exhales audibly.

"You really think Ettinger was talking about Bishop in his book?" Brenda says after we've left his office. "He seems kind of . . . how would you say it, pompous? Maybe he just wants us to think it was Bishop."

"I'm sure he was referring to Bishop," I say. "Because he's scared shitless."

Brenda simultaneously nods her head in agreement with my observation and frowns in disapproval at my profanity.

CHAPTER 10

Lawsuits are just two stories vying for legitimacy as truth, especially lawsuits like *Bishop v. Poniard*, which rely on stale facts and fragments of history that don't fit together. In the next few weeks, Philip, Brenda, and I scour the Internet looking for scraps of information. We try to locate witnesses who disappeared long ago, leaving no forwarding address. We search sleazy websites for dirt on William Bishop that he can't brush off. There's nothing.

Meanwhile, JADS's Chief Executive Officer, the Honorable Walker K. Mitchell (Retired) starts a harassment campaign—a barrage of e-mails and daily visits reminding me that my revenues for the firm are virtually nonexistent, that what accounts receivable I do have are aging, that I shouldn't have taken on such a big case, that Poniard's cosplayers continue to loiter outside the JADS office and that he's holding me responsible. I repeatedly ask them to leave, but they ignore me, getting as close to the JADS entrance as building security will allow.

I wait to receive the original letters between Felicity and Scotty, firing off increasingly threatening e-mails to Poniard but getting no response. Each morning I vow to resign if I don't receive the documents by the end of the day, and each evening I give Poniard an extension.

On this morning, I arrive at the office at seven o'clock to do some research on *Bishop v. Poniard*. This early, there shouldn't be many JADS people around to look over my shoulder. As I'm sipping my bitter cup of JADS hot-plate coffee, a large shadow invades my peripheral vision. I look up to see Judge Mitchell. I should've known he'd be here already. He's tireless, coming in before anyone else and leaving late. Once an underpaid judicial officer, he's now a multimillionaire. He takes two long strides forward and drops a manila envelope on my desk.

"This was left on my chair by mistake," he says. "It's addressed to you."

"Do you have any idea who—?"

"None." Before I can say another word, he's out the door, obviously not happy about my working on something other than mediation.

The manila envelope bears a printed label addressed to Parker Stern c/o Judicial Alternative Dispute Solutions, PERSONAL AND CONFIDENTIAL. There's no postage, no courier logo, no return address. Like an excited child on Christmas morning, I roughly tear open the flap. I reach inside and pull a large Ziploc baggie that contains a smaller envelope, which contains three sheets of paper—the correspondence between Felicity and Scotty. Or, that's what the documents appear to be. I examine the larger envelope. There's no cover letter, not even a buck slip from Poniard saying *here you go*.

I find Felicity's first letter, the one in which she mentions "Billy Bishop." The handwriting is calligraphic but relaxed. I compare it with the handwriting in Felicity's later, undated note, in which she surprises Scotty with a trip to France. Although both notes seem to be written by the same person, the writing in the second seems more frenetic, more deeply etched into the paper. But what do I know about handwriting analysis? I'll have to hire a real expert. I put the papers back into the large envelope and then e-mail Poniard confirming that I've received the letters.

Brenda arrives at work an hour later.

"You look nice," I say, and then scold myself for violating the first rule of anti–gender bias training.

Blushing, she primps her hair. "Oh, thanks. Philip took me clothes shopping."

"He did what?"

"It was just H&M." She puts her hands to her mouth when she realizes what I'm implying. "Oh my god, no, we weren't . . . his wife, Joyce, came with." She takes a deep breath. "I was telling him how much I like working here—working for you—and he noticed I was wearing the same two dresses all the time. He said if I wanted to get ahead I should be more professional and he's so easy to talk to I let it slip that I couldn't afford a new wardrobe. So he insisted that he loan me some money for new clothes and said I could pay him back from my paychecks, which I'll be able to soon because I have a steady job now." She bites at a fingernail. "If I did something wrong, I could take the clothes back."

"No. It really isn't any of my business. Philip is a kind man."

She hands me the briefing for a small mediation that I have scheduled next week. As she's about to leave, the chat program launches.

Poniard:
>Do you have the letters, counselor?

Brenda glances at the screen and says, "I'll come back later." She takes a step toward the door.

"No, stay," I say. "We're all on the same team."

She grins slightly and sits down in a client chair opposite my desk.

PStern
>It's about time. They went to the wrong office. How were they delivered?
Poniard:
>JUST TELL ME THEY'RE SECURE!
PStern
>Yes, I've got the letters. We need to get them tested by the document examiners. Do I have your permission?
Poniard:
>Whatever you need to do . . . just keep them safe and in good condition
PStern
>I will take care of that immediately.

Without a *thank you*, he abruptly ends the chat.

After Brenda leaves, I pick up the envelope, grab my coat, and head out the door. When I get outside, the cosplayers—now gathered in front of the seedy Café Guadalajara because they'd been rousted for loitering in front of JADS—begin waving and shouting at me. I hurry to my car and drive the fifteen minutes to the Community Bank of Marina Del Rey, not far from my condo. The teller accompanies me into the vault and retrieves my oversized 12 × 12 safety deposit box. He uses his key on the lock and leaves me alone. Only when the door closes do I insert my own key.

I haven't opened the box in years, and now I survey its contents: fifteen thousand dollars in cash, because I learned at a young age that you might have to go on the run at any time; my old SAG card, under the name *Parky Gerald*, expiration date July 31, 1990, the year after I became an emancipated minor and went underground at age fifteen; a washed-out snapshot of my mother and me in Big Bear—I must've been eight or nine—throwing snowballs and actually having fun together; a stack of reviews and credits on all my films (I guess it's not as easy to jettison the past as I pretend); an English pewter tie tack in the shape of a barn owl, inexpensive and unfashionable, a gift from Harmon Cherry simply because I once admired it on him. I take the McGrath letters and place them in the safety deposit box. I start to close the lid but instead reach into my wallet and retrieve a picture of Lovely Diamond and me taken at a barbecue last Labor Day. Her arms are wrapped around my neck, and she's looking up at me with genuine love, or so I thought at the time. I'm smiling my best Parky Gerald smile, still mugging for the camera after all these years. I have quite a few digital photos of us, but this is my favorite, the only one I actually printed out so I could keep it with me always. But that particular *always* is over. I drop the photo into the box and close the lid.

Instead of going back to the office, I drive to Venice Beach. Though it's less than a mile away from my home, for the past year and a half I've stayed away from that neighborhood. Horrible memories. After searching for the impossible parking spot near the ocean, I finally relent and park farther inland on Main Street. I get out of the car and walk toward the beach, eventually finding the address of what was once the Windward Bar, where Paula Felicity McGrath was last seen. It's now an organic sandwich shop/juice bar. Then I diagonally cross the street to the Pacific Avenue Hotel, the former flophouse turned upscale beachside inn, where Luther "Boardwalk Freddy" Frederickson supposedly spotted William Bishop driving away with the goons who kidnapped Felicity. There's a valet service and a doorman outside. There are alcoves on the building facade, but I can't conceive of a homeless person being allowed to stand near the wall these days, much less sleep there. I go west until I reach the boardwalk. It's October, and the salt scent of the ocean rides on a clement breeze, but school started weeks ago, so the beaches are empty. I walk north, passing bicycle riders and Rollerbladers, beach bums with overbaked skin, senior citizens in wheelchairs pushed by devoted but bored Filipino attendants. I pass street vendors who despite the sparse crowds have shown up to sell T-shirts and henna tattoos and cheap jewelry and vintage clothing and laser-art seascapes. I pass hot dog stands, pizza joints, seaside bars, beachfront apartments, youth hostels, medical marijuana dispensaries. When I reach the Santa Monica Pier, I'm drenched in sweat. As I walk, I try to learn something about Paula Felicity McGrath, as if the permanence of steel and brick and concrete and water and sand can whisper wisdom if I only listen hard enough.

I'd like to go home but decide to spend the afternoon drumming up some mediation business for my employer and so make the short drive up Ocean Park back to the office. When I pull into the parking lot, I notice that the cosplayers are gathered at the building's entrance, exactly where they're not supposed to be. I start to pull around the building to my assigned space in the back and ask them to disperse, but then I get close enough to hear shouting, and I realize what's really going on. I stomp on the brake, leave the car parked in the middle of the driveway, and sprint over to the entrance. The cosplayers are gathered on one side of the walkway, screaming and shouting and waving their arms like spectators at a bullfight. Some of the people who work at JADS are standing on the walkway near the building, gawking like freeway rubberneckers. My boss, Walker Mitchell, is shouting for someone to call building security and for someone else to call the cops, and my assistant Brenda is alone by the door crying, blood oozing from her knee and down her leg. In the middle of the melee Banquo and some huge biker-type with long hair, a grizzly beard, and tattoos covering both arms are rolling around on the concrete. Just as I arrive, Banquo gets the upper hand and repeatedly punches the biker in the face. I've broken up a few basketball fights, and the trick is to always grab your teammate and not the opponent, because your teammate is less likely to turn and punch you. I run over and grab Banquo's arms, hoping he realizes it's me and considers me a teammate.

"That's enough, Banquo," I shout. "You said you wanted to help Poniard? Well, this is hurting him."

His arm is cocked to strike another blow to the bloodied face of the biker, and as hard as I grip his deltoid and bicep, I'm not nearly strong enough to hold him back. But he relaxes and stands. He looks into my eyes, his gaze a terrifying mixture of anger, surprise, and regret, and for a fleeting moment I feel I recognize him from somewhere other than his role as one of Poniard's hangers-on. But then the sirens become audible and that feeling is gone, and so is Banquo, running toward a beat-up brown Honda—a later model of the car that Felicity McGrath was driving on the day she disappeared. Courtney is at the wheel. He gets in, and they speed out of the parking lot, long gone when the police arrive thirty seconds later.

I go over to Philip Paulsen, who's still comforting Brenda, but before I can ask what happened, Walker Mitchell approaches and points a finger at me, his face almost as white as his hair. "You're done, Stern. Effective this moment. I don't even want you in the building. Let me know where we can send your personal property."

"Judge Mitchell, I—"

"Leave now, or I'll have *you* arrested for trespassing." He gestures toward Brenda. "You're terminated, too . . ." He's obviously struggling to remember her name. "Young lady. Two weeks' severance, and you're lucky to get that."

"Walker, that's not fair," Philip says. "Brenda needs this job." I didn't realize that Philip Paulsen and Walker Mitchell knew each other, though Philip seems to know everyone.

"That is not my problem," Mitchell says.

"Can I get my purse, sir?" Brenda asks. "And a bandage for my knee?"

"No, you may not," Mitchell says. "I'll have someone bring you your purse. As for a Band-Aid, ask the paramedics." He points to the EMTs attending to the biker, who obviously has a fractured nose.

"What happened?" I ask.

Brenda cowers and moves close to Philip. He puts his arm around her. "We have to talk to the police," he says. "We'll explain later. Where can we meet?"

I tell them to meet me at The Barrista Coffee House in West Hollywood. I've used it as an office before. Why not again?

CHAPTER 11

My ex-law partner Deanna Poulos opened The Barrista Coffee House shortly after our law firm fell apart three years ago. Since then, I've spent most of my spare time here. Deanna died almost two years ago and bequeathed the place to her employees. But her estranged parents contested the will. I represented the employees *pro bono*—they'd been Deanna's true family—and avoided a costly lawsuit by buying them out with money that I'd earned as a kid actor. I wanted to give the shop to the employees, but they insisted that I remain a fifty percent owner. That's on paper. Her former top associate Romulo manages the place, and any profits go to the staff. In exchange, the baristas keep my regular table in the back open for me and warm my coffee when it gets cold.

Now the shop is empty, except for a couple of regulars who nurse one cup of cappuccino for hours while they sit hunched over their laptops using the shop's free Wi-Fi, or pounding out the next great screenplay or novel, or mapping out the story of a video game that will rival Poniard's. Philip, Brenda, and I are meeting in the office, a cubbyhole where my late friend Deanna spent so many hours balancing the books and counting cash. Philip Paulsen is sitting behind the desk across from a disconsolate Brenda Sica, who alternately looks down at the floor and up at the ceiling.

"What happened?" I ask.

"I am so very sorry," Brenda says.

"Don't apologize," Philip says. "Just tell him."

She sits back in her chair and begins talking so softly that I have to ask her to speak up. Apparently, the huge man who looked like a biker was a process server who barged into JADS reception and announced in a loud voice that he was serving Parker Stern with papers in *Bishop v. Poniard*. The receptionist called Brenda. When she came out front and told him I wasn't in the office, he called her a liar and started walking toward the back offices.

"That's when I made the big mistake," Brenda says, her voice quavering. "I reached out and grabbed the man's sleeve to stop him because he had no right to go to your office, but he was so big and strong, and when he turned he twisted my arm hard and I lost my balance and fell." She points to a fresh scrape on her knee. "It's fine. I shouldn't have touched him." Her eyes are glistening.

"Typical Frantz bullshit," I say, forgetting for the moment that she doesn't like profanity. "He didn't need to send a process server. Frantz could've had his secretary e-mail the documents, but he has to grandstand, to try to embarrass me with the people at JADS."

"I think it was that Lovely Diamond girl who sent him," Brenda says.

"She wouldn't do that," I say.

I glance over at Philip, who has his head down.

"I'm going to report Frantz to the State Bar and have his process server arrested for assault," I say.

"The story isn't finished," Philip says, using the blue cloth handkerchief he always carries to wipe away the sweat.

"Anyway, the guy threw the papers at me," Brenda says. "Literally, Mr. Stern. I'm on the floor and he threw them at my legs. Then he just left, didn't say he was sorry or anything. I started picking up the papers, and Marnie the receptionist came over to see if I was all right, which I was except for my bloody knee. And then there's this yelling outside and banging on the doors and I see the huge guy fighting with the tall guy in the costume, who's always hanging out in front of—"

"Banquo wasn't supposed to be anywhere near that building."

"I know, but he was out there anyway, and the guy from Frantz's office pushes him, and I guess the Banquo guy defends himself and that's when the fight started."

"I'll fix it with Judge Mitchell once he's calmed down," I say. "I'm sure he'll take you back."

"I already spoke with Mitchell," Philip says. "There's no fixing it."

"What gave you the right?" I say.

"Let's talk in private," he says.

"There's nothing to talk about. You overstepped your bounds, Philip."

"In private, Parker." He says this with a soft voice that carries great authority. Brenda skulks out of the room.

Philip makes sure that the door is completely shut. "Years ago, Deanna and I had a six-week bench trial in front of Walker Mitchell. He and I both worship at St. Paul's."

"So what?"

"I talked to Walker because I was the only hope of saving Brenda's job. You can't do it. It's not just the lawsuit and the cosplayers hanging around. William Bishop threatened never to send any Parapet business to JADS so long as you were working there."

"Whatever they think of me, Brenda doesn't deserve to lose her job," I say.

"The process server is threatening to sue JADS, claiming that Brenda started it. She was probationary. Mitchell doesn't want the headache. He's a cold-hearted man."

Only then do I notice some legal documents strewn all over the desk. "What's this?"

"A motion from our opponents. They're trying to disqualify you on the grounds that you have a conflict of interest. You allegedly represented William Bishop in 1999."

"I started at the firm that year and never worked for Bishop."

"Apparently you did. The hearing is in six weeks. Luckily, the court's docket is full, so we have some time to think about how to oppose it."

"Six weeks is nothing."

We're quiet, except for the sound of Philip's labored breathing. "I've got things to do," he says. "And not here."

As soon as he leaves, I phone Walker Mitchell at JADS, who refuses to take my call and instead e-mails me a formal notice of termination. Then I sit down with Brenda at a back table, order us both coffee drinks, and offer to give her a fifty percent raise if she'll stay and work with me on Poniard's case. After all, she lost her job because of me. Without hesitation or false pride, she agrees. Good. I know she desperately needs an income. And I need her help.

I e-mail Poniard about Frantz's motion to disqualify me and get a terse reply saying, "Fight it."

I take a closer look at the motion to disqualify. Supposedly, in 1999, during my first month at Macklin & Cherry, I represented Bishop in a libel action. Bishop had been arrested for driving a stolen Porsche 911 with phony plates. Except the car wasn't stolen; it had been used in a movie, and Bishop was testing it out to see if he wanted to buy it. The trouble was that the props department had failed to remove the mocked-up license plates used for the film. So not only was Bishop wrongly arrested, but one of the tabloids had reported that he was a car thief. I apparently wrote a research memo analyzing whether he could sue the tabloid for libel. Now Frantz and Diamond are using that anti- quated memo to claim that I have a conflict of interest, that back in 1999 I obtained confidential information about Bishop's reputation that I could use against him today.

I don't remember any of this. It was just a memo, and while Bishop was on the rise, he wasn't the colossus that he is today. But under the law, that might not matter. If my 1999 lawsuit was substantially related to *Bishop v. Poniard*—whatever *substantially related* means— I'll be booted off the case. And I don't want to be off the case. Not with Lovely Diamond on the other side.

I read through the document one more time, trying to jog my memory. As it turns out, Lou Frantz and Lovely Diamond got one thing right—the memo does contain information that might help Pon- iard's case.

CHAPTER 12

I set out early on the two-hour drive to Palm Desert, a community eleven miles east of the more famous Palm Springs and heavily populated by retirees. It's Saturday, so the traffic is light. I've arranged a meeting with Harrison ("Harry") Cherry, Harmon's father and a former entertainment attorney himself. More accurately, I've arranged the meeting through his wife Sonja, who set two conditions before she agreed to let Harry see me. She has good reasons. He's suffering from Alzheimer's Disease, a tragedy all the more poignant because he's always had an incisive mind. Sonja told me that he was at a manageable stage one up until a month ago, but in the past four weeks he's declined. So, I promise not to say anything that could even hint that Harmon is dead—any reference to the loss makes Harry agitated and more confused. And when she says the interview is over, it's over.

The Cherrys live in a retirement community bordering a golf course. The large Mediterranean-style homes all look the same and are all gray and yellow stucco with a white enamel trim. The SoCal deserts spike into the high nineties even during November, and though I'm dressed in jeans and a light cotton shirt, by the time I get to the Cherrys' front door, my shirt is mottled with sweat.

The housekeeper escorts me to the backyard, a lush area with artificial waterfalls and rock gardens and queen palms lining the adobe paths. Harry and Sonja are sitting at a patio table drinking iced tea from tall glasses. Sonja Glanz Cherry, Harry Cherry's third wife, stands up. She's a brunette whose body is a kind of postmodern collaboration between a minimalist personal trainer and a conceptualist breast implant doctor. I know exactly how old she is—fifty-three, a quarter of a century younger than her husband. You'd think that Harmon would've disliked and mistrusted her, but he'd say that anyone who makes his father happy makes him happy, and the rest is just froth.

She leans in as if to give me an air kiss and whispers, "It's one of his good days. So far." She puts her hand on his shoulder. "Harrison, you remember Parker Stern? He works for your son Harmon."

And so the director has yelled action, and I'm to play my part without a minute's rehearsal—which doesn't stop me from shuddering when she refers to Harmon in the present tense. I pretend that I'm a kid actor again, taking an improv workshop in which I have to roll with the oddest cues thrown my way.

"How are you, kid?" Harry says.

I'd be worried that he didn't use my name, except that Harry has always had two ways of addressing the males in the firm, depending on their age—*kid* and *old-timer*. He always remembered the women's names, though. He's dressed in tan slacks and a vanilla golf shirt. There's a large wet spot on the shirt, maybe iced tea but maybe drool. He's tall, much taller than Harmon was, with cottony silver hair and a crooked grin. During my first two years at Macklin & Cherry, he worked there too, as an *of counsel*, an honorific that allowed him to come into the office a couple of times a week and service his few remaining clients. He had Harmon's brilliant mind without the ambition, and some said that Harry was the better person for it.

"Pour the kid a cold drink, Sonja," he says. "Hot as hell out here." She leans forward, but before she can reach the pitcher he grabs it away, fills my glass, and refills his own, liquid sloshing all over the table. Sonja calmly takes a napkin and wipes up the spill.

"What brings you all the way from Beverly Hills?" he asks. I haven't worked in Beverly Hills since the law firm broke up three years ago.

"If it's OK I'd like to ask you some things about William Bishop."

"Of course it's OK, kid. He's suing you, if I'm not mistaken. What did you do to him?"

"Parker is the lawyer for the defendant," Sonja says.

"Yes, of course. I've read about your case. The video game designer. Tough adversary, Billy Bishop. Double whammy that he's represented by Lou Frantz, that son of a bitch." He hesitates. "Did you go to law school with Frantz?"

"Parker wasn't born then, Harrison," Sonja says.

He looks at me with the ingenuous eyes of a tiny child who has no inkling that he knows nothing about life. Then he looks away. "Of course. What do you want to know about Billy Bishop?"

I retrieve my copy of the old memorandum and turn to the last page. Although the memo is confidential, Harry is allowed see it because he helped write it. Like most callow attorneys, when I wrote the memo I focused not on the factual details but on the more fascinating legal theory. I concluded that the tabloid had an absolute right to report fairly and accurately on the arrest. There were attachments to the memo, none of which I prepared. They include a list of court cases in which Bishop had been a party (breach of contract, intellectual property, and labor disputes), a summary of newspaper clippings about his philanthropic activities, and most importantly, a list of movie projects that he was involved in. The initials in the document's footer show that Harry Cherry prepared the list of movie projects.

Like the archived movie database page that Brenda found early on, Harry's list of projects shows that Bishop acted in a film called *The Boatman*. He has a specific date—1979. Brenda can't find a copy of the movie. No VHS tape, much less a DVD. She found nothing on eBay or at websites specializing in rare and hard-to-find videos. None of the film preservation museums has a celluloid copy of the movie.

"Harry, you prepared this list of Bishop's movies," I say, sliding the page toward him. "There's one entry called *The Boatman* that says that Bishop was an actor. What can you tell me about that movie?"

He leans forward and stares at the list. I smell the sharp, spicy scent of cologne, and though I don't detect anything else, I have the feeling that the cologne has been applied generously to mask a fetid odor. I take a shallow breath through my mouth, waiting for him to say something.

Harry checks his watch and stands up.

"What is it, Harrison?" Sonja says.

"Golf with Ralph and Carl and Jeff . . . no, Pete. We're teeing off in five minutes."

"You don't have a tee time today," she says.

"I don't have a . . . ?"

She reaches over and takes his hand. "Sit down, Harrison. We've scheduled this talk with Parker from Harmon's firm. It won't take long, will it, Parker?" The last is delivered in a tone as precise as a scalpel.

"Not long at all," I say. "I'm wondering about the movie that Bishop acted in."

"Ohhh?" The word is a glissando into a falsetto, a cross between a question and a moan. It's a welcome utterance, because it's always been a signal that Harry Cherry is about to launch into an anecdote about someone famous who floundered.

"*The Boatman* is the first movie that Billy Bishop ever produced," he says. "Starred in it with Hildy Gish."

"Who?"

"Directed and wrote it too, believe it or not. Invested his father's money. You know his father?"

"Howard Bishop," I say. "The music lawyer."

"Billy pissed his father's money away," Harry says. "Low budget, shot in a matter of weeks. A modern-day version of the Orpheus and Eurydice myth. You know the story?"

I'm about to remind him that Harmon often used the myth as a parable to teach his associates the value of trusting our superiors but fortunately stop myself. Harmon learned it from his father. "I think I studied it in college," I say. "Orpheus is a great musician. His beautiful wife Eurydice gets bitten by a poisonous snake and dies. He travels to the underworld, hoping to bring her back. The gods of the underworld are so enamored of his music that they agree to let him lead Eurydice back to the world of the living. But on the journey home, Orpheus must not look back at his wife. Of course, he looks back."

Harry nods and smiles a surprisingly lucid smile. "Very good. *The Boatman* was a modern take on that myth. Anyway, when Papa Howard got wind of it, he pulled the plug." He squints his eyes, as if trying to remember. "Film had lots of problems, but the biggest was that Bishop admired Andy Warhol, tried to make it look like the sex and drugs were real, that the actors weren't professionals but a bunch of freaks. Billy wasn't a professional actor, but he was pretty good, actually. Have to be a good actor to accomplish what he's accomplished, producing block-buster movies, the Oscar nominations, and then switching gears entirely and becoming the head of a worldwide conglomerate, you know, the guy doesn't just own a studio and a television network, but twenty-seven newspapers, a record company, and a fucking English Premier League soccer team. And that's only ... almost owned the Dodgers until the commissioner put the kibosh on it. You got to be able to fool a lot of people to acquire all those things. Oh, Billy Bishop is definitely a good actor." He huffs for breath, folds his hands on the desk, and stares at me as though he's about to continue talking. I wait ten, fifteen, thirty seconds.

"How did the father manage to shut *The Boatman* down?" I finally ask.

"Oh, well, Howard . . ." And then a gaping stare with a gaping mouth.

"What about Howard?" I say.

He doesn't answer. He closes his mouth and makes a humming sound. He takes a few audible breaths and shouts, "Felicity McGrath was on that picture!"

Given Harry's condition, I should stay calm, should show no reaction, but my excitement gets the better of me, and I begin to blather. "So Felicity really did know Bishop? Because if you could testify to that, we could—"

Sonja's virulent scowl jolts me into silence.

He leans in close, and his hooded eyes narrow. "Don't tell anyone, kid. No one's supposed to know but Harmon and me. If Howard and Billy find out that I told you, they'll . . ." He stiffens and looks down at his hands, and then looks to each side as if he's being watched. "Wasn't supposed to tell. I shouldn't have told." He looks at Sonja like a contrite third grader and says, "Am I in trouble?"

"Of course you're not in trouble, baby," she says.

He smiles and pats her hand. "You're a good girl, Sonja."

I don't want to upset him further, but I'm so close. Just a little more information. "Harry, tell me more about *The Boatman*. Where can I get a copy? And who's Hildy . . . Hildy Gish?"

His eyes recede in fear, and he shakes his head. "Billy will be pissed. He said not to tell. Harmon . . ." With his index finger he draws a happy face in the condensation on the outside of his iced-tea glass. Then, using the same finger to cover the top of his straw, he pulls the straw out of the glass and dribbles tea across the table in swirls. Sonja grabs his wrist and confiscates the straw. Harry sticks his finger into the tea puddles and draws more curlicues. He alternately looks at Sonja and then at me, turning his head back and forth in a Ping-Pong rhythm.

"*Scavi*," he hisses.

"I don't understand," I say.

He lowers his head and won't look up.

"Harry?" I say.

No response.

I appeal to Sonja. She shakes her head, not in answer but in reproach. Harry snuffles, the tears welling up in his eyes. Within seconds, he's sobbing, the desolate, snorting cry of the decrepit. Sonja reaches out and caresses his back.

"It's OK, sweetie," she says. "Everything's OK. I'm here, Harrison."

He slides over and buries his face in her shoulder. She looks at me and shakes her head.

I stand up, not sure whether to say good-bye, not sure what a good-bye will mean to a man with no memory. It's like attending a funeral, where the object of the ceremony is inevitably absent, oblivious, irretrievable. But there's a difference. Now, the shell of the man isn't lying in a casket but is breathing, moving, uttering sounds, emitting odors. And though he's just as irretrievable as the dead, no dreams of an afterlife can soften the observer's horror.

"Thank you both for your time," I say. "It's good seeing you."

Harrison lifts his head from his wife's shoulder and smiles sadly. "Harmon liked you, Parker. You were his favorite. I miss him. I miss my son." And then the ever-diminishing light in his eyes dims, and he returns to what I realize is a blissful insensibility to the pain that long life inevitably brings.

CHAPTER 13

Philip pokes at the sizzling roast beef with tongs. "Parker, I want you to know that not many people know how to grill tri-tip properly, especially on an open barbecue. I use a simple dry garlic rub, some kosher salt, finely ground pepper, and cook it over the cooler parts of the grill away from the flame. The fat flare-ups give it enough flavor."

Though it's early November, he's taking advantage of the heat caused by the Santa Ana winds. "It's why I moved to Southern California," he says. "To escape the Chicago winters. Backyard cooking and golf year-round." Fortunately, he's wearing a baseball cap—he's a Cubs fan—because otherwise the sweat from his brow would be dripping onto the meat.

As he works, I tell him about this morning's meeting with Harry Cherry. He merely nods his head and hums like a country doctor examining a patient until I get to the part where Harry used the word *scavi*.

"The *scavi* are the tombs in the necropolis beneath St. Peter's Basilica in the Vatican," he says. "I spent a year away curating a Vatican collection and got to know them well. If you ever go to Rome, you must visit. But you have to reserve months in advance."

I know about the Vatican's *scavi* because I looked the word up on my iPhone as soon as I left the Cherrys' house yesterday.

"Harry couldn't have meant the necropolis," I say. "If he meant anything. His thoughts are all tangled up."

Philip's wife Joyce pokes her head out the backdoor. She wears her straight gray hair in a short chili-bowl cut, and the jowls on her round face confirm that unlike so many LA women her age, she's never had cosmetic surgery. She actually could pass for a retired nun. She's plump and is usually all smiles, though not today.

"We're ready to eat when you are," she says. "Come inside."

"We're eating outside," he says.

"No, we are not," she says. "It's too cold."

"It was eighty-four degrees a little while ago."

"The sun's about to go down, and the temperature's already starting to dip. I've set us up in the kitchen." I'm grateful to her—the San Fernando Valley gets cold at night this time of year no matter what the daytime temperature. My long-sleeve soccer jersey kept me too warm for the afternoon, but now a cool breeze is knifing right through it.

I hold a serving plate while Philip puts the beef on it and tents it with aluminum foil. "It needs another rest," he said. "Ten to twelve minutes. Just enough time to finish our salad."

We go inside. Joyce and Brenda are standing at the butcher-block kitchen table, filling up salad plates. Brenda pours red wine, a Malbec from Argentina that I brought, into three of the four glasses and sits down near the empty glass. She and I drove over together from The Barrista. We seem only to have the lawsuit in common, and yet that's OK—I've found that I like being near her. She's earnest and dedicated and idealistic in a way I haven't been since I was a second-year lawyer. And she respects privacy—there's no pressure to talk about my life or to ask about hers.

I toast the host and hostess, Brenda sipping water from her wine glass. She's never said she doesn't drink, but I've never seen her consume alcohol.

"So Joyce, Parker went out to visit Harmon's father Harry yesterday," Philip says. "You met him a few times at firm gatherings."

"Oh yes," she says. "A nice man. Much more relaxed than his son. Though I remember him swearing a lot."

"He's suffering from dementia," Philip says.

"If I get that Alzheimer's or whatever, I hope I realize it and have the guts to check myself out and save everyone else the trouble," Brenda says. "If I live to be old enough to get it, which I probably won't."

We're all quiet, and her neck becomes splotchy. "I'm so sorry," she says. "I don't know what I'm talking about."

I get the impression that Brenda has never been to a dinner party, even a casual one, doesn't know how to make conversation, and so just blurted something out in an attempt to fight her shyness.

"You did nothing wrong," Philip says. "So many people believe that today. All human life is sacred no matter how damaged. The way Sonja still dotes on and protects Harry is proof of that." Philip might have left the priesthood, but he hasn't abandoned his faith. He's consistent in his views—capital punishment and euthanasia are as abhorrent to him as abortion.

"What a depressing thing to talk about during dinner," Joyce says. "I don't know why you brought it up, Phil." She's the only person I've ever heard call him Phil.

"It's relevant to our lawsuit," he says. "Harry has a long history with Bishop."

"Ah yes, the lawsuit," Joyce says, glancing at me with a frown. "I think that's an even more depressing subject."

"Alzheimer's is a terrible affliction," Philip says. "I just try to keep my mind active and hope. That's one of the reasons I decided to go back to work. I don't want my brain to atrophy. It's been good to get back into the game."

Joyce's face tightens, and she purses her lips and raises her shoulders, a woman making a decision. "I have to say this, Parker."

"Not now, Joyce," Philip says in his soft voice.

"No, I have to. I didn't want Philip to go back to work. Or more accurately, I didn't want him to go back to work for you."

I've always gotten along with Joyce. Or so I thought. But I was arrogant back in the firm days. "Joyce, if I've ever said or done anything to—"

"It isn't because I don't like you," she says. "I do. You're a great lawyer, firm in your beliefs. Admirable. And that's the problem. The case is too dangerous. You're a magnet for trouble, and Philip isn't getting any younger. He's had some physical problems recently."

He waves his fork at her and says mid-bite of salad, "I'm perfectly fine."

"Philip, I truly don't want to risk your health. I can find someone else."

"Not as good as I am," he says. "And I say that in all humility. I agree with Joyce. The case is definitely dangerous and you do attract trouble. Which is exactly why I'm working with you. It keeps me young, and it keeps my brain clear and in shape. And besides, you and Brenda need my help. Now let's finish the salad so the tri-tip doesn't rest too long."

For the rest of the meal—which is excellent, even Brenda's chocolate chip cookies—I make sure to avoid talking about the case, which is the only thing I really want to talk about. So we discuss sports and art and politics, though we tread lightly on politics based on some engrained disagreements in views. Brenda knows a surprising amount about comic book and graffiti art (hence her admiration for Banksy, the English street artist)—she only half-jokingly talks about a boyfriend who was a tagger—and makes a strong case for why it should be taken seriously. Later, Philip and I recycle some old stories about Harmon Cherry and other former colleagues that neither of us tires of hearing. At around eight o'clock, Brenda and I announce that we're going to leave.

"Wait," Philip says. "I want to show you something on *Abduction!*"

"I'll clean up," Joyce says. "Just make sure you keep the sound down on that horrible game."

Philip leads us into a small bedroom that he uses as an office and game room. He turns on his television, powers on his Xbox, and connects to the Internet.

"Video games are the new creative medium," he says. "One has to know these things to keep current."

The game launches, depicting an upscale bar, all chrome and glass and din, which I recognize as being located in a Westside mall. Philip maneuvers the viewer toward a man sitting with an attractive redhead in the corner booth. We elbow our way past jostling patrons who form a barrier between the player and the man in the booth. As we approach, it becomes clear that the man is William Bishop. Is the woman Felicity McGrath? We don't know, because just as we get close, Bishop's facial features melt and rearrange themselves into those of a faceless demon. The woman transforms into a gap-toothed crone with warts.

Brenda looks at the screen with hands on hips. "How strange," she mumbles.

"You're telling me," Philip says. "I've been stuck in this bar for days. No one online has solved it either. Just when you think Poniard is making a point . . ." He takes a couple more passes at approaching the Bishop character, but the same thing happens. He shrugs. "Maybe next time."

I move close. "Philip, listen, about what Joyce said, I really don't want you to do this if—"

He puts a fatherly hand on my shoulder. "My wife is a worrier. I'm loving this and grateful that you have the confidence in me to let me work on such an important case."

CHAPTER 14

For days, Brighton has rattled the front gate outside the rundown building, pressing the intercom button over and over again. A woman with an old hag's voice keeps saying, "Go away, we don't want any!" He's tried circling around to the back alley and climbing the concrete wall, only to have suffered deep wounds from the barbed wire. He knows this because when he disturbed the wire, blood started dripping down from his POV onto the screen, and his movements were restricted for a suitable healing period—Poniard's way of penalizing the player for stupidity. There seems to be no solution to this level. Brighton has gotten so frustrated that he seriously might give up on *Abduction!*

Then, on a Saturday, he comes home from an under-12 league soccer game, in which he's scored two goals but has also gotten a yellow card for shoving this overgrown kid who pulled his shirt to stop him from scoring a hat trick. The HF Queen made him play soccer, but of course she doesn't show up at games, always too busy. So Bugsy watches from the sideline and shouts advice, though he's never played the game himself. At this game, he got a red card and a one-game ban from watching because he cussed at the linesman. Afterward, they went for pizza, and that's when Brighton remembered Leon's Pizza Parlor in *Abduction!* He's gone inside there just once, but it seemed like a dead end, a module leading nowhere populated by cardboard characters who don't react, who just sit and eat pizza. Besides, all the action is in the upscale Scott's Bar across the street, where everyone is looking for the mysterious "Scotty," and where William the Conqueror himself sometimes sits in a corner booth drinking scotch with a beautiful woman. This seemed like an important opportunity the first time Brighton saw

Bishop there, but when Brighton approached the table, the Conqueror dissolved into a pig in a business suit. Poniard has created the perfect diversion with that fancy bar, because ninety-nine out of a hundred people will search there and ignore other possibilities. That's what Brighton did until he and Bugsy went to get pizza after the soccer game.

Now, he opens the door to the pizza parlor, passes by a couple of scruffy non-interactive characters scarfing down an extra-large pizza topped with what at first looks like olives and anchovies but turns out to be scurrying cockroaches and black mold. Absolutely disgusting. No wonder Poniard has posted a health department "D" rating in the pizza parlor's window. He probes and prods the place until he gets the idea to explore the restroom, remembering that Poniard's earlier games featured drains and sewers and storm pipes as passageways to other worlds. He has to knock a grumpy pizza chef unconscious with a rolling pin to get into the bathroom, but once he does he plunges into the toilet and flushes himself into darkness.

Swirling algae and murky water, a pinpoint of light far in the distance. He swims through wads of toilet paper, fighting off a couple of gigantic sewer alligators that Poniard has thrown in just for sport. He can almost smell the rank water, feel the bacterial chill on his skin as if he were wearing one of those haptic suits he's read about in *Ready Player One*. Why didn't he remember that Poniard tries to make you feel everything when you're in his world, including nausea and revulsion?

He reaches the light and emerges through a breach in the wall, the sewer water pouring into the room. He's entered a space just beneath a photograph of a short gray-haired man with a moustache who's posing with a totally buff African American man standing in a boxer's pose. There's writing on the photo that reads, *What's up, Doc? Thanks for everything. We both champs*, and then a signature that Brighton can't recognize.

He turns around to find the other walls filled with photographs of the guy with the moustache. There's a large receptionist desk in the middle of the room. When he maneuvers the mouse around the desk to investigate, he finds that all the drawers have been pulled out. The floor is strewn with papers that have fake video game writing on them. Two of the wall photos have fallen, leaving gleaming shards of broken glass that reflect light so brilliant that Brighton wonders if the glass is really a radioactive mineral. The soundtrack starts blaring out creepy music—creaks and squeals of a violin, punctuated with an eerie string-bass line, the kind of music they play right before someone is brutally murdered in one of those old black-and-white movies that Bugsy likes to watch. He moves the mouse and taps the keyboard gingerly—he doesn't want to die and have to start the game over.

He finds a closed door on the right. He tries the knob, not expecting it to open—too easy. There's a loud *bash-boom*, and from the other side of the wall a man moans what sounds like an "awwww!!!" of aggrievement and surrender, and Brighton reflexively tries the knob again, and this time a woman squeals, her scream reaching a crescendo and then morphing into a piercing electronic screech that makes Brighton let go of the mouse and cover his ears for fear that his eardrums will burst.

The HF Queen bursts into his room and says, *What the hell was that?*

Brighton didn't know she was home. He points to the screen. The animated door opens of its own accord, and the screen draws the viewer into a back office. Brighton manipulates the mouse, but he has no control. This is now a cutscene. An old woman lies face up on the floor, her legs twisted under her in a grotesque knot. There's a scroll-handled dagger stuck in her chest. Her uninhabited eyes stare at the viewer, and even if you move so she'll stop looking at you, those eyes follow you everywhere.

The man in the chair moans again. "I've been gut shot!" And then he dies a video game character's death, dissolving into glittering pixels and nothingness.

"Oh my god," the HF Queen says, and she actually puts her arms around Brighton and draws him close. "What happened?"

Brighton shrugs and wriggles out of her grasp. He isn't sure whether he's killed a level boss or whether something in the game has gone terribly wrong.

CHAPTER 15

Two days after the Paulsen dinner, Herman "Bud" Kreiss and his wife Isla are found dead in their Century City office. She was stabbed several times in the chest, and he died of multiple gunshot wounds. I phone the police and tell them that I have information that could implicate William Bishop in the murders. A callow detective comes out to the coffee shop and takes my statement. The stories in the media report that the police department has no leads but speculate that the Kreisses were killed by one of the many spouse abusers or deranged fans or hardened criminals with whom Bud Kreiss clashed while guarding his celebrity clients. The list of suspects is endless.

Poniard, however, doesn't hesitate to name William Bishop as the killer. The day after the bodies are discovered, *Abduction!* plays online in a modified form. A level that challenged the player to find Kreiss's office has become a cutscene, in which the viewer passively watches Bishop stab Isla and shoot Bud Kreiss in the stomach.

The Kreiss murders are horrifying, but with a lawyer's perverse narcissism, I keep thinking that we've lost our most important witness. I also feel an odd sense of responsibility—would they be alive if I hadn't showed up at their office that day?

I send a spate of e-mails to Poniard but don't get a reply until the next morning. I'm already on my third Barrista macchiato.

Poniard:
>Hey, Parker Stern. You e-mailed me. Responding
PStern
>Your accusation that Bishop killed the Kreisses. Frantz will amend the
*   complaint to add that to the defamation claim.*

Poniard:
>*No worries counselor—truth is a defense*
PStern
>*There's no evidence that Bishop has anything to do with it.*
Poniard:
>*The Conqueror obviously found out that Kreiss was going to finally tell the truth . . . so he had him killed*
PStern
>*Speculation.*
Poniard:
>*Truth*
PStern
>*So you keep repeating. But where's the proof?*
Poniard:
>*The Felicity/Scotty letters . . . Bishop denies they exist, which proves he's a liar, that he's covering up*
PStern
>*Yes, Bishop is a liar. But that doesn't make him a killer.*
Poniard:
>*What Kreiss told you was solid proof. And now he's dead. That's no coincidence*
PStern
>*It's my professional advice that you stop making disparaging statements about William Bishop, true or not. It's too late to avoid potential liability, but if you keep this up, you're going to look bad to the judge and jeopardize your case.*
Poniard:
>*Duly noted counselor. Consider your ass totally covered. Bye*

Almost knocking my coffee cup off the table, I put my fingers on the keyboard and try to cyber-shout *Wait, I'm not done talking to you!* but the chat program flashes *Poniard has signed off.* I want to throttle my client. But who is my client? As his fans must have done, I try to picture him in the flesh. A pierced, tattooed scofflaw with a James Dean face? A plump albino misfit who lives on Cheetos and beer? A Harvard-educated investment banker with a unique hobby?

My cell phone rings. Caller ID shows that the call is from Frantz's law firm. I tap the *answer* button.

"Parker, it's Lovely Diamond." As if I wouldn't know. Her tone is formal, as it usually is to people other than me.

"Another frivolous motion?" I say.

"Your client is blaming Bishop for the Kreiss killings. It's bullshit."

I clench and unclench my fingers. "So I'm right. You did call to threaten me."

"No, it's . . . no one knows I'm calling. But that horrible video game showed the Kreiss murders before they happened."

It takes me a moment to process the fact that she's implicating my client in murder. "Sounds like I'm getting an advance preview of Bishop's new propaganda campaign."

"I'd never lie to you."

"Oh, really? Then tell me why you left me."

"Goddamn it, Parker. The game showed the murders before they happened."

"Sounds like you've been playing too much *Abduction!*, Ms. Diamond."

"If there's one thing you should've learned about me it's that I don't play games. Your client knew about the murders beforehand. Draw your own conclusions. And . . . and watch out for yourself." She clicks off, though I don't realize it until I've repeated, *Hello, are you still there?* three times. Her voice lingers like a coming-of-age song that can move you to tears decades after you first hear it. I stare at the phone, willing it to ring again and wondering whether she's truly called me out of concern.

I power on my laptop and launch the e-mail program, sending a message to Poniard. "URGENT. WE MUST COMMUNICATE **IMMEDIATELY**!!!" While I wait for a response, I search the Web for anything substantiating Lovely's claim. Nothing at first. But within thirty minutes, reports surface that *Abduction!* depicted the murders before they occurred. And then the speculation explodes with volcanic magnitude. Poniard's supporters accuse Bishop of trying to frame Poniard by hacking the game. Others maintain that Poniard is clairvoyant and was trying to warn Kreiss. Still others call Poniard a murderer. One blogger points out that Isla Kreiss was killed with a dagger—also called a *poniard*.

Homicide detective Angela Tringali—a thin, plain woman with short brown hair who looks more like a real estate broker than a police officer—shows up at The Barrista at opening time and interrogates me for an hour about how Poniard could have predicted the murders. I explain why Bishop had a motive to send someone over to kill the Kreisses—Bud was going to come clean about Boardwalk Freddy, the witness who saw Bishop drive away from the scene of the abduction. I don't know whether Lovely Diamond called her or whether she simply responded to the rampant Internet chatter. Harmon Cherry would say that a lawyer is at his most strident when advocating for a client he doesn't trust, and at the moment that's true for me—when Tringali treats my story dismissively, I rudely invoke the attorney-client privilege and tell her to leave, which only causes her to order a patrol car to park in front of the shop and scare the customers away.

So I sit alone at my back-corner table watching the only three customers in the place nurse their lattes and sap our Internet bandwidth. At about eleven o'clock, Brenda comes inside carrying a large shopping bag. She walks over to me and sets the bag on a chair. She doesn't remove her sunglasses.

I tell her about the visit from the police detective and the cops' suspicions about Poniard—which are also my suspicions.

"But the evidence is on our side," she says. "And he's our client." She has the typical naïveté of someone who hasn't been around the legal system. She truly believes that someone has to be right and someone has to be wrong. It doesn't always work that way.

"The truth is that we don't have a client at all," I say. "We're representing a ghost. Maybe worse, a murderer."

"You don't believe that."

"Why do you say that?"

"Because it would be so easy for you to quit, but you haven't. You think you're staying on the case because of that blonde lady lawyer, but you're not. Not anymore. You're doing it because Bishop's filthy dirty. He's lying about not knowing Felicity. He denies that the letters are real. He worked with her on *The Boatman* in 1979, and he's lying about that, too. And poor Detective Kreiss put him at the scene of the crime, and he gets . . . I've watched you work. You don't give up until you see justice done."

She just described me perfectly. Or maybe not. Maybe I haven't quit the case because I simply need to stay in the public eye as a way of compensating for having no family, no friends, no law firm, no future as a trial lawyer—and no Lovely Diamond. Now these black thoughts coalesce and take aim at Brenda Sica's knockoff Oakleys.

"Will you take those glasses off, Brenda? It's hard to talk to someone when you can't see their eyes."

She lifts her hand and removes the sunglasses, and I'm immediately seized with guilt. Her right eye is mottled blood-purple. The caked-on makeup, intended to hide the contusion, only accentuates it.

"Who did that to you?"

"No one did anything to me."

"Please don't say you walked into a door."

She puts the sunglasses back on. "I'm going to say it's none of your business." She's never spoken to me in that tone before.

"No one should do that to a person. If there's anything I can—"

"Here's what you can do for me. You can watch these." She lifts the shopping bag onto the table and goes to the back room.

I open the bag to find a DVD of *The Fragile Palace* and VHS tapes of the other four films that Felicity McGrath starred in between 1983 and her disappearance in 1987. Brenda has been searching for all but *The Fragile Palace*, Felicity's breakout movie, for weeks. The boxes for the lesser-known movies are scratched and without shrink-wrap. Brenda obviously bought the movies over eBay or from online merchants who specialize in used videos. I'm irrationally disappointed— there isn't a copy of *The Boatman*.

I examine the cover art for *The Fragile Palace*. A sepia image of a sultry Felicity stares at me, the right side of her face in full focus, the left side feathered and blurred to a cloud white. Her lips are parted orgasmically; she has coruscating, opium eyes. And the log line, *Too hot to touch . . . Too cold for love.*

Because of Felicity's disappearance, *The Fragile Palace* has become a cult classic. I've seen it more than once and so am more interested in the other movies that Brenda has found. But something about that contrived cover image of Felicity makes me want to watch the movie again. So I start to insert *The Fragile Palace* into my computer's DVD drive, but instead I pick up the shopping bag and go into the back room. Brenda is so engrossed in whatever's on her computer screen that she jumps when she sees me. She's taken her sunglasses off and now reaches for them, but she puts them down again, apparently realizing how silly it would be for her to wear them in dim light. She lowers her head, as though that could possibly hide the bruising.

"Did you watch any of these?" I say, making sure to look directly at her.

"I didn't. I wanted to get them to you right away."

"But surely you've seen *The Fragile Palace.*"

"Not the kind of thing I watch."

Lately, Romulo and I use this room for storage, and it's surprisingly large, so large that when Deanna was alive, she'd sometimes clear it out and use it for private parties. The room can comfortably hold twenty, though Deanna would fit twice as many people inside. I unlock a cabinet on the far wall, revealing an expensive HDTV entertainment center—a vestige of happier days.

Brenda widens her eyes and winces. "I thought they kept coffee grinders up there."

I find the remote control, power on the system, and insert *The Fragile Palace* into the DVD player. I bring in two chairs from the main room and put them side by side in front of the big screen TV.

"Come on," I say. "Sit down."

Brenda gives a timorous shake of the head. "I have lots of work to do."

"It can wait. We'll sit in the dark and watch movies as if we're in a movie theater. No popcorn, but I can get us some cookies and scones."

When she still hesitates I go to the main room and ask Romulo to have someone bring us pastries and coffee. When I come back in, I take Brenda's hand and lead her to the television. I bow and make a show of pulling out her chair for her. Giggling in spite of herself, she sits down and crosses her legs. When the barista comes in with the food, I dim the lights and hit *play* on the remote.

In *The Fragile Palace*, Felicity plays Molly, a young housewife who turns to sex and drugs out of boredom and plunges into inevitable degradation. The film is a combination melodrama/sexploitation flick, a cheesy rip-off of Buñuel's *Belle de Jour*. But Felicity was brilliant. She used her icy, detached screen presence to show with frightening clarity how the most ordinary person can be destroyed by her hidden desires. As I watch, there's something odd—Felicity's voice sounds familiar to me. Did she and I perform together in some TV commercial or sitcom pilot that never made the Internet movie databases?

Though I was only eight or nine years old when the movie came out, I was an industry insider, so still remember the outrage of critics and fans who believed that Felicity deserved an Academy Award nomination, that she was robbed because the Establishment would never allow an unknown actress whose previous films had bordered on soft-core porn to compete with the likes of Shirley MacLaine, Debra Winger, and Meryl Streep.

When the movie ends, I get up to turn on the lights.

"Not yet," Brenda says. "Please."

I sit down.

"She was awesome," Brenda says. "I had no idea." She looks down at her hands, which are folded in her lap. "Mr. Stern . . . Parker . . . would it be OK if we watch the others? I think we should watch them to really get to know her." She points toward the shelf. "There's a VCR player, right?"

I nod. Deanna ran a full-service establishment in every way. I power on the tape player and switch the video input. It makes sense to watch the other films. In a way, we're representing Paula Felicity McGrath as well as Poniard. These movies are the main record of her life. We spend the afternoon and evening watching Felicity's movies in the makeshift Barrista Movie Theater, I scarfing down pastries and guzzling coffee, and Brenda sipping at chai tea lattes and daintily nibbling on scone crumbs.

Three of the four later movies are shoddy rehashes of *The Fragile Palace*. The directors of these films seemed to think that *The Fragile Palace* worked not because of Felicity's talent, but because of how good she looked naked. Some of the sex scenes in the later films are so gratuitous and explicit that I can feel Brenda's discomfort. Can she feel my arousal? How could Felicity have made such dreadful career choices? If she had a manager back then she should have fired him; if not, she should have hired one.

After eight dismal and increasingly bleary-eyed hours watching Felicity's career decline, we launch *Meadows of Deceit*, her last film. I don't think either of us wants to see it—the descending spiral in Felicity's life is already too obvious, too disheartening—but like marathon runners in pain, we've come this far, so why not finish?

From the opening scene, it's obvious that *Meadows of Deceit* was Felicity McGrath's last-ditch attempt to break out of the good-girl turned druggie-slut roles. An indie film released in 1986, the year before her disappearance, the story is set in England and Scotland of the late 1930s. Felicity stars as Patricia Marlowe, an aristocratic young Englishwoman who rebels against her controlling mother, an elitist who's infatuated with Hitler's Germany. Patricia runs off to rural Scotland, where she takes a position as the village schoolteacher and falls in love with Hadley Rossiter—played by an actor named Samuel Turner. Rossiter is the handsome son of a local farmer. They plan to be married, but when Germany invades Poland, he enlists in the RAF, gets shot down during the Battle of Britain, and goes missing over Dunkirk. Patricia returns to London, appealing to her well-connected mother to get information on Rossiter's fate. The mother confirms that Rossiter is dead. Despite her mother's entreaties to marry someone of her own class, a desolate Patricia devotes herself to the war effort, vowing to return to Scotland and her schoolchildren someday. When the war ends, a blind Rossiter returns, having spent the war years in a German prison camp and a military hospital. It turns out that Patricia's duplicitous mother knew all along that Rossiter was alive.

Meadows of Deceit ended Felicity's career. The critics panned the film as a flabby melodrama and flayed Felicity for daring to take on a role beyond her abilities. One reviewer called her a starlet without acting chops, a born floozy who couldn't play a sober virgin convincingly for five minutes, much less a hundred and ten. Revising history, they questioned her performance in *Fragile Palace*, attributing her success to luck and a good director.

They didn't get it—Felicity was magnificent. A few of the critics grudgingly admitted that her British accent was passable, when in truth it was so authentic that if you didn't known better you would've thought she was a member of the Royal Family. But they mistook her remarkable control for a lack of effort, her spontaneity for a lack of discipline. They didn't see, perhaps refused to see, how she could elicit a deep emotional response with the crook of a finger or a blink of an eye. And there was something else—her voice. I performed with many fine actors in my career, listened to many more with a professional ear, and I've never heard a voice so mellifluous, yet so resonant.

In the end, the problem with Felicity's performance in *Meadows of Deceit* was that movies aren't circumscribed by the opening fade-in and the end credits. Rather, the actor's past performances, even her personal life—especially her personal life—color what the viewer sees. On the screen and in life, Felicity had played the bad girl, and the critics couldn't envision anything else.

When the movie ends, I turn to Brenda. She's crying.

CHAPTER 16

Two weeks later, on the Monday before Thanksgiving, Brenda and I take the elevator to a level below the parking garage. The doors open to a dark, fusty corridor that contains an electrical room, a building supply room, various closets, and the Macklin & Cherry archives. We former firm partners can't recycle the files, because they might become relevant someday—in a malpractice suit against the firm for some old representation, in a rights dispute between a studio and a screenwriter's heirs, or in any number of other unforeseen legal battles. In some sense, a law firm breakup is like a divorce with children involved—you can never end the relationship.

The elevator opens to a security desk, behind which sits a ruddy-faced man in his forties, dressed in a powder-blue security guard shirt and a sea captain's cap, which he keeps on his head indoors because he thinks it makes him look more official.

He greets us with a formal scowl until he recognizes me. "Parker Stern? Hey, man. Long time no see." He speaks in a West Texas drawl, though he's lived in California for thirty years. He shakes his head. "How about those Lakers, huh? You can't stop the aging process." He loves the Lakers, loves basketball in general. In our younger days, he and I played on the firm's basketball team together. He wasn't much of an athlete, had a beer gut and no stamina, but at six-three, two hundred and forty pounds, he could bang bodies and grab rebounds no matter how out of shape he was. He's probably put on another twenty pounds since I last saw him.

"Good to see you, Roland." I introduce Brenda and say, "OK if we look through the old firm files? We're working on a case and need to search something."

"All yours," he says. "You still got your old key? I don't think anyone changed the locks."

Brenda and I walk to the end of the hall and enter a poorly lit room, which smells of mold and dust and parched paper. The rickety Casablanca ceiling fans merely rearrange the heavy air. I hear only our own footsteps and the rattle of those overhead fans. In the old days, Philip Paulsen would spend days on end down in this dungeon, supervising massive document productions. But he's not with us today because his wife Joyce put her foot down, worried that the air would harm Philip's lungs.

"I do not like it down here," Brenda says.

"It's fine. Just a storage room."

"Creepy, creepy. Should we really be down here, anyway? I mean, is it ethical?"

"I was a partner in the firm. We have every right to be down here." That's what I argue to myself. The legal niceties aren't so clear. I might have been a former partner of Macklin & Cherry, but I'm also Bishop's adversary and am about to rifle through his files.

I lead her to a cubbyhole that once served as an office for the people who worked in the archives. These days, someone comes in once a week and dusts the place, and an outside service retrieves documents as needed. The obsolete Gateway desktop computer is still there, and even better, it boots up. I launch the equally outdated document management program and enter my old password.

"Damn," I say.

Brenda lowers her head, as she does every time I curse.

"The password's not working," I say. "Either they locked me out, or I forgot . . . I couldn't have forgotten."

"It's been a long time, Mr. Stern, right?"

I try the password again—*childstar*, one that I'll never forget. It still doesn't work. I try as many variations I can think of—lowercase, all caps, initial caps. All the while Brenda peers over my shoulder, chewing on a thumbnail.

"I can't get into the system," I say. "We'll have to search the files manually."

"They're arranged in alphabetical order?"

"No, by client number, unfortunately."

"Do you remember Bishop's client number?"

"That's why it was so important to get into the digital index. We'll just have to look at the labels."

She puts her hands on her head and sighs, and then says, "OK, let's go. How about I start on one side and you take the other. And . . . could I take this side? It's so dark in the back, and I have nightmares about rats."

I make my way to the far side of the room and survey the rows upon rows of file folders. I use my hand to brush away the cobwebs, and when I open a file, I check for black widow spiders that might be lurking in the crevices of a Redweld expandable. On another day, I might be fascinated by ancient contracts for the services of Stanley Kubrick, Steve McQueen, and Elizabeth Taylor, but now they're just annoyances. There are no files for *The Boatman*, no files that have anything to do with William Bishop, Parapet Media, or any of his other companies. He and his corporations were clients of the firm for years. Someone scrubbed this place clean—no, not someone, Bishop's lackeys. I'll have to ask Roland on the way out if he has a record of Bishop's people being here.

Brenda's shriek echoes off the rafters. I run back to her side of the room. I don't know if I'll have to kill a rodent or fight off one of Bishop's thugs.

She's sitting in front of the computer, her smile brighter than the ceiling lights.

"Are you OK?" I ask.

"I'm great." She hands me a file folder.

The tag says Hilda Marie Johnson, a name that means nothing to me.

"It's the real name of an actress named Hildy Gish," Brenda says. "You told me that Harry Cherry mentioned her, right?"

I nod. "How did you figure this out?"

"The computer. I searched for *Hildy*, but there was nothing, but there was an entry for *Hilda*, and it's close, so I pulled the file."

"How did you even get into the computer?"

"Your password, *childstar*. It worked with an initial cap and a *question mark* at the end. A lot of these programs make you have capitals and a special character. So I just capitalized the first letter and tried some punctuation marks and the question mark worked and I got in right away."

"But I was sure that I . . ." Then I remember that in the last years of the firm, the new fascistic head of the IT department forced all the lawyers to make their passwords more secure. He probably made me change mine. My case assistant is certainly resourceful.

"They wiped this place clean," I say.

"Well, they missed this one." She hands me the file folder.

The file shows that several times during the eighties, William Bishop hired Hildy Gish to act in his movies, all before Felicity disappeared. Gish obviously wasn't a big-time actress, so most of the agreements are simple day-player contracts. When Brenda shows me the document at the bottom of the file, I struggle not to shout. I'm looking at Hildy Gish's acting contract to appear in *The Boatman*. Whoever sanitized the file for Bishop obviously didn't know Hildy Gish's real name. What makes me want to pump my fist in triumph is that, attached to the contract, is *The Boatman*'s cast list.

William Bishop had everything to do with this film. But despite what Harry Cherry said to me, Felicity McGrath's name isn't listed as a member of *The Boatman*'s cast. When Brenda realizes this, she lets out a disappointed groan.

What I feel is not disappointment but another emotion entirely. Because other words on this long-forgotten piece of paper cause a frenzied jolt of electricity to surge down my spine.

"Could we get out of this place now?" Brenda says.

I tuck the Hildy Gish file under my arm and go to the door. The moment I open it, a scream comes from down the hall, the hideous falsetto of a male in agony. I close the door to a crack and look out. The only parts of big Roland's body that are visible are his arms and lower torso, enough to see that he's sprawled out lifeless in his chair. Two men, one tall and one short, both middle-aged muscular, draw away from him and head toward the door, not running but walking with purpose, like masters of efficient slaughter. These guys are professionals. They've overpowered a two-hundred-and-sixty-pound roughneck before he could get out of his chair.

"Let's go," I say. "Now!"

"Oh my god, oh my god," Brenda whimpers.

Still clutching the Gish file with one hand, I grab her wrist with the other and lead her back to the so-called office with the desk and the computer, no place to hide in itself, little more than an alcove. The file room door rattles. They've got Roland's keys, and they're trying them in the lock. After only a few tries, I hear the door swing open.

A thick industrial curtain covers the entire back wall, the kind that's suspended from a track in the ceiling and that can slide to separate the office from the rest of the file room. I take hold of the hem, lift it up, and tell Brenda to crawl behind. She looks at me as if I'm daft. The footsteps on the concrete floor are getting louder. But maybe we've gotten a break—the men seem to be meticulously going up and down the file stacks looking for us. She has no choice, and once she's gone behind the curtain, I follow her under. The stench of dust and mold and decaying insect parts and rodent droppings is nauseating, and I try to hold my breath. Brenda's breathing is so loud and labored that she's on the verge of hyperventilating. I fear that the men will hear her gasping for air and find us. She presses her body against mine, evidently thinking that we're going to try to avoid those men by hiding behind the curtain, but I push her away—I'm not foolish enough to think we can win a game of hide 'n' seek behind some filthy drapery.

In the darkness, I feel along the wall, hoping that my memory of a drunken night eight years ago is still clear enough to find what I'm looking for. And there it is—the handleless door in the drywall. I push hard, and it opens inward with a scraping sound. I hope those guys are far enough away that they didn't hear it. I pull Brenda inside and shut the door tightly. There's a lock, but only one of those cheap sliding latches that you get in the hardware store, the kind that wouldn't survive one blow from those guys. I lock it anyway.

Though there's a light switch, I'm not about to turn it on, so it's black in here. I feel my way to the end of the short hall and find another door, but it's locked. I'm not about to jangle my keys trying to unlock it. This far below ground, it's dank and cold. Or maybe it's just the fear that's making me shiver. Brenda presses her body against mine. I put my arm around her and hold her tightly, not for any amorous reason—mortal terror is only sexually arousing in the movies—but so those guys won't hear her teeth chatter. Harry Cherry claimed that underground rivers run through Beverly Hills, and with a straight face, Harmon would insist that it was true. I never believed them, but now I hear the babble and whoosh of rushing water. It's probably just the plumbing, or the blood rushing through my veins at Mach speed.

I try to keep still, to keep Brenda still, to comprehend the footsteps and the murmured words of the stalkers on the other side. As so often happens when you try to focus on one thing for too long, my mind wanders, and I recall the night I learned about this door. My late partner Deanna Poulos and I had won a major trial that day and had celebrated by hitting more than a few Beverly Hills bars for a tequila taste test. After a night of doing shot after shot, we returned to the building at about midnight and got in the elevator to retrieve our cars, though neither of us should have even thought of driving. But instead of going to the parking level, she pressed the button for the archives.

"There's something I want you to do for me—or rather to me," she said. Although Deanna preferred to sleep with women, we'd have these occasional trysts that she called *sport fucking*—we fooled ourselves into believing we could dismiss the act's significance by making light of it. She was one of those people who consciously aspired to be known as wild and edgy, and the alcohol fueled that goal. She took me to the archives, opened the curtains, and showed me this door, which she'd learned about from Philip Paulsen during a document production.

"I always wanted to fuck in a cave, and this room is like a cave," she said with a drunken logic that made sense to me only because I was also drunk. So we went inside and had sex almost fully dressed and standing up. The next morning I arrived at work with a raging hangover and had to listen to an equally hungover Deanna berate me for agreeing to go along with something so unsexy and crass.

Now the footsteps get louder. The slaps of shoe leather on concrete are arrhythmic, which means that both of them are close. There's a scraping and tapping, no longer coming from floor level but higher up, and I'm certain that one or both of them are feeling along the curtain to see if we're hiding behind it. Fortunately, the door has no handle. Will they feel the door seams or lift the curtain high enough to notice the door? Brenda is holding her breath and trying not to shake. Her heavy perfume seems to have saturated whatever air is left in this place, and now I worry that Bishop's men will smell it.

The sounds stop, and there's grumbling, and the footsteps fade, and one of the men says what sounds like, "We'd better get out of here," and eventually there's the heavy thud of the front door shutting. I don't think we've been hiding for more than ten minutes, but I've lost track of time, and I make sure we stay in that dark room for twice that long. Finally, I motion for Brenda to stay put, open the door gingerly, slide out, and lift up the curtain, my heart in a race with my panting lungs. I slowly creep out and look up and down the stacks, but I don't see anyone. I doubt they'd lie in wait, which gives me comfort. I knock on the wall twice, and Brenda opens the door, pulling so hard that the scrape of wood against concrete reverberates throughout the file room. I take her hand, and we run for the door.

When we're sure the corridor is clear, we hurry over to the desk, where Roland's huge body has somehow slipped to the floor. I bend down next to him, and as I reach out to feel for a pulse, there's a loud gurgle of breath that makes me flinch.

Roland opens his eyes, shakes his head, and says, "Holy shit, those guys were good. A Taser gun and some kind of sleeper hold . . . shit, my head's spinning." He makes a move to stand, and when I tell him to sit he shakes me off, so I help him up as best I can, no easy task given his girth. He goes over and sits behind his desk, and then asks me to give him his cap, which for some inexplicable reason he perches on his head. I pick up the phone and dial 911, asking for both the cops and an ambulance.

"They were looking for you, Parker," Roland says. "When I told them I hadn't seen you, they said they'd followed you here. I told them that you'd come and gone. Guess they didn't believe me."

Only when the paramedics arrive do I realize that I no longer have the Hildy Gish file, and I'm about to go back inside the archives to get it when I notice that Brenda is carrying it.

"You left it on the floor of that horrible, wonderful room," she says. "I wasn't going to let it out of our sight."

CHAPTER 17

Roland has no record of anyone from Bishop or Parapet Media coming to look at files, though there are always work people coming in and out of the place. After talking to the police—they made clear that they didn't take me seriously when I said William Bishop was behind the attack on Roland—I want Brenda to go home or back to The Barrista, but she refuses. "I'm part of this more than ever," she says.

So we drive to Topanga College together. The young man at the information booth tells us that Nate Ettinger is teaching a seminar. We find the classroom and stand in the back of the room. Ettinger looks at us in surprise but doesn't break cadence, continuing his lecture about legitimate uses of film and art as tools of political persuasion. He praises the aesthetics of Nazi filmmaker Leni Riefenstahl, he believes that Oliver Stone is a great thinker, he maintains that celebrities like Ronald Reagan and Arnold Schwarzenegger are prototypes for future politicians. By the time his lecture is over, I want to punch him. Actually, I've wanted to punch him since I saw *The Boatman* cast list.

After class, he speaks informally with some students and then comes over and greets us with a big smile, though he isn't happy to see us. He sits across from us, pats the outside of his plaid sport coat, and takes a half-bent billiard pipe out of the inside pocket. Smoking is prohibited in college classrooms, but he lights up anyway. "To what do I owe this unexpected visit?" he says.

"I was overcome with the sudden urge to ask you what it's like to work for William Bishop," I say.

The smile remains on his lips but leaves his eyes. "I wouldn't know. I never worked for him. He didn't give me the opportunity. When he took over the studio I was working at, he killed my movie in its infancy."

"Oh, you did work for him," I say. "On *The Boatman*. I have the list of cast and crew. And it's interesting—the typewritten credits sheet lists you as an associate producer, but someone crossed that out with a pen and listed you as the lighting and sound man. Which was it?"

He jerks his head back and drops the pipe, not bothering to pick it up.

"Let me see it," he says.

I slide it over to him. He scowls at the piece of paper and slides the list back to me with aggression.

"Lighting and sound?" he says. "Sure, why not."

"Why the lying?" I say.

His shoulders slump, and he sighs like a man accepting news of a serious illness. "Do you know that after the film was shut down, two of his goons showed up to search my apartment to make sure I didn't have any copies? Frightened my girlfriend, tore up the place, and threatened to break my legs if they found out I had a copy. That's why I lied to you and that's why I won't discuss that movie or McGrath or Bishop."

"Who sent them?" I ask. "Bishop?"

He crosses his arms. "I won't discuss it."

"Did Felicity McGrath act in *The Boatman*?" I ask.

He just stares at me.

I blurt the next words out—a lawyer's primal instinct. "Last time we were here, you said Felicity slept with many men in Hollywood. Did they include you?"

Ettinger raises his hand in denial, but there's also a fleeting braggadocian glint in his eyes that answers my question in the affirmative.

Brenda goes to the other side of the table and sits beside him. "I know this is scary," she says. "But we really need your help. Can you at least tell us whether Felicity acted in the movie?"

"I cannot," he says.

"There's another person we're interested in," I say. "The cast list says that an actor named Bradley Kelly was in *The Boatman*. Is that the same guy who started the Church of the Sanctified Assembly?"

Ettinger closes his eyes, takes a deep breath, and nods. "Another reason why I won't talk about it."

Though I was certain that it was the same Kelly, Ettinger's confirmation causes a glaucomatous fog to descend, one of the many symptoms of my courtroom stage fright. The late Bradley Kelly was the charismatic founder of the Sanctified Assembly, supposedly a divine prophet who traveled to a parallel universe and drank of the celestial fountain of all truth. He also seduced my mother and persuaded her to join his sham religion because she had business savvy that he didn't. Through her, he got access to the money I earned as an actor. She dragged me into that world, and there I stayed until age fifteen, when I escaped the abuse and terror. After that, I became the Assembly's sworn enemy. I'm still their enemy.

A young woman comes into the classroom and walks over to Ettinger. "I thought we had office hours, Professor. Did I get the time wrong?"

"No, Madison. You have the correct time. I unexpectedly got tied up. But I'm done with my meeting now. Let's get some coffee and talk in the plaza." He stands up and without saying good-bye escapes through the door.

"He isn't only afraid of Bishop," Brenda says. "He's afraid of the cult."

"He should be."

She grabs my sleeve. "We'll figure this out. I'll find addresses or phone numbers for the people who worked on *The Boatman*. And we have Philip Paulsen, and he's awesome."

I nod. There's something I haven't told Brenda. It's about another actor whose name appears on *The Boatman* cast list. His name appears on page 2, near the bottom:

Little Cupid . . . . *Parky Gerald*

Was I really in that movie as a four-year-old? Did I know Felicity McGrath?

As soon as Brenda and I leave the campus and get back into my car, we call Philip Paulsen on the speakerphone to update him on the day's developments. He uncharacteristically loses his temper over Bishop's

Gestapo tactics. After we convince him that we're OK, he says, "I'm down at the County Hall of Records. I've been looking at records the entire day." His breathing is so labored that I'm certain he's drenched in sweat from sitting in that stuffy old government building, where air-conditioning and adequate circulation are only aspirational. He would've been safer in the Macklin & Cherry archives.

"You're working too hard," I say. "Which is exactly what Joyce doesn't want. What *I* don't want."

"I found something," he says. "Felicity McGrath had a child."

"Rumors were that she was pregnant," I say. "We already knew that."

"No. She bore the child two years before her disappearance."

Brenda half squeals, half gasps. Because Philip delivered the news in his pastoral monotone, it takes me a moment to understand its significance. When it does, I swerve halfway into the other lane, earning a long, hostile honk from an affronted Audi. I pull over to the curb and cut the engine.

"Go ahead, Philip," I say.

There's the whoosh of his breathing on the other end of the line. "OK," he says. "There's a birth certificate for a baby girl named Alicia Courtney Turner, born December 21, 1985. Mother, Paula McGrath. Father, Samuel Turner. Unmarried."

I shudder when I hear the middle name—the same as the cosplayer who believes she's Felicity. I'd take it as another one of her make-believe games, except she couldn't possibly know that Felicity had a daughter.

"The actor who played Rossiter in *Meadows of Deceit*?" I say. "Have we tried to find him?"

"We did and he's dead," Brenda says. "Died in 2005 of AIDS."

"Why didn't the media pick the birth up?" I say. "Or the cops?"

"The birth certificate was filed under seal," Philip says.

"Whoa, that's probably illegal," I say.

"Someone had to have *mucho* clout to get it done," Philip says. "Like our boy Bishop."

"Bishop wasn't that powerful in the mid-eighties," I say. "I doubt he could—"

"Maybe his father?" Philip says.

It doesn't seem likely that lawyer Howard Bishop had that kind of power. But it doesn't seem likely that he could have quashed *The Boatman*, either, and Harry Cherry claims he did.

"How did you manage to get a copy?" I ask Philip.

"I have a connection," he says. "That's all you need to know. I'm going to do some looking for Alicia Turner."

"Go home," I say. "If not for yourself, for me. Joyce will kill me if you don't take better care of yourself."

"I'll let you know what I find," he says, and the connection goes dead.

"I'll look on the Internet for this Alicia girl," Brenda says once we're back on the road. "She's young, so maybe she's on Facebook. Maybe she knows something about what happened to her mother."

"If she even knows who her mother was," I say.

CHAPTER 18

Brighton slides the cursor across the screen and simultaneously presses the tilde key to cast a spell on a Komodo dragon that bears an uncanny resemblance to William Bishop. The giant lizard is wearing leather puttees and jodhpurs and is carrying an old-time movie director's megaphone. Bugsy says he's dressed like Cecil B. DeMille, whoever that is.

"Pause that thing," Bugsy says.

Brighton hits the *pause* key.

"That damn game of yours," Bugsy says in that perpetually stern voice that doesn't necessarily reflect his true mood. "It resurrects the dead. Some things should be left alone."

Brighton doesn't understand Bugsy's point, but he resumes playing the game, sensing that this will rile Bugsy up, which is perfectly OK because he's learned that Bugsy likes nothing more than to be riled up. It gets him *pontificating*, the HF Queen says.

"In my day, there were sharp lines of demarcation between reality and illusion," Bugsy says. "Novels and films were fantasy worlds where you went to escape reality, to laugh, to scream, to cry, to cogitate, to fantasize, all without consequence. Now what do you have? So-called 'reality' television, where you try to glorify your own existence by scoffing at someone else's, never mind the observer effect, which means, because I'm sure you don't know about quantum physics, that the very presence of the camera changes the reality so you're not seeing reality at all. And then there's your *Abduction!* game, supposedly pure illusion but seemingly affecting the world outside the screen in adverse ways. Although the logical theory is that this Poniard fellow is the murderer himself."

Brighton doesn't care what anyone says—Bugsy, the HF Queen, the bloggers, the media, anyone—Poniard isn't a murderer. Brighton's belief in his hero's innocence is absolute, and it's not just because he's ten years old like Bugsy whispered to the HF Queen when *she* called Poniard a killer. No, Brighton knows Poniard through the video games, and as violent as they are, the games preach *non*violence, fairness, justice.

"What're you guys up to?" the HF Queen says.

Brighton starts. He didn't hear her come in. She's always sneaking up on him lately. She's still in her work dress, but she's taken off her high heels and is barefoot.

"What else?" Bugsy says. "The kid's brains are getting pickled in cyber-brine with this game."

"You are the one who told me to let him play it," she says.

"You should know better than to listen to me," Bugsy says.

She leans over to look at the screen and rests her hand on Brighton's shoulder. He hates when she does that, all the more so because her hand feels soft and firm at the same time.

"How're we doing on this level, kiddo?" she asks.

Brighton shrugs. A man with coal-black hair and a Do-Right jaw kneels down in front of a fountain that spews an iridescent emerald-green liquid, clearly toxic because each time a drop splashes on the ground, there's an angry sizzle, a billow of smoke, and a deep fissure where the liquid has landed. But then the kneeling man stands up, mugs for the camera, and smiles. He has gorgeous pure white teeth, so bright in fact, that capillaries of light beam off his incisors and bicuspids, a silly effect more worthy of a Saturday morning cartoon show than a Poniard masterpiece. He walks over to the lethal fountain, and though the waters engulf him, he's unharmed. He clasps his hands in a kind of prayer position. *I am Cad Belly, the keeper of the Celestial Light*, he says. *We all must bathe in the healing waters of the Celestial Fount. The pure will be cleansed; the evil shall perish.*

"Seriously?" the HF Queen says.

"This Poniard fellow has some big *huevos*," Bugsy says.

"No, he's crazy," the HF Queen says.

The Queen's fingers tighten on his shoulder, but she doesn't say anything else. Before she came home, Bugsy had taken one look at Cad Belly and started pontificating about the Church of the Sanctified Assembly, calling it a cult that worships money and celebrity and holds Bradley Kelly up as a divine prophet. He also said that the Assembly *isn't beyond silencing its critics by any means necessary, if you know what I'm saying.* Of course Brighton knew what he was saying—Bugsy always sounds like a gangster.

On screen, Cad Belly takes a step toward the camera and spreads his arms, as if to embrace his congregation. *I am now sanctified, cleansed by the Fount. All ye are commanded to partake of the Fount or ye shall perish by it.* And suddenly, his face hardens into white granite, and his skin flashes neon reds and ambers and blues, and like a radioactive Bruce Banner he explodes out of his suit and pounds a fist on his now bare chest. He snarls and uses his perfect white teeth to tear a crease in the thin air as if it were a flimsy curtain, and he disappears into nowhere— an *alternate universe*, Bugsy calls it.

"They're going to holler bloody blasphemy," Bugsy says. "And this time, they'll be right."

The HF Queen shushes him. The Komodo C. B. DeMille appears and shouts, "Take One, Scene One! Action!" The words *STAGE FOUR: THE SKANKTIFIED ASSEMBLAGE* appear in mauve lettering on the screen.

Brighton tries to open the doors of a bejeweled cathedral, behind which scores of unfortunate men, women, and children are held captive in cells, chained and brainwashed by ruthless underbosses who all look like Cad Belly. (You can tell the prisoners are being brainwashed because the jailers use a chainsaw to open the prisoner's skull, after which they remove the brain, dip it in soap suds, scrape it against an old-fashioned washboard, hang it on a clothesline, and put it back into the prisoner's head. After that, the prisoner—now wearing a sign that says *devotee*—walks around in circles with a loopy smile and cow eyes.) The fingers of Brighton's left hand fly over the keyboard, while his right hand makes impossible mouse turns, disintegrating guards and casting spells to unlock doors.

"The kid's like a fucking Segovia on that thing," Bugsy says.

"Language, Dad," the HF Queen says, without taking her eyes off the screen.

Brighton likes the compliment, though he has no idea who Segovia is. Meanwhile, he never misses a keystroke. This is an easy level, another signature element of Poniard's games. Rather than make the stages ever more difficult like most games, he mixes in easier levels. Brighton has read a few blogs claiming that Poniard is like a drug pusher, that he designs his games to ensure that even the mediocre player will get "high" once in a while and keep playing. In the end, Brighton liberates all of the Skanktified Assemblage's prisoners.

"My god," the HF Queen says. "That son-of-a-bitch Poniard is not only a murderer, he's suicidal."

Then comes the concluding cutscene, in which Komodo William Bishop yells *Cut! And that's a wrap!* His eyes shoot daggers at the game player—literally. He laughs, his double-bass hoot so loud and malevolent that it causes Brighton's subwoofer to rattle the walls and windows like a California quake.

CHAPTER 19

I spend three days trying to get Poniard's attention so he can explain the addition of the *Skanktified Assemblage* level to *Abduction!* That's wrong—there is no explanation for taunting a formidable cult that wouldn't hesitate to destroy you. Finally, during morning rush at The Barrista (if you can call it a rush):

Poniard:
>*I know you're upset at me, counselor, but I had to do it. It's a lead, and it's a shitty little level anyway . . . not much time to put it together*
PStern
>*You HAD to antagonize the Church of the Sanctified Assembly? You HAD to hint at Bradley Kelly's involvement so you could you blow the element of surprise? Bishop and Frantz didn't know about Kelly or The Boatman. Now they might figure it out.*
Poniard:
>*The public is my audience. They have millions and millions of brains, the best Internet there is, more powerful than a super-computer. They can help us solve this . . . but I have to give them the facts, keep the pressure on Bishop. And* Abduction! *is in part procedurally generated*
PStern
>*What's procedurally generated?*
Poniard:
>*An algorithm determines what happens depending on individual players, so my audience can actually change the game and hopefully find out what happened to Felicity. Which means we win the lawsuit*

PStern

>You know nothing about the law or how it works. And the fact that you added this level so quickly plays into the hands of those who say you killed Bud and Isla Kreiss.

Poniard:

>Whatever

PStern

>Did you know about The Boatman *when you hired me? That I was in it? Are you playing me with all this?*

Poniard:

>Nothing about The Boatman. *You found that*

PStern

>Did you suspect the Sanctified Assembly?

Poniard:

>No proof just vague rumblings—rumor & innuendo, as you lawyers call it

PStern

>That's insanity!

Poniard:

>Also, I worried that you wouldn't take my case if I mentioned the Assembly. Because of your trial against them. I'm sure you agree they deserve whatever I say about them . . . creepy fascist cult. I'm not scared of them, and I know you aren't, Parker Stern

PStern

>You're so wrong. Only a fool isn't afraid of the Sanctified Assembly. They're relentless and will try to find out who you are and make you pay for this. And I don't mean in court. They're orders of magnitude better at that than William Bishop, with all his resources. And by the way, there's no evidence that the Assembly has anything to do with McGrath's disappearance.

Poniard:

>Bradley Kelly

PStern

>Kelly was a working actor, so of course he appeared in movies. That doesn't mean that the Assembly is involved. Your imagination is getting in your way. You're hiding something from me. What?

Poniard:
>I only hide what I need to hide, just like you
PStern
>You've drunk at that well once too often, Poniard. You and I are dif-
    ferent. Do you know why?
Poniard:
>I'll take the bait
PStern
>I've never used my secrets to manipulate others.
Poniard:
>LOL. The ONLY reason anybody keeps secrets is to manipulate
    others. Just have patience . . . the game will reveal all
Poniard has signed off.

What to make of Kelly's and my involvement in *The Boatman*? I don't remember that film—I was four or five years old, constantly working since I'd turned three, and my memory of most of my performances at that age is long gone. *The Boatman* was supposedly filmed in 1979, a year after Kelly's journey through a crease in the universe that allowed him to find the Celestial Fountain of All That Is, which transmitted the Celestial Laws to him. Although Kelly ever after proselytized and gradually formed his clandestine cult of wealthy devotees who treated his lethal propaganda as truth and willingly engaged in his warped Assembly rituals, the Church of the Sanctified Assembly wasn't formally founded until 1987. It's never occurred to me before—why would it?—but 1987 was the very year in which Paula Felicity McGrath went missing. Is there really a connection?

I go into the back room where Brenda is working at her computer. As I tell her about my chat with Poniard, she continues to stare at the screen and type on her keyboard.

"What are you doing?" I ask.

"I've been researching this Sanctified Assembly."

"You hadn't heard of them before?"

"Sort of. I knew you had a big case against them. But I had no idea how scary they are. Some ex-members claim that the Assembly uses these good-looking chicks as bait to lure them in and take all their money. Supposedly the Assembly believes that suicide is caused by contagious germs. Some say that once you're a member, you can't leave the church even if you want to, that if they can't shut their critics up by using the courts, they'll do it by threats, beatings, blackmail, even murder. One judge who ruled against them was found dead a few weeks later, supposedly a hiking accident, but no witnesses. The Assembly tries to get celebrities to join so they can attract new members. And they hate you, Parker." She finally stops gazing at her monitor and turns to me. "So, I was thinking. Is it possible that Bishop is a Sanctified Assembly member?"

The sudden confluence between stored data and flash memory sparks an insight that I should have had long ago. When Brenda and I interviewed Bud Kreiss, he told us that on the night of Felicity's disappearance, Bishop drove up to the scene of the abduction in a blue Mercedes-Benz. Bradley Kelly required all Assembly employees to drive blue Mercedes. The Sanctified Assembly believes that blue is the color of the celestial angels' wings.

CHAPTER 20

I t isn't that I haven't gotten job offers during the past couple of years. After my trial against the Church of the Sanctified Assembly, firms large and small called and asked me to head up their trial departments. I received offers of full partnerships, seats on management committees, seven-figure guarantees. Or I could've opened up my own shop, picking and choosing my cases. I don't lack for potential clients who are eager to hire a lawyer who's taken on one of the most dangerous and powerful organizations in the country. But I didn't do any of those things. Paradoxically, though being with Lovely Diamond helped blunt the crippling stage fright, it also took away my desire to continue in a job that institutionalizes struggle against an adversary. And now, she's my adversary.

Precisely at nine o'clock, I retrieve the Felicity/Scotty letters from my bank safety deposit box and take them to a rented suite in the Manchester Airport Hotel on Sepulveda Boulevard near LAX, right under the flight pattern. The location is more convenient for both of the document experts, who'll fly in, test the letters, and immediately fly out to another venue and another case. Besides, I can't have the inspection take place at The Barrista, and I'm not about to do it in my condo—not with Lovely there.

We've both hired expert consultants. QD examiners, they're called, because they examine questioned documents. They arrive together precisely at ten o'clock, the time that Lovely has scheduled for the inspection. Tops in their field, they're on opposite sides of almost every important lawsuit where document authenticity is at issue. They repeatedly perform parallel Electrostatic Detection Apparatus investigations, sample ink and paper using polypropylene-capped tubes, and examine handwriting for forgery. Middle-aged former college science professors who've become wealthy serving as professional witnesses. They both wear gray business suits, brown-rimmed eyeglasses, and oxford shoes, and they have matching haircuts, as if they've been thrown together so often they've unwittingly become mirror images of each other, though my expert is a woman and Lovely's is a man.

We wait for Lovely while they bicker over who has the better ink library, an argument that must've repeated itself a hundred times. Lovely is twenty-five minutes late. She's wearing a cutout peasant blouse and black jeans, as if she's taking the day off. Her blonde hair, which she usually wears up or in a ponytail during work hours, falls loosely almost to her shoulders.

"Kind of you to join us," I say.

"Let's just get this over with," she says. "I have a busy day." She looks around the room and says, "Didn't bring that pretty little assistant of yours?"

"Let's get started," I say to the experts.

The QD examiners nod at each other and go over to the table on which I put the documents. They start with the first letter to Scotty, dated May 4, 1987, a few months before Felicity McGrath's disappearance: *As always, you worry too much. Bad vibrations. It's just make-believe, remember? And Big Bad Billy Bishop has our Backs (how's that for alliteration?) Anyway, my darling, he's my insurance policy. Stop worrying. Free ticket out of purgatory. So relax while I enjoy for once.* Using a blunt hypodermic needle, they each take six miniscule samples, which they put in a vial. To add the solvent, one expert uses a syringe and the other a small-volume pipette, leading to another obviously well-worn argument between them. When they poke holes in the words *alliteration* and *worrying*, I cringe, because as tiny as the samples are, I haven't asked Poniard's permission for such destructive testing. They take six samples from the second letter, which is undated but obviously written shortly before Felicity's disappearance: *Surprise! You're going to take that trip to Paris you've always dreamed about. The tickets have been reserved in your name. The flight leaves in three days. Au revoir, my sweet.* This letter is shorter, so the sampling is even more invasive. Next, trying to determine whether the type of paper existed in 1987, they examine the document to see how it fluoresces under ultraviolet light. For exemplars of Felicity's signature, they use copies of a handwritten shopping list that the cops found in Felicity's apartment, which they'll compare to Poniard's letters.

The process takes a little over an hour. Lovely and I sit on opposite sides of the room, she working at the standard hotel-issue Formica desk, and I on the nubby sofa, which must harbor renegade bed bugs, because after a while my skin begins to crawl. She reads on her iPad, confers with her expert, and doesn't look at me once. I review a stack of documents as a pretense, getting nothing accomplished. All the while, I try so hard not to look at her that she's all I can think about. I feel her every move, know without looking when she lifts a hand to brush a strand of hair off her face and when she crosses and uncrosses her legs. It's torture that I wish would last forever.

The experts pack up and head off to their next assignment. Lovely gets up to leave but turns to me and says, "Your client is unstable. Dangerous."

"And yours is a lying psychopath."

She closes her eyes, no more than an extended blink and walks over to me. I'm certain that she's about to shred me with her sharp-ice voice, or worse, turn around and storm out. She raises her right arm as if to strike me, and I think, *Lovely, if you do slap my face I'll welcome the touch of your flesh on mine*, but she doesn't slap me, only lays her hand gently on my cheek, and it's then that I learn that it's not a myth, that the heart is truly the reservoir of love and emotion, because my own heart gambols and twirls and finds a jubilant equilibrium I thought was gone forever. I draw her close and we kiss, the heat of her body a paradox, new and familiar. When she abruptly pulls away, I once again get confirmation about how easily I delude myself.

She walks over to the ratty sofa, falls into the cushions, and buries her face in her hands. I stand there, my arms outstretched in confusion or maybe supplication. She looks up at me, but she isn't crying. The blue flecks in her gray eyes radiate pristine light.

"I'm going to tell you why," she says.

I sit next to her. Maybe, just maybe, after it's all said, she'll come back to me.

"When I was twenty years old, I got pregnant."

The machinery that operates my brain freezes up. I strain to understand what she just said. At the time, she was performing in porn movies. "How did you—?"

"How do you think?"

I reach out to her again. She pulls away and says, "Don't!"

I suddenly recall a story about how, as a second-year law student, she nearly got into a physical altercation with her pro-life constitutional law professor over abortion rights. "You had an abortion," I say. "And that's why you and Professor Sommer—"

"No."

"That's not why you went after Sommer?"

"No, I didn't have an abortion."

"I don't—"

"I had a child. Have. He's ten years old."

She begins speaking cathartically, delivering a primal confession to the heavenly shrink, one she must have wanted to share forever. She'd been in the business for a year, and there was this film shoot on a yacht in international waters. Unlike most of the other performers, she'd never partied much, but this time she drank and did drugs and forgot to swallow her estrogen/progestin. She did three gangbang scenes worth $1,800 each, so of course didn't know who the father was. And how could she possibly paternity-test twenty-nine suspects even if she'd wanted to, which she didn't because they were all slime? When she missed her period, she pretended that doing porn was like long-distance running where the female parts of your body shut down, and when she finally went to the ob-gyn the ultrasound so clearly showed it was a boy. Why had she said yes when the doc asked her if she wanted to know the gender? Once knowing, it somehow felt so wrong to end it (emotion knows no politics), and she waited and waited and waited so long to choose that there was no choice to be made.

"My aunt took him in," she says. "My mother's older sister. Like the rest of my mother's family, she disowned my mom because of my father, hated me even worse for what I was doing. She'd never been married, no kids, so I guess she thought this was her only chance for a family. But there was one condition—my father and I could have nothing to do with the kid, no contact, not even payment of child support. My father told her to go fuck herself, said he'd raise the boy, but . . . I agreed, Parker. Best for all concerned. I was twenty, a child myself, though I'd been doing the least childlike things you can imagine. The boy didn't know I existed, my aunt told him some bullshit story about. . . . And then, not long ago, she died of a heart attack. Ed and I are his only family. So I gave up my apartment, moved in with my father, quit the US Attorney's Office, and went back to work for Frantz because he's letting me have flexible hours."

The words she doesn't say reverberate like a saboteur's bomb: *And I broke it off with you*. But I finally understand. When we were together, I made it no secret that I didn't want kids, that my childhood was so dysfunctional that I didn't have the wherewithal to be a parent, that in my late thirties I was getting too old to be a father. She swore that she didn't want children either, that so many people have kids out of obligation and expectation and not true desire for a family and end up miserable and full of regret. Only, I realize now that she didn't mean a word of it, and neither did I.

"You should've told me," I say. "I'll help you with this. I don't even need to work. Together, we can—"

"That's exactly why I didn't tell you, because I knew you'd say that, to be noble."

"I'm not being noble. I love you."

She looks at me for a long time with a sad frown. "Everything's changed. I have a responsibility to my son. And you're too dangerous."

My spine straightens with a jolt, as though one of the document experts' blunt hypodermic needles penetrated the base of my skull. "I don't have any idea what that means."

Her shoulders go slack. She takes an audible breath, and fixes her eyes on me wearily. "You court danger. The case against the Sanctified Assembly. And now Poniard. Two people are already dead, your client probably killed them, your life's in jeopardy, and you keep plowing forward. You make it unsafe for the people around you, and I can't have that happen to my child." She sounds like she's been talking to Joyce Paulsen.

"They're just lawsuits, Lovely. And you were involved in both of them."

"Exactly. I was just like you. But not anymore. I can't afford to be. As for the *Bishop* case, I thought it would be an easy default judgment, a no-brainer. Until you got involved, and then it became perilous for both of us. I won't expose my child to that. As soon as you're disqualified—"

"I won't be."

"As soon as you're disqualified, there'll be a lull. I'll tell Lou that I'm off the case." Her eyes, now a slate color, are as unyielding as I've ever seen them.

I go to the window and stand with my back to her, watching a 747 with a *Federal Express* logo fly low on its final approach to LAX. Whoever built this hotel did a good job of soundproofing. I can barely hear the jet engines. And yet, the noise is still there, as if I'm perceiving the annoying sound not with my ears but with my skin. No matter how hard you try to shut out the bad things they always seem to find another way in.

She points to the letters. "I hope you're going to keep those in a safe place. Lou will want them for trial."

"Count on it."

She packs up her things and goes to the door. Just before she opens it, I say, "Your son. What's his name?"

She pauses for a long time, considering whether to share even this innocuous bit of information.

"It's the only thing I demanded before I let her take him," she says. "That I be the one to name him, that he keep my last name. At least there would be that. His name is Brighton. Brighton Diamond. He loves to play your client's horrible game. He's kind of a master at it actually. Drives me crazy."

And despite the agonizing pain that oozes out of the marrow in my bones, I actually hear myself laughing out loud as she closes the door.

CHAPTER 21

If William "the Conqueror" Bishop is really who Poniard says he is, how hard would it be for him to send out some of his people to steal Felicity's letters and make it look like a carjacking? Now that the document examination has ended, I want to stow the letters back into my safety deposit box immediately—no, sooner than that. Fortunately, I'm only a couple of miles away from the bank. Unfortunately, I'm driving not an armored Humvee but an aging Lexus that's overdue for an oil change.

As I'm about to pull out of the hotel parking lot, my cell phone chimes, announcing a text message from Philip Paulsen.

Meet me at Cranky Franks @ 12:30. I have a lead on Alicia Turner.

What's up? I reply.

Can't talk or text now. Tell you when you get here.

So instead of going to my bank to secure Felicity's letters, I drive to Cranky Franks, located downtown near the campus of the University of Southern California. Cranky Franks is one of LA's historical landmarks—literally. No matter that it's a hot dog stand that sells the city's tastiest combination of sodium nitrate, meat trimmings, and fat, and the greasiest French fries in the state. It's also a monument to LA's mostly lost vernacular architecture—the stand itself is the shape of a giant hot dog. When, in the early eighties, the landlord announced his intention to evict Cranky Franks and build a parking structure, the neighboring college students nearly rioted, causing the City Council to intervene and give the stand historical-landmark status. In our Macklin & Cherry days, Philip would lead the iron-stomached among us—I was one of them at the time but no longer—on periodic excursions to Cranky Franks, until his wife Joyce made him stop after his first heart attack. Like a lush hiding his alcoholism by hitting the bars mid-afternoon, Philip evidently still sneaks out to Frank's to satisfy his cravings.

The 105 Freeway is clear, so it takes me only twenty minutes to get to Cranky Franks. There's never any parking in the area. That's why the landlord wanted to demolish the hot dog stand and build a new structure—in LA, parking lots generate far more revenue than fast-food joints. So I find a spot several blocks away. Off the college campus, the gangs rule the neighborhood. Cranky Franks isn't far from where Reginald Denny was beaten during the Rodney King riots of 1992. Rumor has it that the university has made deals with the gangs to keep the immediate neighborhood near the campus safe. I've parked significantly out of that safe zone. So even though it's high noon, I make sure to check my surroundings. I keep my eyes forward and walk quickly, but not so quickly as to seem fearful. At times like this, I thank my mother for developing my acting ability.

A half block from the hot dog stand that wonderful smell of chili and grease hits my nostrils, and I relax when I see the long line of people. I hope that Philip has already ordered a spicy dog with grilled onions and extra chili for me, but that didn't happen, because his car is parked at the curb twenty yards ahead and he's inside, waiting for me. If a person can be too polite, Philip Paulsen is.

He must be listening to someone speaking because though he's looking right at me he doesn't acknowledge me when I wave at him and shout in a football-tailgating voice, "Hey, Philip, let's score those dogs."

So I go up to his car and rap on the passenger-side window and without waiting for a response open the passenger side door. I'm about to slide in next to him when I see the gaping wounds in his chest, the crisscross slashes marking his neck, the crimson stains on his white dress shirt, the hideous blood spatters on the windshield that in the blinding sun I at first mistook for the droppings from a passing flock of crows.

CHAPTER 22

I call the cops and spend the next two hours telling them what I can about the lawsuit and Philip's involvement in it. Once the medical examiners leave for the morgue with his body, I volunteer to call his wife Joyce, but the cops order me not to and say something about police investigative protocol. So I drive to the bank to secure the Scotty letters in my safety deposit box and then to The Barrista. I have no memory of the car ride, though I must have made it, because I'm standing in the coffee-house storeroom, tears streaming from my face and my left hand aching from the punch I took at the drywall that separates this room from the back office. Just as Joyce said, I'm dangerous—I'm as responsible for Philip's death as the person who stabbed him.

When Brenda comes into the store, I'm sitting at a table icing my hand and drinking a macchiato. I don't think to wait until we're in private but blurt out the news in a half-shout, half-sob. When she comprehends, she stands up and staggers backward a step, gaping at me as though I killed Philip myself. She examines her hands as if checking for blood, looks up, and wordlessly asks the ceiling joists or God above for an explanation. Her eyes overflow, her cut-rate brown mascara tracks muddy twin trails of anguish down her cheeks, and she crumples onto a wooden chair. She cries silently for a minute and then grabs her backpack and hurries out of the shop.

I stay at The Barrista late into the night, working behind the coffee bar, busing tables, ringing up the cash register, and when I return home late that night, I force myself to fight off sleep so that the persistent vision of the slashed-up body of Philip Paulsen won't invade my dreams as it's invaded my consciousness. And yet I do sleep and can't awaken from the gruesome nightmare that seems eternal.

William the Conqueror will pay for this.

—⁓—

The next day, I learn details from Detective Tringali, the cop in charge of the Kreiss homicide. Philip was trying to dial 911 before he died. Though it was daylight on a crowded street, there were no witnesses. He suffered four stab wounds to the torso and a cut to the throat. The coroner's conclusion as to cause of death is hemorrhagic shock as a result of injury to the heart by a double-edged knife.

A poniard is a double-edged knife.

As I did with the Kreiss killing and yesterday at the crime scene, I suggest that Tringali look into whether William Bishop had anything to do with Philip's murder.

"We'll check out all leads, of course," she says because it's the politically correct thing to say. "Right now I'm more interested in your client's involvement. Have you and your client had any discussions that could shed light on what happened to Mr. Paulsen?"

"Attorney-client privilege, detective. Just like the last time." I hesitate, but not long enough. "Is there anything in my client's video game about the Paulsen killing?" I've just revealed that I don't trust Poniard.

"We were going to ask you about that, counselor."

"I have no idea how to play that game."

She's quiet for a long time, debating whether to make me suffer because I haven't helped her. She takes pity on me. "There's nothing in the game that we can find. Yet."

Good thing for Poniard, because if Philip's death were depicted in *Abduction!* I would scour heaven, earth, and cyberspace to track down my client and expose him to the world.

"I trust that if you discover something before we do, you'll let us know," she says.

"As long as it's not privileged. What do you think happened?"

"Chances are that Mr. Paulsen was the victim of random violence, with robbery the motive. His wallet was gone. There's been a rash of crime around that campus lately. Rough area."

"Yeah, but in broad daylight so close to a crowded diner? Some stranger just opens his door and starts stabbing him?"

"Paulsen's wife and friends say he was kind to a fault. He probably played Good Samaritan for the wrong person."

Neither of us believes it.

—⁓—

Philip's funeral takes place three days later, on the city side of Griffith Park at a Catholic cemetery old enough to have the diverse rough-hewn headstones that mark not just lost lives but a lost era. There's a large crowd there, people bridging Philip's two careers.

Brenda has been inconsolable the past couple of days but doesn't show up at the funeral. I try her cell phone, but she doesn't answer. The service begins, and Philip is eulogized as loving husband, loyal friend, canon law expert, fly fisherman extraordinaire, and crackerjack paralegal who knew more about a case than most of the attorneys he worked for.

After it's over, I get in the long line to pay my respects to Joyce. As I get closer I see that her lips are frozen in one of those rote half-grins you see at funerals, but I'm sure the only reason it looks anything like a smile is because her sunglasses conceal her eyes. When I reach her, she frowns.

"Oh, Parker, he so liked you," she says. "He'd tell me you always needed help but wouldn't ask for it. So when this time you asked him to work on this case of yours, he knew how desperately you must have needed him, couldn't say no, couldn't bear to let you down."

"Joyce, I'm so sorry. About what happened of course, but I want to apologize for asking Philip to—"

She holds up her hand. "Don't you dare! You did nothing wrong, and Philip was a bull-headed man. It was his choice, not yours. I just wish . . ." She reaches out, gives me a soft handshake, and turns to the next person.

I walk back to the parking lot, waiting for the core emptiness to fill again with anger and guilt—the emotions that spur action. But the void is filled with grief, and I wait for the tears to stop before I start the car, all the while wondering where Brenda is.

—⁂—

I drive down Los Feliz Boulevard, intending to turn right on Franklin and head back to The Barrista, but before I reach the intersection, a car changes lanes in front of me and hits its brakes, and I have to hit mine hard to avoid a collision. I want to move to my left, but I'm flanked by another car that won't give me room. I check the rearview mirror. A third car is tailgating inches behind my back bumper. There's nothing to my right except sidewalk. All three cars are blue Mercedes.

Just as I get to the intersection, the driver in the car next to me honks his horn twice, lowers the passenger window, and gestures for me to turn left instead of right. He eases off, giving me room to change lanes but now follows close. I make the left turn, not that I have much choice.

Surrounding me like middle-of-the pack NASCAR racers, my entourage forces me on a twenty-minute drive downtown. Just before we reach Figueroa, we turn into a long driveway and stop at a high-security gate. When the gate swings open, I gun my Lexus and kiss the bumper of the Mercedes in front of me. It's not a gentle kiss. The driver stops his car and gets out, the cords in his neck so taut that they appear about to snap like over-wound guitar strings. He's wearing a black suit, red tie, and sunglasses, the standard livery of Church of the Sanctified Assembly thugs. I roll down my window and give him my best Parky Gerald smirk. "Just take me to Quiana."

He almost rips his sunglasses off his face. Behind the Assembly-mandated poker face, his eyes smolder. There are some names that you don't take in vain around devotees of the Sanctified Assembly, and Quiana Gottschalk's is one of them. After all, that person supposedly doesn't exist.

He starts to say something but thinks better of it, instead walking back to his car and beginning the slow crawl toward the main building.

When we stop, the three drivers hurry over. The guy whose bumper I hit pulls my driver's side door open, grabs my arm, drags me outside, and shoves me against the car. I don't resist. That would be unwise. He pats me down while the other two search my car. Only when they're satisfied that I'm not carrying a weapon or a recording device do they back off.

We pass through the massive gilded doors. I wait in the foyer, an entryway in theory only because the room is as large as my entire condominium, with a Carrera marble floor and a huge gallery chandelier with Bohemian crystal and a platinum finish. Two of the dark-suited drivers come inside and go to opposite sides of the room, assuming identical poses. They stand like the Queen's Guard, rigid posture, arms to pinned their sides, faces forward. There's a clack of high heels on marble, and Quiana Gottschalk, the shadowy cofounder and mysterious elder of the Church of the Sanctified Assembly, walks toward me in a zip-line. Without breaking stride, she slaps my face hard.

I force myself not to react. As a child, I had years of practicing how not to react. I say in my calmest voice, "I guess we can add assault and battery to the false imprisonment charge, don't you think? Mother?"

She tries to slap me a second time, but I grab her wrist. She's petite, weighing about a hundred pounds, so it's easy to deflect her blow. The two guards start forward but stop in their tracks when she raises her free hand.

I release her arm. "To what do I owe the pleasure, Harriet?"

"Your defective behavior continues to break my heart, Parky." She tinkers with the bun in her brown hair, adjusting the rubber band and pulling her hair so tight that the skin on her forehead becomes even tauter, something that seems impossible given the cosmetic surgery she's had.

Harriet Stern's tryst with Bradley Kelly saved her from what seemed like an inevitable death from a drug overdose or suicide. Together, they found a loophole in the Coogan Act, the law that protects child actors from unscrupulous parents, and used my trust fund to finance Kelly's new church. Through Kelly's messianic charisma and my mother's business acumen, they built one of the fastest-growing religions in the world. I call it a cult. They separate adherents from their non-believing families, extort money from devotees in the guise of tithing, seek to infiltrate governments and powerful corporations, and believe that disease results from spiritual impurity. When they started, their so-called rituals were illegal and perverse. They returned my money only after I escaped their clutches at age fifteen, became an emancipated minor, and threatened to expose secrets that would have put them and other Assembly founders behind bars for the rest of their lives. Since then, Quiana Gottschalk has become a recluse, a goddess, someone whose very existence the Assembly denies to the outside world.

"I hold you responsible for the gutter blasphemy that's all over the Internet," she says. "Put a stop to it."

"I'm not in the mood for this, Harriet. I just came from the funeral of a dear man who was murdered on my watch."

No condolences. Assembly devotees don't offer condolences to the family and friends of a nonbeliever. "This Poniard creature shouldn't be your client," she says. "As long as he is, you'll be held responsible for anything he says about us."

"You had your soldiers bring me here just to tell me that?"

"I want you to know how serious this is. I'm only one person. My influence extends only so far. You're not popular with the Assembly."

We stare at each other for a long time. Finally, I say, "Tell me about *The Boatman*, Harriet."

Her eyes widen, and behind the surprise I see the complexity that is, and has always been, my mother. She's calculating whether to lie, and that already tells me a lot.

"You're as resourceful as ever, Parker."

"*The Boatman*, Harriet. I was in it, remember?"

"You were only in one scene." She takes a slow, relenting breath. "It was a play on that Greek myth . . ."

"Orpheus?"

"Yeah, a modern version, supposedly. Except, it had already been done by Marcel Camus, Tennessee Williams, Sidney Lumet. Billy Bishop's father wasn't happy, and he was the main investor. At some point, production shut down, and then Howard Bishop's people came in to destroy all the dailies, the rough cuts. They were worried about videotapes, new technology. They visited everyone personally and made certain no one had a copy."

"Howard Bishop was a lawyer. How did he have the power to—?"

"He was a man with dangerous friends."

Of course. The music industry and the mob were still closely connected in the late seventies. Howard Bishop must have called in a favor. Still, why would Nate Ettinger be frightened after all these years?

"My sources tell me that Felicity McGrath was one of the actresses," I say.

Harriet arches her indelible eyebrows. "That annoying McGrath girl did not act in *The Boatman*."

At first I think that Harry Cherry's revelation was the product of a senescent mind, but then I realize that Harry never said that Felicity *acted* in *The Boatman*. He only said that she was *on* the picture.

"If she didn't act, what did she do?" I ask.

"She was supposedly the writer and director."

"At twenty years old?"

"She was a manipulative, coquettish dilettante, a little girl pretending to be an artiste."

So now I know one truth about Felicity McGrath—she was a prodigy, the creative force behind whatever *The Boatman* was. My mother gave it away by singing the word "artiste" in a sharp falsetto that was meant to convey sarcasm but that instead revealed envy. Harriet always wanted to be an artist and a great man's love, and no matter how grand her position in the Sanctified Assembly hierarchy, she's neither.

"Any reason to believe that Felicity disappeared because of her work on that movie?" I ask.

"How would I know?"

"There's a world of secrets you know that you don't reveal. How about sharing this one? Is William Bishop an Assembly Devotee? He drove a blue Mercedes in 1987."

The sentries have for a while blended into the statuary, but when I ask this question, the guy on my left takes a halting step forward before righting himself and clasping his hands in front of him. Nothing is more top secret than the Assembly's membership roll.

She shakes a finger at me as if I were eight.

"Then tell me about Nate Ettinger," I say.

"Who?"

"He's now a film professor, but he worked on *The Boatman* as a grip. You apparently knew him quite well."

"I wouldn't have had anything to do with a grip."

"He was very handsome back then. And it wasn't on *The Boatman* where you and he . . . became close. It was on *Climbing Panda Hill.*"

She smiles a wistful smile in recollection. "Oh, you mean Nathan. He was never a grip. He knew how to make movies. I thought he was destined to make it big, so I . . ." She crosses her arms and prunes her lips indignantly, exactly as she did in the old days when she was concealing something. "This is my personal business."

"Can you at least tell me what Ettinger did on *The Boatman*? I'm not sure whether he was an associate producer or just a grip."

"It depended on who you asked, Bishop or that girl. Bishop didn't like him. I think he was jealous."

"Bishop was jealous of Ettinger, or Ettinger was jealous of Bishop?"

She shrugs, but for Harriet Stern that means not that she's uncertain of the answer but that it's time to move on to another topic.

"Did you meet Kelly on *The Boatman*?"

"That movie inspired Bradley to . . ." She looks at the sentries and catches herself. So, she has secrets from them, too.

"That movie inspired Kelly to do what?"

"I'm not going to discuss Bradley with you, may his divine memory shine in the celestial firmament."

I roll my eyes Parky Gerald style. "I wish you'd never met that man."

"He saved my life."

"And tried to destroy mine."

She lowers her eyes, a gesture that's the closest she's ever come to showing remorse for exposing me to the predatory Kelly.

"Who else was on the movie?" I ask.

She shrugs, whether in ignorance or refusal I'm not certain.

"One last question," I say. "Did I have contact with Felicity McGrath?"

She lifts her eyes to the ceiling and then lowers them to check her Lady Rolex. My mother always had a short attention span, and now I'm boring her.

"Please, Harriet."

She sighs melodramatically. "You were an adorable, talented child, and she directed every scene, or tried to. So yes, you worked with her."

"Am I free to go?" I ask.

"You've always been free to go. You only came because you chose to."

"Did you tell that to your private militia?"

I turn to leave, but she grasps my arm. Her eyes are suddenly hooded with fatigue. "Make your client leave us alone, Parky."

CHAPTER 23

Poniard has disabled *Abduction!* When Brighton logs on, all he sees is a slideshow—images of Philip Paulsen, the poor old man who got stabbed while working for Poniard's lawyer Stern. When Bugsy first saw the graphics he whistled through his teeth and said, "This guy's a fucking video game Rembrandt." In one picture, Paulsen is carrying a square brief case; he has a golden halo and angel's wings. In another, he's dressed like a Catholic priest. In a third, he *is* an angel hovering over the ruins of a sci-fi-looking city. The slideshow is accompanied by sad organ music, which Bugsy calls a dirge.

Brighton once overheard Bugsy tell the Queen that "Dumping Stern was the biggest fucking mistake of your life," to which she replied, "Father, keep your voice down and if you ever say that again I'll move out and take Brighton with me. Anyway," she continued, "Parker is probably fucking his assistant." To which Bugsy said, "Keep your voice down and what else did you expect after the way you've treated him?"

The Queen keeps calling Stern a fool, keeps saying that Poniard knew about the Kreiss killings before they happened. The Queen says that Poniard is insane. But why would even a crazy Poniard murder his supporters? In a video game, you don't kill your helpers because, whether you're crazy or not, it makes the game boring. And video games can be hacked. The funny thing is that the Queen was on her cell phone one evening telling her boss exactly that. Playing "devil's advocate," she called it.

Then one night, Brighton is sitting in front of the computer screen, mesmerized by the rhythmic patterns that the Paulsen images make. He's watched them so many times that he now recognizes that Poniard calibrated the brightness of the images to change in time to the music, so that if you watch the show in the dark, the light seems to dance a dark ballet off the walls. At one point, he mindlessly jiggles the mouse. The image of Paulsen dissolves, the screen turns to black, and there's a new level—Stage Five: Vengeance.

CHAPTER 24

After leaving the Assembly's Grand Temple, I head for The Barista, hoping to fill Brenda in on the news about Felicity and *The Boatman*, but she's not there. She doesn't answer her cell phone, doesn't respond to texts or e-mails. I'd go to her home, but I don't know where she lives. I call the head of human resources at JADS to see if I can get an address or convince her to contact Brenda herself, but she hangs up on me.

Meanwhile, I get an e-mail message from my document examiner that the Felicity letters to Scotty are authentic. Better yet, Lovely's expert doesn't dispute their authenticity, almost unheard of in litigation. I e-mail Poniard the news and get back an *of course what else did you expect?* and an abrupt sign-off.

The next morning, just before nine o'clock—my self-imposed deadline for alerting the cops and calling the local hospitals—Brenda walks into the coffee shop. I don't recognize her right away, because she's wearing a gray zippered sweatshirt, pink T-shirt, tattered blue jeans, and cross-trainers. No makeup, her hair unkempt in a half ponytail. Today, the dark rings around her eyes are from fatigue, not over-applied eyeliner.

"I missed you at the funeral," I say.

One of the baristas brings her a black coffee, unusual, because Brenda normally drinks only bottled water and a cup of tea in the afternoon. "I tried, I really did, but I can't handle funerals. Especially his. So I was working."

"I wasn't scolding you. I was worried."

Her eyes are filmy from grief and lack of sleep. "I'm sorry I came to work dressed this way. I look awful. It's unprofessional."

"It's a coffee house, Brenda, not a courthouse."

"Philip was going to take me Christmas shopping. He told me he needed help picking out a present for Joyce."

Christmas is two weeks away. I've noticed, of course, but I haven't paid attention. Before my mother became entangled with Bradley Kelly and the Church of the Sanctified Assembly, her views on God's existence and form reflected those of the man she was sleeping with. Whatever her creed of the month, she wasn't big on celebrating the holidays. I was never sure of my ethnic background, because my mother lied about hers and I never knew who my father was. I still don't. Each year, she bought me an expensive Christmas present. Of course, she used my money to do it. And while the Sanctified Assembly purports to respect Christmas and Christianity, it redefines the story of Christ's birth to fit into Bradley Kelly's discovery of the celestial fount. Since the day I escaped the cult, the weeks between Thanksgiving and New Year's have meant loneliness interspersed with alcohol-laden parties. I did enjoy the way tough-girl Lovely Diamond celebrated Hanukkah—how she knew the candle-lighting prayers by heart in Hebrew and English; how she made greasy, overdone potato latkes topped with dollops of sour cream or apple sauce; how she insisted we dance the hora to the *Oh Hanukkah* cassette her mother had bought her during first grade. That holiday came early this year, and the eighth day has come and gone. Did Lovely do anything differently because her boy is with her?

I tell Brenda about our document expert's favorable opinion. Like me, she finds little joy in it. "I've spent the day working on the Boatman cast list," she says, and starts to tell me what she's found, but I motion for her to follow me into the back room where it's private. She sits down in her chair, and I perch myself on the edge of her desk.

"There's someone who isn't listed on that document that should be," I say. "Felicity McGrath. She wrote and directed the movie."

I've jolted her into wakefulness more quickly than any cup of coffee could. "Did Ettinger tell you this?"

"A confidential source. Someone who'd go to the grave before testifying."

Her shoulders slump, and I know she wants to probe further, but to her credit, she doesn't.

"The cast list," she says. She gives a rundown on the present whereabouts of *The Boatman*'s cast and crew. There weren't many involved, not surprising for a low-budget film that never made it into post-production. William Bishop, Bradley Kelly, and Nate Ettinger are accounted for. Six others have dropped out of sight, including Hildy Gish and child actor Parky Gerald. Four others are dead, three of confirmed natural causes, one in a boating accident.

"But I've found something else," she says. "It's probably stupid, but..." She shrugs, embarrassed.

"Tell me."

"A movie curse," she says. "You know, like *Rebel Without a Cause* where James Dean, Natalie Wood, and Sal Mineo all died violent deaths? So did the young stars of *Poltergeist*. Actors who've played *Superman* have had terrible luck. The same with *Rosemary's Baby* and *The Exorcist*, on and on." She twists her coffee cup back on forth on the desk.

"You don't truly believe *The Boatman* was cursed, do you?" Once upon a time, *I* would've believed it. When I was a child my mother repeated every one of these curses, scaring me to death—I acted in movies, after all, and what if my movie were cursed and I'd be the next to die?

"Who knows what's true?" she says. "But that's not the point. Sit down and look." I pull up a chair next to hers. In only a matter of minutes she shows me what she found—the "Orpheus & The Wise Guy" curse, one website calls it. Its subject is a mysterious, classic film that never saw the light of day because it angered an organized crime leader who proceeded to kill everyone who worked on the movie. The film was high art despite the unbridled depiction of hardcore sex and illegal drugs, a precursor to the films of Lars Von Trier and other edgy filmmakers who blur the lines between fantasy and reality. There's no information about cast, crew, or plot, much less an association with Bishop or McGrath. The story is a wisp of legend scudding along on a vast cinematic ocean.

"What made you think of this?" I ask.

"Lucky, I guess. I was looking up movies and the mafia and Orpheus, and it just . . ."

"But even if this is *The Boatman*, how does it help?"

"The Mafia angle, maybe?"

"I wouldn't have any idea how to contact anyone who . . ." That's not true. There is someone I can talk to—if he doesn't kill me before he hears what I want him to do.

CHAPTER 25

"Let me get this crystal clear in my mind," Ed Diamond says in his clipped, educated Brooklyn accent. "You want me to pump some racketeers for information, the knowledge of which could not only endanger my life but would help you in your lawsuit against my own daughter?"

"That's about right," I say.

He brushes back his thinning gray hair, and somehow the gesture signals reproach. He's dressed in his familiar polo shirt, corduroy slacks, and biker's leather jacket, still playing the movie director, though as far as I know, he's retired from making porn. But he's cut the ponytail that he's worn for decades. Is this because his grandchild now lives in his house?

"You have quite the large balls, Parky."

"Please don't call me that." I glance around the room. The Barrista isn't crowded, and the closest customers are three tables away. It's one of the few times I'm happy about the sparse patronage. "I'm trying to get to the truth. I wouldn't have called you if someone else could help me."

As someone who started producing porn in the 1960s, Ed Diamond necessarily had underworld connections, couldn't have plied his trade safely without them. He used his shady contacts to provide important information to me once before. But that was when Lovely and I were on the same side.

"Why would I help you at Lovely's expense?" he asks.

"Because she recently told me that you like me."

He takes an aggressive drink of coffee and presses his lips together as if he's tasted something bitter, and it's not the coffee. "I'm supposed to hide this information from her?"

"I'll leave it to you to decide whether the risk to her and your grandson is too great."

"A low blow to mention the kid. Such manipulation is beneath you."

"It's not manipulation. I've talked to people who still fear for their lives after thirty-five years."

"I'll tell you what. I'll look into it. And here's why. William Bishop was one of the bluenose pricks who kept me from getting a job directing mainstream movies. If he's dirty, I want the public to know it." His voice has gotten so loud that I raise a finger to my lips to shush him, which only annoys him more. "If Lovely's backed the wrong horse, so be it. And I do worry about her. And Brighton." He pauses. "I worry about you, too."

I shrug. We're both embarrassed by that last admission.

"No promises," he says. "If I learn something, maybe I'll tell both you and Lovely, but maybe I'll tell neither of you. Or maybe I'll tell one and not the other, and that could be Lovely and not you."

"I'll take that risk." So I tell Ed Diamond what I know about *The Boatman*, which is precious little—that it was supposed to be a modern myth produced and directed by William Bishop and Felicity McGrath, that it was rumored to contain hardcore sex and actual drug use on camera, that William's father Howard Bishop must have called in a favor to have production shut down, and that the movie might be the subject of an Internet rumor.

"There's one thing I'm not clear about," I say.

"Only one?"

"Many. Bishop's father was just a lawyer. How could he have the clout to intimidate so many people who worked on the movie?"

He laughs out loud. "Howard Bishop wasn't just a lawyer. He was the New York mob's main liaison to the entertainment industry and the unions. He didn't just have connections to the mob; he was one of its bosses."

"My research doesn't show that Howard Bishop was anything other than an attorney."

"Not everything gets on the Internet, goddamn it. Howard Bishop was a master at hiding his true life behind bespoke silk suits, good table manners, and an Ivy League law degree. He conducted business out of his law office and at the Brown Derby restaurant. He did have a lot of recording artists as clients, sure, but they were not his primary business focus. As for why the truth hasn't come out in more recent times, you must know better than I that William Bishop is very good at suppressing information. A chip off the old block. I only know about Howard because of what I did for a living. I unfortunately had to deal with him, or I would've never gotten a film made. Now, is there anything else I need to know before I risk my life for you?"

"I've told you everything." It's a lie. I haven't told him about the cast list or Ettinger or my mother.

He fidgets with his empty coffee cup. I've already exhausted his quite limited reserve of patience.

Brenda comes out of the back room and walks over to our table.

"Sorry to interrupt," she says.

"Then why did you?" Ed says.

"It's no problem," I say. "Mr. Diamond was just leaving."

She hands me a piece of paper. I put it on the table without reading it.

As soon as she's back in the storeroom, Ed says, "Is that the girl you're boning?"

"I'm not—"

"Lovely thinks you are. And if you're not, you should be. She's hot, in a ghetto sort of way."

"I'm not interested in Brenda."

"My point is that you should not sit around and pine for Lovely. It'll do neither of you any good. She's confused, and she's stubborn, and as you know, that's a bad combination where my daughter's concerned. My word of advice to you is go on with your life, litigate your case, and see what happens. Because if you don't, she'll resent you and never go back to you. And do not let your guard down. She'll cut you off at the knees to win this lawsuit." He shoots up out of his chair and begins walking to the exit. I accompany him out of the shop—well, follow him, because Ed Diamond always walks quickly and with a purpose. When we get outside, he points to the cosplayers loitering on the grassy strip near the sidewalk.

"Friends of yours?" Ed says.

"Obsessed fans of my . . ." What I see startles me, but I try to stay expressionless.

He leans in and whispers, "I'll be in touch, Parky. Or maybe I won't."

Only when he's driven away do I walk over to the cosplayers. Among the group are Banquo and Felicity/Courtney, dressed in the same clothing they were wearing when I last saw them.

Banquo bows. "Mr. Stern, Esquire."

Courtney's giggle lasts too long.

"After the fight at the JADS building, I didn't think I'd see you two again," I say.

"Water under the proverbial bridge. Courtney and I—"

"It's Felicity!" she shouts.

He takes a deep, impatient breath. "*Felicity* and I have been traveling to Poniard conventions in San Diego and Monterey. You know, there were a couple of characters dressed up like you, Mr. Stern. I'm surprised that none of them are here."

"You shouldn't be here."

This, too, makes Courtney laugh.

I go back inside the shop and sit down across from Brenda.

"I don't trust Diamond's father," she says.

"We have no choice."

She shrugs and hands me the paper that she brought to me earlier. "You left this on the table for anyone to see. The customers shouldn't know our business."

It's a court order. Judge Triggs has scheduled the hearing on the motion to disqualify me for one week from today.

CHAPTER 26

The cutscene interferes with Brighton's game play like a malicious denial-of-service attack. He jabs at the keyboard and wiggles the mouse, trying to get control of the game again, but he can't. It must be a hack. The half-assed graphics and lame scary-movie music couldn't come from Poniard.

There's an establishing shot of a gray oblong office building, the courthouse where the Queen has her case against Poniard. Brighton is carried in circles around the building a few times. There's a pixilated dissolve, and he's inside the dank courthouse. He skims down the darkened corridor on a dizzying Steadicam ride and ascends one rickety escalator after another. The moving staircases make ungreased grating sounds that get more and more annoying as he ascends. He's thrown off the last escalator with a lurch, landing near a sign that says *Seventh Floor, Departments 70–79*. He's catapulted through a heavy door marked *Private: Judges Only*, the crash so violent that the door flies off its hinges and spins toward the viewer with decapitating intent. Door after door is thrown open until he comes to a sign that says *Chambers of the Honorable T. Tedford Triggs*. Brighton presses the escape button on his keyboard over and over, but there is no escape. A horrible off-kilter cello screeches, and he's pulled into a back office.

"*Mom, come quick!*" Brighton cries. It's the first time he's called her *Mom*. He promised himself he'd never do that, but this was pure reflex, so how can you blame him?

She comes through the door and says, "Brighton, it's late, you have school tomorrow and I have to be in court early—"

He points to the screen.

"Oh shit," she says, and goes to Brighton's desk, picks up his cell phone, and dials 911, and while she talks to the emergency operator in measured tones, Brighton can't take his eyes off the monitor, where a large black man dressed in a judge's robe is being stabbed with flying dagger after flying dagger. His belly screams are ghastly. Blood spews out of his torso, neck, and limbs. There's fake laughter like you hear on old TV shows, as if the judge is the victim of a carnival knife-throwing act gone terribly wrong.

CHAPTER 27

If I'm able to avoid disqualification, it will be because Lovely Diamond made a rookie mistake. I intend to argue that by going forward with the document experts' examination of Felicity's letters to Scotty, she legitimized my representation of Poniard and so waived her client's right to have the judge kick me off the case. It's a hyper-legalistic argument, but it could work. I don't relish taking advantage of her inexperience, but I want to stay on this case, and Ed Diamond advised me not to hold back.

When Brenda and I arrive at Judge Triggs's courtroom, I expect to find the usual crowd of reporters and onlookers lined up waiting for seats. But the entire corridor is deserted except for a lone bailiff guarding the courtroom doors. For a moment, I think that I've gotten the day wrong.

"We're here for an eight-thirty hearing in *Bishop v. Poniard*," I tell the bailiff. "I'm the attorney for the defendant."

"I know who you are," he says, and I wonder if that scowl is his ordinary expression or if he's saved it just for me. "Report to Department 44."

"But Judge Triggs ordered last week that we were to—"

"Department 44, sir." His command reverberates down the empty hallway. I'm about to call him on his rudeness, but Brenda takes my arm and guides me back toward the escalator. She's showing better judgment than I. According to Harmon Cherry, the only thing worse than antagonizing the judge is alienating the courthouse staff. We take the escalators down to the fourth floor, and I hear the buzz of voices before I see the reporters, and court watchers, or the cosplayers who've gathered outside Department 44. Usually this crowd is borderline unruly,

175

but now they're uncharacteristically subdued, because there are four uniformed LAPD officers, along with homicide detective Angela Tringali, standing in front of the courtroom door. In her drab pants suit, she looks more like a court clerk than a cop.

Tringali approaches, puts a hand on my shoulder, and leans in close. "We need to talk, Mr. Stern," she whispers. "Immediately."

"What about?"

"Give me a break, counselor."

I shrug and spread my arms in confusion. "I don't know what you're talking about." I glance at Brenda, who shakes her head, obviously as confused as I am.

Tringali stares at me with eyes that have as much emotion as a pair of beer-bottle caps. "I'm having trouble believing that, Mr. Stern. I'm sick of your stonewalling."

"I said I don't know what the hell you're talking about, Detective. Now, if you'll excuse me, I have a motion to argue."

On cue, the courtroom door opens, and a bailiff I've never seen before pokes her head out and hollers, "Is the attorney for the defendant here yet? The judge wants to see counsel in chambers."

"Yeah, I'm here," I say.

"You'd better come talk to me right after," Tringali says.

Only then do I see the small placard on the right side of the door: "Judge Anita T. Grass." My muscles tense, but not from stage fright. Unless Judge Triggs is just borrowing this courtroom for the day, we're going to be stuck in front of a judge who despises me.

Before she became a judge, Anita Grass built her client base by selling herself as a pit bull litigator and crack trial lawyer who made life miserable for her opponents. She tried her best to live up to that reputation by crossing the ethical line whenever she felt it necessary. A couple of years before my law firm split up, I defended a movie studio against her writer-client's claim that the studio stole his script about adolescent zombies in love. The movie was a blockbuster, and Grass sought to recover all of the profits of the film, which tallied into the hundreds of millions of dollars. At a contingency fee of forty percent, a win for

Grass, or even a substantial settlement, would've allowed her to retire a rich woman. She pushed so hard for settlement that I realized she was afraid to go to trial. So I convinced my client not to negotiate. The week before jury selection, Grass screamed at me hysterically for refusing her client's settlement demands. It turned out that I'd read her perfectly— she'd oversold both her ability and her trial experience. She related to the jurors worse than any lawyer I'd ever seen. Not only did the jury return a verdict in my client's favor, but the judge also sanctioned Grass for hiding key documents. The verdict and the sanction order received a lot of media attention, and Grass was humiliated. She blamed me. I wasn't the only lawyer surprised when she was appointed to the bench two years later. Her questionable ethics and lack of civility should have disqualified her. But she had a powerful ally—Louis Frantz, to whom she'd referred business in the past.

Brenda takes a middle-row seat, and I follow the bailiff into chambers. I expect the stage fright to come on any moment, but instead I feel a slight rush of adrenaline, the welcome kind that used to fuel my performance in bygone days when I was at my best in a courtroom. Maybe bleak reality has blunted irrational fear.

I walk through the chambers door to find Anita Grass behind her huge desk wearing the dill-pickle expression that passes for her normal mien. Her mousy hair is so short that from behind she could be mistaken for a man. Her steel-framed bifocals are perched on a grotesque turned-up nose, the product of a botched rhinoplasty. Her eyes are small and uneven.

Lou Frantz and Lovely Diamond are already sitting in easy chairs across from the judge. I nod to them, but only Frantz nods back. Lovely stares forward, her hands folded in her lap. She's wearing a dark gray pantsuit, unusual, because she ordinarily wears a skirt to court.

The judge directs me to sit in the remaining chair.

"You're late, Mr. Stern," she says.

"It's only eight-twenty-two," I say. "Judge Triggs set the hearing for eight-thirty upstairs on the seventh floor. So technically, I'm eight minutes early . . . Your Honor."

Her already hooded eyes narrow to tight slits, and I think she's about to admonish me, but instead she picks up a document from her desk. "We're going to talk about certain things informally so the news media won't disrupt us. Depending on what happens, we'll put this on the record."

"I object," I say. "The media has a right to be present during official court proceedings."

"Objection overruled," she says. Not even the Constitution can stop Anita Grass from exacting vengeance.

"I'll start by handing you all an order," she says. "Follow along." She gives us each a copy of a one-page single-spaced minute order and begins reading aloud.

In Chambers:

On September 16, 2013, Plaintiff William Bishop filed this action for defamation against Defendant, the individual known as Poniard, arising out of accusations in Defendant's video game *Abduction!* that Plaintiff was associated with the disappearance of Paula Felicity McGrath, an actress who went missing in 1987. The case was assigned to T. Tedford Triggs, Superior Court Judge. On October 24, 2013, Plaintiff brought a motion to disqualify Plaintiff's attorney, Parker Stern, for an alleged conflict of interest in violation of Rule of Professional Conduct 3-310. The Court set the matter for hearing on December 19, 2013.

Late in the evening of December 18, 2013, Judge T. Tedford Triggs received a call from Homicide Detective Angela Tringali alerting him that the Los Angeles Police Department had received a 9-1-1 call from Ms. Lovely Diamond, one of the attorneys for Plaintiff William Bishop. Ms. Diamond reported that the video game *Abduction!* had portrayed the murder of a character with the exact likeness of Judge Triggs. Detective Tringali informed Judge Triggs that two LAPD patrol cars were en route to his residence to protect him from any violence. Detective Tringali further informed Judge Triggs that she considered the depiction in the video game to be a credible threat because a potential witness in the case, Herman Kreiss, and his wife Isla, had previously been murdered, allegedly after their deaths were depicted in the video game.

In light of the foregoing, Judge Triggs cannot preside over this matter objectively and hereby recuses himself. Plaintiff's pending motion to disqualify Parker Stern shall be determined by the judge who is designated to assume responsibility for this matter.

IT IS SO ORDERED.

Dated: December 19, 2013 _____

J. Tedford Triggs,
Superior Court Judge

Since Philip Paulsen was killed, the only way that Brenda and I can monitor *Abduction!* is by trying to keep up with the blogs, because neither of us is any good at playing the game. But we've been so busy that we missed this development. We shouldn't have. My hands start quivering so violently that I have to put the order down on the judge's desk to stop it from fluttering. This isn't courtroom stage fright but rather rage at William Bishop. I've finally become convinced that Poniard has nothing to do with this. Judge Triggs ruled in our favor on both matters that were before him. His disqualification helps Bishop, not Poniard, especially since Grass is his replacement. And Bishop has the resources to hack the video game.

I glare at Lovely until she catches my eye. Neither of us will break the stare. The distrust that each of us has of the other's client has widened the rift between us. Now she finally seems like a true adversary.

"Any questions?" Grass says but doesn't wait for an answer. "No? Then I'm going to turn to the motion to disqualify Mr. Stern. I reviewed the motion and opposition papers this morning, and I'm ready to rule."

She's going to order me off this case. There's no way that she'd give up the chance to brand me an unethical lawyer. I want to stay on this case more than ever. I represent not only Poniard's interest but also the memory of Felicity McGrath.

"I'd like to be heard on the motion to disqualify," I say.

"We won't have oral argument, counsel," Grass says. "Nothing you could say will change my mind."

"Then I want to have your order announced in open court in front of the media and a court reporter," I say. "Open access to the courts is required, and I want to make my record to memorialize for the Court of Appeal that you're refusing to allow oral argument."

"Denied," she says.

Frantz leans forward and jovially slaps his hands on her desk. "I'm going to save you some time, Judge Grass. Although we continue to believe that Mr. Stern has a conflict of interest, we withdraw our motion to disqualify and consent to Mr. Stern's continued representation of the defendants."

The judge sits back in her chair, trying to process this. I glance again at Lovely and notice the slightest flush just above her cheekbone in the shape of a small rosy star that probably only I notice, physical evidence of remorse, one of her least favorite emotions. I told her a long time ago about my run-in with Anita Grass, and she's told Frantz. They want me to stay on the case because they know that the judge will do everything she can to destroy me. Ed Diamond was right—Lovely is going to litigate this case as if I'm just another lawyer. *Scorched earth, baby*, she once said after a defense lawyer tried to take advantage of her when she was at the US Attorney's office.

Grass takes her glasses off and rubs her eyes, unable to hide her disappointment. "Although I was prepared to disqualify Mr. Stern, it's your call, Mr. Frantz," she says. "At some point, we'll schedule trial, to be tried by the court, not a jury according to the record."

I stand, but Frantz remains seated and says, "It's good to see you, Anita," to which she replies "Same here, Lou." I exit chambers, leaving my adversaries to have a pleasant chat with their friend the judge.

The courtroom is empty, except for Brenda, who's still sitting in the same row. She looks like a forlorn child. When I walk over to her, I see tears in her eyes.

"Thinking about Philip," she says. A tear rolls down her cheek.

As if she were my daughter, I pull my shirt cuff over my palm and use it to caress the tear away. She doesn't recoil, just smiles sadly. At that moment, Lovely Diamond comes out of the back room carrying papers under her arm.

"I forgot to give you these," she says, her eyes seething with reproach. "Do I give them to you or your . . . assistant?"

We look at each other, my silence conveying that I don't owe her an explanation. "Either of us is fine," I say. "Brenda and I are a team."

"I'll take them," Brenda says. As if literally closing ranks, she moves so near that our bodies touch. "And you know what, Ms. Diamond? I think you're being very disloyal to Mr. Stern."

"I don't give a flying fuck about what you think," Lovely says. She turns sideways so her back is toward Brenda and says, "I never got a chance to tell you how sorry I am about Philip Paulsen. You used to say such nice things about him. I'm sorry that I never got a chance—"

"You should be sorry that your client murdered him," Brenda says.

"Are you going to let her talk to me like that?" Lovely says.

"Is there anything else we need to discuss?" I say.

Lovely's jaw goes half-slack. She slowly shakes her head and leaves the room without waiting for Frantz, who's evidently still in chambers schmoozing the Wicked Witch of the California Judiciary.

"She's not nice," Brenda says as she skims Lovely's legal pleading. "A trashy mouth."

"She's—"

"Oh, my." Brenda hands me Lovely's document. It's a formal notice scheduling Poniard's deposition for Monday, December 30, 2013, eleven days from now, to take place in the offices of Louis Frantz. The notice demands that Poniard appear in person, in violation of Judge Triggs's order early in the case. The scary part is, now that Anita Grass is the judge, I don't know if Judge Triggs's order is in effect anymore.

When we leave the courtroom, the reporters surround us and

ask why Poniard wants to kill Judge Triggs. I take Brenda's arm and push through the inner circle of media reps and the outer ring of court watchers. Then the crowd magically parts and creates an opening, through which Detective Tringali and a uniformed police officer emerge.

"Mr. Stern, Ms. Sica, you're coming with me now," Tringali says.

CHAPTER 28

Detective Tringali takes us to police headquarters, where she interrogates me about the threat on Judge Triggs and about the Kreiss and Paulsen murders. I don't answer, repeatedly invoking the attorney-client privilege and emphasizing that it would make no sense for Poniard to attack our supporters. I especially don't want to talk about Philip, don't want to revisit yet again the discovery of his shredded body, especially after I've gone over the story with the cops many times. They've made no progress on finding his killer, undoubtedly because they refuse to investigate William the Conqueror. Tringali demands that I provide her with Poniard's mailing address and phone number, refusing to believe that I don't know them. When I insist that she investigate Bishop's role in the murders and the threat on Judge Triggs, she responds that the department is following up on all possible leads.

"I'm beginning to think that you and the department are in Bishop's pocket," I say. "Just like your predecessors were back in 1987 when Bud Kreiss was kicked off the force."

If this were an earlier era, she'd have a couple of burly jailers take me into a back room and teach me a lesson, but instead she exacts her revenge by keeping me in the interrogation room another hour while she comes in and out and asks the same questions over and over. When she finally lets me go, I find Brenda waiting for me in the lobby. She says they questioned her for only fifteen minutes.

We get back to The Barrista just as the lunch rush is ending. Brenda goes into the back room. I order a coffee, sit down at my usual table, and boot up my computer. Improbably, my client is there as soon as the Yahoo! chat program launches.

Poniard:
>*The Triggs level was a mistake*
PStern
>*Please tell me you were hacked.*
Poniard:
>*I'm responsible for anything that appears in my video games*
PStern
>*Are you saying that you included the Triggs level? And the Kreiss level?*
PStern
>*Was your server hacked?*
Poniard:
>*I'm Poniard*
PStern
>*Answer my questions!*
Poniard:
>*Asked and answered, I am Poniard*
PStern
>*Well, Poniard, I want you to shut* Abduction! *down immediately. Enough is enough.*
Poniard:
>*Not until justice is done*
PStern
>*People's lives are at stake, and besides that, the damn game is hurting our chances of winning a lawsuit.*
Poniard:
>*A game can't kill anyone*
PStern
>*Many think video games kill, and that yours is the most dangerous.*
Poniard:
>*I will NOT disable the game, not until we know its outcome*
PStern
>*Don't you know the outcome already? It's your game.*
Poniard:
>*No. You and the players are responsible for how the game ends*
PStern
>*Well, here's something I don't control—Frantz and Diamond have scheduled your deposition for December 30th, 11 days from now. And he wants you to appear in person.*

Poniard:

>*Judge Triggs's order says I don't have to do that*

PStern

>*Judge Triggs recused himself today because of the threat against him. The new judge, Anita Grass, dislikes me—so much so that Frantz withdrew the disqualification motion so I could stay on the case.*

Poniard:

>*Good news*

PStern

>*Not so good. She's biased against me, which means she's biased against you.*

Poniard:

>*It's good because I want you as my lawyer. Nothing else matters. And OK, because you say it's important, I'll appear for deposition via Skype video, I am not a California resident so they can't make me come in person, right?*

PStern

>*Seriously? You'll appear by video?*

Poniard:

>*Yep*

PStern

>*I'm stunned. You're serious? You'll appear on a Skype video and show your face? The deposition will be tape recorded and could be publicly available in the court record.*

Poniard:

>*Make sure the deposition is kept confidential!*

PStern

>*Of course. But why agree to this now? After all this time?*

Poniard:

>*Desperate times, desperate measures*

PStern

>*Very good.*

Poniard:

>*There are conditions. Only you and one opposing counsel can be present at the deposition. And it takes place at a neutral site so I can verify by webcam that there are no others present and no bugs*

PStern

> *This won't work. They'll insist on Frantz deposing you, but he won't know the case like she does, so they'll want her there to help him. As the plaintiff, Bishop has a right to be there. And I'll need my assistant Brenda there. And a court reporter, of course. They'll also want it in their office.*

Poniard:

> *Only one of Bishop's attorneys, you, and the court reporter; they'll take the deal rather than get no video deposition at all*

PStern

> *Unlikely.*

Poniard:

> *Then no deposition; I'll send you details about how to connect w/ me on Skype. Bye*

PStern.

> *Poniard, wait! In the future, you MUST alert me about what's happening in* Abduction! *so I'm not caught by surprise again. Philip Paulsen could play the game well, but I can't.*

Poniard has signed off.

A chat with Poniard always raises more questions than it answers. Has he really lost control over his own game? Why has he agreed to the video deposition? The Poniard that I've been dealing with these past months would never allow it, despite the murders of Kreiss and Paulsen. Once again, I've deluded myself into believing that I know something about the entity on the other side of the Internet routers. When you're communicating through a computer screen, the other person seems so close, but he couldn't be more anonymous, a formless blank in an endless stream of bytes. That's what our information age has wrought—a sense of intimacy when all is distant, a sense of familiarity when everyone's faceless, a sense of omniscience when nothing's clear.

I go into the back room to tell Brenda about the chat. She's hunched over her computer keyboard. Her hair is flyaway, her eye makeup smudged from sweat, which glistens on her brow as if she's channeling Philip Paulsen. *Abduction!* is playing on the monitor.

"I beat Level One," she says wearily.

CHAPTER 29

The only way to get my opponents to agree to Poniard's conditions for appearing at a video deposition is to entice them into asking for a favor first. As soon as I sign off with Poniard, I notice William Bishop's deposition for the law offices of Parker Stern, also known as The Barrista storeroom. After a flurry of e-mails with Lovely that start out detached and professional and end up harsh and threatening, I agree that I'll take Bishop's deposition in his office at the Parapet Media Corporation complex in the San Fernando Valley. In exchange, Poniard will be deposed at a neutral location with only one of Bishop's lawyers, the court reporter, and me present. Both sides will keep the very existence of the deposition strictly confidential so the media won't learn of it. It doesn't seem like Bishop is getting much for what he's giving up, but corporate moguls like him will do almost anything to stay on their own turf.

Once the deal is done, I e-mail Poniard repeatedly, asking for a Skype meeting or at least an Internet chat so that I can prepare him for the deposition—explain the procedure, identify pitfalls, and practice a cross-examination. I get identical replies—*no need, counselor, I got it covered*. While William Bishop suffers from the arrogance of power, Poniard suffers from the arrogance of fame, and that's worse, because while power always has some currency behind it—money, friendship, favors owed, the ability and willingness to do violence—fame is counterfeit, subject to the irrational whims of a faceless public.

On Christmas Eve we close The Barrista early, and I impulsively ask Brenda if she has plans, tell her that there are a lot of good restaurants that stay open on Christmas Eve, that one in particular on the Santa Monica Pier has great food, good martinis, and a panoramic view of the bay. "My treat," I say. "And there's no problem getting a table with an ocean view. I know the maître d.'"

She forces a smile, mumbles, "Thank you, I've never been to a place like that," and tells me she's spending the holiday with her sister. I didn't know she had a sister. At closing time, she says a hurried "Happy Holidays," almost runs out the front door, and disappears.

I spend the evening alone in my condo, sipping the remainder of a bottle of single-malt Scotch that Harmon Cherry gave me one Christmas and performing Boolean searches on the Internet—all variants of *The Boatman* AND (*William Bishop* OR *Felicity McGrath*). On Christmas Day, I walk the deserted beaches from the Marina Peninsula to the Santa Monica Pier, the general area of Felicity's disappearance. I pose irrelevant, rhetorical questions that merely enlarge the voids in my life. How is Lovely Diamond, a devout Jew, struggling to accommodate the background of her son, a child raised by a decidedly non-Jewish great-aunt who condemned Lovely's mother's marriage to a Jewish pornographer? Where does Brenda's sister live? How has my mother and her team of propagandists connived this year to pervert Christmas and expand the power of the Church of the Sanctified Assembly?

CHAPTER 30

On the morning of December 30, a day when even the most contentious lawyers are hibernating in Mammoth or Maui until after the New Year, I drive to the Manchester Airport Hotel for Poniard's deposition. I'll be accompanied at the deposition not by a live witness but by a Dell laptop, two external computer speakers, and a fifty-five-inch high-definition monitor. The court reporter will capture the video of the session on her computer hard drive.

During the fifteen-minute ride from the marina, I continually check the rearview mirror to make sure that I'm not being followed. If word were to leak out, the media would like nothing better than to crash the deposition of the elusive individual known as Poniard. I leave my car with the valet and go to the elevator. The deposition will take place in a twenty-sixth-floor suite. Opposing counsel and I already have key cards, delivered to us yesterday. As I walk across the immense business hotel lobby to the bank of elevators, I feel a hand on my shoulder, and a man says in a broken-steam-pipe whisper, "Keep your eyes forward and walk past the elevators and through that far door." The plier-like grip sends a burning sensation up my neck, discouraging any dissent. Until I glance up at the man.

"What the fuck, Ed?"

"Just keep walking, Parky. I'll explain when we get outside. I don't want Lovely to see us together. Nor do you."

"How would Lovely . . . ? You mean *she's* the one taking the deposition? Not Frantz?" I can't believe Bishop would let Lovely Diamond, a junior lawyer, handle the most important deposition in the case, though, granted, she isn't your ordinary junior lawyer. I also shouldn't have acknowledged that there is a deposition. That's supposed to be top secret.

"Frantz doesn't know shit about the lawsuit. And anyway, she's good. Great. You have your hands full. Now let's go."

It's been two weeks since I met with Ed Diamond and asked him to look into *The Boatman*, and I'd given up on him, figuring that he didn't learn anything, or worse, that he'd obtained some essential information and shared it only with Lovely. Now, he virtually pushes me out a service door and into an alley behind the hotel where service trucks crash and bang while making morning deliveries. A good place to make sure no one overhears our conversation.

"I have something," Ed says.

"Why the hell did you wait until now? And how did you know about the deposition? It's confidential. Did Lovely—"

"I'm her father. She lives in my home."

"Still—"

"She didn't tell me. The kid figured it out."

"How? He's what, ten years old?"

"Because he's smart. Perceptive like his mother, which makes things difficult, let me tell you. But that's neither here nor there. Do you want to hear what I have to say or not?"

Over the din of the linen trucks and the Dumpsters and the voices of the hotel laborers, he tells me the story of *The Boatman*.

CHAPTER 31

Although the suite is supposed to be in the hotel's nonsmoking wing, it reeks of stale tobacco smoke. The furniture is standard-issue hotel drab. There are stains on the metallic-gray acrylic carpeting. Lovely sits on the right side of the couch, and I take a seat all the way to the left, far enough away from her to put some space between us. Despite the distance, I smell her orange blossom and ginger perfume. She's started wearing it again, as if a suitable mourning period for the death of our relationship has passed. Her deposition outline and laptop are on the coffee table, and she has to lean forward to reach them—hardly the optimal ergonomics for asking questions and taking notes.

Twelve feet across from us, the huge LED monitor sits on an audiovisual stand on wheels, a rat's nest of wires and cables cascading from its rear and connecting into a surge-protected power outlet and an Ethernet wall jack. Poniard will appear on that screen in a kind of reality TV–style reveal. The court reporter, Janine—a professorial woman in her late fifties whom I've known for years, Macklin & Cherry's favorite court reporter—is the only person whom both Lovely and I trust to keep this deposition confidential. She sits to our left in a folding chair, half-facing the huge monitor so she can watch Poniard's lips and then turn to us when we speak on the record. She pulls her silver hair back—she's shunned cosmetic surgery and hair coloring but still looks youthful because she keeps fit biking and riding horses—and stretches her pianist fingers in a kind of pregame warm-up ritual. Her stenography machine and notebook computer are perched precariously on a room service tray that serves as a makeshift table. Also on the tray is a webcam with a lens wide enough to include Lovely and me in the shot that Poniard will see on his end.

For an exorbitant fee of $199.99, the hotel has provided us our own secure Internet connection. We also have our own Skype account, to be used only for this deposition and then immediately closed. Poniard insisted on setting it up, and after two days of nasty e-mails back and forth, Lovely and Lou Frantz finally capitulated.

Poniard agreed to sign on at ten o'clock sharp. We wait, Lovely and I staring at the sky-blue Skype wallpaper, complete with wispy clouds. Janine is sitting only a few feet from me, and when I lean forward I notice that she's reading a paperback edition of *Abraham Lincoln: Vampire Hunter*.

"The book is much better than the movie," she says without turning around.

At 10:05, Lovely crosses her legs and begins bouncing the top one up and down. She twirls a strand of hair around her finger. At 10:10, she shakes her head, making her silver earrings wobble. "I'll give him ten more minutes and then I'm out of here. I knew this was all a big joke."

"If you do that we'll take the position that you've waived the right to depose him," I say. "Twenty minutes is nothing. Especially when your boss is never less than forty-five minutes late for a depo."

"Ten more minutes."

Janine never takes her eyes off her novel.

At 10:18, Lovely checks her watch and makes a move to pack up her deposition outline, but then the box *Poniard is video calling* pops up on the screen, and my hands begin to tremble as if I were in court for an argument, so it's a good thing Janine is in control of the computer. She deftly moves the cursor over the green *answer* bubble and clicks the left mouse button. A window opens, but there's no image yet, only a black background and a maddening white circular arrow tracking in a clockwise direction with the words *Starting video* underneath.

The window suddenly expands and flickers. He's looking down at us.

Because the picture is too large for the quality of the video feed, it's gauzy and slightly choppy. But it's more than clear enough to reveal that Poniard is in his mid-twenties, maybe even younger. He certainly fits within the stereotypical demographic for a video gamer, and for some reason I find that disappointing. It explains a lot, though—the brashness, the snarkiness, the testosterone-driven iconoclasm that's gotten him into so much trouble. He's handsome, almost pretty, with longish brown hair, a pale complexion, smooth rosy cheeks (he probably shaves every third day), full lips, and a long, straight Irish nose. His chin is firm and full, almost regal, and his dark, inward-looking eyes peer at us intensely below thick dark brows that save him from looking effeminate. I've confirmed one fact. The photograph that Brenda found early on of the tall man known as Vladimir Lazerev—rumored to be Poniard—isn't the person on this video screen.

All the Internet chats that I've had with Poniard take on different aspects now that I've seen his face. He's retroactively more credible, more authoritative. The appearance of an attractive face after so many impersonal conversations can miraculously reshape past perceptions. He'd make an appealing witness—if I could convince him to come to trial.

Lovely gazes at the screen. She looks neither smitten nor antagonistic but rather puzzled. Janine has that tabula rasa expression of a court reporter who's emptied her mind of all thoughts so she can mechanically process the words of others.

"Good morning, Mr. Poniard," Lovely says.

"It's just Poniard, Ms. Diamond," he says. He speaks with an aristocratic British accent. So now the three of us in this room have information millions of fans and media reporters have been dying to know for some time. I can already feel the weight of the secret pressing on my insides. All my other secrets will have to make room.

"And while it's morning where you are, I will not concede that it's morning where I am," he continues. "You are not entitled to know where I am."

"I'm going to admonish you, Mr. Poniard," Lovely says, "that if you're going to make smart-ass comments like that, we're going to be here all day, and probably back again another day. I don't think you want that to happen."

"You ought to censor your own comments if you're so anxious to finish, counsel," I say.

"Have we met before, Poniard?" Lovely asks.

"Certainly not," he says. "I'd remember meeting such a beautiful woman."

"Please swear the witness in," Lovely says.

Janine administers the oath, and though she's recited the words thousands of times, I detect a slight tremor in her voice. She's obviously read up on the case and my client.

Poniard agrees under penalty of perjury to tell the truth.

"State your full name for the record," Lovely says.

"Poniard."

"Your legal name," she says.

"I object and instruct the witness not to answer in accordance with Judge Triggs's order prohibiting questions about his identity," I say. I make the same objections to questions about Poniard's address, phone number, e-mail addresses other than the one listed on his public website, location of his web servers, place and date of birth, and educational and occupational history since high school. Despite my repeated objections, Lovely seems delighted with the way the deposition has started, probably because she doesn't want Poniard to answer these questions. Rather, she wants to go to Judge Grass after the deposition and ask her to overrule Judge Triggs's order that let Poniard keep his identity secret.

"Poniard, did you create the video game called *Abduction!*?" Lovely asks.

"Oh, I most certainly did. I'm the writer, producer, director, designer, graphic artist, and so on." There's an off-putting arrogance not only in his words but also in his tone. But I've known from the start that Poniard is arrogant.

"How would you describe the game *Abduction!*?" she asks.

"It's a multiplayer online game dedicated to solving the mystery of how and why your client William Bishop kidnapped and, I believe, murdered Paula Felicity McGrath."

"What evidence do you have that William Bishop kidnapped Felicity McGrath?"

"I'll object on the grounds of attorney-client privilege regarding any information that Poniard learned from me," I say. That will stop him from testifying about my finding *The Boatman* cast list. I want to keep that a surprise for as long as possible.

"There are the letters between Felicity McGrath and Scotty showing that she was involved with William Bishop just before her disappearance and that she was afraid of him," he says.

"Where did you get those letters?" Lovely asks.

"From Scotty," Poniard says.

I lurch forward in my seat, a show of emotion that has no place in front of the opposition. Janine glances up at Poniard but quickly looks away, clearly embarrassed that she reacted. While on the record court reporters try to act not like human beings but like extensions of their steno machines. I'm sure Lovely noticed Janine flinch, but she doesn't react, just keeps looking at Poniard with cold, unblinking eyes. If I were sitting next to my client, I'd take a break and pull him out of the room to find out why he blindsided me. When I asked about Scotty months ago, he pleaded ignorance. This is what happens when you don't prepare. I should've refused to let the deposition go forward unless he and I had a videoconference or at least a phone call.

"Who's Scotty?" Lovely asks.

"I won't answer that," Poniard says.

"But you know his identity?"

"Yes." Again, he's more honest with Lovely than he is with me. Harmon Cherry once talked about what he called the deponent's mini-Stockholm syndrome, a client's self-destructive tendency to want to please the adversary during cross-examination. I've never had a client suffer from that until now.

"What's Scotty's full name?" Lovely asks.

"I won't answer that," he says.

Lovely turns to me and says, "Mr. Stern, I insist that you disclose the name of this Scotty person."

"I can't do that," I say.

"Then we'll pay another visit to Judge Grass and make a motion to compel. And I'll seek sanctions not only against your client but against you for withholding relevant evidence."

"Do what you have to do, Lovely," I say.

"Call me *Ms. Diamond.*"

"Thanks for the clarification," I say. "Because I certainly don't know who you are anymore."

Her lower lip droops in a slight pout of injury. She's made the mistake that so many young lawyers make—thinking you can separate life and the lawsuit. It can't be done—the lawsuit *is* your life.

"Don't quarrel, children," Poniard says. "Ms. Diamond, Parker can't tell you about Scotty because he doesn't know who Scotty is." He hasn't looked at me once, which is good, because I don't want him to appear that he needs my help to testify. But I don't think he's really looking at Lovely, either. His eyes seem to be riveted on a spot on the wall between us.

Lovely shakes her head, incredulous. "Who's Scotty, Mr. Poniard? What's his name?"

"I won't tell you who Scotty is no matter what you do," he says.

Over my objection, she asks ten more questions designed to get at Scotty's identity, all slight variants of the first question but none similar enough that I can object that the question has been asked and answered. She's trying to wear Poniard down, to get him to slip up or, short of that, make him look completely intractable. I taught her the technique.

Lovely checks her notes, glances at Poniard, check her notes again, and watches the screen for a long time without asking a question. Poniard looks back down at her. She shoots up out of her chair and says, "Let's take a short break."

"We've just gotten started," I say.

Instead of arguing, she sits back down on the couch and turns her laptop computer completely away from me. She feverishly inputs keystrokes and stares at her own small screen for a while.

"Is everything OK?" I ask.

She brushes the hair out of her eyes and lowers her head in a glower, a look she reserves only for people she holds in contempt. She's never given me that look. "Back on the record," she says, expectorating the words.

Lovely waits for Janine to get ready and then says, "Poniard, would you be willing to trade your kingdom for a horse?"

"Objection," I say. "You accused him of being a smart-ass before, and now you're—?"

Poniard holds up his hand. "I'm afraid Ms. Diamond has won this level," he says. "She is, indeed, as highly intelligent as I've heard. More so. I would imagine that people tend at first to dismiss you because of your beauty and background, but they clearly shouldn't. You know who else that happened to, Ms. Diamond? Felicity McGrath. Which is why you should empathize with her much more strongly than you do."

I feel as if I'm at a dinner party where everyone suddenly begins conversing in Chinese.

"How could you go along with this charade, Parker?" Lovely says.

"Oh, my dear Ms. Diamond," Poniard says. "The poor man doesn't have a clue, any more than he knows who Scotty is. You're much more astute than he, I'm afraid."

She appraises me for a moment and softens. "Not more astute. Just more realistic about who and what you really are. Your attorney has a trusting side that gets him into trouble. It's also what makes him a great lawyer."

"I'm in the room," I say. "What's going on?"

"Let me ask some questions," Lovely says. "We'll get it on the record."

I want to object, but I can't think of a reason.

"Poniard, that's not really your face I'm seeing on this Skype session, is it?" she asks.

"No, it is not," he says.

"What Mr. Stern, the court reporter, and I are seeing is a digitally animated face."

"Correct."

"In fact, a replica of the face of King Richard the Third of England."

"Also correct."

"King Richard's body was found under a parking lot in February of 2013?"

"Yes."

"And archaeologists created a computer reconstruction of King Richard's face from the skull that they found?" Lovely says.

Poniard nods.

"And the face we're seeing on the screen is the reconstructed face of Richard the Third, and not your face, isn't that right, Poniard?"

"Bull's-eye, Ms. Diamond."

"And we're not hearing your actual voice either?"

"Right about that, too, counsel."

"You don't have an English accent in real life, do you?" she asks.

"I'm not going to answer that," Poniard says. "You're not entitled to know that about me under Judge Triggs's order. Is she, Mr. Stern?"

"What technique are you using to make the animated character respond to my questions?" Lovely asks.

"I'm using a proprietary 3D facial animation system that I developed that speaks and gestures in real time and that responds to the emotions and inflections in my voice."

I should end this right now, but I'm too rattled to speak.

"So basically, you're the puppeteer and we've been watching the puppet," Lovely says. By the accusatory look she gives me, she clearly thinks that Poniard is controlling more than one puppet.

"That's a crude way of putting it," the talking head says. "But close enough."

"Remarkably lifelike," Lovely says. "I wouldn't have known if I hadn't remembered the news reports about how they discovered King Richard's body after so many centuries."

"This is what I do," Poniard's avatar says. "I'm good at it."

All this time I've been staring at the screen speechless, but now the intense heat of humiliation rises, and my voice spasms with rage. "We're taking a break."

"We'll break when I'm done with this line of questioning," Lovely says.

"We're taking a break or this deposition is over," I say.

At any other deposition, Janine would just go off the record, but she seeks permission from Lovely, who's in total control now. I hope Lovely will refuse my request and let me end the deposition so she can run down to court and complain about the trickery. But she's too savvy for that. She knows that a delay will only give me a chance to fix this disaster. "Five minutes," she says.

Once Lovely and Janine have left the room, I say to Poniard, "What the fuck is going on?"

The avatar frowns. "I thought that I should give the judge and jury a voice and a face."

"You've committed a fraud on the plaintiff and on the court."

"Oh, come on, counselor. Judge Triggs ordered that they couldn't inquire into my identity. That allows me to disguise my voice and appearance."

"You're a worse lawyer than you are a witness, which is saying something."

"Diamond seems to think the whole thing's funny. And it is, if you think about it."

"That's the last thing she thinks. She's not your friend or even your worthy opponent. She's burying us, damn it. She's gotten you to refuse to identify Scotty, which gives her ammunition to go down to court and argue that you're not meeting your discovery obligations. That refusal alone can result in a judgment against you."

"No judge would rule against me just because I—"

"Anita Grass would. In a heartbeat. But tell me this—why did you lie to me about Scotty and then blindside me with the truth in a deposition?"

"Because I wasn't under oath when I was chatting with you. I'm not telling anyone who Scotty is, so why get you all hyper about it?"

"I'm tired of your games, Poniard."

"Tired or not, we've established long ago that you're not quitting the case no matter what. You're in love with your hot opposing counsel. Seeing her, that's understandable. And you'll stay on the case because you want to know what happened to Felicity, because you don't want Bishop to get away with what he did to her."

There's a hard knock on the door. Before I can respond to it, Lovely comes in, followed by Janine.

"Five minutes are up," Lovely says.

She asks a series of questions that hammer away at Poniard's deception about appearing on Skype. Then she leads him through various scenes in *Abduction!*, asking about solutions to the various levels. He testifies only as to the levels that the public has already solved and says that he doesn't know the solutions to future levels.

"Didn't you create all the levels for *Abduction!*?" she asks.

"No," he says.

"Which levels didn't you create?"

"I did not design the levels where Bud Kreiss was murdered or where Judge Triggs was stabbed."

"How did those levels get in the game?"

"My server was hacked."

"By whom?"

"By your client, Ms. Diamond. Or, more accurately, by his minions at Parapet Media."

"How do you know?"

"Who else would it be?"

"I'm taking this deposition, so I don't have to answer your questions, even though you have to answer mine," Lovely says. "But I will answer that one. I think you created those levels, Poniard, and that you did so in some misguided attempt to lay blame on my client. Which is the same reason that you killed Bud and Isla Kreiss. You did kill Mr. and Mrs. Kreiss, didn't you?"

She waits for the obvious objection, as does Poniard. Even Janine turns away from the monitor and looks at me expectantly.

"Poniard can answer the question," I say. "Unless he thinks he should plead the Fifth." I've just committed malpractice, but I want to hear the answer, and I have the best chance of getting it now. Lovely shakes her head in disbelief, and Janine inhales audibly and turns back to look at the screen.

The puppeteer, whoever that is, makes the avatar shake his head in sadness. "I shouldn't dignify your ludicrous and insulting question with a response, Ms. Diamond. But the answer is no. I didn't kill anyone. Your client did."

"There's hasn't been a lot of dignity in this entire deposition," Lovely says. She goes on to ask a series of innocuous questions about how Poniard creates video games, during which he gives us a primer on game design. Just after asking a question about the type of software a designer might use to create high-quality graphics, she says, "Did you know that Felicity McGrath had a daughter named Alicia?" Most junior lawyers follow a predictable script, but Lovely has already learned the technique of suddenly switching to another topic to catch the witness off guard.

A heavy sigh comes out of the speakers. "Yes, she had a daughter."

"Have you ever met her?"

"Yes."

"Under what circumstances?"

"I can't answer that."

"Can't or won't?"

"Won't."

"Do you know where she is now?"

Poniard waits a long time before answering. "I certainly do, Ms. Diamond. But I'm not going to reveal her whereabouts."

"Why not?"

"Because she's in hiding, and I feel I'm duty bound as a soldier and a revolutionary and a proponent of the truth to protect her. Which means I'm not about to expose her to William the Conqueror and his private army of thugs."

CHAPTER 32

New Year's Day has come and gone. I went to a New Year's Eve party at the home of a former Macklin & Cherry partner, a disaster because his wife tried to fix me up with her recently divorced sister who wouldn't stop asking questions about *Bishop v. Poniard*, the Church of the Sanctified Assembly, and the celebrities I've represented. Worse, everyone decided they wanted to watch DVDs of cheesy old movies from our hosts' collection, one of which happened to be my big hit *Alien Parents*. It wasn't all that coincidental—most of them grew up loving that movie. I left after the opening credits, mumbling, *Sorry, I never liked that kid*, and stayed up until midnight nursing a Hennessy cognac at a Scottish pub in Marina del Rey populated by septuagenarians who knew all the verses to "Auld Lang Syne."

Now I spend my days preparing for William Bishop's upcoming deposition, where I'll use Ed Diamond's information and hope that Bishop will be so shaken that he'll drop his lawsuit in exchange for confidentiality. I haven't even told Brenda about my conversation with Ed. The element of surprise is crucial. I just hope that Ed hasn't told Lovely in a fit of remorse that he kept the information from her.

It's a Tuesday evening, and as a favor to a former law professor colleague, I'm scheduled to speak tonight at St. Thomas More School of Law to a group of law students who want to become entertainment lawyers, just like every other law student in Los Angeles. I took the gig last August while I was still working at JADS and before *Bishop v. Poniard* disrupted my life. I'm tempted to make up some excuse about flu-like symptoms, but when I say that to Brenda, she says, "Don't cancel. It'll be good for you to be around other people and away from the case."

"Law students aren't other people," I say. "All they'll want to hear about is *Bishop v. Poniard* and my trial against the Sanctified Assembly and the horrible fallout from that. I don't want to talk about any of it."

"Give your presentation tonight. You made a commitment. Trust me, it'll be good for you."

So I go and find myself sitting on a dais in a large lecture hall and watching the room fill to capacity, probably more because of the free pizza than out of interest in what I have to say. The heavy aroma of pepperoni grease, garlic, and cardboard makes my stomach churn, and while my stage fright has never seeped outside the confines of the courtroom, I always worry that it will someday.

My law professor friend told me that the presentation would be informal, that I wouldn't have to prepare and could just answer questions, but when he announces to the gathering that I'll speak on how best to pursue a career as an entertainment litigator, I realize that I'm going to have to lecture for forty-five minutes.

Like a basketball player who hits a desperation jump shot at the buzzer because there's no expectation of success, I make my improvised presentation work. I lose myself in my personal history—interviewing with mid-size Macklin & Cherry though I'd intended to work at a large national firm, joining a first-year class with some of the smartest—and, as it turned out, most troubled—young lawyers that I've ever encountered, and thriving as a trial lawyer because I both loved to perform and wanted to do justice. I talk about the washed-up pop singer of the early sixties who asked if I could send a limo to pick him up and take him to his deposition, about the client who hated his former business partner so much that he wanted me to schedule the deposition on a boat because the ex-partner got seasick, about the lessons in law and life that I learned from Harmon Cherry. I touch on *Bishop v. Poniard*, though I tread lightly and am amused to learn that no one in the room, not even the serious video game players, have gotten further than the second level. Philip Paulsen really was a brilliant man. I even tell them about my late partner Deanna and how she left the practice to found The Barrista, of which I'm now a part owner.

After I finish speaking, I take questions, most of them focused on how to get a job in an entertainment firm or at a studio. The one awkward moment is when a snarky, heavyset young man in the second row asks about the murders of Paulsen and the Kreisses. Some of the students hiss and boo, and the room bursts out in applause when I refuse to answer. I feel for the kid—even his forehead is flushed.

When the Q&A session ends, some of the students approach and try to hand me their résumés—I don't take them. Others pose questions that they didn't want to ask in front of an audience. The man who asked me about the Kreiss and Paulsen murders apologizes and then lingers. At some point, the students and I get into a discussion of the history of defamation law—they're surprised to learn that historically, libel lawyers were viewed as gutter dwellers, their status lower even than ambulance chasers, until segregationists tried in the early 1960s to use libel laws against civil rights advocates, at which time defamation law took on a constitutional dimension and libel lawyers became exalted in the profession.

"This is so fascinating," a young woman with short black hair and huge round nerdy-girl glasses says. "We didn't study any of this in torts or con law. Is there any chance we can get coffee somewhere and talk more if you're not too busy, Mr. Stern?" She extends her hand. "I'm Kat." She has the firm grip of someone who's studied how to make a good impression.

"We could go to the cafeteria," the chubby man says.

"The coffee there sucks," Kat says. "How about we go to your coffee place that you talked about. The . . . ?"

"The Barrista," I say. "Two Rs, a pun on *barrister*. But the shop is in West Hollywood. Kind of far."

"Fifteen minutes away at this time of night," Kat says. "It's in the direction of where I live anyway. Are you guys up for it?"

The others nod. I learn that the chubby guy who asked the indiscreet question is named Dylan, and the others are Lucy and Thomas. I suspect that some of them are more interested in job leads than in an arcane legal discussion, but I like law students. Lovely Diamond was my law student only a short time ago, though it seems like forever.

On the drive to The Barrista, I wonder how many of them will actually show up. They all do. Kat arrives first and sits across from me. The other three arrive together. I buy them the first round of coffee, and we talk about topics ranging from whether the First Amendment offers too much protection to the libel defendant, to how to get a job as an entertainment lawyer, to whether the Lakers will make the playoffs, to whether video games cause violent behavior among children and teens. A little before closing time, Brenda comes out of the back room and starts to wave, but then her face goes blank, and she turns on her heels and quickly walks out.

An hour later—where did the time go?—Romulo announces it's closing time. Now it's just the four law students and me, and we all groan. I haven't lost myself in the law like this in a long time. Thomas and Lucy are shy (Lucy laughs nervously after she makes a point, even if it isn't funny). Dylan, the chubby kid, is callow and earnest, enthusiastic about the law but not quite knowing what it's about. Kat is the most poised and the smartest. She quickly grasps the legal and practical issues behind an argument.

At 12:30 in the morning the three who arrived together leave, and it's just Kat and me in the dark, empty room. She takes a pack of chewing gum out of her purse and offers me a piece.

"For the coffee breath," she says.

I'm not sure if she's making a joke until she says, "I was talking about mine, not yours." She unwraps a stick of gum, puts it in her mouth, and chews daintily.

"Thank you *so* much for meeting with us here," she says. "You must be so busy with your case and all. I can't lie, I'm not sure I really want to be a lawyer, but my parents want me to so. . . . They're both lawyers and assume I'll be one too. It's seemed so boring all my life, even in law school, but you make it sound so interesting. Meeting all those famous people. But you've been in some horrible situations. The murders and the violence, the death of your friend who started this place . . . so wonderfully creepy and exciting."

This woman knows nothing about life and even less about death.

She'd think differently if she were the one who stumbled upon the body of a saintly man like Philip Paulsen. "My colleague, my friend was murdered recently," I say. "You must've read about it. His death wasn't exciting, it was horrible and mundane and bleak."

"You have to admit, there are two things that people like in their entertainment. Violence and sex. Movies, music, video games. Especially your client's video games. Poniard's video games are very sexual, don't you think?"

She puts her elbow on the table and rests her chin in her hand, giving a coquettish look. I didn't see this coming. I sit back to put some distance between us, trying not to offend her.

"It's late," I say. "I've enjoyed talking to you, Kat."

She starts to get out of her chair, and I think she's going to leave, but instead she slides into the chair next to me, and only then do I realize that her olive skin isn't natural but the result of bronzer and heavy makeup. Her face is inches away from mine, and I can smell the gum on her breath, feel her exhalations on my cheek.

"Your ex-girlfriend was a law student, right?" she asks. "Now she's your opposing counsel? She must be a great fuck, an ex-porn star and all. But you know what? I'll bet you I'm better. You want to find out?"

She puts her hand between my legs and starts fondling me. I stand up so quickly that my chair tips over and crashes to the floor.

"You're going to have to leave now," I say.

She moves close again. "You're going to make love to me, because that's what I want. And if you don't, I'll call the cops and say you lured me here and tried to rape me after the others left."

"I'll take my chances." I pull out my cell phone out, but she slaps my hand so hard that I drop it.

"You really don't know who I am, do you?" she says. "And you've been searching for me so hard."

"I—"

"I'm Felicity's daughter, of course." She takes a step back and pulls her sweater above her breasts; she's not wearing a bra. "Don't you want to fuck Felicity's daughter, Parker?"

"Who the hell are you?"

"I told you, I'm—"

"Cover up!" The voice reverberates off the ceiling. Standing inside the front entrance is an imposing man dressed in a brown bomber jacket and dark sweatpants. My heart rate accelerates like the engine of a top fuel dragster. I should've locked the door when the other students left. Then I recognize the man as the cosplayer Banquo.

The woman frowns and lowers her sweater. Banquo walks over, grabs her hair and pulls hard, and I wince at his abuse until the wig comes off and I see the red dreadlocks pinned to her scalp.

I feel like I've spent the evening with Clark Kent and was fooled by a flannel suit and a pair of horn-rimmed glasses. Despite the disguise, I should have recognized her. I was enraptured with my own words, with the students' adulation. She was cunning—she exhibited less hero worship than the others, not more. She's a marvelous actress.

"I'm very sorry for Courtney's behavior, Mr. Stern," Banquo says. "It won't happen again. Will it, Courtney?" He sounds more like her parent than her friend or lover. Though he still speaks with some kind of accent, it isn't quite British.

Courtney stares at me defiantly. Her eyes seem to suck up whatever light exists in this dim room and reflect it back in taunting spears of derision.

"What's this crap about Felicity's daughter?" I ask Banquo.

"She's confused," Banquo says. "Takes the game a little too seriously."

"It's true," she says. "I look just like her." She unpins the dreadlocks and shakes her head. "Don't you love my beautiful red hair? I got it from my mother."

There is a resemblance. But that's the whole point of the dress-up game she's been playing, right? Besides, Courtney, or whatever her real name is, has already proved that she's a chameleon.

"Shut up," Banquo says to her.

"Did Felicity McGrath have a daughter?" I ask, already knowing the answer from Philip's research but wanting to find out what they know.

"You can find any kind of rumor on the Internet," he says. "But we don't really know anything. We just like to pretend."

"Who are you? Really?" I ask. "Do you work for William Bishop? Is this some kind of attempt at sabotaging me? Because if it is, Bishop's wasting his money."

Banquo bows. "We're merely humble followers of the prophet Poniard. Nothing more sinister than that. We revile William the Conqueror. We won't trouble you again, Mr. Stern."

"And that means you don't hang around The Barrista anymore. If you do, I will get the cops involved."

"Of course, sir."

He places his hands on her shoulders and guides her toward the door. When she gets to the exit she shouts, "You'll never find out what happened to my mother! You're unsettling her soul! Let her rest in peace!"

He pulls her outside roughly, and I don't like it. I hurry to the front door, but they're moving quickly and she seems to be going willingly. After they've walked a block she starts stumbling back and forth across the sidewalk as if she's drunk, though she didn't consume anything but coffee in all the time we were together. I watch to see if they'll get into a car, but they walk two blocks down Melrose, turn left on Robertson, and disappear. Are they going to catch a bus this late? I've lived in the city my entire life, and I don't even know if buses run at this time of the morning.

I lock the front door and leave out the back, hurrying into my Lexus. On the drive home I think of all the questions I should have asked—what are their real names, where do they live, how do they survive? Are they a couple? Banquo, whoever he is, barely has control over her, and at times he seems abusive. I should've called someone to try to get her help.

CHAPTER 33

Felicity's back, the first time since Level One. The HF Queen says "Game Over," that Poniard's beaten, which means that no one will ever find out what happened to Felicity. How could they if the judge shuts the game down? An injunction, the Queen calls it. When Ed said, "You're counting chickens, Lovely," she said, "Not this time." She won't tell why she's so sure.

There's a big fight at school—a *brouhaha*, Bugsy calls it. The parents who hate Poniard are down on the teachers because one of the kids was found playing *Abduction!* on a library computer. *Violent and corrupting*, this one annoying mother keeps saying. The Queen still lets Brighton play the game, but she watches him closely. He's a good player—a great player, in fact—so what he learns could help her case. He doesn't know if he should feel wanted or used.

Felicity sits with her back to the monitor, removing the cornrows from her hair with practiced fingers. The scene pulls back to reveal prison bars. Dressed in orange prison clothes that clash with her hair, she's trapped in a barren cell furnished with a cot, a sink, and an open toilet. Cobwebs cover the ceiling vent. Giant black ants swarm a dented food tray and carry breadcrumbs from a moldy sandwich through a cranny in the wall.

Brighton tests the mouse and executes some keystrokes to get Felicity's attention, but she doesn't turn around. He rattles the bars, jiggles the metal cover on the wall grating, and shakes the ceiling vent, but nothing gives way. He tries to dive down the drain and the toilet like he did when he discovered the dead ex-cop, Bud Kreiss—but they lead nowhere.

If Felicity were real, what would he say to make her turn around and face him? Would he describe how his life has changed, how the Queen magically became less cold-hearted after she told him the embarrassing truth about why she gave him away (which he almost, but not quite understands) and about what Ed used to do for a living? When Brighton asked his grandfather about directing porn, which Lovely strongly advised him not to do, Ed snapped at him, saying in his best Bugsy voice, *I made cinematic art that celebrated the human anatomy and natural acts associated with reproduction just like Renoir painted nudes, but ever since the Japanese invented that goddamn video recorder there's no art to it, and it's worse with the Internet, a Bulgarian in a basement with a cheap digital camera, a couple of streetwalkers, and a Romanian primate with a nine-inch putz.* Ed says Brighton serves two functions—the son he never had and the grandson he always wanted.

The Queen is trying so hard to be nice and act like a real mother, but the more she goes around calling Stern a gullible fool, the guiltier Brighton feels, because he knows that he was the reason they broke up. Bugsy let it slip out, or maybe it wasn't such a slip, because Bugsy wants the Queen and Stern to get back together, which can't happen with the lawsuit going on. Brighton found a couple of YouTube videos where reporters tried to interview Stern about an old lawsuit. Stern's a good-looking guy, but he sounds angry, says *no comment* as if he wants to slug the person asking the question, clenches his jaw and focuses his clear eyes past the camera like he's trying to predict the future. Ed says Stern isn't really an angry man, but serious, dedicated, and loyal, that he'll run through a steel-reinforced concrete wall to see that justice is done. No wonder Poniard hired him. The Queen would do that, too, Ed says. So now she and Stern are sprinting toward that concrete wall in opposite directions, about to crash head-on. The thought makes Brighton want to cry.

He works this level of *Abduction!* for hours. When he gets bored he finishes his math homework and watches the fourth quarter of a basketball game with Ed—the Queen is working late again. After that, it's bedtime, but he goes to the computer and jiggles the mouse and watches Felicity fuss with her hair, removing the cornrows, which exist in an infinite loop. He tries something new, follows the ant trail. Fixing the cursor over an ant with a particularly large piece of bread between its mandibles, he holds down the left mouse button, and in a flash he's inside an ant colony, trapped in a dark tunnel inside the wall. He has to fight many bloody battles with ant soldiers to get to the Queen Ant, leaving severed antennae and insect armor in his wake. The Queen Ant sits on her throne. She looks like Brighton's mother! The Queen Ant regards him with fiery eyes and then raises her sparkling scimitar to strike Brighton dead, but he parries the blow, maneuvers in close, snatches a necklace from around her neck, and escapes another of the swords. He sighs in relief because he doesn't have to kill her—he couldn't have done it.

Brighton examines his booty—not just any necklace but the very cross and chain that Felicity wore in Level One before the kidnapping—a replica of the necklace the real Paula Felicity McGrath wore that horrible night. The necklace flashes light that cycles through all the visible colors of the rainbow, and the ant tunnel morphs into scintillating sky. In a cutscene, Brighton flies on billowy clouds back to Felicity's prison cell, where the necklace floats through the air and wraps itself around Felicity's neck. She turns to face the monitor, her hair now flowing down her shoulders in crimson waves.

"Ah, my rescuer," she says. "You're so smart and courageous." She purses her scarlet lips and puts a finger to her temple, as if deep in thought. Brighton smiles because even though she's in prison, she has makeup on.

"Here's what you must do," she says. "You must find The One who knows about me. The someone who remembers who I really was." The light shimmers from her tears like sunlight off a pond. "I know you're out there. Please come forward. If not for me, for the purity of your soul." She fingers the cross around her neck and then turns her back to the monitor. A new level doesn't launch, but the game continues.

Brighton knows a lot about the lawsuit, of course—Bugsy and the Queen talk about it all the time even though the Queen says she doesn't want to, and Brighton reads the online news reports when the Queen isn't looking. So he understands that Poniard has put out an all-points bulletin on a witness, any witness, who can help his case. But why doesn't Felicity say the same thing at the start of this level instead of waiting until the player has battled killer ants to win the necklace? Brighton thinks he understands—you take things more seriously if you have to fight for them.

CHAPTER 34

Before I can take a sip of my espresso, Brenda puts a document on my table.

"Can this judge really do this?" she says. "Seriously?"

The document reads *Order Setting Trial*, scheduling the trial for March 18, 2014, eight weeks from now. It's too soon. I'll have to present evidence and call witnesses that I don't have.

"What happens if Grass overrules Judge Triggs's order and forces Poniard to show in person?" Brenda asks. "Which he won't, right?"

"She could fine him. Or she could hold him in contempt of court. Or order his website shut down. But knowing her, she'd impose the civil death penalty."

Brenda reacts to my lawyer's jargon with a weary eye roll.

"The civil death penalty means she'll enter judgment against Poniard as a sanction for violating a court order," I say. "And then Bishop can pursue Poniard for tens of millions in damages."

She doesn't say it, but I know what she's thinking—I should never have waived Poniard's right to a jury trial in that first hearing before Judge Triggs. Now, we're at the mercy of a judge who can't stand me.

───※───

Over the next weeks, my opponents and I engage in procedural skirmishes and discovery battles. Using The Barrista storeroom as my conference room, I take several unproductive depositions of record keepers; retired news reporters; and police department functionaries, including retired Captain Ted Gorecki, the cop who replaced Detective

Bud Kreiss on the McGrath investigation. He insists that there were no suspects in Felicity's disappearance, that she was engaging in risky behavior, maybe even working as a prostitute, and that she probably picked up the wrong johns. He says that Kreiss was demoted not as part of a cover-up but because his affair with Dalila Hernandez, the news reporter, created a blatant conflict of interest. He speculates that even if Bud Kreiss told Hernandez about a person of interest, Kreiss lied to impress her, to make her feel as if she had a scoop on the legitimate newspapers. Throughout Gorecki's deposition, Frantz sits back in his chair and gloats, not bothering to object even to objectionable questions. He clearly enjoys collecting twelve hundred dollars an hour watching Gorecki walk all over me. Let him gloat all he wants. When I have the chance to sit across the table from Bishop, watch him swear to tell the truth, and ask him questions that he doesn't want to answer, none of my adversaries will gloat.

CHAPTER 35

On Valentine's Day, I get my chance to interrogate Bishop. It's raining. It wasn't supposed to rain until tomorrow morning, and now LA drivers who've forgotten how to navigate in a storm or who probably never knew jam up Wrightwood Drive, my favorite shortcut over the Hollywood Hills to the Valley. It's one of those rare days where you set the windshield wipers to high for a reason other than spreading washer fluid, where the hairpin curves threaten to send you skidding off a cliff and down into the canyon, where you hope to hit flat land before the whole hillside comes down and buries you in an avalanche of mud.

It's also a Friday. Ordinarily, I don't like Friday depositions because most of the deponents mentally start their weekend at the lunch break. Today, though, this could work to my advantage if Bishop focuses not on my questions but on his Gulfstream IV flight to his private ski mountain near Park City.

The Parapet Media complex in the east San Fernando Valley wasn't always an enemy camp. As a kid, I made four movies on this lot, long before Bishop acquired it. I arrive at the main gate with fifteen minutes to spare. The guard asks for my driver's license and directs me to pull over to the side so other cars can pass. It takes so long for him to let me inside that I'm quite sure Bishop's people ordered him to make me wait. I park the car, and with a flimsy retractable umbrella in one hand and my briefcase in the other, half-run from the parking lot into the Dark Fortress—that's what they've called the office building ever since Bishop acquired the studio. The umbrella does nothing to keep my woolen suit dry; if anything it makes the drops coalesce and pour down on my slacks. I take the elevator to the top floor, where the doors open to a lavish reception area. Half of the raised fifty-foot ceiling consists of irregular glass triangles that form a skylight—self-cleaning, according to an article I read—that illuminates the entire floor, even on a dark, rainy day like this. The architect furnished the reception area in molded fiberglass chairs, a glass-and-chrome coffee table, and burgundy leather sofas. The walls and weight-bearing pillars are matching Italian marble. A tree-sized ficus shoots up out of the middle of a vast oak reception desk, far enough behind the receptionist to keep her safe from falling leaves. Every other plant in the room is a variety of fern. I read somewhere that Bishop's wife loves ferns.

I announce myself to the receptionist, who frowns, presses some buttons on her phone pad, and whispers into her headphones, all the while looking past me. She knows why I'm here. Five minutes later, a lithe young woman greets me with a flight attendant's smile, revealing straight, bleaching-gel teeth. She satisfies the major qualifications for a top executive's assistant, even in this era of anti-gender bias and anti-harassment law—she's pretty and perky and has intelligent eyes. She'll be a secretary—more accurately, an executive assistant—only until she sells her first script or earns a promotion to creative executive or gives it all up in frustration and enrolls in business school.

"May I get you water or coffee?" she asks, the words articulated without breaking the smile.

I decline. With my churning stomach, I couldn't consume anything safely. And for a fleeting moment, I actually wonder whether Bishop would tamper with my drink.

She leads me to a large conference room, conceived with a single overriding purpose—to inspire fear and awe. There's a panoramic view of the Santa Monica Mountains to the south and the San Gabriel Mountains to the east. Designed in the Russian classical style, it still feels contemporary. Lavish Corinthian pilasters inlaid with polished chrome articulate the walls. A ceiling mural depicts 1920s Hollywood or, more accurately, Culver City, where most pictures were actually shot in that era.

Janine the court reporter sits at the head of the table. She has her hair pinned in a bun, and she's wearing a stylish gray business suit, as if she's in trial. At Poniard's deposition—at almost every deposition that I can remember her taking—she dressed casually. I never thought she'd break character, behave like someone other than the unbiased functionary charged with recording the truth. When I say good morning she mumbles "good morning" back but doesn't meet my eyes. The videographer is on my side of the table, pretending to test his camera equipment, though he must have set it up a half hour ago.

Bishop sits across the table, wearing a suit and tie. Unlike most witnesses, he hasn't taken off his coat. Lou Frantz, who's sitting to Bishop's left, has already taken his coat off, exposing a red and gray paisley power tie and red suspenders. Frantz turns sideways and whispers something to Bishop, who nods. The two men share many physical features and yet seem nothing alike. They're both tall and slim with silvery hair and deep California tans. But Frantz's hair is thinner, whiter, and isn't quite in place, and his cheap Thirty-Six-Hour Clothiers suit is three sizes too big, making his body seem as if it's drooping toward the floor, an image that either fortuitously or intentionally matches the hangdog expression on his thin face. In contrast, Bishop's hair is slicked back symmetrically, and his tailored charcoal-gray suit, Italian high-collar dress shirt, and yellow silk tie are perfect. His jaw is a firm U-shape, and except for some character creases in his forehead, his face is wrinkle free. It's hard to believe he's seventy-one years old. He really could have been an actor. As always in public, he's wearing his signature horn-rimmed glasses that improbably make him seem not bookish or benign but more intimidating. While Frantz hunches forward a bit, Bishop holds his shoulders level, but not self-consciously so, unlike those men who thrust their chests out and pull their shoulders back because they've read somewhere that good posture bespeaks confidence. While Frantz's demeanor advertises *weight of the world*, Bishop seems to float above the crowd, as though earth's gravity exerts less force on him than it does on the rest of us.

The photographic lights reflect off his thick glasses, so I can't see his eyes. I hope that isn't a problem when he faces me during the deposition—I want to see his eyes. Bishop doesn't acknowledge me but instead keeps talking to Janine, who's apparently describing how her stenography equipment works. Although Bishop has sat through countless depositions and undoubtedly couldn't care less about the mechanics of court reporting, he listens to Janine's explanation as if enthralled. Every powerful person I've met, no matter how odious or evil in real life, has a large reservoir of charm. It's easy for William the Conqueror. He's so feared that all he has to do is behave cordially and feign interest, and even a seasoned veteran like Janine will hold forth about the intricacies of her job and giggle like a tween whenever he smiles or nods his head.

Frantz looks at me with the same gloat that he had during the Gorecki deposition. Lovely sits on Frantz's left, dressed in a gray pin-stripe suit and cotton turtleneck sweater. Her expression is as hard as the granite table in front of her. We nod slightly at each other, as if we're two mourners greeting each other at a funeral.

"You're late, Stern," Frantz says.

"By five minutes, courtesy of the slothful guard at the gate," I say. "Which by Lou Frantz Standard Time is forty minutes early. Would you like me to come back at ten forty-five?"

"Maybe you should use the time to find a Laundromat and dry your clothes," he replies.

"Not necessary," I say. "I'm sure that over the next few hours you'll provide all the hot air I need."

Lovely clears her throat and puts her hand over her mouth to mask a smile, but Frantz notices anyway and looks at her with annoyance.

"Ready when you are," Bishop says. Despite his benign and polite words, his imperious tone leaves no doubt that he's commanded me to get started. I slowly unpack the documents from my litigation bag and meticulously take my time pouring myself a cup of inevitably bad conference room coffee, all to show that I don't take orders from him.

"Let's get started," I say.

Bishop raises his right hand. Even the way he holds it, as if about to bestow some sort of imperial benediction, conveys power. The videographer asks the attorneys to identify themselves, Janine administers the oath, and the witness states his full name—William Maxfield Bishop.

He uses his palm to brush the air above his impeccable silver coif just in case a strand of hair had the temerity to break ranks. I stare at his tanned face and in that moment change my first question. My opponents probably told Bishop that I'd start with his educational background or jump into his relationship with Felicity McGrath. But I ask, "Mr. Bishop, did you have stage makeup applied immediately before this deposition started? Is that why you had them hold me up at the gate? So your studio makeup people could finish applying the greasepaint?"

Lovely doesn't react, but out of the corner of my eye I notice Janine hesitate in her transcription for the briefest of moments. It's enough to verify that I'm right.

"Objection," Frantz says. "Argumentative, not to mention offensive. And particularly ironic given that your client appeared at his deposition as King Richard the Third of England. A criminal, by the way, just like Poniard."

"My point is that our clients both have their own ways of hiding who they truly are. Mine does it with animation and yours does it with the award-winning makeup department of a major studio. Now, answer the question, Mr. Bishop. You have to answer unless Mr. Frantz instructs you otherwise, and he hasn't done that."

"I do instruct him not to answer," Frantz says. "Right of privacy."

"Not even close on the law," I say.

"If you don't like it, take it up with Judge Grass," he says. Which he knows I won't do. But I've made my point. I'm not going to cower in front of the all-powerful William Bishop.

"You told the court reporter that your full name is William Maxfield Bishop," I say. "Have you been known by any other names?"

"William Bishop. Some old friends and my wife call me Billy."

"How about William the Conqueror?" I know very well that Bishop detests the nickname. That's exactly why I asked the question.

You'd think he'd frown, but the muscles in his cheeks soften, and he grins. He'd look like a benign grandfather but for his eyes. It's the stark contrast between those eyes and the rest of the face that makes him look so terrifying at the moment. This must be how he looks just before he detonates his temper.

"That is not a name that I've ever called myself," he says flatly. "It's an invention of people like your client who're in the business of telling lies about me."

"You're called *William the Conqueror* because you have a reputation of being a ruthless businessman who'll do anything to get what you want, correct?"

"My adversaries use that name because they're crass, offensive, and envious," he says. "But let me add that your premise is incorrect. I've always conducted my business in an open and aboveboard way."

"Really, sir? What about illegal hacking of Congressman Lake Knolls's e-mail account? Do you consider that open and aboveboard?" Lake Knolls is an Academy Award–winning actor and ambitious politician who ran into some trouble a few years ago. One of Bishop's tabloid newspapers illegally intercepted his personal e-mails.

Frantz makes a harrumphing series of objections and instructs Bishop not to answer.

Returning to a more conventional approach to depositions, I lead Bishop through his educational and occupational background—he's an alumnus of an East Coast prep school in 1960, a time when the children of even the wealthiest Los Angeles families attended public school. He earned a bachelor of fine arts degree from the NYU Film School and a master's degree in business from the University of Chicago. After that, he worked a series of low-level jobs in a talent agency and on film productions and eventually began producing his own movies. He had a string of top-grossing hits and took over as the head of a studio, which he transformed into the international conglomerate Parapet Media Corporation.

"I'm going to list some names," I say. "And I'd like you to tell me if you know them, and if so, how." I don't expect truthful answers, but I want to gauge his reaction—trial lawyer's poker. "Bradley Kelly?"

"Founder of the Church of the Sanctified Assembly," he says. "If that's the Kelly you mean."

"Also an actor?"

"Debatable. Pretty face."

Interesting. A true Assembly devotee wouldn't speak that way about Kelly—unless Bishop is part of the group's elite Covert Vanguard, with orders to infiltrate the highest levels of business and government and work to increase the Assembly's power and influence.

"Did you ever work with Kelly?"

"He was in some movies I produced. I never had anything to do with him."

"Parky Gerald."

"Cute kid, OK for a child actor, hellish stage mother. He had some bit parts in some of my movies before he got big. Turned twelve and wasn't cute anymore."

Lovely chews on her lip to stifle a laugh. I suppose I asked for it.

"Nathan Ettinger?" I ask.

He frowns. "Always looking for production deals from every studio in town. Much better college professor than a producer."

"Ever work with him?"

"No. He was a producer on the Parapet lot for a short time before I acquired Parapet. Never got a movie made."

"How do you know he's a professor?"

"I have a vast knowledge of the motion-picture industry and all its players large and small," he says without any apparent awareness of how arrogant he sounds. "That's how I've managed to become so successful." More likely he's been keeping tabs because Ettinger worked on *The Boatman*. No wonder Ettinger is frightened.

"Why do you say Ettinger is a better professor than he was a producer?"

"Because he couldn't be worse."

"Hildy Gish."

"Don't know that name."

I go through the remaining names on the list. He denies knowing any of them.

"Paula Felicity McGrath?" I ask.

Without missing a beat, he says, "Felicity McGrath had small parts in a couple of movies produced by a studio where at one time I worked as a mid-level creative executive. I wasn't involved in any of those movies."

Next I show him copies of the letters between Felicity McGrath and Scotty and ask about their authenticity and substance. Despite the document examiner's opinion, he maintains that the letters are forgeries. He says he doesn't know who Scotty is, much less why Felicity would write, "Big Bad Billy Bishop has our Backs" or that he was her "insurance policy."

"Let's turn to another topic," I say. "Earlier when I asked you about your employment history, you didn't mention acting as part of your motion-picture career. Have you ever appeared as an actor? And by that I mean at any time in your life, professionally or otherwise."

"I played Papa Bear in my fourth-grade presentation of *Goldilocks and the Three Bears*." His smile is practiced, intended for Janine and the videographer. "As I recall, we did it in Spanish."

"No other acting roles in your entire life?"

"None that I can think of. Though I didn't have the time to study my fifth- or sixth-grade yearbooks to see if there were any pageants in those years."

"So you've never appeared in a motion picture?"

"Objection, asked and answered," Frantz says.

"Never," he says.

"Have you ever written a screenplay or directed a motion picture?" I ask.

"Alas, never. I don't have the talent for it. I'm a big picture man, pardon the pun." He sits even taller in his chair, something I thought impossible, as if he needs to counterbalance the false humility with a physical show of arrogance.

"What about *The Boatman*?" I say.

"Counsel, I just said I never . . ." There's glitch in his voice. He gives Frantz a sidelong glance. Lovely looks at me with probing gray eyes.

"I don't know what you're talking about," he says.

He knows exactly what I'm talking about—for the first time all morning, he's broken eye contact. Now I'll see how he reacts when I drop Ed Diamond's information on him.

"Let's see if I can refresh your recollection," I say. "*The Boatman* was a movie that was filmed in 1979 but was never released, correct?"

"I don't know of any such movie," Bishop says.

"You were credited as the writer and director on *The Boatman* and also acted in it?"

"Objection," Frantz says. "He's testified three times that he doesn't know anything about this so-called movie."

I hardly hear Frantz, have no awareness of Lovely or Janine or the videographer. At this moment, only Bishop and I are present. "I won't be satisfied until I hear the truth, Mr. Bishop. Now, *The Boatman* was based on the Orpheus and Eurydice myth, wasn't it?"

Like pre-programmed automatons, Frantz repeats the same objection and Bishop the same answer to this and each of my subsequent questions, and Janine pounds soft keystrokes into her steno machine and tries so hard not to react that that the cords in her neck tighten visibly, and the bearlike videographer sits forward in his seat as if he were in a movie theater about to watch the hero and villain do battle at last, and Lovely—well, Lovely keeps her head down and furiously takes notes, and that's when I know I'm doing well, because she has no reason to take notes with Janine here pounding out an instant transcript that appears on Lovely's computer screen almost the moment the witness's words are spoken. Questions aren't supposed to tell a story, but that's exactly what lawyers' questions do, as if we were the original postmodernists, spinning out narratives in an unconventional form. My series of questions recount the tale of *The Boatman* as told to me by Ed Diamond. Bishop plays Miles Boatman, an alcohol- and drug-abusing singer-songwriter with middling talent. Boatman loves Eurydice Jones, played by a little-known African American actress named Hildy Gish. Eurydice is a beautiful but troubled cocktail waitress who works at the hardscrabble dive where Boatman performs. She resists Boatman's naive, awkward advances at first but finally gives in when he sings her a love song he wrote especially for her. After a series of torrid love scenes—the sex is supposedly real—Eurydice suddenly and without explanation breaks things off. A broken-hearted Boatman disappears but returns a year later, hailed by a growing number of fans as a mystical poet and prophet who speaks for his generation as Bob Dylan did for his. Boatman now makes music so hypnotic and transcendent that some suggest that, like blues great Robert Johnson, he's gone down to The Crossroads and sold his soul to the devil in exchange for musical genius.

When Miles Boatman returns to town, Eurydice is addicted to heroin. Gish supposedly shot up on screen using real smack. Eurydice has become the mistress of a vicious mafioso, who's in league with a dissolute parish priest in spiritual control over the neighborhood. Boatman vanquishes the villains and, in a montage dream sequence, reveals to Eurydice that he was about to commit suicide when an invisible force led him on a journey down a river that flows through the far side of the universe. The healing waters cleansed him of the cellular contaminants of alcoholism, self-loathing, and suicidal thoughts and gave him the true power of song and poetry. The movie ends with Boatman guiding Eurydice out of her living hell and to the celestial river so that she, too, can be cleansed.

By the time I finish, Bishop looks ten years older. His makeup has congealed with the perspiration on his cheeks and forehead. He's not a man accustomed to sweating.

"Are you a follower of the Church of the Sanctified Assembly?" I ask.

Frantz's neck elongates like a septuagenarian jack-in-the-box. "You've got to be kidding, pal. You and your client's crazy obsession with the Sanctified Assembly has nothing to do with this lawsuit."

"Answer the question, Mr. Bishop," I say.

"I've heard of that organization," he says.

"*The Boatman* was an allegory for the way the actor Bradley Kelly supposedly started his new religion, wasn't it?" I ask.

"I don't know of any such—"

"You don't know of any such movie? Didn't Bradley Kelly himself appear in it? You cast him as the crooked priest."

"How . . . ?" The word is little more than an involuntary whoosh of air out of his vocal cords.

"Do you have something to add, Mr. Bishop?" I ask.

"Ask a question, counsel," Frantz barks.

"I just did," I say.

"Move on," Frantz says.

"But you didn't really cast anyone on *The Boatman*," I say. "Or write or direct the film. Felicity McGrath did, am I right?"

Bishop doesn't answer, but I don't need him to. This isn't about making a record. It's about forcing him to give up.

"Howard Bishop was your father?" I ask.

"I need a break," Bishop says.

"Why don't you answer my question first? It's not a tough one."

"I want to speak to my counsel." He stands, as do Frantz and Lovely. Bishop points at Frantz. "Not you. Just her."

Frantz sits down, sticks his fingers under his necktie, and pulls at it as if he's strangling. His jaw flaps once, but he doesn't speak. Lovely walks outside with Bishop.

"Let me guess," I say. "Lovely pressed your client on the Skanktified Assembly scene in the video game, he refused to discuss it, and you supported him. And now Bishop realizes that Lovely is the one who knows what she's doing. So he's publicly humiliating you, just like he does to anyone else he considers his subordinate." It isn't nice to kick a man when he's down, but sometimes you just can't help it.

"You're grandstanding, not lawyering, Stern."

"Since you're the grandstanding wizard, I take that as a compliment."

"Fuck you," he says. With fists clenched, he gets up walks out the door. I'm tempted to follow him to see whether he avoids Bishop and Diamond or tries to join them.

All this time Janine has pretended to edit her transcript. Now she looks up and says, "Parker, I don't know if your depositions are making me old before my time because of the pressure or are keeping me young because I never get bored."

"Do you want me to hire someone else next time?" I ask.

"Oh, no," she says. "I hate to be bored."

The videographer is working at his laptop. He's a large man, but he says, "I don't like being scared, and this whole thing is getting scary. I mean we're talking about that girl's disappearance and the Sanctified Assembly . . ."

I point to his laptop. "If you don't like to be scared, I assume you're not playing *Abduction!*" After what happened to Philip Paulsen and the Kreisses, my comment is in tasteless humor, but bad taste can sometimes restore your equilibrium, like a bracing splash of ice water.

He visibly shudders. "No way. Too creepy for me. This whole case is."

When my opponents return a few minutes later, Lovely, not Frantz, sits next to Bishop. In the five minutes since we broke, the droopy bags under Frantz's eyes seemed to have sagged another inch. Bishop sets his jaw and fixes his eyes on me with a slight smile that almost makes him seem amused.

"The seating arrangements are up to you," I say. "But only one person can object or participate, and that's Lou, because he made the first objection."

"I'll be handling the rest of the deposition," Lovely says. "Take it up with Judge Grass if you don't like it."

I don't mind giving in on this one. It won't matter. "Back on the record," I say. "Mr. Bishop, Howard Bishop was your father, correct?"

"Correct."

"He was a music lawyer?"

"Yes."

"But he also did business with a man named Carmine Scibetta?"

"At this point I'll object and instruct the witness not to answer," Lovely says. "Violates his right of privacy."

"The name of his father's business associate violates his right of privacy?"

"His relationship with his father is personal," Lovely says. "I instruct him not to answer."

And so she instructs when I ask Bishop whether Carmine Scibetta was an organized crime figure associated in the 1950s with Los Angeles racketeer Jack Dragna and later with the infamous Mickey Cohen, and whether Scibetta, a devout Catholic and virulent racist, was the prime investor in *The Boatman*, and whether he shut down production of *The Boatman* when he learned that the movie was a propaganda piece for a budding cult that sought to promote itself at the expense of the Catholic Church and portrayed interracial romance to boot.

Finally, I abandon the pretext of asking questions. Let them leave if they don't like it. "Here's what happened," I say. "Mr. Bishop, you were early follower of Bradley Kelly and are a current devotee of the Church of the Sanctified Assembly. In fact, you're one of its Covert Vanguard. Felicity McGrath was also Covert Vanguard in 1979, or maybe she was never with you, was just a kid who wanted to make a movie no matter what it was about." I sense that my voice has gotten too loud, my cadence too fast, that I'm pleading a case to a nonexistent jury with too much passion, but I can't help myself. Frantz objects, and then Lovely does too, but I talk over them. Despite my unprofessional diatribe, they don't get up and walk out; it's as if they're enthralled by what I'm saying.

"By 1987, Felicity's career was over," I continue. "At twenty-nine years old she couldn't get a job as an actress, much less write and direct movies. So she went to you, her old friend and colleague, for help. That's why she wrote to Scotty that you had her back, that you were her insurance policy, that you were her free ticket out of purgatory. When you refused to help her, she threatened to go public about *The Boatman*, a Mafia-financed movie showing explicit sex and illegal drug use. Maybe worse, she'd tell the media that you were a shill for the Assembly. You couldn't let that happen. You were building your career on your image as a man with *family values*, as one of the few Christian conservatives in Hollywood. Not only would your career have been over, but more importantly, the Sanctified Assembly's budding attempt to legitimize itself as a mainstream religious movement would have foundered before it began. You're one of their master spies, and they'll stop at nothing to make sure you don't blow your cover. Like the Soviet KGB, the Assembly holds its spies dear. So maybe on your own, maybe on orders from your Supreme Prophet Bradley Kelly, you and your Assembly goons kidnapped and killed Felicity McGrath. And after you abducted her, you drove away in your blue Mercedes-Benz."

The room falls silent. Janine, who almost never shows emotion during a deposition, sighs so loudly that her shoulders rise and fall. Frantz looks down at the table with a hangdog expression, as if his futile objections have depleted him of energy.

"I'll move to strike Mr. Stern's absurd monologue as improper argument," Lovely says. To my shock, she has the hint of a grin on her lips, the look of a chess player who recognizes checkmate three moves before her opponent does. Bishop actually lets out a thin, high-pitched laugh.

"Do you find something funny, Mr. Bishop?" I ask.

"I do, Mr. Stern," he says. "Your vivid imagination. Your silly questions about a movie that never existed, your absurd fairy tale about McGrath. It's hilarious, actually. All you're missing is proof. During this entire deposition, you haven't showed me a shred of evidence supporting what you've claimed. Because you don't have it."

Now I know exactly what Lovely Diamond told Bishop during the break, as sure as if I'd huddled with them in the hall. As a law professor, I taught Lovely that you gain nothing in a deposition by asking questions without using your evidence, because the witness will just recant the testimony and claim a refreshed recollection once the evidence comes to light. So showing the witness the evidence first is usually the best approach. Not today.

I reach into my briefcase and pull out the cast list from *The Boatman*. I hand it to Bishop without having Janine mark it first. "How about this for proof, Mr. Bishop? A document your minions didn't sanitize when they raided the Macklin & Cherry archives."

Bishop skims the document and begins shaking his head like a batter trying to ward off the effects of a beaning. The shakes almost become tremors.

"Where did you get this?" he hisses. His cheeks puff out like an expanding bag of microwave popcorn. He crumples up the cast list and hurls it at me. The piece of paper bounces off of my forehead, just missing my right eye. It feels great. I pick up the paper and unfold it, sliding it back toward him.

"*The Boatman* is a fantasy that you're trying to exploit," he shouts. "This deposition is over. Stern, get out of my building. All of you get out." With surprising agility for a man his age, he springs out of his chair and walks out the door.

Lovely slumps down, her lips parted in lingering shock, her eyelids narrow slits through which she searches for what went wrong. She looks gorgeous.

Frantz seems oddly energized. "Pack up our documents, Lovely," he says. "And don't you ever forget again that I'm the boss and you're just a second-year lawyer who doesn't know what the hell she's doing. I'll be in William's office." Odds are that he'll smooth it over with Bishop. If there's one thing that Frantz is good at, it's schmoozing clients.

Lovely and I wait wordlessly until the court reporter and videographer leave.

"Where did you come up with this stuff?" she asks.

"Attorney-client privilege," I say. "Which is what I'll say if you serve an interrogatory asking the question."

"Is your mother your source? Did she feed you all this bullshit?" Lovely knows about my past, about my mother, though at the moment I wish she didn't.

I give a noncommittal shrug.

She picks up the cast list and reads it over. "Jesus, McGrath's name isn't even on this."

"Doesn't matter. She was the ghostwriter and director. At nineteen, twenty years old, the brains behind the great William the Conqueror. And I will prove it."

"How?"

I have no answer for that. But maybe for the first time since I took this case, I truly believe it. "I'm not going to reveal my strategy to opposing counsel," I say.

"You have no evidence."

"The cast list shows—"

"It shows nothing. It might embarrass my client, but it has nothing to do with the case, which is all that matters."

"What matters is that Bishop dismiss the lawsuit. He can issue a press release saying that he's proved his point and he'll never find Poniard to collect a judgment anyway. Or his PR people can concoct some better excuse. But he should drop the suit for his own good."

"Oh, Parker," she says. "You just don't get it."

"It's you and your client who don't—"

"Billy will never—"

"So he's Billy now?" Jealousy can surge without warning.

"William will never give up. It's not in his nature. He has too much power to be beaten. He'll stop at nothing to . . . and he's in the right. He didn't do what your client says."

"You're right about one thing only," I say. "I do believe that he'll stop at nothing."

CHAPTER 36

Three and a half weeks until the trial begins, and I still don't have a shred of admissible evidence of Bishop's involvement in Felicity's disappearance. Poniard won't budge on revealing Scotty's identity or Alicia Turner's whereabouts or on telling me what these people know. I've gotten so frustrated with my client that I've stopped e-mailing replies or responding to chat requests.

This morning at The Barrista has been hectic—I've been research-ing the law, drafting the trial brief, responding to the other side's spate of motions to keep evidence out, none of which Brenda can help me with—and it gets more frenzied when she comes running out of the storeroom and shrieks, "Parker!" She collides with Romulo, who drops a tray of lattes, the crash of shattering glass resulting in the awkward applause that always follows such a restaurant mishap. Brenda doesn't cower, doesn't apologize, doesn't seem to notice.

"Parker, you'll never guess—"

I hold up my hand, concerned that she's about to divulge something confidential to everyone in the place. She cranes her neck and looks around the room, eyes blinking like a drying-out inebriate becoming aware of her surroundings. The customers and staff are gawking. Only now does she go to help Romulo clean up the spilled coffee and broken glass.

"Oh, my, I'm so . . ." She bends down to help clean up.

"It's OK, I got it," he says, clearly unhappy with my assistant. On the best of days, Romulo and others on The Barrista staff view her pres-ence in the shop as an annoyance.

"Yeah, OK, sorry," she says. "I owe you. Parker, come into the back room with me."

When we're inside the storeroom, she claps her hands and bobs up and down like a joyful nine-year-old who's just unwrapped her biggest birthday present. She gestures toward her computer screen, which shows an e-mail message sent via a website that Philip Paulsen set up to receive unsolicited e-mails about the case. I haven't looked at the site since it launched—not after reading the messages from obsessed Poniard fans, spammers whom Bishop probably hired to flood the system, and kooks who claimed to have sighted Felicity McGrath over the past twenty-five years at locations ranging from an In-N-Out drive-thru in Lodi, California (Felicity was slinging double-double burgers animal-style), to The Borghese Museum in Rome (she was volunteering as a docent). Evidently Brenda has continued to monitor the website.

This e-mail's subject line is "The Queen Ant," and the body reads, "Learn to Act, Stage, Screen, Earn Money as an Extra in the Exciting Entertainment Industry—Taught by a Trained Actress—Echo Park Actors Studio."

"A virus or a Trojan horse," I say. "Bishop's cyber-attack."

"I thought so at first. But then I . . ." She clicks on the link, which spawns a garish website that announces its worth in blaring blue and red oversized printing that has no subtlety, no finesse—a kind of nineteen-fifties discount-groceries ad transplanted into cyberspace. The left side of the page is in English, the right in Russian Cyrillic. Inside the distracting mess of testimonials and puffed claims is the black-and-white photo of a raven-haired, wrinkle-free woman who calls herself Marina Shalamitski.

"Who is she?" I ask.

"No idea. But we have to check her out, right?"

"This is Bishop hacking us. Or if not that, a kook who wants attention."

Her quick half-shrug conveys uncharacteristic impatience. "This woman is reaching out to us. Parker, *please*." She bites her lower lip like an ingénue in a chick flick, and I wonder if it's calculated, because despite what you read in novels, women rarely bite their lips that way.

"Get your things," I say. "We might as well visit Madame Marina."

From the outside, the Echo Park Actors Studio looks as grungy as its website. Located a few miles east of Hollywood, the studio occupies one unit of a dilapidated square gray stucco commercial building across the street from the Los Angeles Police Department's Echo Park division and three units away from Apex Bail Bonds. I expect to meet not an acting teacher but a scam artist promising to make movie stars out of heavily accented Russian greenhorns, desperate dreamers who've fled abuse or boredom or depression, and innocent young bumpkins unaware that this era's true stars appear not in movies but in reality TV shows.

Brenda and I enter into a darkened room that smells like a combination musty gymnasium and patchouli-scented ashram. At the back of the room is a small stage. Folding chairs are stacked against the wall.

The woman who calls herself Marina Shalamitski looks up at us from a collapsible table that serves as a makeshift desk. She's dressed young, in dancer's black leggings and a pink sweatshirt with a silk-screened picture of a green springing deer on the front—the logo for John Deere tractors. The cosmetic surgery can't hide the woman's true age—late fifties or older.

"How may I help you?" she asks without a trace of a Russian accent.

"Parker Stern and Brenda Sica," I say. "We're here ... we're here about the Queen Ant."

There's no sign of recognition. Does she not know what I'm talking about or has all the Botox made even the slightest show of emotion impossible?

I'm startled by the appearance at the stage door of an antiquated man. His bald pate is mottled with liver spots. A fringe of white hair forms a wispy semicircle around his skull, and his goatee looks as if strands of a cotton ball have floated over and stuck to his chin. An irregularly shaped wen bulges from his brow, making him look like a hideous fairy tale troll. He wears hearing aids, and not the modern high-tech micro brand but large, unsightly, flesh-colored buttons. Behind thick bifocals his eyes are so puffy that the lids look glued together. He shuffles over in a walker that gets traction from fluorescent yellow tennis balls stuck on two of the legs.

"Your business isn't with my wife, it's with me," he says in a voice that's shockingly resonant and youthful. And that's how, despite his mask of decay, I recognize him—Clifton Stanley Gold, former Broadway actor, second banana in innumerable fifties and sixties sitcoms, for years top-row middle-square on the TV game show *Hollywood Squares*, and once the preeminent acting teacher outside of New York City. His students included child star Parky Gerald.

There's no way he could recognize me. The last time I saw him I was eleven years old, with a prepubescent voice, smooth cheeks, and blond hair. He'd certainly remember my mother, though. He repeatedly kicked her out of his acting studio—for shouting at him because he gave another actor the lead in a scene from *The Boy with Green Hair*, for showing up drunk to drive me to an audition, and for trashing his teaching methods in front of my fellow students and their parents. The last incident resulted in my expulsion. The memory of her behavior embarrasses me to this day, and I find myself looking down at my hands as if I were still that child and he'd just chided me for ignoring his direction.

"You're here about the e-mail," he says. "I'm Cliff Gold."

Marina puts her hand on his shoulder and says, "What's this about, Clifton?"

"Mr. Stern is a lawyer," he says. "And this young lady is . . . ?"

Brenda introduces herself.

"I represent a video game designer and artist known as Poniard in a lawsuit," I say. "The case was brought by William Bishop, the chairman and CEO of Parapet—"

"We know who William Bishop is," Shalamitski says. "What's that have to do with us?"

"I e-mailed Mr. Stern," Gold says. "I want to tell them some things about Paula McGrath."

His wife grips his upper arm, and not gently. "Clifton, what could you possibly know about some silly lawsuit?"

"I know something about Paula," he says. "They deserve to hear what I know. Marina, leave us alone."

Shalamitski shakes her head. "Clifton, I really don't think you should—"

"We really need to talk to him, miss," Brenda says in a dismissive tone.

"Forgive my colleague's abruptness," I say apologetically, more to seem reasonable in front of Gold than to placate Shalamitski.

"Give us some time," he says to his wife. She reluctantly goes back to her table. Gold gestures toward the folding chairs stacked near the wall. "Mr. Stern, if you'd assist me."

I grab two chairs, Brenda takes a third, and we set them up near the stage. Gold tries to get into the chair without assistance, but he's so feeble that Brenda has to help him.

"I've been following your lawsuit in the news," he says. "My youngest granddaughter plays your client's video game, and I asked her to show me what all the fuss was about. I saw the level that you were just referring to where the Paula character—she's called Felicity, of course, but I call her Paula because that's who she was when she started taking lessons from me as a thirteen-year-old middle-schooler from the neighborhood, exactly my granddaughter's age, incidentally—where the Paula character makes an appeal for help. And the video game character is absolutely right—Paula deserves closure. So with my granddaughter's help I e-mailed you on that website of yours. My granddaughter didn't think I should be too specific with all she's read about in the news, so . . ." He takes a peek over his shoulder. "Besides, I knew Marina wouldn't like it."

Could it be that after all these months, Poniard's attempt to use *Abduction!* to gather information has finally paid off?

"What can you tell us about Felicity's . . . Paula's disappearance?" I ask.

He tells us how "Paula" was the most talented student he ever had, a triple threat who was not only a brilliant actor but also a talented writer and director. He'd wanted her to go to New York and perform in live theater to hone her craft, but she wanted only to work in films and become a mega-star. After they clashed over her career direction, she stopped taking classes. Years after their falling out, she showed up not long after the *Meadows of Deceit* debacle and asked him to help change her image and resurrect her career.

"That was early 1987," he says. "We worked together on and off until she disappeared. At first she seemed serious, dedicated. But then, she started to deteriorate, drinking, maybe worse. A couple of months before her disappearance, she started boasting about this magnificent new movie she was working on, a picture that would not only restart her career but leave a legacy. Very grandiose statements."

Felicity's roommate Natalie Owen said that on the day of the kidnapping, Felicity had mentioned going to a night-shoot for some unidentified film.

"Paula would share no details about this so-called project, would become agitated if I pressed her," Gold says. "But here's the interesting thing. On one occasion—to be honest, the words seemed to slip out inadvertently—she claimed that she was working with Billy Bishop, that he was 'making it all happen.' It didn't make much sense, because Bishop was an A-list producer by then, and there was no way he'd work with box-office cyanide Felicity McGrath."

"We have information that in the late seventies they worked on an unreleased picture called *The Boatman* together," I say. "Maybe Bishop hired her for old time's sake?"

He considers this. "I don't know about *The Boatman* or any other project they worked on in those early days. But they did both take classes from me around that time. Before either of them was anyone. And I shouldn't say this but—" He tilts his head and looks at us, the practiced pause of a gossip who wants to feel that he parted with the salacious information reluctantly—"they often traveled to and from class together, and they played opposite each other in some passionate love scenes. I'm a good teacher. I can usually tell what's acting and what's real. Their body heat was genuine. Paula might have been a good enough actor to fool me, but not Billy."

"Would you testify to that in court?" I ask.

"About their being in my acting class together, of course. About an affair, not on your life. Billy's still married to the same woman, and after all, it's just my educated speculation. I never peered into their bedroom window. But I'm not sure any of this helps you." A stage actor's pause. "Her behavior was erratic in the weeks before she disappeared. As I told you before, she would often come to class drunk or hungover. Other times she was hyperactive. I worried about cocaine. There were a lot of men, I think, though that was nothing new with Paula. I was frightened for her."

"None of that means she wasn't working with Bishop," Brenda says.

"True, but it doesn't make sense," he says. "She claimed to be working with a top commercial producer on a movie that was as confidential as the Manhattan Project. Nonsense. In my view, the entire story was a fantasy, a wish that a troubled mind came to confuse with reality. Their romantic relationship makes that scenario more likely. Paula was reliving her past glory."

"It doesn't matter if it was true about the movie or not," Brenda says. "Bishop denies knowing McGrath."

"Yes, I read that," Gold says. "That's why I came forward. I expect others are frightened. There was a lot of bully in Billy Bishop even back then. I'm too old to be afraid." His jaundiced eyes are glistening. "You know, some speculated back then that Paula picked up those men at that bar, slept with them, and afterwards took her own life. I don't dismiss that. Her obsession with this imaginary movie was manic in its intensity. I realize with the benefit of hindsight that Paula was probably bipolar. During the worst of her mood swings, she could suffer from delusions. She was subject to dark bouts of depression. The disease began to manifest itself in her late teens, I see now, just as she was becoming successful. It was triggered by the untimely death of her mother. It probably explains her remarkable creativity. But in the days before the disappearance, she was ready to crash, and I fear . . ."

Brenda rustles in her seat, half-stands, sits again, and puts her hand on her forehead as if trying to ward off a migraine. "Mr. Gold, she did not commit suicide. There was blood on a pylon. A witness saw . . ." Fortunately, she catches herself before revealing our theory of the case. She's been a true believer from the start. I'm glad, because it counterbalances my ingrained cynicism.

"Murder is certainly a possibility," Gold says. "But you know, murder, suicide—after all these years I don't know which is worse."

"Suicide is worse," Brenda says. "Much, much worse."

I'm not so sure. As horrible as suicide is, there's individual choice. Among the many reasons that murder is abhorrent is that it's so damned unfair. Brenda and I have never discussed this, really haven't talked about anything important beyond the case. You can spend days and nights with a person, but the gaps in what you know are immeasurable.

"Do you have any reason to believe McGrath was involved with the Church of the Sanctified Assembly?" I ask.

"Paula? I highly doubt it. She did not take direction very well and certainly wouldn't take it from a hack like Kelly. I taught Kelly only once and bluntly told him he didn't have talent. Only years later did I learn that I'd disparaged a "divine prophet." But I can't believe Paula would have anything to do with Kelly. Paula was about the art."

"What about Bishop and the Assembly?" I ask.

"Billy Bishop worshipped at the church of Billy Bishop, just as he does now." He thinks for a moment. "With one exception—I think he worshipped Paula McGrath."

Not the answers I expected, at least not with such certainty.

We question Gold for another ten minutes. He tells us that he knows nothing about any of Felicity's surviving friends or family. After Felicity disappeared in 1987, he told the cops what he just told us, even told them that he believed that Bishop and McGrath had had an affair. The cops seemed uninterested.

"Our trial starts in three weeks," I say. "We can arrange to get you to court if you need help."

He glances in the direction of his wife. "I no longer drive, but Marina will take me. Just serve me with one of those . . . what do you call them? So I have to show up by court order, and Marina can't . . ."

"A subpoena," I say. "Of course."

I help him to his feet, and he insists on leaning on my arm and seeing us to the door. When we get there, he asks Brenda to bring him his walker. As soon as she's out of earshot he leans in close to me and whispers, "So glad you're OK, Parky. I've worried about you over the years. A glorious coincidence, don't you think?" With a scrawny hand, he pats me on the shoulder, the same show of approval he'd give when as I child I'd nail a scene.

CHAPTER 37

Ever since Poniard decided to play a dead king of England at his deposition, I've limited our communications. I have sent periodic e-mail updates—"Gorecki depo not productive," "Bishop depo went well," "Document examiners testified as expected"—but don't reply when he asks for more detail. No matter how much he pushes, I will no longer share confidential information, haven't said a word about Clifton Stanley Gold. Poniard needs protection from himself. Brenda keeps reminding me that I have an ethical duty to keep my so-called client informed, so I activate the chat program one last time before the trial and renew a futile plea.

> *PStern*
> *>You need to appear and testify at trial tomorrow.*
> *Poniard:*
> *>LOL, counselor*
> *PStern*
> *>No joke. It's never been a joke. It's the only way to win—you testify
>   what Scotty told you about Bishop, what Alicia Turner told you.*
> *Poniard:*
> *>Alicia didn't tell me anything. I'm protecting her from Bishop*
> *PStern*
> *>Still, the other side has a right to question you about her. And if she
>   does know something that can help, you should share it. We have to
>   prove you had a pure state of mind, that you didn't act with reck-
>   less disregard for the truth when you accused Bishop.*

Bishop is a public figure. In the nineteen sixties, the US Supreme Court held that a public figure can only win a libel case if he proves that the defendant actually knew the statements were false or otherwise acted with reckless disregard for the truth. Even a grossly negligent defendant gets off the hook. It's a pro-defendant standard, one that recognizes only the worst conduct should be penalized when speech is concerned. I hope to prove that Poniard didn't act with reckless disregard for the truth because he truly believed that Bishop kidnapped Felicity because of what Scotty and Alicia Turner told him—whatever that is.

> *Poniard:*
> *>TRUTH is a defense, and what I have said is TRUE*
> *PStern*
> *>We can't show that because there's no real evidence that Bishop abducted Felicity McGrath. Bud Kreiss's statement is double hearsay. And we have nothing else.*
> *Poniard:*
> *>Then we have lost*
> *PStern*
> *>We don't have to prove truth to win. Only that you didn't turn your back on the truth by making the accusations recklessly. I need something, anything, that shows that you didn't really believe your charges against Bishop were false.*
> *Poniard:*
> *>You don't get it. If we do not prove that Bishop took Felicity, it's a loss. Showing that to the world is all I care about. That's why I invited the lawsuit in the first place. INVITED it! Because it was the ultimate way to trap William the Conqueror. All this other legalese is meaningless*
> *PStern*
> *>Winning the lawsuit isn't meaningless. This judge won't rule for us, but the appellate court could if you cooperate. We have to avoid a judgment against you. Bishop wants tens of millions. I'm going into court tomorrow and do my best to get the judge to rule in your favor.*
> *Poniard:*
> *>I do NOT care about winning the lawsuit or about saving myself or about money or millions, meaningless trifles. If Bishop pursues me, I'll melt back into the cybersphere to fight again. I'm a guerilla. I wanted to find out what happened to Felicity, but there just wasn't enough time, Bishop was too powerful this time, he'll be weaker the next time. Know this, Parker Stern, it is not your fault, it is mine, my own act of reckless disregard*
> *PStern*
> *>What do you mean?*
> **Poniard has signed off.**

CHAPTER 38

Caught in a cloud of anti-anxiety med side effects and rising fear, I ride the escalator up to Judge Grass's courtroom, step onto solid ground, and freeze when I see the slithering blur of humanity milling around at the far end of the hall. By waiving Poniard's right to a jury when the case began, I committed malpractice—not technically but because my instincts were poor. Back then, we had the fair-minded Tedford Triggs as a judge, but facts change, even judges change, and I shouldn't have been so shortsighted. Now we're stuck with Anita Grass, who hates me and owes Lou Frantz and won't let judicial ethics get in the way of double payback.

My knees buckle and I stumble, almost falling back down the escalator, but Brenda—was she waiting at the top or did she coalesce out of oxygen molecules?—grabs my wrist and with surprising strength keeps me from falling. She leads me not toward the courtroom but down a side corridor. My legs feel heavy while my head drifts upward, as if the laws of gravity apply only from the neck down. We turn left at the end of the hall, but by then the media has seen us and are in pursuit. Brenda presses an intercom button and announces herself. When the door buzzes, she pulls it open and guides me through.

"I've been here since six o'clock setting up," she says. "I made arrangements with Millie the clerk to come through this way so we can avoid the crowd."

"We should go through the front. The reporters are going to think I'm afraid to face them."

"That's not what you're afraid of, is it?"

"Brenda, it's not ... I just felt a little dizzy when I got off the escalator."

"It's OK. If I had to talk in front of a bunch of strangers I'd be afraid too." She's frowning, but she looks more resigned than worried. She rests a hand on my wrist. "You always come through. That's why Poniard has such faith in you."

I notice her light-gray pinstripe suit, white ruffled blouse, and knee-length A-line skirt. She's backed off on the makeup, not wearing the dark eyeliner.

"You look very professional," I say.

"I bought these at a thrift shop. I've been saving from all my paychecks."

We go through the empty jury room into the courtroom, fortunately avoiding Judge Grass's chambers. I doubt Grass knows that her clerk did our side a favor. Brenda has already set out our pens and papers and notebooks and computers and documents.

The air is stagnant, the artificial fluorescence both too stark and too dim. The functionaries who design these halls of justice go to such lengths to ban natural light and fresh air and traffic noises, as if the outside world were antithetical to fairness. For me, pleading a case was once like performing live theater—more exciting, because what happens in a trial isn't make-believe but art for reality's sake. I was in total control. Since the day three years ago when Harmon Cherry died, I've been lost.

I reach into my pocket, take a Xanax out of a vial, and swallow the tablet dry. With all the practice I've had taking these pills, who needs water? They make me numb, but numb is better than frightened.

While Brenda organizes exhibits, I sit with closed eyes, perform useless breathing exercises, and wait for the meds to kick in. They do, sending me into a near stupor. Now I have to fight to keep my eyes open. Brenda prepares in silence, mechanically, and I have the feeling that we're a couple of morticians preparing for a funeral. After this week, she and I will no longer work together—I don't have a law practice. What will she do for a job? I'll certainly give her a great reference, but I don't know how much weight my word carries. And then there's William Bishop, whose power to disrupt a commoner's life is limitless. Will his vindictiveness keep Brenda unemployed?

I don't really notice the time pass, don't see the courtroom filling up, don't become truly alert again until Lovely Diamond walks into the room, followed by Louis Frantz, who makes a show of holding open the swinging gate for her. Frantz and I nod to each other, more out of reflex than etiquette. Lovely doesn't look my way. Bishop isn't with them, and I doubt he'll show up. A financial emperor like William the Conqueror won't waste his time in a courtroom when there's no jury to impress, when the judge is bought and paid for.

They sit down at their table to the right of me. Courtrooms are small, and no matter the emotional and adversarial distance, in physical distance my opponents are only ten feet away. I turn toward the gallery so I don't have to look at them. The seats are almost full, but something's missing.

"No cosplayers," I whisper to Brenda.

"They're here," she says, tipping her head toward the plaintiff's side of the gallery.

There's no one in costume, and I start to ask Brenda what she's talking about, but then I see—the cosplayers are in the middle row, dressed in street clothing. Banquo is sitting near the aisle, eyes forward. He's gotten a haircut, but his black beard is thicker than ever. He's dressed in a yellow cotton dress shirt too large in the neck and too tight in the biceps. He has his antiquated laptop, the one he brought to the very first court session, perched on his knees, and he's typing into it as though he were a member of the news media. Behind him is the Goth Abe Lincoln, dressed in a coat and tie, and Raggedy Ann Dohrn, in a white blouse and jeans. I can't identify any of the others—they appear so different without wigs and makeup and costumes. Are they the clean-scrubbed group in the row behind Banquo? Courtney isn't here, fortunately—at least, I don't think she is, and suddenly the panic begins to surface through the drug-induced froth of my brain, because that woman sat not more than three feet from me in the coffee shop and I couldn't recognize her. Who's to say she hasn't melded into the gallery?

Brenda taps my arm and tilts her head toward the clerk, who's

sitting rigid in her chair, the phone to her ear—a clear sign that Judge
Grass is about to enter the courtroom.

"Let's win this thing," Brenda whispers. "You can do this, Parker."
It's a sign of her naïveté that she thinks of our lawsuit as some ath-
letic event in which a pat slogan can pump you up so that you'll work
miracles.

The clerk replaces the phone in its cradle, stares intently at the door
to the left of the bench, and with a practiced prescience says, "All rise"
a fractionated moment before the chambers door clicks open. A black-
robed Anita Grass steps behind the bench and says, "Trial in *Bishop v.
Poniard.*" She leans forward, rests an elbow on the bench, and gazes
down at me with a look of motherly concern that seems so genuine and
sincere that it has to be feigned. "We'll proceed. If Mr. Stern is feeling
up to it, that is."

Embarrassed titters ripple through the courtroom, accompanied
in counterpoint by a long, uninhibited guffaw that comes from the
throat of reporter Brandon Placek.

"That's horrible," Brenda whispers. At the adjoining table Frantz
watches me, while Lovely keeps her head down, pretending to read a
document. I will her to stand up and walk out of here, but of course
that doesn't happen—she's all in with Frantz and Bishop. The twin triggers of anger and betrayal release hours of pent-up tension and propel
me up out of my chair.

"The defense is more than ready to proceed, Your Honor," I say. "In
fact, we're looking forward to it."

"Very well," the judge says. "Mr. Frantz, please present your opening
statement."

CHAPTER 39

Frantz half-stands and, keeping his left arm behind his back military-style, deftly buttons his suit jacket with only his right hand, a skill that he's honed through thousands of trials. He glances at me and clears his throat, a surprisingly effective beginning. Only the great Louis Frantz can transform a repulsive bodily reflex into an oratorical flourish. His red and gray paisley tie is much too long, falling four inches below the belt, and there are loose threads in the seams of his light-gray coat.

"May it please the Court," he says. "There's a key question in this case, and it's this—who is Poniard? There's no legal name, no face, no voice, only a fraudulent cartoon character concocted during a deposition in a failed attempt to deceive the Court about who Poniard is. This person who hides behind the name Poniard hasn't bothered to show up at trial to defend himself, so we can't ask him who he is.

"So, who is Poniard? The answer is really quite simple. He's a left-wing radical intent on undermining the United States Government and subverting American culture. He's a cyber-terrorist with the same goals as Anonymous, with its hacks into corporate and government computers, or WikiLeaks, with its release of top-secret information intended to harm America."

Frantz walks away from the podium and faces the gallery. He's one of the few lawyers who could get away with turning his back on the judge, but he's such a commanding presence that it seems perfectly natural.

"In furtherance of his political goals, Poniard targeted William Bishop," he says. "Why? Because Mr. Bishop, a man of impeccable reputation, holds conservative political views, values family, promotes democracy and the capitalist system over the welfare state. Because Mr. Bishop has succeeded, as if that's some kind of crime rather than a badge of honor. With actual malice, Poniard employed his *Abduction!* video game as a weapon of deceit, as a vehicle to publish false and defamatory statements about Mr. Bishop to tens of millions of people worldwide." He spins around and faces the judge again. "But in fact, Your Honor, the accusation that Mr. Bishop had anything to do with the disappearance of Paula Felicity McGrath is a complete fabrication, and Poniard knows it. Such libelous speech cannot go unpunished." Frantz quotes Poniard's most inflammatory statements—supporting cyber-attacks on the Department of Defense in protest of the use of unmanned drones, calling for a war crimes tribunal to try two presidents for failing to close the prison at Guantanamo, announcing that his video games entertain only to undermine the Establishment.

Frantz states unequivocally that William Bishop didn't know Felicity McGrath, that Felicity's letters to Scotty mentioning Bishop don't prove such a relationship. Good—he's propagating his client's lies in open court, and his case will disintegrate if I can show that Bishop and McGrath had a relationship.

Frantz launches into an encomium of Bishop, mentioning his decades-long marriage to a remarkable wife, his devotion to family, his charitable works—his Irene and William Bishop Foundation encourages private charitable donations as a substitute for welfare—and his success in building the most formidable media conglomerate in the world.

"Harm to my client's reputation, Your Honor," Frantz says. "That's what this case is about. And through his video game, Poniard has sullied the reputation of a great man, causing him incalculable damages. So in conclusion . . ."

He points to Lovely, who with a few clicks of her computer launches recorded portions of *Abduction!* on the five monitors placed throughout the courtroom. She shows portions of the first cutscene in which Bishop's two goons violently kidnap Felicity. She displays the bloody animated murder of the Kreisses, after which she projects Poniard's Internet accusations that Bishop committed those murders. She plays the Skanktified Assembly scene, in which the cartoon film director is a rat with William Bishop's face. I wonder if her son Brighton helped compile these clips.

Judge Grass gapes at the monitor like a vindictive high school vice-principal deciding a suitable punishment, and I'll undoubtedly be her target. Those in the gallery watch rapt, the silence punctuated by periodic gasps and shocked giggles that draw an evil eye from the judge.

When the demonstration ends, Frantz says, "Your Honor, this disgusting game speaks for itself. When all the evidence is in, we're confident that you'll find for the plaintiff and award substantial damages not only to compensate William Bishop but to punish Poniard for his unconscionable conduct."

Frantz turns and mugs for the spectators before sitting down. Meanwhile, Diamond has left the image of the rat-like William Bishop on the monitor. It's a ploy—they want my first words to Judge Grass to be a request that they take the image off the screen, thus underscoring its power. I glance over at Brenda, who punches something into her computer, overriding the Diamond-Frantz computer system. The monitors immediately go dark.

"Mr. Stern, your opening statement," the judge says.

When I stand I experience a hiccup of fear, but then I glance at Lovely Diamond and gather myself. Though I've written out the first words of my argument in bold letters so I can read them if the fear muddles my speech center, I don't have to use them, can actually move away from the lectern.

"Your Honor, the law is clear that Poniard's video game *Abduction!* is a work of art entitled to full First Amendment protection, just like a book or a painting or a motion picture. Neither is there doubt that to win this libel case plaintiff William Bishop, a public figure, has a heavy burden of proof. He can't win just by proving that Poniard made false statements about him. No, to prevail, Bishop must prove by clear and convincing evidence that Poniard made false and defamatory statements with reckless disregard for their truth or falsity."

Unlike Frantz, who hammered home the facts, I rely on the law.

Sure, I'd like to prove that Bishop kidnapped Felicity, but Bud Kreiss was my only potential witness on truth, and he's dead. So I'll have to chisel away at Bishop's case by arguing that Poniard didn't intentionally turn his back on the truth when he released *Abduction!*

I outline only the evidence that my opponents know about—the correspondence between Felicity and Scotty mentioning Bishop as an insurance policy; Bishop's unqualified denial that the letters are genuine; my document examiner's unassailable conclusion that they're real; Kreiss's statements about homeless Boardwalk Freddy seeing Bishop driving away in a blue Mercedes with the goons who'd just abducted Felicity; the lost movie *The Boatman*. I don't mention Clifton Stanley Gold, my surprise witness, who'll testify that Bishop and McGrath knew each other.

I glance at Lovely, who's still taking notes. After the trial I won't see her again unless by some improbable quirk of litigation we're again placed on opposite sides of some legal dispute. Harmon Cherry was right—no good comes out of making a lawsuit personal.

"Are you finished with your opening, Mr. Stern?" the judge asks.

Only then do I realize that I haven't just been glancing at Lovely, I've been staring at her. "Yes . . . no, Your Honor," I say. "I just want to conclude by saying that at the end of this trial, William Bishop will have failed to meet his burden of proving that Poniard acted with reckless disregard for the truth."

"Very well," the judge says. "Mr. Frantz, call your first witness."

CHAPTER 40

C aptain Theodore Gorecki, Los Angeles Police Department (Retired), Frantz's first witness, could be a villain in one of Poniard's video games, but what kind? His white 1950s-flattop haircut, porcine head, and pug nose, assembled atop a massive barrel body cloaked in a tight gray polyester suit and extra-short red tie, label him a lug who'll be easily vanquished on cross-examination. But his icy-blue grand inquisitor's eyes leave no doubt he's a dangerous level boss. His history with the police department bears that out—you don't rise to the level of captain without being intelligent, competent, and politically astute. At age seventy-three, he still has the cop's facility for answering every question in an official, commanding monotone that makes him sound objective and reasonable. Except that if you believe Bud Kreiss—and I do—Gorecki isn't objective at all; he's complicit in covering up William Bishop's role in Paula Felicity McGrath's disappearance.

Frantz asks Gorecki about his background, eliciting testimony about quick promotions and important commendations for bravery and service to the community. Gorecki testifies that he was the lead investigator in the disappearance of Felicity McGrath and that the LAPD couldn't identify a suspect. He insists that William Bishop was never a person of interest. He expresses frustration and contrition for not being able to solve the crime. "Sometimes the bad guys get away," he says, shaking his head sadly. All in all, it's a convincing performance.

"In 1987 did you investigate whether William Bishop was involved in the disappearance of Paula Felicity McGrath?" Frantz asks.

"We looked into it," Gorecki says.

"Why was that, Captain?"

"Herman Kreiss Jr., one of our detectives, reported that a source put William Bishop at the scene of the crime. We looked into the report, and it didn't check out. There wasn't a shred of evidence that Mr. Bishop had anything to do with McGrath's disappearance."

Then Frantz surprises me by announcing that he has no further questions. He knows I'm going to ask Gorecki about Luther "Board-walk Freddy" Frederickson's statement that Bishop was at the scene. Most lawyers would have tried to defuse my cross-examination about Boardwalk Freddy by asking Gorecki about it first. What kind of trap have Frantz and Diamond laid?

As soon as I stand, Gorecki gives me his cop's iron stare and doesn't break it. I'm sure Frantz told him about my stage fright. No problem—the fear doesn't affect me when I'm interrogating a witness, maybe because I can hide behind the questions and make the witness the center of attention. I show Gorecki a copy of the 1987 McGrath police report and say, "Mr. Gorecki, you testified on direct examination that you investigated whether William Bishop played a role in Felicity McGrath's disappearance, did you not?"

"Yes."

"But there's no reference to William Bishop in the police report, is there?"

"That's correct, sir. We left it out because we didn't think the information Kreiss provided was credible. The police report is a public document, and it wouldn't have been fair to Mr. Bishop to mention it."

"You were trying to protect Mr. Bishop's reputation?"

"Absolutely."

"Just like you're trying to do now."

"Objection, argumentative," Franz says.

"Sustained," the judge says.

"Would it surprise you if I told you that my side subpoenaed all the department's case files for the McGrath disappearance and there wasn't any reference to Mr. Bishop in any document, public or private?"

"After thirty years on the police force and many years in private security after that, nothing surprises me, sir."

"Why wouldn't any of the field notes refer to William Bishop?"

"The information wasn't credible. Why ruin a man's reputation?" It's Gorecki's first slip-up.

"So you did leave something out of the file to protect Mr. Bishop's reputation?"

"I . . . as I said, Detective Kreiss's information wasn't credible."

"Bud Kreiss was an experienced police detective, right?"

"Yes, sir."

"He'd headed up many murder and kidnapping investigations?"

"That's correct."

"Like you, he received commendations from the department."

"Yes."

"In fact, he received the Medal of Valor."

"Yes."

"The LAPD's highest honor?"

"Yes, sir."

"Awarded for conspicuous bravery or heroism beyond the call of duty?"

"That's accurate."

"You never received the Medal of Valor, did you, sir?"

Gorecki's metallic jaw slackens slightly, and he suddenly looks his age. "I did not, counselor." One way of shaking a professional witness is to challenge his credentials, let his own pride undermine him.

"You agree that in 1987, Bud Kreiss was an experienced decorated cop?"

"I do agree with that."

"Doesn't the amount of detail a witness gives increase his credibility?"

"It might."

"Detective Kreiss gave you a lot of detail about William Bishop's involvement, didn't he?"

"Not that I recall."

"He told you that a man name Luther Frederickson—also known as Boardwalk Freddy—saw two men force Felicity McGrath into a Volkswagen?"

"Objection, hearsay," Frantz says. "In fact it's double hearsay—what Frederickson supposedly said to Kreiss and what Kreiss said to the witness."

"Your Honor, it's only hearsay if I were offering Detective Kreiss's statement to prove the truth that any of what he said actually happened," I say, making an argument Poniard would despise. "I'm not. I'm offering the testimony to show that if Frederickson did make the statement, it bears on whether my client acted with reckless disregard for the truth."

Here it comes—Anita Grass will sustain the objection and keep out my strongest argument. And she does open her mouth to say *sustained*, aspirates the *s*, but there's the sound of computer keys rippling in the media section, and she hesitates. "O . . . overruled," she says.

Frantz falls back into his chair—she's stolen victory from him. I think I know why. Anita Grass is ambitious and certainly not someone who'll be satisfied with sitting on the Superior Court for the rest of her career. She might dislike me, but she also doesn't want to embarrass herself in front of the news media and, by extension, the people who elevate trial judges to the Court of Appeal. Still, from her pained expression, the need to swallow the word *sustained* has made her dyspeptic.

Before she can reverse herself, I ask, "Boardwalk Freddy said he saw two men force Felicity into a Volkswagen, correct?"

"So claimed Bud Kreiss," Gorecki says.

"Freddy said the VW sped away toward the Santa Monica Pier, the same place where blood of McGrath's type was found?"

"If you say so. It's been twenty-seven years."

"Would you have remembered better if you'd filed some notes on it, Mr. Gorecki?"

In my peripheral vision I see Frantz standing to object, but before he does the judge says, "That's argumentative, Mr. Stern. I'm going to sustain my own objection."

I hear Brenda sigh in disapproval, the high whooshing sound perilously close to the word "Jesus." She cannot behave that way. If I can hear her, so can the judge.

"Well, according to Detective Kreiss, Boardwalk Freddy saw a blue Mercedes-Benz pick up the two men who'd abducted Felicity McGrath, correct?" I ask.

"I don't recall, sir. I do know that Luther Frederickson—Boardwalk Freddy—suffered from chronic alcoholism and drug addiction, and was a transient who was prone to make up self-aggrandizing stories."

"And I suppose you don't recall Bud Kreiss telling you that the driver stepped out of the car and went into the backseat and that McGrath's abductors got into his Mercedes?"

"You're right, Mr. Stern, I do not recall that." He's trying to keep his cop-as-witness demeanor, but his right knee has started bouncing rhythmically.

I catch Judge Grass glancing at his moving leg. Let's see if I can worsen the restless leg syndrome. "But you do recall that Boardwalk Freddy identified the driver of the blue Mercedes as the movie producer William Bishop?"

"It wasn't credible information."

I'm tempted to ask him why, but you almost never ask a *why* question on cross-examination because you'll most likely get an answer you don't want. So I ask, "If Boardwalk Freddy was right, William Bishop would've become a prime suspect in the abduction of Paula Felicity McGrath, correct?"

"Objection, calls for speculation," Frantz says.

Judge Grass sustains the objection. Of course she does.

"Shortly after he reported Boardwalk Freddy's sighting of William Bishop, Detective Kreiss was busted back down to patrolman, correct?" I say.

"He was demoted, yes."

"Assigned to the graveyard shift?"

"As I recall."

"To punish him for not covering up William Bishop's role in Felicity McGrath's abduction, correct?"

"Absolutely not, sir. Because we need patrol officers to work late night and early morning to protect our citizens. And Officer Kreiss had lost seniority, so we couldn't very well require others to work those hours."

"He was demoted because he wouldn't go along with your cover-up of William Bishop's role in the McGrath kidnapping, am I right?"

He shakes his head and lets out a mocking snort. "You're not only wrong, sir, you're rude and offensive."

"Well, the pretext for demoting him was that he was having a romantic relationship with a newspaper reporter named Dalila Hernandez, whom he told that the LAPD was looking at a person of interest, correct?"

"It wasn't a pretext," Gorecki says, his lips twisted as if he's fighting back a snarl. "Bud Kreiss had a conflict of interest that arose from his relationship with Hernandez, but that was a very small part of why he was demoted."

When Brenda and I interviewed Kreiss, he claimed his alleged relationship with Hernandez was the *only* reason for his demotion. Again, as curious as I am about the actual facts, I don't ask Gorecki what he means. Instead I ask, "Do you know where Dalila Hernandez is today, Captain Gorecki?" Brenda has spent months trying to find Hernandez.

"I have no idea."

"She's disappeared just like so many other witnesses in the McGrath investigation, hasn't she?"

Judge Grass tosses her pen onto the bench. "Another argumentative question, Mr. Stern. No need to answer that, Captain Gorecki. But please answer this—you said the alleged affair was only a small part of the reason why Detective Kreiss was demoted? What was the primary reason?"

Again Brenda sighs, though Grass has asked a legitimate question that Frantz would've asked on redirect anyway.

Gorecki speaks directly to the judge. It's clear that he's been waiting to give this answer all morning. "Detective Kreiss was demoted because he was an alcoholic. His alcoholism affected his ability to perform his job duties. Before his demotion, he'd undergone extensive counseling and had been disciplined more than once. He was intoxicated while on duty several times in the months leading up to his demotion. To put it bluntly, he and Luther Frederickson were occasional drinking buddies. He was lucky he didn't lose his badge." He turns toward me. "Bud Kreiss's struggles are well documented in his employment file if you want to verify this. So his demotion had to do with protecting the citizens of the City of Los Angeles, not with some imagined cover-up that you've made up to try to get your client out of this mess."

So Kreiss wasn't forthright with us. Now I know why Frantz didn't explore the issue on direct. He knew I'd walk right into the trap.

I glance at my opponents' table. Frantz and Diamond are both leaning back in their chairs with arms crossed, as if they're formerly ravenous diners who've just polished off a prime piece of meat.

"You didn't mention Kreiss's alleged alcoholism in your deposition, did you, Mr. Gorecki?" I ask.

"You didn't ask me about it," he says. "I thought you would, but you dropped it. And it wasn't *alleged* alcoholism, sir."

When a witness hurts you on cross-examination, the short-term goal is to look unfazed, and the easiest way to do that is to ask another question immediately, as though the bad answer was innocuous.

"Mr. Gorecki, you told us earlier that after you left the force you worked in private security," I say. "What was the name of your company?"

"Majestic Security Systems," he says. "I was one of the founders."

Next to me, Brenda starts inputting keystrokes into her computer. We were ready for this.

"Do you still work with Majestic Security?" I ask.

"The company was bought out by a large public company several years ago. I'm still a major shareholder and also a consultant. I retired from full-time work three years ago."

"What's your role in the company?"

"Threat management. Protecting individuals who because of their stature may be likely kidnap victims or targets of stalkers."

"The same kind of work that Detective Bud Kreiss did when he left the police force, correct?"

"In broad strokes, true, but Bud Kreiss catered to a different clientele."

"You mean your clients were richer and more important?"

He shrugs.

"Excuse me for one moment, Your Honor, while my colleague projects something on the courtroom monitors," I say.

"Hurry it up, counsel," the judge says.

The webpage of Gorecki's company appears on the courtroom LED screens.

"Your company Majestic Security Systems was acquired by a subsidiary of Parapet Media Corporation, wasn't it?"

Frantz springs out of his seat with the agility of a man half his age. Good—he didn't do a background check on his own witness. That often happens when the witness is an ex-cop—lawyers, even great ones, believe they're automatically credible.

"Objection! Irrelevant," Frantz says. My question couldn't be more relevant, but Frantz is hoping that his friend Anita will sustain his objection anyway. Even she can't go that far.

"Overruled," she says, sounding almost apologetic. She leans back in her chair and crosses her arms, her lips pressed into a one-dimensional line.

"Mr. Gorecki, was Majestic Security acquired by an affiliate of Mr. Bishop's Parapet Media?" I repeat.

His knee bouncing revs up. He folds his arms across his chest so tightly that his undersize jacket looks as if it might split at the seams. His shoulders and arms are still huge, and from the expression on his face, I'm sure he'd like to use them to snap my spine. "We were . . . yeah, a company very far down the Parapet Media chain acquired us. It's a security company. Mr. Bishop didn't run it, probably didn't know about it."

"I'm sure you're wrong about that," I say.

Gorecki relaxes a moment, and his leg stops bouncing. Not for long.

I nod to Brenda, and she projects the Majestic Security webpage titled "Clients and Testimonials" on the courtroom monitors. Over the next fifteen minutes, I get Gorecki to admit that Majestic Securities represented twenty-two affiliates of Parapet Media Corporation,

Bishop's conglomerate, and that Parapet also referred outside business to Majestic. The inference is clear. As payback for covering up his role in Felicity McGrath's kidnapping, Bishop, upon Gorecki's retirement, rewarded the ex-cop with lucrative security work and ultimately made him a multimillionaire.

I finally let him leave the stand. He lumbers past me on creaky arthritic knees, and for a moment I imagine him as an actual level boss in *Abduction!* whom I've just defeated. He did damage to our case with his revelation about Bud Kreiss's alcoholism, but in the end, I avoided the ultimate trap that Frantz and Diamond laid for me.

Or so I think until Judge Grass says, "Mr. Frantz, call your next witness," and Lovely Diamond says, "Plaintiff calls Luther Frederickson," and up to the stand walks Boardwalk Freddy, looking more like a retired Vegas croupier than a one-time derelict who lived on the rough streets of Venice Beach twenty-seven years ago.

CHAPTER 41

Philip and Brenda searched diligently for Luther Frederickson. When they couldn't find a trace, they concluded that he'd OD'd or died of cirrhosis of the liver, or as Poniard believed, was killed by Felicity's kidnapper to silence him. He was the only known witness through whom I could have proved that what Poniard says in *Abduction!* is true. And that's why no plaintiff's attorney of sound mind would have let Frederickson come within fifty miles of this courthouse. Frantz and Diamond are hardly irrational. But they have a powerful client who's accustomed to getting whatever he wants, and Bishop wants not just victory but vindication. In that way, Poniard and William the Conqueror are alike—they're both rich megalomaniacs who'll listen to no one. Frederickson is here to refute what Bud Kreiss told me.

Lovely stands at the lectern, so close that I can smell her perfume. Without so much as a glance at me, she grips each side of the lectern, squeezing so hard that her fingers turn blue at the tips. I'm not the only anxious lawyer in the courtroom.

Frederickson takes the witness stand and swears to tell the truth. We'll see. He's a tall, thin man with a wiry body and a flabby, pallid face. He's mostly bald, with several strands of gray-blond hair combed over to the side. He has an eighties-style moustache, but it doesn't look old-fashioned because he has a strong chin. His eyes are slightly crossed, which is probably why he tilts his head back and squints at Lovely as if using his longish nose as a gun sight. He's dressed in baggy blue polyester slacks and a red and gray plaid sport shirt that doesn't completely hide an ugly scar that runs horizontally across his chest just below the neck.

"What's your name, sir?" Lovely asks.

"Luther Grant Frederickson. Back in the eighties when I was living on the beach they called me Boardwalk Freddy." He speaks in an even Great Plains twang. He points a hitchhiker's thumb at his chest. "Yeah, that's me, Boardwalk Freddy. I got that name from Officer Bud Kreiss, the Venice Beach beat cop, who later became a detective, you know what I mean? When I was on a bender, he'd holler, 'Get off the board-walk, Freddy!' And the name stuck. Of course, I never left the board-walk." His gap-toothed smile makes him look like an elderly Alfred E. Neuman, the cartoon character from those old *Mad* magazines that Harmon Cherry collected.

Lovely returns Freddy's smile, but hers is as forced as his is genuine.

"Let's slow down, Mr. Frederickson," she says. "What do you do for a living?"

"I'm on disability. Have been for many years. I have vision prob-lems, so I can't drive, amblyopia, a lazy eye they call it, since childhood. I'm a diabetic, other problems, bad back, so I can't work much. Had thyroid cancer, but I'm cancer-free. Sometimes I do people's income taxes, simple stuff, kind of like H&R Block, because back in the day before I moved to San Francisco, I was an accountant for the movie industry. Of course, I was on food stamps after that, and then on the streets. But mostly I can't work anymore."

"You were living on the Venice Beach boardwalk in July 1987, correct?"

You're not supposed to lead your own witness, but there's an excep-tion for background questions, which this is. I stand and object anyway just because Freddy's first rambling answer broke Lovely's rhythm, and I want to see if I can throw her off some more. I'm ready to duck and cover in response to what I expect will be Judge Grass's rebuke for my spurious objection—I used the same technique against her when she and I were trial adversaries—but to my surprise she says, "Sustained."

"It's foundational, Your Honor," Lovely says. "I'm just trying to save time."

"Don't argue with my rulings, Ms. Diamond," the judge says.

Brenda slides a document over to me, a computer printout from a website called Following the Law, one of those supposedly anonymous forums where disgruntled attorneys can complain about judges with impunity. Seven people say that Judge Grass dislikes attractive female lawyers. Of course—she's the girl who didn't get invited to the prom and has exacted revenge ever since. Did Frantz's team fail to discover this tidbit? Or, maybe they did find it. Lovely has dressed more conservatively since Grass became the judge—pants instead of skirts, neutral colors, less makeup. But while Brenda can make herself look plain, Lovely can't. Not to mention Lovely's porn past, which must disgust a repressed feminist like Grass. So Lovely Diamond and I are vying to see which of us the judge dislikes least.

Lovely takes a tension-reducing deep breath. "Mr. Frederickson, where were you living in July of 1987?"

He nods solemnly and proceeds to show that the judge should have allowed Lovely's leading question. "Well, before I was living in Carthay Circle and went up to Haight-Ashbury during the Summer of Love, which was 1967, you know what I mean? I lived in the Haight until it got raunchy and then tried a commune in Mendocino, and after that came apart when some of the founders went capitalist and started selling weed commercially, I moved to Telegraph Avenue in Berkeley, where I lived throughout the seventies, but things were never the same up north after the Stones concert at Altamont, you know what I mean? I was there, and let me tell you, the Hell's Angels were out of control. And after that I moved up to Humboldt County and then Seattle . . ." He spends the next few minutes describing his travels after leaving Seattle and won't stop even though Lovely tries to interrupt him. Eventually, he testifies that from January of 1985 to July or August 1987, he was homeless in Venice Beach.

Listening to the man's ramblings, I realize that had my mother not seen the Celestial Light and instead continued to drink and abuse drugs into middle age, Boardwalk Freddy is the person she'd have become. Some would call it "drug burnout," but that's not Freddy's problem. The fire still burns but erratically, as if fickle winds alternately fan the flame and threaten to extinguish it. I doubt that in her short tenure at the US Attorney's office, Lovely faced a witness as uncontrollable as Boardwalk Freddy Frederickson. From the way Lou Frantz keeps looking in her direction and grimacing, there's no way he saw this coming—which means that Lovely prepared Frederickson for trial on her own and will take the blame if he falters.

"Let's focus on my questions, Mr. Frederickson," Lovely says. "Can you do that?" She's trying to sound warm and ingratiating, but the frustration comes through.

"Sure, I can focus, Blondie," Freddy says. "I do tax returns."

Judge Grass employs an aggressive head turn and a sharp look to stifle the gallery's laughter.

"Mr. Frederickson, in the summer of 1987, did you know who Felicity McGrath was?" Lovely asks.

"Sure did. She was a famous actress and also started hanging around the Tell Tale Bar in Venice."

"When was that?"

"Maybe April, May of 1987. I saw her all the time, because that was my territory, panhandling, sleeping there. Warm sea breeze, fresh air. Sunny California."

"Can you tell us what Ms. McGrath was doing the times you saw her?" Lovely asks.

I object to the question as calling for a narrative, but the judge overrules me.

"Most of the time she was hanging out at the Tell Tale Bar drinking and picking up men," Freddy says. "That was the rumor, because they wouldn't let someone like me inside the bar, you know what I mean? A lot of the street people thought she was a hooker, but I knew who she was from the movies; I thought she was down there working on a film or something, scouting locations and what not. Celebrities didn't hang out in that part of Venice in the eighties. Dangerous place, not like now. Felicity was pretty kind for an actress, like one time she bought me a burger and fries, just out of the blue, you know what I mean? And a few times she slipped me a five-dollar bill. Real sweet kid, so I don't think she was hooking or anything, just lonely, or maybe liked to bang tough guys or something." There's no logic to when Freddy stops talking, the length and content of his answers apparently determined solely by faulty brain chemistry.

Lovely narrows her eyes like a teacher's pet trying to focus on a lecture while a jackhammer breaks up asphalt on the playground. "Tell us about the night of July 23, 1987," she says.

"Yeah, the night of July 23, 1987. I was leaning against the wall of the Pacific Avenue Hotel, in one of the alcoves, trusty shopping cart by my side. I couldn't sleep, been drinking muscatel, which kept me awake, not like the Thunderbird did. It was a warm, beautiful night."

"Were you drunk?"

"Always. And I was probably on something illegal, too."

"If you were drunk or on drugs, how can you remember anything about that night?"

"Felicity McGrath went missing that night. I was maybe the last person to see her. You don't forget a thing like that, you know what I mean?"

"What did you see, Mr. Frederickson?"

"I saw Felicity arrive at the Tell Tale Bar about eight, eight-thirty. Weird, because she hadn't been there for a while, not for weeks, so I was surprised to see her show up. She was dressed to kill . . . I mean, bad choice of words, but real sexy, real beautiful. She was making a big scene before she went inside, flirting with the bouncer, some of the guys on the street, acting like a flighty character in one of her movies or something, though this was real life. Oh, I do remember this—before she went into the bar that night, she kissed a woman, Eunice, who really *was* a whore, working the cheap hotels and bars. Well, Felicity goes inside and stays there for a few hours, and I forget about her and I'm trying to sleep but can't because that bum's vino is burning an acid hole through my intestinal linings, and then about eleven-thirty out of the Tell Tale comes Felicity with these two scary-looking toughs I never saw before. One tall and one short, both with dark curly hair."

"Was she resisting?"

"Nah, she was laughing, giggling, touching them, real flirty. They were putting their arms around her, kissing her, feeling her up. She must've been drunk or high to let them do that in public."

"What happened next?"

"They went to this car and drove away down Speedway Avenue. And that was it, the last I saw of her, you know what I mean? The last anybody saw of her. I told all of it to the cops back then."

"Do you recall what kind of car?"

"I don't recall."

"Do you know who William Bishop of Parapet Media Corporation is?"

"Of course. Your client, William the Conqueror."

More laughter from the gallery, which Lovely ignores. "Did you know who William Bishop was in 1987?"

"Sure did."

"How?"

He launches into a long history of his work experience, how he was once a CPA who'd worked in the movie industry as a production cost accountant. He testifies that he was attached to three of Bishop's movies, though he only saw him on the set a few times.

"Now, on the night of July 27, 1987, did you ever see William Bishop at Venice Beach?" Lovely asks.

"I don't recall that, ma'am."

"And did you ever see Mr. Bishop—?" Lovely stops talking, because Lou Frantz is leaning over and almost imperceptibly shaking his head. Through gritted teeth, he whispers, "Sit down."

I get it. Frantz doesn't like Freddy's answer. He expected an outright *no*, not an *I don't recall*. Frederickson not only rambles; he's unreliable. Lovely has managed to fire the loose cannon that's Boardwalk Freddy Frederickson without the weapon turning on her and her client, but Frantz doesn't want to risk even one more volley. Lovely's cheeks flush pink, but she smiles through the embarrassment and says, "Thank you, Mr. Frederickson. I have no further questions."

"Your witness, Mr. Stern," the judge says.

Lovely gathers up her notes and sits down. She expected a clean direct examination that would eviscerate our best argument, but her examination was anything but clean.

The law is a vulturine profession, and I intend to feed off Lovely Diamond's mistake in bringing this uncontrollable witness to court. For the moment, I'm once again the Parker Stern who existed before Harmon Cherry died, the arrogant gunslinger who would win unwinnable trials, the rising star who believed that pleading a legal case was the most elegant sport of all and that he was its next Michael Jordan.

When I go to the lectern, Frederickson crosses his legs, clasps his top knee with his hands, and waits with an earnest expression. Because this is cross-examination, I, unlike Lovely, can ask leading questions. But I don't start with one. I have nothing to lose with this witness, and that's liberating.

"Mr. Frederickson, how did Ms. Diamond find you?"

"Oh, she didn't find me, I found her," he says. "This buddy of mine from AA, he works at a body shop over in Mar Vista, he's telling me about this video game, the one that your client put out, and I tell him I know something about Felicity McGrath's disappearance, and my buddy tells me about the lawsuit and says he thinks I'm a character in the game, so I say can I see the game, and he says sure, so I go over to his house and he goes on the Internet and shows me the game, and there I am in the first scene, so I called up Mr. Louis Frantz's office, and they put me through to Ms. Diamond, and I tell her I want to sue just like William the Conqueror did, you know what I mean?"

"Let me get this straight," I say. "You called Mr. Frantz's office because you want to sue Poniard?"

"Yeah, like I told you, my buddy from the body shop—"

"Mr. Frederickson, please stop," I say. It's a courtroom bark, just this side of civil, as nuanced as delivering a line in a stage play. It works—he stops talking.

"Objection," Lovely says. "The witness should get to finish his answer."

"Mr. Stern is controlling his witness," the judge says. "Something that you should learn how to do, counsel."

Lovely glares at the judge, her gray eyes iceberg-cold.

"And you, Mr. Stern," the judge says. "If you use that tone of voice in my courtroom again, I'll sanction you."

Frederickson, who's been watching the interplay like a tennis spectator who doesn't quite understand the game, says, "Should I finish my answer?"

"No!" the judge and I say simultaneously.

"Listen to my question, sir," I say. "Can you do that?"

He nods, for the moment compliant.

"Why do you want to sue my client?" I ask.

"I want to sue for libel because that video game makes me look like a bum!"

Even the judge laughs at this answer, as does Frantz. Only Lovely doesn't smile.

"Did they agree to represent you?" I ask.

"Didn't say yes, didn't say no."

"They wanted you to testify in this case first, am I right?"

"Yeah, something like that."

"Stringing you along so you'll testify the way they want, don't you think, Mr. Frederickson?"

Lovely objects, but before the judge can rule, I say, "Let's move on to something else. You knew Detective Bud Kreiss very well back in 1987, didn't you?"

"Sure."

"A fair man? Told you to get off the boardwalk but never made you leave?"

"Yeah, he was a good guy. Especially for a cop."

"Do you think he was a liar?"

"No, he was a straight-up guy."

"Was Detective Kreiss lying when he reported that you said you saw the two men from the Tell Tale Bar forcing Felicity McGrath into a Volkswagen Rabbit and then saw the two men leave with William Bishop?"

He uncrosses his legs and straightens up in his chair. "I don't remember anything like that."

"That's not what I'm asking you, sir. I'm asking whether you think Bud Kreiss was lying when he said those things."

"Objection, hearsay. Calls for speculation," Lovely says.

"Sustained," the judge says.

"I should be allowed to cross-examine this witness on his opinion about Bud Kreiss's veracity," I say.

"It's speculation, counsel," she says. "Move on, unless you're finished with the witness."

I get as close to the witness as I can without letting go of the lectern. No matter what you see on TV, you can't approach a witness without the judge's permission, and there's no way that Grass will let me get close to Frederickson. "Did you or did you not see the two men who were leaving the Tell Tale with Felicity McGrath force her into a car?"

"I don't remember, sir," Frederickson says. He's suddenly not the clown he's been all afternoon. He's uncrossed his legs and is sitting forward, his expression solemn, his thick lips pressed together, a church worshipper determined to catch every word of the sermon.

"And did you or did you not see William Bishop drive up in a Blue Mercedes and leave with those selfsame men?"

"I don't recall that."

"Well, you told Detective Bud Kreiss that's what you saw shortly after Felicity McGrath went missing, didn't you?"

"I . . . I don't remember what I told Bud Kreiss."

"So you might have told him that you saw Bishop leave with the men who took Felicity?"

"No, I . . . I don't recall. I was a drunk, a heroin addict, back then, you know what I mean?"

"Well, didn't you tell Ms. Diamond during direct examination that you'd never forget that night because that's the night Felicity McGrath was taken?"

"Objection," Diamond says. "The record speaks for itself."

"Sustained," the judge says.

"Oh, come on, Your Honor," I say. "That's not even a valid objection. And this is cross-examination and, as you said, a court trial."

"Don't push me, Mr. Stern," the judge says. "And hurry it up. Let's move this case along."

I hack away at Frederickson for another ten minutes, trying to get him to concede that he might have told Kreiss that Bishop was at the scene. I explore the Sanctified Assembly angle, hoping that he rehabbed at one of the clinics that the Sanctified Assembly runs to "cleanse the cells of contaminants" that lead to alcohol and drug addiction, facilities that serve as recruitment centers to build the Assembly's membership. Frederickson insists that he's only been to Alcoholics Anonymous, even offers to show the court his chip. I ask him whether he knows Ted Gorecki, whether Gorecki strong-armed him, and though he refers to Gorecki as The Gorilla, he denies that anyone threatened him if he told the truth. As for his own disappearance in 1987, he claims that the publicity surrounding Felicity put the fear of God in him, set him out on his long road to recovery. With each question he hardens his position. He's a lot tougher than he seems. You have to be tough to survive what he has. So I try another approach.

"Mr. Frederickson, if you'd told Detective Kreiss that you saw William Bishop at the scene of Felicity's kidnapping, would you have been lying?"

"I . . . I don't know."

"Did you lie to an LAPD detective back in 1987?"

"I wouldn't . . . I don't remember much. My memory, a tippler's fog they call it, you know what I mean? I was maybe confusing it with those other times, when . . ." He catches himself, but too late.

"What other times, Mr. Frederickson?"

He glances sidelong at Lovely.

"Ms. Diamond can't help you, Mr. Frederickson," I say. "What other times?"

He sits back and clamps his jaw shut. Brenda scribbles something on a Post-It and hands it to me, and when I read it, I ask her question immediately.

"You mentioned earlier that you thought Felicity McGrath might be down in Venice filming a movie. You saw William Bishop working on that movie with her, didn't you?"

He gapes at me as if I have clairvoyant powers rather than a smart administrative assistant with good instincts.

"There were a couple of times when . . . early on where I thought Felicity and a guy who looked like William Bishop came down to Venice together."

I would've expected the media's keypads to click in excited response, for the spectators to rumble in shock, but the courtroom falls silent, as though everyone must calibrate their brains to absorb this information. Not only has Boardwalk Freddy provided evidence that William Bishop and Felicity McGrath knew each other, but he's placed them together. Which means that Bishop has lied all this time. Better yet, I've exposed the lie through his own witness.

"What else did you see?"

"Felicity and the Conqueror went into the Tell Tale, came out, looked around," he says.

Lovely pops up, a reflex, and because she has no grounds to object she tries to save face by saying, "Your Honor, I'd ask that the witness refer to my client as *Mr. Bishop.*"

"Oh please, Ms. Diamond," Judge Grass says, her lips turned down in judicial disdain.

Lovely sits down. She's only helped underscore the power of Freddy's testimony. I don't feel sorry for her, not one bit, and the absence of sympathy makes me exceedingly sad.

"Go on, Mr. Frederickson," I say. "You were telling us about Felicity and the Conqueror."

"Yeah, both times when I saw them together, Felicity was carrying what looked like—it was early 1987 and what did I know?—but it looked like she was carrying some kind of miniature movie camera, pointing it everywhere, like she and Bishop were working together on a picture or something. Like a home movie, not a movie movie that you'd see in theaters. But it wasn't one of those old Bell and Howell cameras I had when I still lived with my family and I took silent movies of the wife and kids, and we . . ." he shrugs and holds his shoulders up for a while, as if the upward motion will squeeze the nostalgia out of his brain. "Anyway, Felicity's camera was more modern, you know what I mean? She'd try to hide it, like that old show *Candid Camera*, but I saw her with it, saw her take it inside the bar. Bishop was in disguise— baseball cap, sweatshirt, jeans—but I knew it was him. Maybe that's what I told Bud Kreiss, instead of what you said I told him. Maybe." He lowers his head and lets it fall to his chest, and for a split second I fear he's dropped dead, that my cross-examination killed him. But I'm not *that* good.

"No further questions," I say. This couldn't have gone better, and I silently celebrate until I realize that there's something not right about his testimony. I've always thought that if Bishop kidnapped McGrath, he did it to keep her quiet about *The Boatman* years earlier, that she was blackmailing him. If that's what happened, why would they be hanging out at the beach together taking pictures?

When Lovely half-stands to ask questions on redirect, Frantz places his hand on her arm and almost forcibly pulls her back into her chair. "Nothing further," he says.

"We'll recess until tomorrow morning," the judge says.

I expect the cosplayers to stand up and cheer, but they file out respectfully with the rest of the gallery. Banquo doesn't look at me until he gets to the door, but then he stops and gives me a solemn nod. Every woman in the gallery starts to resemble Courtney, and yet I don't think she's here.

"Omigod, omigod, omigod," Brenda says under her breath.

One of Harmon Cherry's favorite sayings was *Pigs get fed, hogs get slaughtered*. It got so that the associates would roll their eyes when he said it—behind his back of course. He credited the words to his father, Harry, who got them from who knows where. William Bishop has always been a hog. It's high time he got slaughtered.

CHAPTER 42

Poniard:

>*@BrandonPlacekTinseltown just tweeted "Abduction! trial shock: witness puts Bishop/McGrath together shortly before her disappearance. Witness denies seeing abduction; is he lying?" It's all over the internet, on social media*

Poniard:

>*Answer me, Parker Stern. You've had plenty of time to get back from court and check your computer. I waited an hour after court ended and another 30 minutes to reach out to you. LA traffic isn't that bad*

Poniard:

>*All reporters on Twitter are unanimous, news stories coming in, they think Boardwalk Freddy helped our side, that Lovely Diamond blew it, you were strong. You exposed William the Conqueror Bishop as the liar we know him to be*

Poniard:

>*Come on Parker Stern, I just want to Congratulate you and get your thoughts on tomorrow*

Poniard:

>*???*

Poniard:

>*???*

Poniard:

>*OK, I get that you're pissed at me. I know I've been a difficult client . . . but I've only done it to get to the truth, and I am not against you. I never have been*

―ɱ―

Brenda wants us to take a belated curtain call through the court-room's front entrance this morning, but Harmon Cherry would never allow premature celebrations, and neither will I. She assumes that one good day in court will lessen my stage fright, but it's just the opposite—yesterday we had nothing to lose, and today we do. The fear that I've felt these past years has merged with my cells. Sometimes, like yesterday, it will remit spontaneously, but that's emotional fool's gold, because it will return.

Still, I walk into the courtroom this morning clear-headed and on steady legs—until I see William Bishop and Lovely Diamond sitting at counsel table, reviewing my handwriting expert's report. I lean against the edge of the table to steady myself, pretending to survey the courtroom. The Conqueror looks like he's spent the past few weeks tanning and like he had a recent appointment with a sculptor to style his flawless gray hair. He and Lovely are whisper-distance away from being cheek to cheek, his left hand resting on her back between the shoulder blades as if they're dancing some sort of attorney-client waltz. She glances up when Brenda and I put our things down but dismissively goes back to reading the document. Is it my imagination, or does she lean in closer to Bishop?

The click of the front door lock startles me, though it isn't even that loud. Lou Frantz walks in, his suit coat flung over his shoulder as if it's the end of the day, not the beginning. The bailiff fends off the media and locks the door again. Frantz's open-mouthed grin makes him look like a pit bull deciding whether to snap.

"How're the jangly nerves today, Stern?" he says.

"Much better now that I remember it's only you I have to go up against, Lou," I say.

"Just a heads-up—I'm handling the witness today. Good luck on getting your objections sustained." He goes over and sits with Bishop and Frantz.

After five minutes pass, the bailiff unlocks the doors and lets first the media and then the general public in. People rush inside and vie for the best seats as if this were some discount white sale at a cut-rate department store. Yesterday's cross-examination made the trial a hotter ticket than it already was—that, plus the chance to see William the Conqueror testify live. Only minutes before we're scheduled to start, the bailiff has to eject two courtroom regulars who start shoving each other in a dispute over who gets to sit in the front row. The cosplayers, again dressed in everyday casual, find the same seats on the plaintiff's side. Still no Courtney as far as I can tell. Again, Banquo barely acknowledges me. One would think that he and his cohort were rooting for Bishop.

Among the spectators racing for seats are Ed Diamond, who's holding the hand of a wiry child wearing blue jeans, a gray UCLA football T-shirt under an unbuttoned blue-and-white-striped flannel shirt, and Nike sneakers. The boy's medium-length blond hair is styled in a helmet shape with long bangs that extend to just above the eyebrows. It's a haircut that you'd see on a child actor, which this kid could be with his good looks and expressive blue-gray eyes. It must give Lovely comfort that the boy looks just like her and not like his anonymous sleaze-ball father. They're not experienced courtroom watchers and so are about to lose the chance to find seats. I catch Ed's eye and point to two empty seats in the first row right behind me.

Once they've laid claim to the seats, the boy stands up and waves, trying to get Lovely's attention, but she's focused on a legal brief and doesn't look up. Her obliviousness annoys me, maybe because she so bluntly told me I wouldn't be good for the boy. I reach over and shake Ed's hand.

"Welcome to my world," I say.

"We're here to support my daughter, not you, Park . . . Parker." His smirk reveals that almost calling me *Parky* wasn't a slip of the tongue. Needling is a bodily function with this man. He puts his head on the boy's head. "This is my grandson Brighton. Brighton, this is Mr. Stern."

"I know," the boy says. "Stern is Poniard's lawyer."

"It's *Mr.* Stern," says the man who a moment ago almost called me *Parky* in public.

I extend my hand to the boy, though I don't know if that's the proper way to greet a ten-year-old. I haven't spent much time around children, didn't have a normal childhood myself. He takes my hand and pumps it up and down once, keeping his eyes focused on my ribcage.

"A pleasure meeting you, Brighton," I say in a stilted tone that I don't use with adult strangers.

He glances at Lovely as if to verify that she isn't watching. "I love Poniard's games. They're awesome. You know Poniard, right? I mean I know you know him, but do you *really* know him? Because my *mother* says you don't really." He says the word "mother" as though it's a distasteful medication.

"Don't be rude, kid," Ed says gruffly. "Mr. Stern has more important bovine to broil than us two insignificant bulls."

Brighton giggles and then looks up at me and says, "Sorry for being rude."

"Apology accepted," I say. "And to answer your question, your mother's right. I don't know Poniard. He's a genius, and no one really knows a genius."

Lovely finally looks up at the gallery, and when she sees us, slams the document down on the table and comes over. Though I'm no more than two feet away from her, I feel less present than a dust mote floating in the stale air.

"We talked about this, damn it," she says in a harsh whisper that draws more attention than if she'd spoken in a normal voice.

"This'll be more educational than anything he could learn in that academy for spoiled brats," Ed says.

Brighton smiles at her hopefully. "We're here to give you—what did Ed call it, to lend you *moral support*?—after your bad day yesterday." When he realizes that I, her opposing counsel, could hear him say that, he makes it worse by covering his open mouth with his hand, a similar though less exaggerated version of one of my signature movie moves when I was Parky Gerald.

"You're dragging me down by being here, boy," she says in an awful serpentine whisper. "Go to school and let me do my work without worrying about you."

The boy lowers his head. I'm sure he'd like to hide so no one can see his embarrassment, but the courtroom is full.

I shake my head in disapproval, which causes Lovely to half-spin and face me. "This is none of your goddamned business."

"It's just that you sounded exactly like my mother." I couldn't have said anything more disparaging. Lovely and Ed both know how Harriet mistreated me.

"You don't know what you're talking about," Ed says. "Lovely's a great mother."

"You're right, I don't know what I'm talking about," I say. "But whose fault is that?"

A mortified Brighton sits down, lifts his feet onto the seat, and tries to curl into himself like a frightened pill bug. Ed puts his arm around him. Lovely is about to snap back at me, but the clerk calls the courtroom to order. Lovely glares at me one last time and hurries back to her side of the table.

Only then do I notice what I haven't been noticing—the stage fright that had been triggered by seeing Lovely and Bishop together has subsided. Is this respite as simple as not wanting to embarrass myself in front of Lovely's father and son?

Anita Grass walks in and says, "Do you have a witness, Mr. Frantz?"

"The plaintiff calls the individual known as Poniard," Frantz says. He waits for the buzz to die down, checks his watch, and waits some more. He sighs and says, "I guess we'll have to settle for Poniard's deposition because he doesn't dare show his face in these parts."

Lovely presses some buttons and launches artfully edited video segments of Poniard's deposition. The spectators ooh and ah at how real the King Richard III computer graphics look. Judge Grass focuses not on the graphics but on Poniard's attempt to deceive the court and on his refusal to testify about Felicity's daughter Alicia Turner and the mysterious 'Scotty.' When the video presentation ends, she says, "Mr. Stern, give me one good reason why I shouldn't enter judgment against your client for perpetrating a fraud on the court and refusing to answer relevant questions."

"I don't condone what my client did," I say. "But his artifice wasn't successful, and there's been no prejudice to the other side. Your Honor can draw whatever inferences you think best about Poniard's credibility, though I chalk his behavior up to immaturity. But to decide this case on a procedural technicality would be unjust, especially in light of what happened yesterday."

I notice Frantz whispering in Bishop's ear and Bishop vigorously shaking his head no. Frantz shrugs and says, "I guess this is one of the few times that Mr. Stern and I agree on something. Mr. Bishop, too, wants this case decided on the merits."

So despite yesterday's debacle with Frederickson, Bishop still wants not simply to win but to prove he's right.

The judge lifts her eyebrows into twin arches of incredulity and says, "Go ahead, Mr. Frantz. It's your case to try."

Frantz uses the next forty-five minutes to examine two witnesses about how Poniard's video game actually damaged Bishop's reputation. They're legally unnecessary—you don't need a witness to prove that *Abduction!*'s allegations of kidnapping and murder were harmful—but surprisingly effective.

Frantz's first witness, Father Ernesto Martinez, also known as the Celebrity Priest because he stars in his own reality TV show, testifies that he has serious doubts about whether his church should accept Bishop's contribution to build a new school that would bear Bishop's name. Through him, Frantz brings out Bishop's philanthropy and religious devotion, in that way undermining my claim that Bishop is a devotee of the Church of the Sanctified Assembly—the Catholic Church has strongly condemned the Assembly.

As Frantz predicted, Judge Grass overrules all my objections, supposedly because "there's no jury and I know the law, I can sort out the evidentiary issues later, so stop wasting my time, Mr. Stern." That doesn't stop her from sustaining his objection when during cross-examination I say, "Don't you agree, Father, that someone acting as an undercover agent for the Sanctified Assembly would feign devotion to another religion?"

The second witness is a Parapet Studios employee who works as a techie in the post-production department. Though he's actually in his late-twenties, he looks like he just got out of high school. As soon as he takes the stand he begins exhibiting symptoms that I know well—quivering hands, halting speech, flop sweat. He testifies that he's an inveterate gamer, a fan of Poniard—he corrects himself to say a *former* fan—who began playing *Abduction!* when the game first appeared online. He says—actually stammers—that when he saw the opening cutscene depicting Felicity's kidnapping, he played the clip for his coworkers. Before each answer, he shifts his eyes and looks sidelong at Bishop, who with arms crossed gazes at the back wall. Bishop has clearly ordered this man to atone for his sins by coming to court and testifying under oath that he believed—but only for a moment—that his boss of bosses was a murderer. I don't bother to cross-examine the poor guy.

Then Frantz stands, buttons his coat, tugs at his sleeves, half-turns and winks at the gallery, and announces in his divine baritone, "The plaintiff calls William Maxfield Bishop."

Bishop stands with that elegant posture, all the more impressive because most men his age hunch over from the weight of the years. He springs up to the witness stand, where he faces the clerk and raises his right hand before she asks him to. In reply to whether he swears to tell the truth, his "I do" is loud and unequivocal. Without being asked a question, he's taken ownership of the room, just like he takes ownership of everything else. Anita Grass smiles a respectful, nonjudicial smile. Why not? Bishop has unlimited wealth and controls much of the media and so could advance her career.

Over the next two hours, William the Conqueror, with Frantz as his de Beaumont, makes the courtroom his Hastings, using lies as his arrows and charisma as his sword. He gives a long and detailed account of his life, leaving out the fact that his father, Howard Bishop, was an LA crime boss. He lists his charitable works, describes his enchanted family life and his forty-year marriage in the face of Hollywood temptation. And then to the merits:

"Did you know Paula Felicity McGrath personally?" Frantz asks.

"Absolutely not."

"What about the letters that Felicity wrote to 'Scotty' mentioning you?"

Bishop shrugs his broad, square shoulders. "I didn't know those people and don't have a clue why they would mention me, unless it was because I was a successful producer whom they hoped to meet. In this town, people turn pipe dreams into close personal relationships."

"What about Luther Frederickson's testimony that he saw you and McGrath together?"

"Sadly, the man's mind must have suffered from the alcohol and substance abuse. Never heard of the Tell Tale Bar, never hung out in Venice."

Frantz even asks about a topic I thought he'd avoid at all costs. "Did you work with Ms. McGrath on a movie called *The Boatman*?"

Bishop gives a disdainful chuckle perhaps gleaned from those old acting classes. "Of course not. But when Mr. Stern asked me about that movie at my deposition, it sounded familiar. Since then, I remembered that it's some silly Hollywood movie myth, a film that never existed."

"What about the document that purports to be a cast list for *The Boatman*?"

"Documents can be fabricated very easily these days."

And the final act of this staged fairy tale: "Mr. Bishop did you have anything to do with Paula Felicity McGrath's disappearance?"

He leans forward, keeping his upper body straight, his face earnest and sad. "Absolutely not. That's a fantasy made up by a madman for his own political reasons. This Poniard fellow is nothing but a terrorist who's spread the basest of lies to the world. And he's injured me, Mr. Frantz. Despite my assets and my past successes and whatever good works I might have done, he's damaged my reputation with my friends and family and coworkers and the public. It's an assault, but unlike a physical assault, I couldn't hire security or build fences to shut out the danger. I could heal from a physical assault, but I'll never get over this. It hurts, Mr. Frantz. It hurts."

After this last answer, Bishop removes his horn-rimmed glasses and dabs at his eyes with a cloth handkerchief that he pulls from his pocket. The Conqueror is a far better actor than Clifton Stanley Gold gives him credit for. I glance over at Lovely Diamond, whose own eyes have misted over. Is she part of the show, too? Judge Grass is nodding her head in sympathy.

"Incredible," Brenda says under her breath.

Behind me, a child's voice says in a loud whisper, "She's winning again, right, Ed?"

Frantz says he has no further questions.

As soon as I'm on my feet, I ask, "Mr. Bishop, are you now or have you ever been a member of the Church of the Sanctified Assembly?"

"Objection," Frantz says. "Violates Mr. Bishop's right of privacy. It's offensive to ask a man about his religion."

"Sustained," the judge says.

"Are you aware, sir, that the penalty for perjury in the state of California is a felony punishable by a maximum of four years in the county jail?" I ask.

Bishop keeps his body still, doesn't even blink. Only his mouth moves. "Whatever it is, it's not relevant to me, Mr. Stern, because I've told the truth."

"Last question, Mr. Bishop," I say. "Where's your wife?"

"Pardon me, sir?" he says, twisting his shoulders as if trying to loosen a kink in his back muscles. For the first time this morning, he's nonplussed.

"I asked you, Mr. Bishop, where your wife is. Because if you have this wonderful marriage, wonderful family, if you've suffered such grave harm at the hands of my client, why isn't your wife of forty years here to support you? I'd think she'd be in the first row right behind you. Where are your children and grandchildren?"

It doesn't bother me that the judge sustains Frantz's shouted objection. All I care about is that the reporters are still pounding on their electronic devices.

"Nothing further, Your Honor," I say.

When Bishop steps down, Frantz announces in a grandiose tone that the defense rests.

"All right, Mr. Stern," the judge says. "Be prepared to put on your case after the lunch break."

I turn and look out at the gallery. My key witness—my only witness—isn't here in court. My imploring eyes fall on Ed Diamond, who's still sitting in his chair. He knows what I'm asking, because he shakes his head and mouths the words, "No fucking way, Parky."

CHAPTER 43

I labor in the empty juror's room while Brenda runs to the courthouse cafeteria to bring us some lunch. As she did yesterday, she returns with an assortment of inedible fare—an overripe banana that's more black than yellow, a cold roast beef sandwich with wilted lettuce on desiccated whole-wheat bread, a carton of low-fat blueberry yoghurt that's a month past the expiration date, and an extra-large cup of bitter drip coffee. The anti-anxiety meds have destroyed my appetite, so I take only the coffee, but Brenda insists that I eat something, virtually force-feeding me some of the sandwich. She swallows a few spoonsful of yoghurt without enthusiasm. Neither of us dares touch the banana. We don't talk about this morning's testimony. Especially in this age of glitz and celebrity and meaningless sound bites, image can trump the truth, and that's what happened when Bishop usurped control of the courtroom and through his kinetic personality single-handedly undid the damage that Boardwalk Freddy did to his case. So we go over our direct examination of Clifton Gold and hope that his wife Marina really will get him to court in the next few minutes.

Outside in the courtroom, there are footsteps and the creaking of folding chairs and voices that multiply and rise and fall and comingle so that individual conversations are indiscernible. It's the sound of a matinee audience returning after intermission, formal and awkward before the show started but now relaxed and confident. I open the door slightly and peer into the courtroom. He's here—Clifton Stanley Gold, dressed in an elegant gray silk suit and white turtleneck. He's supported on one side by an elegant black beech-wood cane, and on the other by his wife Marina, who in her vanilla silk blouse and black slacks would look very nice but for the vicious scowl on her collagen-enhanced lips. I go over and take Gold's hand, a soft touch rather than a handshake, because he seems so brittle I worry that even the slightest squeeze will break his bones.

"Thanks for coming," I say.

He bows slightly. "In the words of Aristotle, 'At his best, man is the noblest of all animals; separated from law and justice he is the worst.' I have a duty to tell what I know."

"Thanks for bringing him," I say to Marina.

Her indelible scowl deepens. Without a word, she crosses her arms and, diva-like, turns her back on me.

Brenda takes Gold to the assistant's bench immediately behind us so that he doesn't have to walk far to get to the witness stand. Ten minutes before we're supposed to start, Bishop and Frantz come into the courtroom, smiling as if they'd just topped off nine holes of golf with a country-club lunch. Bishop doesn't look our way, so I don't know if he notices Gold, much less recognizes him. Lovely follows thirty seconds later, but she's not smiling. Right behind her are a sheepish Brighton and a recalcitrant Ed Diamond. Ed and Brighton take the same seats on my side of the courtroom.

At one twenty-nine, the courtroom doors open, and a tall man walks in. It takes me a moment to recognize him as Nate Ettinger. He's again dressed like the professor he is, in a camel-hair coat, navy-blue slacks, powder-blue cotton shirt, and a red bow tie.

I nudge Brenda. "What's he doing here?"

"No idea. But now you can call him as a witness. Didn't you once say that you don't have to subpoena a witness who shows up in court?"

She's right on the law but not on strategy. "It's never going to happen. He's so scared he'll testify to anything just to please Bishop."

"I disagree."

"Fine, but I'm the one with the law degree."

She shrugs, but from the blasé pirouette that follows, I can tell that it was a dismissive, not a contrite, shrug.

Millie the clerk walks in, followed by the judge, who nods at me as soon as she takes the bench.

I go to lectern, but instead of addressing the judge, I look at Bishop. "The defense calls Clifton Stanley Gold."

Because the ceiling lights are reflecting off Bishop's lenses, I don't actually see his eyes widen, but I know they have because the black frames move visibly up and back and stay there until his jaw slackens. As Brenda helps Gold circumnavigate the boxes and tables and desks that pose hazardous obstacles on his way to the witness stand, Bishop whispers to Frantz, his mouth moving like a manic auctioneer's.

"I object to this witness," Frantz said. "We received no notice at all that he was going to be called."

"Is this true, Mr. Stern?" the judge asks.

"Yes, Your Honor, but we found him about the time plaintiff found Luther Frederickson, who wasn't disclosed to us and yet who was allowed to testify."

She shakes her head. "Mr. Stern, I don't think—"

A lawyer should never interrupt the judge, but our case turns on this moment. "The timing doesn't matter anyway," I say. "This witness is being called to impeach Mr. Bishop's testimony this morning, and under the rules I had no obligation to disclose him."

She takes a breath to speak but thinks better of it. She shuts her eyes for a moment. "Very well, counsel. But the testimony better be solely for impeachment." She glances over at Frantz apologetically.

Meanwhile, Gold has completed his arduous journey to the stand. He was a slight man in his prime, and with the shrinkage from age, his head barely clears the railing. I can see only his nose, his thick bifocals, the ugly growth on his brow, and his mottled bald skull with its dried-dandelion fringe. But when he swears to tell the truth, his voice fills the room.

The gallery is silent at first. Most people don't recognize Gold's face or even his name—he hasn't had an acting role in twelve years and isn't wearing the light-brown toupee that covered his head in a mini-pompadour when he performed in sitcoms and on game shows. But there are whispers of recognition from the older spectators when I elicit testimony about his Tony Award in the early sixties for playing the lead role in a modern version of *Timon of Athens*, and a second Tony as a featured performer in a revival of *South Pacific*, and finally oohs of surprise when he mentions his TV roles and his stint on the *Hollywood Squares*. And then I spend time focusing on his career as an acting instructor. The list of well-known stars that he's taught is massive; four of his students have won Oscars, sixteen have won Emmys, and another eight have won Tonys. After every third question, I look at Bishop, who obsessively stretches his neck and pulls his shoulders back and down, elongating his spine, as if he's in the midst of a Pilates workout. His jaw is clenched, and his fists balled up in rage. I can't let myself forget how dangerous this man is.

"Do you know William Bishop?" I ask.

"Once upon a time I did. Billy Bishop was one of my acting students."

"When was that?"

"The late nineteen seventies."

"Who else was in his acting class?"

He names twelve more people, three of whom went on to have successful acting careers. It's a helpful response, because in one sentence he both bolsters his credentials and confirms that he has the keenest of memories. Then he pauses—for drama, I hope, but then I begin to worry, because he's scanning the room as if confused—until his eyes fall on Bishop. "Also in that acting class was Paula McGrath. Better known as Felicity McGrath."

The spectators shuffle in their chairs, trying so hard not to react that at some point there's a collective exhalation of air that sounds percussive. I haven't taken my eyes off Bishop since I asked the question. He's staring at Gold not with malevolence but with a kind of basset-eyed embarrassment, and now he looks exactly like hangdog Lou Frantz, who's sitting in his chair fuming, ineffectual. Lovely Diamond is looking up at me with what I interpret as reluctant pride. Or maybe that's how I want her to react, to have her think I'm the primal male who's overcome her resistance by sheer force. And then I catch Bishop silently mouthing some words to Gold.

"Your Honor, Mr. Bishop is trying to communicate with the witness during my direct examination," I say. "I object to any attempt to intimidate Mr. Gold."

Frantz jumps out of his chair and shakes a finger at me, but before he can speak, Gold says, "Billy . . . Mr. Bishop . . . wasn't threatening me, Mr. Stern."

"Then what was he doing?" I ask.

"I'd rather not say."

"I'm afraid you'll have to."

He looks at me with disappointment, but takes a labored breath that seems to make his whole body shudder. "He mouthed the words 'Please, you don't understand.'"

"How do you know that's what he said?"

"My hearing has deteriorated over the past years. I can see facial expression and body movement, still hear emotional intonation in voices, but sometimes the words are unclear. I've learned to lip-read."

I question him in more detail about Bishop and McGrath, establishing that they often arrived at and left acting class together, that they performed on stage as partners, and that they played love scenes opposite each other. As was Gold's wish, I don't ask him to speculate about an actual romantic relationship. I pass the witness.

Lou Frantz's cross-examination can make a saint look like a serial killer, and he won't hold back because of Gold's advanced age. But this time, he makes not a scratch in Gold's pristine testimony. His attempt to make Gold seem like a disgruntled has-been, bitter about Bishop's failure to help him, backfires when Gold testifies that he turned down offers to act in three Parapet Media movies because he didn't like the scripts. Frantz tests Gold's memory with rapid-fire questions about the past, but the answers only confirm that Gold has an acute mind. When Frantz suggests that Gold has come to court and lied about Bishop because he wants the media attention, Gold bursts out in a phlegmy laugh and says, "I was a working actor seen by millions of people for five and a half decades, Mr. Frantz. You can still see me on the classic movie and TV cable stations once or twice a week. I'm eighty-seven years old. The last thing I need or want is more fame, not to mention that I wouldn't perjure myself to get it." With a lilt in his voice he says, "In fact, I wouldn't perjure myself for any reason."

Frantz finally gives up, one of the few times I've seen it. He leans over and confers with Lovely. When she slides him a Post-It note, he nods and asks, "Mr. Gold, when was the first time you communicated with Mr. Parker Stern, Poniard's attorney?" It's an afterthought question, one that Lovely probably suggested only because I scored points asking something similar of Boardwalk Freddy Frederickson.

Gold says, "Well, I e-mailed Mr. Stern through his website and then he came to my studio, and . . ." He pitches forward and gropes for his cane, which falls to the floor outside the witness box. An alert Brenda retrieves it for him. Leaning on the cane for support, he looks at me, stricken.

"Did you understand my question, Mr. Gold?" Frantz says.

Gold sits and waits, his eyes glued to mine. If I thought he looked old before, now he looks a hundred.

My brain compresses and throbs, my past and my future two sides of a vise crushing the present beyond recognition. I wish I had that cane because I'm about to swoon. But I brought Gold here, exposed him to this question, and I'm not going to have a good man perjure himself for me. Even though we could get away with it. So I force myself to say in as firm a tone as I can muster, "Please answer Mr. Frantz's question, Mr. Gold. Fully and accurately."

He nods in gratitude. "I first met Mr. Stern in nineteen eighty or nineteen eighty-one. His mother brought him to my acting studio. He was at the time a working child actor who went by the name Parky Gerald. He later became a big star."

As the years have gone by, I've tried to convince myself that the public has forgotten me, that my efforts to hide my past have been unnecessary acts of egotism. The reaction in the courtroom—the *omigod*s, the *isn't he dead?*s, the *holy fucking crap*—prove otherwise. Clifton Stanley Gold remains on the witness stand with eyes closed, as if not seeing me will shut out the noise and the guilt. Marina

Shalamitski still scowls. Bishop and Frantz huddle together, undoubtedly trying to find significance for their case in what Gold just revealed. Lovely Diamond gapes at me with her beautiful mouth half-open, her eyes filling with tears.

Brenda puts a hand on my shoulder. "I'm not sure what's going on. You were the kid in *The Boatman*?"

Without taking my eyes off of Lovely, who's looking back and wiping away the tears, I nod.

There's a loud boom up front, and the room quiets down, all eyes searching for the bomb. Judge Grass, who doesn't have a gavel on the bench—most judges don't these days—slammed a thick volume of California Rules of Court on her desk as hard as she could, and she's poised to do it again.

"There will be silence in this courtroom, or I'll call the bailiffs to clear it," she says. She looks at me. "Let me get this straight, Mr. Stern. You were the child actor Parky Gerald? The kid who divorced his mother and disappeared?"

"That would seem to be an accurate statement, Your Honor." I still can't bring myself to simply answer yes.

"Heavens," Judge Grass says, her sparrow's face suddenly moony and girlish and wistful, emotions I thought genetically beyond her reach. "My sister Julia had such a crush on that kid, posters in her room, fan magazines. I was two years older, but even I thought he was . . . Julia passed four years ago, and I . . ." She gathers herself and says in her normal peremptory voice, "Any further questions of the witness, Mr. Frantz?"

"Not at this time, Your Honor," he says in a gruff, yet befuddled tone.

"Mr. Gold, you're excused," the judge says. "We'll take a ten-minute recess. When we come back I expect that everyone will have settled down. I won't tolerate any further noise or outbursts. We have a trial to finish." She leaves the bench and disappears into chambers before we can stand.

Brenda waits for our opponents to exit the courtroom, says she has to follow up on something, and leaves as well. I sit at counsel table for a minute, two minutes, five, pretending to make notes and to thumb through court pleadings. Finally, I stand and turn toward the gallery. Not a single spectator has left the courtroom. The reporters, the regulars, the clerk, the bailiff, the cosplayers, Ed and Brighton Diamond— they're all staring at me.

CHAPTER 44

Throughout the ten-minute break, which turns into twenty minutes, reporter Brandon Placek taunts me mercilessly with questions about my childhood. Turns out he's the right age to be a fan but wasn't. It doesn't stop him from searching the IMDb website and asking me about all my flops, about my "divorce" from my mother, about my whereabouts between my disappearance at fifteen and my starting law school. This is the real reason why I hid my identity all these years—I don't want anyone to associate me with Quiana Gottschalk and the Church of the Sanctified Assembly. Ed Diamond, who's sitting two rows in front of Placek, finally turns around and tells him to shut the fuck up.

Brenda almost sprints in, her pumps clacking on the industrial linoleum.

"Where have you been?" I ask.

"Talking to . . . come into the jury room."

"We're about to start."

"Come with me now!" She grabs my arm and pulls me up. Alone in the jury room is Professor Nate Ettinger, sitting in a plastic shell chair with aluminum handles. He stands when he sees me, tugs on the sleeves of his coat, tightens his bow tie, and snaps to attention.

"I want to testify and tell the judge what I know," he says.

Brenda, who's twirling a strand of black hair around her index finger, tries to suppress a grin.

"Look, Mr. Ettinger, you shouldn't testify just because my assistant pressured you to."

"Brenda didn't pressure me to do anything. I approached her. That's why I came down to court, to see if maybe I should . . . And then Clifton

Stanley Gold gets up there, and as elderly and frail as he is, faces down Bishop. I . . . I couldn't live with myself if I walked out of this court-room still a coward. It's time to stop hiding from that man. Too many years." He makes an effort to meet my gaze, to appear steadfast, but his irises wobble with indecision. He could make a disastrous witness. I dislike his academic arrogance, his puffed show-biz credentials, his con-trived professor's wardrobe, and Judge Grass will probably dislike him for the same reasons. Lou Frantz smells fear like an alpha coyote, and he'll destroy Ettinger if he detects even a trace of trepidation.

"We're doing too well," I say. "I don't think—"

"Don't deprive me of the chance to redeem myself," he says. "I beg you."

"Poniard would want you to put on the strongest case possible, right, Parker?" Brenda says. "He'd even want you to gamble. That's who he is, right?"

"You don't win a lawsuit by gambling," I say. "That's why people like Poniard hire lawyers."

"Well, let's do an analysis of the evidence then," she says. "Sure, you proved Bishop to be the liar we knew him to be, proved that he knew Felicity, but it's like you're always telling me . . . a liar isn't a murderer. Nate . . . Professor Ettinger can talk about *The Boatman*, about all the threats and stuff. He can establish motive."

"Brenda, I—"

"I'll come through," Ettinger says. "I owe it to myself and to Felicity McGrath. I'm an effective speaker in front of an audience. I'm always lecturing, of course."

That's what I'm afraid of. Still, Brenda is right—we do need more evidence. And Harmon Cherry would preach that the evidence always trumps instinct. "OK," I say. "We'll try it. But if things aren't going well, expect me to cut it off."

As we're about to go back into the courtroom, Ettinger grabs my sleeve. "You know, we worked on a movie together," he says. "Not just *The Boatman*. I associate produced and did some second unit direction on *Climbing Panda Hill*, though you probably wouldn't remember me. You were good. I knew your mother very well."

"You and a hundred other guys," I say, rolling my eyes. That's another reason why I don't like him.

When we get back into the courtroom, Judge Grass has already taken the bench. Bishop, Frantz, and Diamond are in their places, looking listless and wrung out.

"You're late, Mr. Stern," the judge says. "Unacceptable." Despite the words, this isn't the same Judge Grass as before the recess. Before, her eyes radiated a harsh fluorescence whenever she looked at me, but now that light is softer, more diffuse, more ambiguous in its judgment. The happy events of childhood take root in our core and return not as memory but as emotion, raw and immediate. Anita Grass the girl was star-struck by Parky Gerald; Anita Grass the woman still is.

I apologize and explain that Ettinger is another last-minute impeachment witness. A cowed Frantz doesn't bother to object. Ettinger takes the stand, but unlike the courageous Clifton Gold, looks everywhere but at Bishop's cyber-knife stare.

All I have to do is ask a few foundational questions, and Ettinger launches into a wonderful lecture on the joint Bishop-McGrath production of *The Boatman*—how he worked on the film as an associate producer, how Bishop produced and starred in the film, how Felicity McGrath wrote and directed it though Bishop took all the credit. Like my mother did, he describes the movie as a modern version of the Orpheus and Eurydice myth about a down-and-out musician who goes through hell, sees the light, and becomes a prophet. He adds important new information that triggers shocked *ahhs* and titters through the gallery and starts Bishop's bowed head shaking continually: the actors engaged in hardcore sex on camera and ingested actual illicit drugs, just like the "Orpheus & the Wise Guy" curse said. Bishop insisted that the movie pay homage to Andy Warhol and The Factory, according to Ettinger. He recounts how production shut down suddenly and how Howard Bishop threatened to harm anyone who talked about the movie. He testifies about the rumored long-term affair between Bishop and McGrath. Brenda did well in lobbying me to call him to the stand.

There are only two small bumps. He disagrees when I suggest that

The Boatman was a depiction of Bradley Kelly's founding of the Church of the Sanctified Assembly, and he blurts out that, as a four-year-old, I was in the movie. "You were a very cute, well-behaved little boy, Mr. Gerald," he says unctuously. "I thought you were dead, the victim of foul play."

I try to ignore this and move on, but the judge has to silence the laughter.

Throughout my direct, Bishop has repeatedly whispered in Frantz's ear, and Lovely has typed feverishly into her computer. When I pass the witness, Frantz stands and says, "Just a couple of questions, Mr. Ettinger. You worked on a movie called *The Volcano Paradox*, didn't you?"

"I produced that movie," he says.

"Isn't it the case that you weren't the producer but actually received only a minor co-producer credit?"

He puffs out his chest and pulls at the lapels of his coat. "I was cheated out of my rightful credit. I produced that picture, but the head of the production company stole it and invited me to sue him. Of course, I couldn't afford to defend myself. But the IMDb credit is correct."

"You don't like Mr. William Bishop, do you, Mr. Ettinger?"

"I wouldn't . . ." he shifts his eyes toward Bishop and then looks at me. I won't meet his glance. "No, I don't like him, but not because he fired me. It was because his father threatened to harm me if I revealed anything about *The Boatman*, and the son embraced the threat so he could hide the embarrassing things he did on that movie. I've been frightened ever since—until today, when I decided to stand up to him."

"In 1982, didn't Mr. Bishop fire you off a movie project called *The Wailing Saint of South Philly*?"

Ettinger looks at the judge. "Your honor, I think this trial has exposed Mr. Bishop as a pathological liar. As to *The Wailing Saint*, he didn't fire me; I quit when he took over the studio because I didn't want to work with a man who'd threatened me, a hypocrite who projected this clean public image and all the while cheated on his wife and hid what he'd done on *The Boatman*. It was just as well. He would've turned *The Wailing Saint* into schlock, anyway."

It's not precisely what Ettinger said when we first met in his office, but he wasn't under oath then. Now, it's the perfect answer, and for one of the few times ever, Louis Frantz doesn't have a quick rejoinder. He asks a few questions trying to attack Ettinger's answer about the *Wailing Saint*, but Ettinger remains firm. The testimony wasn't perfect, but almost.

"Anything further, Mr. Stern?" the judge asks.

I'd like to be able to call Poniard, Bud Kreiss, the full cast and crew of *The Boatman*, but all I can say is, "The defense rests."

The judge asks Frantz if he plans to put on a rebuttal case, and when he answers in the negative I expect him to begin closing argument, but instead he says, "Your Honor, the plaintiff moves that judgment immediately be entered for the plaintiff and against the individual known as Poniard. We've shown that there is absolutely *no* admissible evidence that Mr. Bishop had anything to do with the disappearance of Paula Felicity McGrath."

"That's absurd," I say. "We've proved that Bishop had a motive for the kidnapping—covering up his humiliating involvement in *The Boatman* so he could save his career and his marriage, and secretly pimp for the Church of the Sanctified Assembly."

An otherwise impassive Bishop rocks forward and back in his chair.

"I object to that foul language," Frantz says.

"What's your client going to do," I say, "sue me for defamation?"

"That's enough, counsel," the judge says. "Were you finished, Mr. Stern?"

"No, I was not. We've established that Bishop was cheating on his wife with McGrath, that they were still spending time together in Venice in eighty-seven just before McGrath disappeared, that she wrote letters to Scotty referring to Bishop as her insurance policy. Then there's Bud Kreiss's report of what Luther Frederickson told him, which given what's happened in this courtroom you shouldn't discount even if it is technically hearsay. Not to mention that Bishop perjured himself ten times over."

"Mr. Stern, I have a question for you," the judge says. "Other than knowing about the Scotty letters, was your client aware of any of these other facts when he released his video game?"

"He knew that . . ." What did Poniard really know? I have no answer.

"I didn't think so," she says. "Here's how I see this case. Despite Mr. Bishop's shocking behavior in this court—"

"It's not just shocking, it's perjury," I say.

"That may very well be, counsel, but let me finish. Despite the plaintiff's behavior, there's still no evidence that he had anything to do with McGrath's disappearance. The fact that he knew her doesn't prove it, taking acting classes and working on a film with her doesn't prove it, the fact that his father threatened people doesn't prove it, and even lying in court doesn't prove it. So you haven't shown that Poniard's statement is true. And you've just admitted to me that we don't know Poniard's state of mind when he released the video game. All he'll admit to knowing about are those letters, and they don't provide a basis for the accusations against Mr. Bishop. So how can we say Poniard acted with anything other than reckless disregard for the truth?"

Though everyone in court now must believe that Bishop had a role in Felicity's abduction, the judge's legal analysis isn't wrong. Some judges would ignore the technicalities and seek to do justice, but not this judge. Her crush on Parky Gerald only goes so far.

I'm desperate. And sometimes an ember of understanding smolders beneath the slag of defeat and reveals itself in the sheer act of pleading for mercy. "Anita—sorry, I mean, Your Honor—there's one more avenue I just realized I can pursue. How about giving me until Monday to bring in additional evidence of Mr. Bishop's role in the Felicity McGrath disappearance? We'd be missing only two court days. It's the fair and just thing to do after Bishop's behavior."

We look at each other, and while a few years ago it would've been an awkwardly brutal stare-down between bitter adversaries, now it's a kind of reconciliation.

"You can have until Monday, counsel," she says. "We're adjourned until then." She leaves the bench so hurriedly that she far outdistances Lou Frantz's angry bark of protest.

I don't know whether Anita Grass has done me a favor or called my bluff. I am sure that she wouldn't have given me the extra time if she didn't have an abiding affinity for Parky Gerald, child star.

The media starts shouting questions at Bishop and me, so both sides remain sitting at the table until the bailiffs clear the room. My opposing counsel and their client walk not toward the front door but toward the jury room. Before Bishop exits, he stops in front of me and says, "Stern, you don't know what troubles you've stirred up for everybody." His words snap whip-like, ominous.

"Communicate with me through your lawyers," I say.

Brenda isn't as restrained. "Don't you dare threaten us," she says, a newfound ferocity in her tone. Her shoulders hunch in an angry shrug, and she clenches her fists. "Look where your threats and your crimes have gotten you, Mr. Bishop. Your life as you knew it is over—your empire will crumble, your squeaky-clean reputation has been exposed as a fraud. What's your oh-so-loyal wife going to do when she hears about you and Felicity?"

"Stop now, Brenda," I say.

Bishop towers over her, and now he leans over and comes within six inches of her face. She doesn't recoil.

"You may be right about what I face, young lady. But what does or doesn't happen to me is the least of my worries right now." He straightens up, tugs at his lapels, and walks out.

Once the jury room door closes, Brenda starts gulping for air, almost hyperventilating. Her chest heaves with each breath. She lowers her head and raises her dark eyes to look up at me, a show of contrition. She wraps her arms around herself and visibly shudders. "That was *so* scary."

"You brought it on yourself," I say. "You should never engage the opposing party like that, and certainly not someone as dangerous as Bishop."

"Maybe so," she says, dropping her hands to her sides. "But it felt wonderful."

As soon as Brighton gets home from the *Poniard* trial, he goes to his computer and logs onto *Abduction!*, more out of habit than of interest. Luckily, the HF Queen hasn't gotten back from court.

In the past week, *Abduction!* hasn't offered anything new, just repetitive cutscenes and old levels. Maybe it's because the trial is an adventure, role-playing, and strategy game all rolled into one. The judge and the witnesses are obstacles and level bosses. The lawyers are both characters in the game *and* the game players. He now understands better why the HF Queen says she loves practicing law, though no one likes to get pounded the way she did today. But maybe she isn't beaten after all, because in the end the judge said she'd probably rule in the Queen's favor—unless Stern succeeds in his quest to bring in more evidence. Poniard was right about one thing—William the Conqueror is a big fat liar—worse than a liar, Ed said in the car driving home, though he made Brighton promise not to repeat that to the Queen. Which means that the Queen is on the wrong side of the case, but Brighton doesn't blame her for it. It seems that the legal profession is like chess—sometimes you play white and sometimes you play black.

Brighton makes a couple of cool mouse maneuvers, and a new stage of the game appears on his monitor. It's the courthouse, but it's less a higher level than some kind of dead-end mod, a simplistic *beat 'em up* game featuring bloody fistfights among Stern, Frantz, Bishop—and the HF Queen. The player can choose to control one of the lawyers or Bishop but can't control the judge, who resembles a giant crow with a skinny face, massive beak, and black wings made out of her judicial robes. The crow-judge squawks at the lawyers and from time to time hits them with a huge gavel for no reason. Brighton's stomach has been rumbling for an hour because the trial was too exciting for him to take time to eat lunch, but when he sees his mother get hit in the face and suffer a broken nose, his guts twist like an over-coiled spring and his appetite vanishes.

But it feels to Brighton like something's missing from the scene—what, he can't say.

CHAPTER 45

According to John 8:32, the truth shall set you free, but the truth threatens to make me a prisoner. Yesterday after court, the media followed me home and tried to get past security and into my parking lot. It's still early in the morning, but the tabloid reporters and paparazzi are already milling around the front gate. They all want to interview Parky Gerald all grown up.

Last night, I spoke with Harry Cherry's wife Sonja, begging her to bring Harry to court to testify about William Bishop and *The Boatman*. "We'll deal with the Alzheimer's," I said. When she refused, I asked to meet Harry at their home. When she said no to that, I foolishly threatened to subpoena the old man. She made a rude comment about Parky Gerald's acting ability, told me to "fuck off," and hung up the phone.

Despite the phone call with Sonja, I have to find a way to see Harry Cherry and pick at the slivers of his shattered memory. So at a little before nine o'clock, I drive out of the building in my neighbor Amber's Toyota Prius—it's a good thing that as a little girl, Amber loved Parky—and set out on the drive to Palm Desert.

It takes me three hours to leave the smog of LA for a dry desert heat that taxes the air-conditioner on my neighbor's hybrid. When I reach Ontario, I input Brenda's number, intending to tell her where I'm going, but I abort the call. I've already exposed her to enough danger, and if I get the information I need, things will be even more risky. I don't want Brenda to end up like Philip Paulsen.

I turn onto the Cherrys' street and start to pull up to the house, but then I see Sonja walking toward her BMW. I speed past and tour the cookie-cutter neighborhood—admittedly, they used a high-class cookie cutter—and return to the Cherrys' place five minutes later.

I ring the doorbell. No answer. I ring again and then a third time. Maybe Harry doesn't live with Sonja anymore. Maybe she put him in a facility. It's been four months since I've seen him. Could he have deteriorated that much? Or maybe she was simply being proactive. He's not going to get better, and she's a young woman. Would she be that cruel?

I turn to leave when the door opens.

"May I help you?" The man looks like he's in his early thirties, mean-street handsome, with black hair, swarthy skin, and a fitness-center body. The talons of an eagle or falcon tattoo bleed out from under the sleeve of his white medical polo shirt, which he wears tucked into white medical-attendant slacks.

"My name's Parker Stern. I used to work with Mr. Cherry. I was wondering if I could speak with him."

"I know who you are, sir. Mr. Cherry is unavailable."

"Mr. Cherry might be able to help me in a trial I'm handling."

"He can't help you, sir. He can't help anyone."

"Harmon? Harmon, is that you?" Harry's voice sounds like a wood rasp scraping a two-by-four. He shuffles up next to his caretaker. The cottony hair has thinned even more since last November, and what remains is flyaway and coarse. His dim eyes have retreated deeper into their sockets. Last time I saw him, he still stood straight, but now he lists to the side with what looks like a scoliotic twist of the spine.

Philip Paulsen would abhor what I'm about to do. "Yeah, it's me, Pops," I say. "I just came by for a quickie consult." Which is how Harmon Cherry always approached his father for advice. But it's not only words that I'm plagiarizing. Harmon spoke in a clipped cadence and a nasal tenor, making him sound like a laid-back California version of the old movie actor Edward G. Robinson in his gangster days. Clifton Gold encouraged his acting students to mimic, and at the law firm I was renowned among my colleagues for my dead-on Harmon imitation. At one firm party, I was drunk enough to give in to entreaties to do the impression for Harmon. I'm sure the colleagues who encouraged me didn't have my best interests at heart, but Harmon laughed so hard that he sprayed salivary froth all over my friend Rich Baxter. And now I've used that voice with Harry.

The attendant shakes his head. "Harry, you have to come inside." He starts to shut the door on me, but I push back against it.

"Got a very important question for ya, Pops," I say. Harmon always described his questions to Harry as important. His career success had surpassed that of his father, and he always seemed to feel some guilt about it.

The young man's reserve of calm, which must be vast to deal with Alzheimer's patients, has dissipated. "No way, man, that's just wrong."

He's about to shut the door, but Harry half-elbows his way past him. "What'ya got for me, son?" he says, leaning in with what looks like keen interest. When he puts an arthritic hand on my shoulder and kisses me on the top of the head, I struggle not to flinch. I reach out and pat his shoulder twice, just like Harmon would, even in front of clients. As someone who grew up without a father, I looked at such shows of affection with uncomprehending awe.

The caretaker is glaring at me. But I sense he won't do anything to upset Harry and so won't abruptly separate him from his long-dead son. But how long before Harry's deteriorating brain cuts the cord of this senescent delusion?

"Where's the scavi, Pops?" I ask. "I'm looking for it."

Harry tilts his head to the side like a bemused puppy.

"The scavi, Pops?"

Now Harry whimpers like that puppy, and I know I've lost him.

"You'll have to leave or I'm going to call the cops, man," the caretaker says. "You should be ashamed. What you're doing is cruel."

"Beverly Hills River," Harry says. And then it becomes a whiny, geriatric Aeolian incantation—"Beverly Hills River, Beverly Hills River, Beverly Hills River, Beverly Hills River . . ." Mucous tears overflow his eyes.

"Forgive me," I say to the young man. "Tell Sonja I'm sorry. It's just this lawsuit, it's made me . . . I'm sorry."

The young man conveys through aggressive silence that he doesn't forgive me at all. He takes hold of Harry's shoulders and firmly but kindly turns him around and shuts the door.

Not until I get into Amber's car and start the engine do I realize that Harry Cherry gave me exactly the answer I came for.

CHAPTER 46

Normally, the drive from Palm Desert to Beverly Hills takes over two hours, but I make it in eighty-three minutes, thanks to my illegal use of the carpool lane. I park at a meter off Linden Avenue and "Little" Santa Monica Boulevard, get out of my car, and walk the four blocks to Macklin & Cherry's old office building on Camden, passing the familiar Eddie Dalton's Hair Salon and VIP Manicures by Antoinique, and a new women's shoe store that didn't exist when the firm broke up. I don't think anyone's following me. I enter my old building through a side door and hurry to the elevator, which I take down to the archives. The doors open to reveal Roland at his desk. He flinches when he sees me, reaches into his desk, pulls out a handgun, and aims it at me, his hand wavering with a fear-induced palsy. I hold up my hands and take a step back. "Whoa, Roland, it's me."

He lowers the gun, as relieved as I am. His fair cheeks splotch neon red, and his oil-drum chest deflates. "Jesus, Parker, you scared me shitless. Ever since those guys showed up people are supposed to call ahead."

"I never knew you kept a gun down here."

"I didn't." He looks around as if to make sure no one is listening, though I don't see anyone else in the vicinity, "I'm not supposed to have it. But I'm not going to . . . you know." He reaches behind his head and massages his neck. "Say, you weren't followed this time, were you?"

"No. I made sure of it." Actually, I'm not sure of anything.

"What can I do for you?"

"Do you know about my trial?"

"Can't say that I do. Is it in the news? You had a lot of cases in the news. You know, the NBA season's ending, hockey's in full swing, MLB spring training ... I don't much like the news. Sports, talk radio are OK, but ..." He shrugs his fat, sloping shoulders contritely.

That's good. If he doesn't know about the trial, he won't recognize the danger.

"Roland, I have a favor. I need to get something from inside the M&C archives."

"Go ahead. Your key should still work. I tried to get building management to change the locks after those assholes attacked me, but they didn't want to spend the money, claimed it was a one-time thing."

"I don't want just to get into the archives. There's this other room ... I might need one of your keys."

"Look, Parker, I'm not supposed to leave my desk."

"Please, Roland. It's important."

He shakes his head.

"I can score some Lakers playoff tickets. They're yours."

"Lower level, center court?"

"Absolutely." I'll have to pay exorbitant broker's prices, but I don't care.

He reaches into his desk and takes out an old-fashioned jailer's key ring with a dozen keys attached. He makes a labored attempt to stand.

"Do you have a flashlight in there?" I ask.

He slowly lowers himself back into the chair, takes a long aluminum flashlight out of the bottom drawer, and stands up again.

"And bring your weapon," I say.

He rolls his eyes to the ceiling as if looking for divine guidance, lets out a snuffling belly sigh, and retrieves the gun.

I insist that we walk down the hall side by side. If he's behind me and gets startled I worry that he'll shoot me; if he's ahead of me and gets startled I fear he'll turn around and shoot me. I open the door to the archives and we go inside. The room smells moldier than ever, like the underside of a freeway bridge after a rain. We pass the massive file shelves and go back toward the alcove that has the computer on which Brenda found the Hildy Gish file with a cast list for *The Boatman*. The dirty industrial curtain still conceals the back wall—and the hidden door that saved Brenda and me from Bishop's henchman.

"What the . . . ?" Roland says.

"A secret cave." That's what Deanna called it that night we had sex in there. "But I'm interested in what's behind the far door."

There's a light switch, but when I flip it on, nothing happens. No surprise—I doubt anyone has come in here in years other than Brenda and me, and we weren't about to change the light bulb. Roland turns on his flashlight. We walk to the end of the room, where there's another door. I try it, but as I suspected, it's locked. I try my office key, but it doesn't fit.

Roland hands me the flashlight and the gun, which shakes as much in my hand as it did in his. He starts trying different keys. It's quiet except for the jingling of metal on metal and the rush of flowing water, the same sound I heard when Brenda and I were hiding. This is what Harry Cherry had to mean when he kept repeating "Beverly Hills River."

The door unlocks on the eighth try. Roland pulls it open gingerly, and I shine the flashlight inside, revealing a decayed, water-stained staircase—undoubtedly riddled with termites—leading downward.

"Those steps aren't going to hold you, much less a big guy like me," Roland says.

I hand him his gun. "This might take a while, so don't wait for me. I'll need your flashlight and the keys."

He hands them over and wastes no time leaving the room.

I shine the flashlight down the stairway again. Eleven steps. I will myself to stay feathery on my feet, curse all the scones and muffins and puffed pastries that I've sampled at The Barrista over the years. The first three steps creak but hold, but the fourth cracks when I place my left foot down. There's no railing, so I steady myself by bracing my right hand against the concrete wall. I take a long stride to the next step without testing it and then say "screw it" and skip every other step. They hold—all but the last, which shatters from the rot, injecting sharp splinters into my leg. I shine the flashlight on my shin and pull out the large ones, ignoring the blood that's running into my shoe.

The flashlight beam reveals a small rectangular room with file cabinets on two sides. The room is damper than the humid main archives. I stop and listen—the sound of flowing water is louder, but I still don't know if it really comes from underground streams or the building pipes or the city sewer system. It doesn't matter. This has to be Harry Cherry's *scavi*—the truth of Paula Felicity McGrath must be entombed here.

Fortunately, the file cabinets are marked alphabetically, the ink fading but still legible. I try the file drawer marked *A–B*, looking for *Bishop* or *Boatman*. I riffle through the files, but there's nothing I care about, just old original contracts between long-shuttered production companies and former megastars whom few people under sixty-five remember. The only hopeful sign is that all these files involve sensitive transactions that either Harry or Harmon Cherry handled. This room belonged to them. None of us at the law firm had any idea.

I go to the *M* cabinet, looking for McGrath. Again, nothing. The same with *P* for Parapet Studios. Why was I so sure? Harry Cherry's mind isn't right. I consider starting with the first cabinet again and going through every file, but that would far exceed the battery life of this flashlight, might take me past Monday's court hearing—assuming Bishop's goons didn't find me here first. Then on impulse, I open the cabinet marked *T–U–V*, and there they are, filed under *T*—two sealed files marked *Highly Confidential—H. Cherry's Eyes Only* stuffed into a fraying red accordion file labeled *The Boatman*.

CHAPTER 47

I leave the office building and go back to my car, carrying the file under my arm like a running back afraid to fumble. People on the street keep staring at me, glancing down, and I'm sure they're focusing on the files, that Bishop's goons are following me, biding their time. Then I realize that they're looking at my torn dress slacks and bloody shin. I make it to my car and drive back to my condo, catching every red light between Beverly Hills and Marina del Rey. The drive in late-afternoon traffic takes thirty minutes, but it feels three times longer.

When I reach my complex, I avoid the reporters by pulling into my security garage and hurrying up the stairs. My shin throbs with every step and stings when the ocean breeze hits the exposed wound. I go inside my condo and rip open the first manila envelope. It's a videocassette tape with a faded label that says *The Boatman*. So someone kept a copy after all. I open the second package—another cassette tape, but this one unlabeled.

The last time I used my antiquated videotape player was two years ago, when Lovely wanted to watch a Parky Gerald movie and I had an anxiety attack when I saw Sanctified Assembly founder Bradley Kelly appear on screen. I'm surprised that the machine turns on when I hit the power button. I take the tapes out of the Redweld folder, insert the one labeled *The Boatman* into the player, and reach for the *play* button, but I can't bring myself to press it. My finger remains suspended over the device, poised in horrible equilibrium by the opposing forces of curiosity and fear. Is it the anticipation? A primal, superstitious belief in that old movie curse? The unwillingness to bring this game to an end? My hand begins to tremble, and I feel as though I've entered a courtroom unmedicated and unprepared. I take a deep breath and press *play*.

There's a black screen but no credits, so this is a rough cut, not a finished film. Music starts playing. Beethoven's second movement of his Piano Concerto no. 4, also called *Orpheus in Hades*. I'm partial to alternative rock, but Harmon Cherry liked classical music and made us listen to it because he thought it helped our analytical skills.

Dissolve into the sleazy bar where Hildy Gish as Eurydice Jones is in the restroom, shooting up smack over a toilet. Gish is dark-skinned and sexy, a remarkable casting choice for the still-bigoted Hollywood of the seventies. She was either a superb actress or, as Nate Ettinger testified, injected actual drugs. She makes the act of getting strung out erotic, harrowing, heart-wrenching. She's one of the cast members who disappeared. Where is she?

On my high-definition monitor, the old analogue picture is elongated, warped, infused with a pixilated fuzziness that can't live up to the capabilities of my state-of-the-art LED screen. Despite the limitations of the analogue medium transplanted to a hi-def screen, it's obvious that the movie is beautifully filmed, shot predominately in muted blues and grays, deep-focus clarity, so though the film is in color, the viewer has the crisp, noir feeling of black and white. The director has immense talent.

Eurydice returns to the bar to speak with a forlorn Miles Boatman, who's playing piano—William Bishop in his mid-thirties, but playing younger and getting away with it. And over the next eighty-seven minutes, the movie plays out just as Ettinger and Ed Diamond's sources said it did—Boatman's love of Eurydice goes unreciprocated, so he embarks on a journey to the far side of the universe, becomes a prophet, returns, and rescues Eurydice from hell.

The masterful writing and direction makes the film profoundly disturbing. I want to puke when Bradley Kelly comes on the screen as the corrupt priest, delivering every line in the smarmy, overly dramatic style that made him a pretty-faced hack on the movie screen but a modern-day Mesmer to his real-life devotees. Kelly proved that religious charlatans don't have to be particularly good actors. The movie's proselytizing for the Church of the Sanctified Assembly increases my angst—I well know the Assembly's tenets, and *The Boatman* is a gospel for Kelly's nascent religious movement. That didn't stop the film from depicting rampant drug use and graphic sex. Eurydice shoots heroin in three separate scenes. In another scene Miles Boatman—Bishop—snorts what's supposed to be cocaine. I had a small part as the child of a prostitute, virtually abandoned to the bar patrons and fawned over by Eurydice. In a shocking scene, especially for 1979, a drunk, distraught Boatman and the dissolute priest played by Kelly kiss passionately on the lips. So much for Bishop's well-publicized opposition to gay marriage and Kelly's tenet that homosexuality is a curable result of cellular contamination.

Later, Bishop and Gish appear in a lurid scene involving full-frontal nudity and passionate coupling. Bishop has an erection, actual, not prosthetic—reason enough for him to later suppress the film, which would have destroyed his newly minted image as a defender of family and conservative values. Still, Ettinger's testimony that the film depicted hardcore sex isn't quite accurate—it's unclear whether the love scenes are real or simulated, a testament to the director's skill.

The film ends abruptly, as if Howard Bishop shut down the film just before the director could splice in the end credits. And without the credits, how can I prove that Felicity McGrath directed this? Still, I now understand why someone would want to shut this film down. It blasphemes the Catholic Church. It makes Bishop look like a fraud and hypocrite. His getting a hard-on in that love scene would be enough to make him a laughingstock. Not to mention his kiss with Bradley Kelly. *The Boatman* truly would've destroyed Bishop's reputation.

I eject *The Boatman* and insert the second cassette. The leader runs for so long I conclude that the tape is blank and reach over to hit *stop*. But then there's the main title—*Satan's Boatman—A Film by Paula F. McGrath*—followed by the same Beethoven theme from the first movie.

The scene fades in to Felicity McGrath—not the 1979 version, but older, the age at which she appeared in her last film, *Meadows of Deceit*. She's wearing a floppy hat and Jackie-O shades and is sitting with her legs curled up in a lounger. The scene takes place on a deserted stretch of beach. Was this what Boardwalk Freddy saw her filming in Venice?

"Hello, I'm Paula," she says. "I'm a filmmaker. I was an actress until it all went awry. But I was really something once." The camera cuts to a still photo of her from *Fragile Palace*. Just like when I watched her earlier films, her voice sounds eerily familiar, aural déjà vu. Even after this bit of dialogue, you know this woman is in control, one step ahead. If this is the real Felicity McGrath, she's nothing like the ingenue gone wrong in *Fragile Palace* or the English virgin in *Meadows of Deceit*, or the sexy, wise-cracking skank in Poniard's video game.

"I grew up in Springfield, Illinois," she says. "I ran away to Hollywood when I was fifteen, escaped my food-stamp mom and her crack and her boyfriends. I met a man who said he could get me into modeling. I was a fool to trust him with all the creeps out here, but I was like a lot of young girls, naive and stupid. The joke is, he was legit. I was modeling at fifteen, doing TV and movies a year later. I had to lie about my age, of course, and some said the movies were porn, even investigated the producers for having me engage in underage sex, but it wasn't true. I've always been an actress, not a slut." Her full lips are slightly asymmetrical when she smiles. She takes off her glasses and stands. The camera moves backward as she walks forward. "Be forewarned—what you're about to see, what you're seeing now, what you've already seen, is artifice, a ruse perpetrated on you, the audience. Deceit is the essence of art—the very word *artifice* comes from the Latin *to craft art*. I'm a craftsman—well, craft*woman*. Our role is to deceive and in that way to expose deceit—and to always be truthful." It's a melodramatic Orson Welles–style radio intro, cheesy and old-fashioned even in the 1980s, but it works because of McGrath's passionate delivery, her candid beauty; she's not wearing makeup, or maybe the stage makeup makes it seem that way. "This is my film. I've operated the camera, set up the lighting, edited the raw footage, written the lines, directed the action. So, if you don't like our particular truth, blame me." She relaxes, slumps her shoulders, and says in an almost bored voice, "Cut and print it, e—" Her last words are cut off when the scene shifts.

I press the pause button and rewind. McGrath was probably saying *effect* when she was cut off, a broadcast term. When I hit play again, my suspicion is confirmed—the opening scene transitions by overlapping with the next—a *wipe effect*, it's called.

The first scene from *The Boatman* from the earlier tape comes on. Or so it appears. But then I notice the differences. In certain scenes Bishop overplays the part, seems smarmy where in the first version he seemed sincere. Hildy Gish is stronger, less a victim than someone striving to heroically change her life. There's an additional brutal and troubling scene where Bishop forces himself on Eurydice. It's then that I understand that McGrath reshot and reedited the film to make it not a tribute to Bradley Kelly but an attack on him, an exposé revealing him to be a fraud—not a prophet, but Satan's Messenger, a devious predator who relies on deception and violence to get what he wants. McGrath was shooting this the very year that Kelly announced the formation of his Church of the Sanctified Assembly. McGrath made Eurydice braver, the victim turned heroine. Former hero Miles Boatman became the villain.

At the same time, she's protected Bishop's reputation somewhat. The embarrassing scene showing him sexually aroused is gone. The sex in which he's involved is clearly simulated, mainstream R-rated fare. And somehow, she's made him look like a much better actor than he was in the original.

My theory has always been that William Bishop is part of the Sanctified Assembly's Covert Vanguard. If so, why would he go along with this brutal attack on the divine Bradley Kelly?

At some point, *Satan's Boatman* loses continuity, becomes a mishmash of unconnected scenes, unedited dailies, multiple takes. McGrath obviously never finished her reshoot. Ninety-two minutes in, the scene shifts to the bar's kitchen after last call, and though I can't prove it, I'd bet my condo that this was shot at the Tell Tale Bar in Venice. Eurydice is sitting on a chair, polishing her toenails. Miles Boatman walks in holding a workout bag. He initiates the cinematic ritual that had been reenacted in countless edgy movies since Andy Warhol—no, since Otto Preminger directed *The Man with the Golden Arm*: liquefying the drug in a spoon by heating it over a stove burner, fashioning a leather belt as a makeshift tourniquet, tapping the syringe to rid the solution of air bubbles, and plumping up the veins in his arm with his fingers. He makes a move to inject himself, but Eurydice grabs his arm and says in a sultry voice, "Ladies first, baby." He kisses her quickly, preps her arm, and injects the needle into her vein.

There's no context to any of this, no connection to anything in the plot that's come before. I hope that the rest of the tape will reveal how McGrath intended to make the film coherent.

Hildy Gish acts out the orgasmic heroin rush. With a junkie's droopy eyes, she gazes at Boatman and begins panting. A horrible gasp emanates from her throat, so harsh and painful that it sounds like a special effect rather than anything human. When Boatman bends over to check on her, she projectile-vomits all over his shirt. Is this real or a rip-off of the infamous scene from *The Exorcist*? Eurydice's eyes flutter and roll white. She falls back hard on the kitchen floor. Bishop grabs her shoulders and gives her a gentle shake, and when she doesn't respond, he says, "Hildy, sweetie, are you OK?"

Once Bishop breaks character, any faint hope that this scene was scripted evaporates. Gish convulses, the seizure rattling her limbs. She foams at the mouth. There's a hideous gurgling sound of a person drowning in her own saliva. The convulsions stop, and Felicity McGrath, dressed in a work shirt, blue jeans, and baseball cap, runs in from offscreen and puts her ear to Gish's chest.

"She's not breathing, Billy. Do you think she swapped the . . . ? I told her not to."

"No," Bishop says. "No." It's more a moan than an answer.

McGrath administers CPR, while Bishop stands by helplessly, wringing his hands like a frightened, ineffectual child, making whimpering sounds. Seconds and then minutes pass, but neither calls 911. Why didn't they call 911? Felicity halts her attempts at reviving Gish and presses her fingers into Gish's neck, searching for a pulse. She drops her arms and begins sobbing. Bishop raises his hands to the sides of his head, elbows splayed like a buzzard's wings, and lets out a doleful bellow. He abruptly lowers his arms, looks into the lens, and sprints forward. The movie world shakes and spins, and the screen goes dark.

———𝕸———

Lovely Diamond answers on the third ring. "We have to talk," I say.

"About what."

"Your client. I've got proof of his guilt. I wanted to show you first in case . . ."

There's a long silence. "I don't believe you. What do you—?"

"We'll have to do this in person. I'm at my condo."

"Not there." She's right—too many memories.

"The Barrista," I say. "Ten forty-five. We can do this after everyone has left."

"That works," she says, and hangs up.

———𝕸———

I arrive at The Barrista at 11:05 p.m. It took longer than anticipated to evade the paparazzi and the press. I had to borrow a different neighbor's car, a Land Rover. Before last week, he probably wouldn't have loaned me a cup of sugar. Being a celebrity does have its benefits.

Though I'm twenty minutes late, Lovely hasn't arrived yet. Has she changed her mind about coming?

The shop is empty. Romulo and the rest of the staff are polishing the chrome espresso makers and wiping down the tables, getting ready to close. When he sees me, he gives me a big smile. The other baristas glance at me shyly.

"You're an actor, huh, buddy?" he says "That little kid. I remember that little devil. My sisters loved him." He pats me on the back. "All right."

"Has Brenda come in today?" I say.

"Not today or yesterday." His smile broadens. I'm sure he'll be very glad to get his storeroom back.

One of the baristas brings me a shot of espresso. I smell it as if it were a fine Bordeaux. I take a sip, and it's even better than wine. I've been living on courthouse swill, and I've missed this.

Lovely still hasn't arrived by the shop's 11:30 p.m. closing time. She sends a text saying she's on her way. I tell the staff to leave, that I'll close up.

She finally arrives at 11:40, wearing a blue hoodie, plaid shirt, blue jeans, and a floppy green felt hat. She sits down across from me.

"Sorry I'm late," she says. "The kid's . . ." Her gray irises darken, a storm warning to herself not to pursue this line further. "William Bishop's not a criminal."

I heft the package containing the *Satan's Boatman* tape. "I have proof that he's a murderer and abducted McGrath to cover it up."

"Billy . . . William wouldn't do something like that."

"Are you sleeping with him? Is that what this is about?"

She looks like someone who's been stung so many times by this question that she's immune to its venom. "Did you sleep with your roly-poly little assistant?"

"Is the blonde slut jealous?"

The voice from the storeroom sounds like Brenda's, but the woman who walks out isn't Brenda, it's Courtney the cosplayer, dressed like video game Felicity McGrath, red hair in dreadlocks, tight jumpsuit. My first reaction is that the gun in her left hand and the knife in her right are props. But when I look into her eyes, I know better.

"I'd say, 'Don't scream and nobody will get hurt,' but it would be a lie," she says, and then moves across from me and directly behind Lovely.

"Courtney, what's this about?"

She points the gun at me. "My name's *Felicity*!"

"OK, Felicity." I raise my palms in conciliation and keep them there. "I'm on your side. I'm trying to find out what happened to you." I'm stretching my acting ability in an effort to sound calm but also to avoid a patronizing tone that could set her off.

She shakes her head. "People who disturb lost souls have to pay for their sins. You're disturbing my . . ." She shuts her eyes and shakes her head violently. "You're disturbing Felicity's soul with all your probing and digging and asking questions, all those people looking at old, dead history that should stay . . ." Her jaw clenches, and she looks as if she's about to pull the trigger.

And then it all becomes clear. I've made a grave miscalculation. I struggle to keep my eyes from blinking and, against all reason, slowly lower my raised hands.

"Philip Paulsen," I say. "It was you."

She smirks proudly. "The priest was bothering Alicia Courtney. Bothering, badgering her, invading her privacy."

"And the Kreisses?"

"He was going to help you win your case, trouble Felicity's soul so she couldn't rest. You have to die, Parker." She shakes her head again, but this time as if dazed. I have to keep her talking.

I tilt my head toward Lovely. "Let her go. She's my adversary, which means she's been trying to keep Felicity's soul at rest."

Courtney's icy chuckle makes my legs quiver. "She's not going anywhere. You think I'm stupid or something? Anyway, that blonde bitch saved the black-assed judge."

"What did Judge Triggs have to do with—?"

"That judge was going to help you win." Courtney uses the barrel of the gun to motion toward Lovely. "He ruled against *her* in court. I haven't figured out if this girl is a level boss or collateral damage like the cop's wife. It matters, you know. You get points off for collateral damage but a bonus for killing a boss. Which are you, Ms. Diamond? I think a boss, because evil hides behind beauty."

Lovely looks at me with her lips clamped together as if she's trying to stifle a scream. But her hands are also balled up into fists, and I fear that she'll try to fight. She wouldn't stand a chance.

"So you're telling me that if Poniard wins the lawsuit, somehow Felicity's soul will be damaged? I think it's the exact opposite. I think if I win the lawsuit, we'll be closer to getting to the truth, and the truth will set Felicity's soul free, will bring closure to—"

"Shut the fuck up!" Courtney says.

I stop talking, try not to shrink away, not to break eye contact.

She regards the weapons in her hands with a puzzled expression. "It's so important for the player to choose the right weapons before starting a level. The battle is often won and lost because of the right weapon." In a childish, sing-song tone, she says, "A knife for your friend, a gun for the cop, a knife for his wife 'cause a gun would go pop!" She sneers and jabs the knife in the air toward Lovely. "I would've had that judge if this porn-slut whore hadn't warned him."

I stand slowly, hands up, to divert her attention toward me. If I can somehow get the gun, I'll deal with the knife just so Lovely can run.

"Sit down!" Courtney shouts. Good. She's focused on me now.

I don't sit down. It's not an immediate risk, because she wants to talk some more, explain her demented actions like the psychopath she is. If she didn't want to talk, she'd have killed us both already. Lovely tries to stay still; she's a strong woman, but her lips are trembling.

"Let's talk about this, Felicity," I say.

She laughs derisively and shakes her head. "Don't patronize me, Parker. I've told you already. I'm Felicity's *daughter*. She lives on through me. I am my mother. We're all our parents. There is something I want to tell you, though, before I kill you both and move on to the next stage. You'll think this is hysterical."

The door to the back alley cracks open slowly. Who is it? Romulo or someone else on the staff who left something behind? Brenda? I circle to my left, clockwise around the table, and fortunately Courtney circles in the same direction, which was my intent, because now the rear door is out of her line of sight.

"Stop moving, goddamn it!" she shouts.

I put my hands up. "You wanted to tell me something, Courtney . . . Felicity? Something that would make me laugh?"

She looks at me with demented glee. "Did you know your—?"

A huge mass crashes through the alley door and lunges at Courtney, all the force directed at the hand carrying the gun, which clatters to the floor and slides away. A woman shrieks—I don't know if it's Courtney or Lovely. Lovely jumps up, runs to the storeroom, and slams the door shut. I dive for the gun and retrieve it, look for Courtney, but my only target is the indistinguishable ribbon of intertwined bodies. Then it's no contest because the powerful Banquo Nixon knocks Courtney unconscious.

He stands up, holding the knife. "Oh god, Mr. Stern, I didn't know, I really didn't know, I couldn't believe she ..." He's speaking not in his normal British accent but with a slight Russian accent.

His face has been slashed from the corner of his mouth to just below his left ear.

"She cut you pretty bad," I say. "You'll need the paramedics to get you to the hospital." I reach over and smooth away some of the whiskers of his thick beard. He just keeps looking at Courtney and apologizing to me.

The heavy beard covers a birthmark—identical to the one in that fuzzy picture Brenda found so long ago of the person many suspect of being Poniard.

"Vladimir Lazerev?" I say.

Sirens blare in the background. Lovely must have dialed 911.

"I have to leave," he says.

"Are you—?"

"I'm no one important. Please don't tell them I was here. Tell them you were the one who knocked her out. And ... and don't hurt her. Sorry, Mr. Stern."

He turns and runs toward the back door, doesn't stop when I shout, "Poniard, wait!"

Though I beg her not to, Lovely insists that she'll tell the cops about Banquo, understandable because I won't reveal why I want to keep his involvement secret. But when the police arrive, she parrots my version of events—Courtney hid in the storeroom, came at us, and I disarmed her.

The cops don't leave until one-fifteen in the morning. Lovely and I are alone.

"Now will you admit you're wrong about Bishop?" she says.

I hold up the *Satan's Boatman* tape. "Let's watch this. Then we'll talk."

We go into the back, and after *Satan's Boatman* has finished, Lovely Diamond asks me for a favor that I should immediately refuse. But, of course, I don't. I can't.

—w—

I don't get back to my condo until three in the morning. Rather than going to bed, I launch the computer and send Poniard a message—*Are you all right?* There's no reply, and there's still no reply when I wake up with my head on the desk three hours later. I try to get some sleep in my bed, but it's hopeless. So I shower and drive back to The Barrista, ignoring the pursuing reporters and photographers, who already know about last night's assault. I wait for Brenda to show up, and when she isn't in by nine-thirty, I text her. I get a message back that she's ill and won't be coming in today, maybe won't come in tomorrow either. *So sorry, Parker,* the message ends. There's no mention of last night's attack. At least I know she's OK, that Courtney didn't go after her before coming for me.

Next, I call Detective Tringali, who takes my call immediately. I don't tell her about *Satan's Boatman.* Like a fool, I promised Lovely I'd wait. I do ask about Courtney.

"Very preliminary information," Tringali says. "The forensics people say that the gun this suspect Courtney Doe was carrying—"

"What did you say her last name was?"

"We don't know. We're calling her Courtney *Doe,* like *Jane Doe.* Anyway, preliminarily, the bullets from her gun match those that killed Bud Kreiss. The knife is consistent with the blade that killed Isla Kreiss and your friend Mr. Paulsen." She goes on to say that there's no apparent connection between Courtney and Bishop, that Courtney is profoundly disturbed—one of the police psychiatrists thinks she's suffering from schizoaffective disorder, whatever that is. Courtney keeps repeating that she's Felicity McGrath's daughter but otherwise won't identify herself, keeps babbling on about video game wars and evil level bosses and wicked lawyers and porn-star bitches trying to rile up Felicity's soul. The cops have no leads on her true identity—no fingerprints, no arrest records, no missing persons reports. It's as if she sprang full-blown out of nowhere.

The last thing Tringali says before we end the call is, "I loved your movies when I was a girl."

I pour myself the third Brazilian Bob-o-Link of the morning and wait for Lovely Diamond to call. Fifteen minutes later, someone comes over to my table and drops a heavy box on it, startling me. I look up to see Joyce Paulsen, Philip's wife.

I stand and say, "How are you doing, Joyce?"

"Hanging in there, thank you for asking." It's a rote, meaningless answer to a rote, meaningless question.

"Did you talk to the police? They think they've . . . they *have* captured the woman who killed Philip."

"They said she attacked you and Lovely Diamond. Are you all right?"

"We're fine."

"It's so horrible, what happened to my Philip. You know, he used to chat with those people when he came to see you, the ones who dressed up like characters from your client's video game. He mentioned the one who . . . he said she dressed up like Felicity McGrath, insisted that everyone call her Felicity. Said she was a pretty girl, but so very troubled. I think that's why she was able to get so close to him the day he . . . The police said it could've been someone he knew. Anyway, he felt sorry for her. I do, too."

"I don't."

Joyce frowns, as if I've dishonored Philip's memory.

I ask her to sit, offer to buy her some coffee and a pastry, but she says, "I can't stay. When the police came by a few months ago looking for evidence, I showed them Philip's case files, but they said something about attorney and client confidentiality, that you have the right to review them. But I was so . . . it just slipped my mind. When they came back today, they asked again. I still hadn't passed the files on to you, so I just boxed everything up and here I am."

"Thanks. It's good to know that the cops are honoring the attorney-client privilege."

"Well, you take care, Parker." She raises an index finger. "There's something else." She reaches into her pocketbook and hands me a USB flash drive. "Philip was so good with technology, and I'm . . . what did he call me, a Luddite? I had my young neighbor copy all his e-mails about the case on this . . . gizmo. He didn't read them, though, I made sure of that, just made copies. The police said once you finish reviewing the documents for the confidential things, call Detective Tringali and they'll come pick up the nonconfidential documents."

When she leaves I put the box and the flash drive in a cabinet in the storeroom. The Poniard case is over, or it should be.

I glance around the room, trying to find a way to kill time. As a kind of homage, I decide to watch one of Felicity's movies—not her hit *Fragile Palace*, but her ultimate Hollywood defeat, the wonderful disaster *Meadows of Deceit*, where she plays the aristocratic young Englishwoman who runs off to rural Scotland, becomes a village schoolteacher, and falls in love with the Scottish farmer, played by Sam Turner, the father of Felicity's daughter.

When Turner first comes on screen, I hit the pause button, rewind ten seconds, and play the scene again. Why didn't I see it earlier? "Scotty" has to be *Sam Turner*. Felicity nicknamed him based on the character he played in *Meadows of Deceit*.

I power on my laptop and find the first letter from McGrath to Scotty, undated but written sometime before May 12, 1987, the date of Turner's reply. Turner had obviously warned her not to trust Bishop. In her letter, McGrath disagrees, telling Turner that what she's working on is "just make-believe" and that Bishop is her insurance policy, her "ticket out of purgatory." In other words, Bishop would help her get her career back by working with her on the film and could provide insurance against anyone who was after her. The Sanctified Assembly? Howard Bishop's criminal organization?

Turner isn't buying it, and he says so in his letter of May 12, 1987. He tells her she's treading over old ground, dangerous ground. "This isn't some phase," he continues. "He's one of them, which means he's dangerous." Bishop was one of what? The Sanctified Assembly? The LA mob?

And then, as Turner predicted, things went bad. So Felicity wrote Turner that she was sending him and the child to France. "You're going to take that trip to Paris you've always dreamed about. The tickets have been reserved in your name. The flight leaves in three days." A trip to Europe on three days' notice wasn't a vacation; it was an escape.

Sam Turner was Alicia's father, but he sure doesn't sound like Felicity's lover. Turner died of AIDS in 2005. In a fit of blatant stereotyping, I launch Google and search "Sam Turner actor gay" and discover that he was one of the first uncloseted gay men in Hollywood, coming out at the expense of his career. He moved to France in the late 1980s, just like McGrath asked him to do, and stayed there until his death. So what? A gay man could have fathered McGrath's daughter.

We missed this information about Turner because Philip Paulsen was murdered. He was investigating Sam and Alicia Turner, and that part of the case got lost after he died and the trial date came upon us so quickly.

I hit the rewind button, but before the tape is out of the cassette, my cell phone rings.

"It's me," Lovely says. "It's all arranged. Four o'clock."

CHAPTER 48

William Bishop lives in the Sunset Hills above the Chateau Marmont, the hotel favored by actors and rock stars, and most famous as the location of actor John Belushi's fatal overdose on a heroin-cocaine speedball. In the late seventies, there was a nice concierge named Janelle who looked after me when my mother was partying with the celebs.

I wend my way up an impossibly narrow private road, clear security, pull into a large masonry driveway, and park near the front door. Bishop lives in a Bauhaus-style resort house with a view that spans from downtown to the ocean. He also owns a house in Brittany, a brownstone in New York, and a farm in Australia. When this is over, he'll probably have another home—state prison.

A butler of sorts or maybe a bodyguard—the man somehow looks both refined and urban tough—leads me through a living room and into a study. Many would-be movie moguls cover the walls of their rooms with posters and awards, but not Bishop. I do recognize an Edward Hopper painting and a huge Jeff Koons rendering of a family with puppies. Lovely is sitting on an antique French Louis XIII Aubusson-upholstered sofa that, according to media reports, cost Bishop $150,000. The serene landscape is embroidered needlepoint—flat-weave tapestry, they call it. I learned all of this from Brenda's research. I hope she shows up at The Barrista tomorrow so I can fill her in on what's happening—the parts I can share.

"No Frantz, right?" I say.

"You said you didn't want him here."

"It wouldn't be the first time you've surprised me. And you haven't told Bishop about the tape?"

She's about to snap back at me when Bishop enters the room. He's dressed in white slacks and an open-collared plaid sports shirt. It's the first time I've seen him without a coat and tie, and now I notice that, though his suntan looks good from the neck up, his chest is leathery and wrinkled, freckled with liver spots and warts, as if the years of sun damage skipped his face and coalesced in this one spot.

"What's this about, Stern?" he asks. I thought he'd look defeated, but he seems resolute, his eyes hawk-like. Neither of us sits down. He uses his height to great advantage. I take a couple of steps back so I'm looking across from, not up at, him.

"We're going to watch a movie together," I say. "I'm sure you still own a VCR."

"I don't have time for your games," he says.

"The movie's called *Satan's Boatman*." I hold up the videotape.

His cheeks blanch, and he falls into the sofa.

"I've made digital copies of the key scene and saved them to various places in the Cloud," I continue. "So don't think about using strong-arm tactics."

"William wouldn't do something like that," Lovely says. "He's—"

"Your client already sent people after me," I say. "They followed Brenda and me to the Macklin & Cherry file room."

"Is it true, William?" she asks.

"They had orders not to hurt anyone," he says. "They just wanted what belonged to me."

"Orders?" I say. "Tell that to Roland the security guard. He was hit with a Taser and choked." I hold up the tape again. "Showtime, Bishop. After we watch it, I'm going to call the cops."

"Why haven't you done that already?" he says.

"I'm doing your lawyer a favor. Call it . . . professional courtesy. Now, where's the videotape player?"

His skin takes on a corpse-like pallor. He begins shaking his head slowly.

"You killed Hildy Gish," I say. "And then you kidnapped and killed McGrath because she was going to tell the cops."

He just keeps shaking his head.

"I'm done," I say.

Lovely grabs his sleeve. "William, please."

He takes a shallow breath, more like a gulp. "OK. OK." Another gulp. "Someone infiltrated the movie and substituted lethal drugs for the saline solution in the needle."

"How convenient," I say. "But I'll play along. If it wasn't you, there are only two possibilities. The first is your father's associates."

"My father's *associates*, as you call them, stopped caring about *The Boatman* as soon as I paid them their investment back with double the interest. And after my father died, I didn't have to keep the movie hidden to satisfy him. But I kept the threat alive because I'd changed my life and had a reputation to protect. Even so, in eighty-seven I was willing to jeopardize that reputation so Paula could make her picture. So no, my father's clients had nothing to do with Hildy's death."

Though I don't find his story plausible, McGrath did make him look better the second time around, as if she was trying to protect his reputation.

"So that leaves the newly organized Church of the Sanctified Assembly," I say. "Kelly got wind of the reshoot and sabotaged the production so his new church wouldn't have been strangled in its crib."

"Kelly wasn't involved," Bishop says.

"Why are you so sure? Because you're a devoted follower of the Assembly?"

"I was never a follower. Neither was Paula. Brad Kelly was a clown. Who ever thought he'd become a deity?"

"*The Boatman* was a propaganda piece for everything Kelly preached," I say.

He laughs harshly. "You understand nothing, Stern—as smart as you think you are."

"Oh, he's proved that he's pretty smart," Lovely says in a voice so soft that it magnifies her disgust with Bishop.

Bishop's glance of irritation is parried by Lovely's sarcastic fake smile. He takes a weary breath and says, "Paula wasn't using Kelly's ideas. *He* was using *hers*. She wanted to make a movie about a Utopian prophet. That's what *The Boatman* was originally. She thought the concept up all by herself. At the time, Kelly's so-called religious thoughts were all confused. Oh, he had these nonsensical ideas about a celestial fountain and a parallel universe—sounded like a goddamned schizophrenic if you ask me—but after *The Boatman*, he created a coherent story. He changed it around, used it for his own purposes, but he plagiarized Paula's art to do it. It pissed her off, too. So in the reshoot she decided to make him look like the asshole he was. But mostly she changed the plot for the art, decided that the original was unrealistic, that she'd been too young and naive in seventy-nine to understand the world's unfairness. Paula was about her art, not about some cult that Bradley Kelly invented." He pauses. "You're the one obsessed with the Sanctified Assembly, Stern."

I don't enjoy admitting it, but he makes sense. Kelly was a face man with crazy ideas, a persuasive speaker, but not an intellectual. He always needed someone smarter to help him. That's why he took up with my mother.

"Then who tampered with that needle?" I ask.

"It must've been someone working with Paula. But you have to understand that I wasn't around for most of it. Paula wanted it that way. I scouted the location—that's what Frederickson was talking about at trial—and was there for only a couple of days of reshooting with Hildy. Most of my scenes were recut from rough footage Paula and I kept, even though my father had forbidden it. Paula reshot the picture on a shoestring budget, with people coming in and out for small jobs. She even operated the camera. I offered to finance it all, but she didn't want that, not after what happened in seventy-nine with *The Boatman* being shut down because of me. She used all her own savings for *Satan's Boatman*, spent so much that she could hardly pay her rent. And still, she wouldn't take a nickel from me. When Hildy . . . after the thing happened, I asked Paula to tell me who had access to the props and the saline, but she was trusting, protective of everyone she worked with. She insisted no one would betray her like that and was afraid I'd hurt an innocent person if she named names. She was right, I would've hurt someone. And she thought . . ." He hangs his head.

"Tell it," I say.

"Paula believed Hildy or I put the real thing in the syringe. I was the one . . . in the seventies, I admired Warhol, how his actors would actually have sex or take drugs on screen, and yet it all worked within the plot. I was a foolish child, and my father, God love him, knew that. So did Paula. She never went along with that craziness. By nineteen eighty-seven I'd outgrown it. But Paula was never quite certain of that." He shrugs helplessly. "I didn't know what was in the syringe."

"The girl was dying," Lovely says. "Why didn't you call 911?"

"It was too late, Hildy was already dead. And as for the body . . . there was no proof that we weren't really using heroin. Paula wanted to call the cops, but I would've lost my career, my family, my reputation. So I asked her not to. Paula and I, we . . . we loved each other, but we could never. . . . So we moved Hildy to a room upstairs from the bar. Her real name was Hilda Marie Johnson. That's what her driver's license said. She had drug problems in the past, no family, she wasn't a big star, so we let . . . the cops just thought she was a junkie who'd OD'd." His perfect shoulders slump. As if in purely mechanical response, Lovely exhales, the sound so loud that it might be taken for a sob.

"Your fairy tale left something out," I say. "What happened to McGrath?"

He stares at me for a long time and then relents, a physical surrender. "I . . ." He squints his eyes hard. "Do you know her movie *Meadows of Deceit*?"

"Of course."

He gives me a hard look. "She loved that picture, was obsessed by the way it ended."

It takes me some time to process what he's saying, and when I do, I shake my head. "I don't believe you."

"It's true," he says.

"I don't understand," Lovely says.

"He's saying that McGrath is alive," I say. "That it was all a ruse. Just like the dead pilot in *Meadows of Deceit* was alive at the end."

"That's absurd," Lovely says.

"The whole scene at the beach was staged," Bishop says, his voice barely above a whisper. "A phony kidnapping produced by Hollywood's top filmmaker William Bishop and directed by the brilliant Paula McGrath. Her wild behavior in the Tell Tale Bar, the goons, the blood on the pier—McGrath's actual blood, voluntarily donated—the lost shoes and jewelry, all scripted so she could disappear forever. After Hildy died, Paula wasn't about to live her life as if nothing happened. I could, but not Paula. She was braver than me. She wanted to escape this Hollywood life, to become someone else. She no longer wanted to be an actress, didn't want to be a writer or director, didn't . . . didn't want to be a mother. She said she was unfit, never wanted to have the kid in the first place. She was despondent, and I . . ." He shrugs helplessly.

Lovely's gray eyes emit a serrate glare. "What the fuck, William, did you force that poor girl to have the baby and then to abandon it two years later?"

"Paula wasn't someone you could force into anything."

Lovely shakes her head in disbelief and then stands and walks to the other side of the room, as far away from Bishop as she can get without leaving.

"The 'Scotty' in those letters," I say. "Sam Turner?"

"Yeah, Paula called him Scotty," he says.

"Are you the girl's father?" I ask. "Because I don't think Sam Turner was."

Any residual bravado leaks out of him like air from a punctured tire. He fully deflates, becoming old and frail in an instant.

"You never saw her, never even looked for her after Turner died, did you, Bishop?" I say. "What was it? If you pretended Alicia didn't exist, she wouldn't? Is that how it works for you?"

"I always made sure Sam Turner had plenty of—"

"Don't justify your behavior by telling me you provided for her financially," I say. "I don't understand people like you."

"I do," Lovely says softly.

There's a difference—when her son Brighton was born, she was twenty years old, trapped in a sordid lifestyle. When Bishop's daughter was born, he was twice Lovely's age and on his way to becoming a billionaire. But I leave it alone.

"Did you know that Lovely and I were attacked last night?" I ask.

"One of those crazy followers of your client," he says. "Killed the Kreisses and your paralegal—crimes you and your client falsely accused me of committing."

"She says her name's Courtney," I say. "Claims to be Felicity's daughter. There is a resemblance. And Courtney's the daughter's middle name."

He shrugs helplessly. "I can't believe she'd... Your client. He claims to know where she is."

"Poniard won't tell me."

Bishop nods sadly.

"If this fable were true, why wouldn't you just have asked McGrath to come forward?" I ask. "She could've cleared matters up in an hour."

"She would've come back if she really knew what was going on," he says. "She's a recluse, too fragile, too sheltered from the outside world. Being back in the spotlight, hounded by the tabloids, picked apart by the online vultures would kill her. I wouldn't do that to Paula to save my own skin. I did it before, but not again. You must understand what I'm saying now that the world knows you were Parky Gerald."

I'm not about to let Bishop make this about me. "One last question," I say. "Given what you just told me, what possessed you to bring a lawsuit and expose yourself to all this public scrutiny?"

"How could I not? What would I have told my wife, the board of directors, the shareholders?" He glances at Lovely across the room. "Lou Frantz told me it was a slam-dunk winner."

"That's what he said when he thought you were an honest man," she says.

We're all spent, quiet for a long time. Finally, I say, "Here's what you're going to do, Mr. Bishop. You're going to dismiss the lawsuit against Poniard right away. And you're going to..." My eyes fall on the *Satan's Boatman* cassette on the end table. For some reason, the movie's bizarre opening scene projects on my brain. And then I see it.

"I need to use your VCR," I say. "I know you have one."

"Stern, I told you I didn't want to see that—"

"No. I only want to watch the beginning. I need to ask you something about it."

CHAPTER 49

Nate Ettinger rocks back in his office chair and puffs on his unlit pipe. "I'm glad I could play a small role in finally exposing Bishop for the criminal he is. Of course, it was Clifton Stanley Gold who was the brave one." He leans forward and clasps his hands loosely. "You've freed me, Parker—you and Brenda. I'm so grateful that she convinced you to let me testify. For the first time in years, I no longer feel cowardly. And Bishop can't harm me anymore." He frowns. "He can't, can he?"

"No chance," I say.

He sits back again, relieved. "You said on the phone there were a few loose ends I could help you with."

"Something in your book on eighties Hollywood," I say, picking up the copy I brought and turning to the section on Felicity McGrath. "I was just wondering how you knew that Felicity McGrath was born in Springfield, Illinois."

"I can't remember specifically, but I did a lot of research, so it must have been out there somewhere.

"Actually, my staff and I couldn't find anything like that."

"I'm an academic. Research is my job."

"Well, I'm an attorney and research is my weapon. I wouldn't have missed information like that."

"What's this about, Stern?"

"It's about the fact McGrath made up a fictional city of her birth for the opening scene in *Satan's Boatman*."

"Why would she do that?"

"Who knows why a writer does anything? Maybe she didn't think coming from North Hollywood was exciting enough. The only way you could've believed she was from Springfield, Illinois, was if you saw the movie. Or worked on it with her."

"This is some sick practical joke, right? In honor of the unlikely reunion of Parky Gerald and Nate Ettinger after all these years?"

"Not only were you on the set of *Satan's Boatman*, you were the one who substituted heroin and cocaine for saline in the syringe that killed Hildy Gish. You just thought that it would be William Bishop who died. He was the one who was supposed to take the first needle. But he and Gish ad-libbed at the last moment and the drugs went into Gish's arm."

"You're insane, Stern."

"About the needle being meant for Bishop? I watched the scene. He was going to inject himself. And Bishop told me that they improvised at the last minute. Or, if you mean, where did I learn that McGrath was only *pretending* to be from Illinois, I finally remembered that Clifton Stanley Gold told me McGrath started with him when she was a thirteen-year-old still in middle school. Turns out that McGrath was a Valley girl. The story about being a runaway was McGrath's embellishment—she was a wild, restless teenager, threatened to run away, but Gold made her stay home in exchange for acting lessons. But there was nothing about Springfield, Illinois, until *Satan's Boatman*. You didn't do your homework, Professor."

"Get out of here, Stern, or I'll call security."

"I wouldn't do that, E."

"What did you call me?"

"*E.* That's what Paula McGrath always called you, right? I got that from Bishop, too. She started calling you that way back in seventy-nine, on the set of *The Boatman*. And you know what? She calls you that in the *Satan's Boatman* video, says, 'Cut and print, E.' You operated the camera for that scene, didn't you?"

The muscles in his forehead knit together to form an ominous glower. He isn't a benign college professor anymore.

"And then there's Luther Frederickson," I say. "Bishop and I have gotten to be very close. You know, *the enemy of the enemy is my friend,* and all that? He admitted to me that he paid off Boardwalk Freddy to disappear. Helped him through rehab and everything. It turns out that Frederickson wasn't just a panhandler and a transient, he was a businessman. It seems our lapsed accountant was supplying drugs to half the junkies on the beach. And he says that he sold you the heroin and cocaine not long before Hildy Gish died. Of course, he thought you wanted it for recreational purposes, had no idea until now that Gish even OD'd."

"I told you, Stern, you're crazy. Why ever would I do something so horrible?"

"You know, it's not something that I like to acknowledge, but by genetics and upbringing I'm a bit of a conspiracy theorist. So when something goes bad, I think big—Mafia, Sanctified Assembly. I fight against the tendency, but . . . in my defense, there were a lot of things in this case that confirmed my biases. But as my mentor Harmon Cherry used to say, evil is most often mundane, personal—and so trivial. You worked on the original version of *The Boatman* and thought you deserved way more credit than Bishop gave you. Then, a couple of years later, Bishop took over the production company you were with, discontinued development of all your projects, and fired you. He never liked you, thought you were a no-talent fake, that as a producer you had no taste. He took away your chance at succeeding in Hollywood. And here you are, stuck teaching as an untenured professor at a small-time college. That's motive."

Ettinger presses his lips together.

"Then McGrath contacted you in 1987 about reshooting *The Boatman*. You thought it was going to be your opportunity for glory. Or maybe you just saw it as the chance for payback. So you read the scene where Bishop and Gish were both going to pretend to shoot heroin—Bishop was going to go first—and you spiked the vial with real drugs. But the actors changed the scene and Gish died. After that happened, I'm sure you really were afraid that Bishop would find out what you did and come after you. Then you conveniently showed up at the trial and volunteered to testify against him because you could make sure he was implicated once and for all in Felicity's disappearance. You could finally help ruin him forever."

There's a clatter under Ettinger's desk, and when he raises his hands above the ledge he's holding a gun. I didn't see that coming, though I should have—he's been afraid for years that William Bishop's men would come after him, undoubtedly more so because of the lawsuit against Poniard.

What I feel is not fear but an odd sense of bewilderment. I'm an attorney, dedicated to resolving disputes in a nonviolent way, and yet this is the second time this week that someone has pointed a gun at me.

"Don't be ridiculous, Nate," I say. "You're not going to shoot me in a crowded office building."

"Stand up," he says.

I stand. He clumsily takes off his sport coat, drapes it over his arm, and uses it to conceal the gun. Unlike Courtney, he can't keep his hand steady, and I realize that his jitters are just as dangerous as her psycho-pathic calm.

"Outside," he says.

I open the door and step into the corridor. He follows, and as soon as he's out the door, two uniformed cops grab him and wrestle him to the ground. Standing over them with her service revolver drawn is Detective of Homicide Angela Tringali. At the moment, she no longer looks like a real estate broker.

"Damn it, Stern, this isn't what I had in mind when I agreed to let you do this," she says.

"It worked, didn't it?"

Yesterday, I met with Tringali in person, telling her that I had information relating to the McGrath disappearance, could help her solve a homicide—but not McGrath's. When she pressed for details, I refused to reveal them unless she let me spend some time alone with the unnamed killer to try to elicit something incriminating. Ettinger's mistake about Springfield, Illinois, and even Frederickson's statement about selling the drugs, isn't strong proof of guilt. She demanded that I tell her what was going on, but I wouldn't unless she agreed to my demands. After shouting at me for five minutes and threatening me for two, she relented, but only if I wore a recording device like I did in that silly movie where I portrayed an eleven-year-old undercover agent. An hour later, I played her the *Satan's Boatman* video clip depicting Gish's death and explained why I believed Ettinger was responsible.

Now, she shakes her head. "You didn't get him to say anything useful and he could've—"

"Here's my free legal opinion, Detective. The fact that he pulled a gun and tried to move me to another location is admissible evidence of guilt. I just made your case miles easier."

"I had nothing to do with that," Ettinger shouts and then realizes even saying that is too much.

The cops read him his rights and lead him out in handcuffs. I lean against the wall to keep from falling until everyone has left. Then I let the enormity of what happened wash over me. On wobbly legs, I make my way down the hall to the men's room, where I hide in a stall and vomit. When it comes right down to it, having a revolver pointed at you is far more debilitating than a case of courtroom stage fright.

CHAPTER 50

Brighton keeps trying to launch *Abduction!* in the hope that Poniard will bring Felicity back for a sad farewell. It's silly, but he needs to say good-bye. The only image on the screen is William the Conqueror in prison stripes, even though the HF Queen says that Bishop isn't really going to jail. Brighton thinks Bishop is a bad man, but the HF Queen says that he's just weak, that all that money and power meant zero.

And then, on the day after that college professor is arrested, he clicks on the link and Felicity appears. Not Sexy Felicity, not Weepy Felicity, but Warrior Felicity in jeans, a leather jacket, and a baseball cap. Brighton laughs joyfully at the sight of her. She's holding a compact high-tech movie camera in one hand and a long sword in the other. A bowed stringed instrument—a cello or a bass maybe—and a thunderous kettledrum play creepy war-movie music in the background.

Her eyes pulse three animated spears of lights. "*Abduction!* is over," she says. "But not the quest. That'll never be over until you find out what happened to me. And you *will* have the chance." She stabs the sword hard into the ground, raises the camera, and points it at the viewer. "I'll be waiting for you."

The screen goes black. A white death's skull momentarily flashes on the screen and then explodes into words:

BETRAYAL!
The Sequel to Abduction!
A Game by Poniard
Watch for It

CHAPTER 51

Once the cops arrest Nate Ettinger, *Satan's Boatman* quickly becomes public. Bishop preemptively dismisses his lawsuit against Poniard, resigns from his position at Parapet Media, and acknowledges that he moved Hildy Gish's body to cover up his involvement in her death. His PR people issue a contrite press release, apologizing for his lack of judgment. He promises to devote the rest of his life to philanthropic causes. To deflect attention from the truth about McGrath's disappearance, he accuses Ettinger of abducting her. Fine with me.

The public pronouncement only increases the scorn and ridicule directed at him. The Sanctified Assembly predictably condemns the movie as blasphemous fraud and threatens to sue Bishop for defamation and copyright infringement for pirating and perverting the teachings of Bradley Kelly. Long-time enemies and former supporters alike call Bishop a hypocrite, a disgrace. That's also fine with me—William the Conqueror should atone for his sins.

On each of the next two days, Brenda texts me to say that she's still suffering from the flu. It's not until Thursday that she shows up at The Barrista. She makes her way through the crowd of onlookers who're willing to spring for a cup of coffee and a muffin just to get a look at Parky Gerald, or if they're too old or too young to care about that, at the man who vanquished William Bishop and exposed Nate Ettinger. Romulo has stationed a brawny barista at a table near me to keep people away.

Brenda looks like a person who's been ill—unwashed hair pulled back in a slapdash ponytail, no makeup, a long pink T-shirt, tattered blue jeans, and sneakers. I smile and wave, but she walks past my table and into the storeroom. I get up and follow her inside.

"Is everything OK?" I ask. "If you're still not feeling well, you can—"

She wheels on me. "Why is Bishop free?"

"Because he's innocent. Courtney, that crazy cosplayer, murdered Philip Paulsen and the Kreisses. Some bizarre delusion that our winning the lawsuit would disturb Felicity's soul. And Ettinger killed Hildy Gish."

"Why should I believe any of it?"

"Uh, because Courtney's knife matched the stab wounds in Philip and Isla Kreiss and the ballistics test show that the gun killed Bud Kreiss?"

"So say the cops. You know how far you can trust them. They're in Bishop's pocket."

"Jesus, Brenda, that maniac tried to kill Lovely Diamond and me. And Ettinger—"

"Ettinger is taking the fall for Bishop killing Gish. The Conqueror murdered Felicity to cover that up. Felicity would've gone to the police."

"It's not true," I say. "*I* was the one who figured out that Ettinger committed the murder, not the cops."

She shakes her head incredulously. "Bishop could make it happen with a wave of his emperor's wand."

"Ettinger pulled a gun on me."

Her silence is not just fraught but downright hostile.

"That still leaves Felicity," she says. "Why does Bishop get to walk on the kidnapping?"

"Because he didn't do it."

"How do you know?"

"Brenda, I . . . I can't tell you that."

Her eyes contort in contending emotions of shock and anger. "After all this time, you don't trust me? After I've given my life to your case?"

"I do trust you . . . I just . . . I can't tell you."

"Why not?"

"There are reasons."

"Did Bishop pay you off, too?"

"Who do you think you're talking to?"

"I don't have any idea. I thought I did." She takes a step back and puts her hands on her hips. For the first time since a trembling Brenda Sica walked into my office last September, I've lost her.

She goes to the table, reaches into her knapsack, and hands me a sheet of legal paper with some writing on it. "While I was out sick I made a list of what we have to do to shut things down. Hopefully we can get it all done today so I don't have to spend an extra minute in this place."

I look into her eyes for any sign of doubt, but they're unwavering. Can I blame her? I've withheld the truth: Bishop's condition for giving me information is that I can't tell anyone, not even Brenda. I take her list and return to my table outside. She's right—the sooner we wrap things up, the better. Her list is thorough—*pay court reporter's invoice, pay videographer's invoice, retrieve demonstrative exhibits from court file, send client "case and representation are terminated" letter, retrieve "Scotty" letters from Marina Community Bank and arrange for return to client, send client final invoice, close client trust account on receipt of payment, file bill of costs for trial within statutory limit, shut down Law Offices of PS website, settle invoice with website host, archive case file.* The last entry says *pay six months' rent to The Barrista and give bonuses to The Barrista staff for all the trouble we caused.*

I set the list down, take a sip of cold coffee, which is OK, because our coffee tastes good no matter what, and pick up the list again. Something's not right. In fact, it's all wrong. I bolt up out of my chair and hurry into the storeroom, where Brenda is sitting in front of her computer, apparently reconciling a bank statement.

"We need to talk," I say.

"What is it?" There's a sandpaper edge to her voice that stops me cold.

Shock leads to clarity, or an illusion of clarity that sometimes results in the perfect course of action. Parker Stern said that, not Harmon Cherry. I open the cabinet and take out the box of documents that Joyce Paulsen brought me last Monday.

"What's that?" Brenda asks.

"Just some crap I have to look through." I take the box to my table and rifle through it, finding copies of pleadings in *Bishop v. Poniard*, LexisNexis printouts, legal research memos—all familiar material. I feel around the box and locate the computer flash drive that Joyce gave me. I insert the drive into my laptop's USB port and double-click on the file, which launches in Outlook as a series of e-mails from Philip Paulsen.

I don't have to scroll down to find what I'm looking for because it's the first message—it was sent the day Philip died. Philip sent the e-mail to himself, a standard practice of his for collecting data. The subject line reads, "*Bishop v. Poniard*—Meeting w/ USC Assoc Dean." That's why he was at Cranky Franks that day—he'd been at USC following up a lead on Alicia Turner.

The e-mail contains an attachment, a copy of a 2004 newsletter touting the university's joint Computer Science/Cinematic Arts program—number one in the nation, according to the headline. Philip must've sweet-talked one of the administrators into letting him search the department's database and scan the document. I don't see anything relevant on the first three pages of the newsletter, but on the fourth page, there's an article on the May 2004 departmental video games competition. When I scroll down the page a bit farther and see the photograph of the winners, my arms start flailing, and I knock my coffee cup over, spilling its contents all over my keyboard. I don't care. As long as the monitor still works.

With coffee-soaked hands, I carefully lift up my laptop and take it into the storeroom. Brenda is typing away at her computer. She doesn't look up.

"Look at me," I say, and not in a gentle voice.

She looks up.

"How did you know Felicity's letters to Scotty were stored at the Community Bank of Marina del Rey."

"I . . . you told me they were. When they came in." What a wonderful actress she is.

"I told only one person in the world."

"Mr. Stern, you definitely told me the letters were at that bank." So sincere, so ingenuous.

I walk over, set my laptop down on table beside her, and point to the screen. "Take a look. This is what Philip Paulsen wanted to show me when he asked me to meet him for lunch the day he was killed."

She turns to the screen and stares at the photograph, and what frightens me most is that she shows absolutely no emotion. Though they were members of the team that won the competition to design the best video game at the best program in the country, only one of the people in the photo is actually smiling. That was the large young man on the left, identified as sophomore Vladimir "The Mad Russian" Lazerev, First Assistant, who at the time didn't cover his unsightly birthmark with a beard. His specialty is listed as "software engineering." He has his arm around the girl in the center, a pretty redhead—Melanie "The Artiste" Oliver, Second Assistant—a freshman and game designer in the Cinema Arts department, but clearly the delusional, murderous cosplayer who goes by the names Courtney and Felicity. And on the right is a small, voluptuous brunette who's the only one of the three looking directly into the camera, as if in challenge. She's curled the corner of her full lips up in a scornful smirk—Alicia "The Dagger" Turner, Team Leader, software engineering, game design, and though ten years younger, unmistakably my assistant, Brenda Sica.

"You called yourself 'The Dagger' then," I say. "And later you refined your nickname to something more obscure, more ominous. I didn't know what a poniard was until you hired me."

She looks at me and shrugs. "I guess this means game over, Parker Stern. You win."

"Nobody wins here. But I will take you to see your mother."

Her smirk becomes frozen in the ether, and her disbelieving eyes study me for a long time.

"It's true," I say.

And only then does this strange woman's mask disappear, melted by tears that reflect the first genuine show of emotion that I've seen from the individual known as Poniard.

CHAPTER 52

North of Santa Monica Beach, the Pacific Coast Highway becomes primitive. Fires, floods, and landslides foil the residents' fruitless attempts to swindle nature. The dwarf mountains rise over the Pacific, the hills blanketed by coast live oak, toyon, sycamore, chamise, California lilac. The ocean, a murky green-blue at the Santa Monica pier, becomes ever more pristine after Topanga Canyon, and by Zuma the sea has turned a deep azure just as the mountains become less habitable.

I roll the windows and inhale the fresh salt air, feel the offshore breeze on my skin. I could've taken the freeway and saved an hour, but something about this route will help cleanse the grime and horror of the past months. And I'll have more time to try to convince Brenda—I can't bring myself to call her by any other name—to explain the unexplainable. She hasn't spoken in the twenty minutes since we left The Barrista.

"You should've told me," I finally say. "It would've made things easier."

She blinks her eyes twice and continues to stare out the window in a kind of catatonic derision. Is she angry with me? You'd think she'd be ecstatic about my legal services. I've accomplished far more than she expected. Is she angry because Courtney—real name Melanie Oliver—is in jail? She should be grateful, because I haven't told the cops who Courtney really is, haven't implicated Banquo. Or maybe she's silent for another reason entirely. Maybe there's nothing for her but the game, and now that her game with me has ended, there's a void. If that's true, maybe it's the key to getting her to communicate.

"When Poniard first contacted me back at JADS and I thought the firm's computers had been hacked," I say. "You were just chatting with me from outside my office, right? Logged in on the firm's system. No hack at all?"

With a slight upturn of the lips but still staring out the window, she says, "I had to alter the firm's system to use the handle 'Poniard' and make sure that our chats weren't logged by JADS's IT Department. But that little tweak only took ten minutes. Easy peasy."

"And all the Poniard chats? What for?"

"You had to believe that there was a client out there."

Something still doesn't make sense. "There were times you were with me when Poniard initiated the chat. How . . . ?"

Now she condescends to share a smug smile. "Vlad *did* hack into the JADS system. Just to see if he could. It didn't take him long. He's good at following a script. It ensured you wouldn't suspect me."

"And you just walked the Scotty letters into Judge Mitchell's office?"

She tips her shoulder and smiles. "My favorite part was my deposition. That technology is the future, something Vlad and Melanie and I have been working on . . ." The smile fades. "I underestimated your girlfriend, though."

She *is* all about the game—so unlike her Brenda character. Trying to know another person is like trying to gauge the taste of food by looking at the packaging. Worse, we use our imagination to invent the packaging. But that's the way it has to be—if we continually questioned who others really are, we'd soon go mad. Still, there's a calculus we make about other humans, an estimate based on the perceived ratio between their personas and their souls. In my estimation, this woman is closer to the snarky, arrogant Poniard of the chat room than to my sweet assistant Brenda.

"I asked you this before, but now you can tell me the truth," I say. "Why me?"

"Oh, my father—Sam—was always ranting about William the Conqueror Bishop and his hypocrisy and his dirty secrets, railing against Bradley Kelly and the Sanctified Assembly. Just as I told you, you'd done well against the Assembly and Frantz. But mostly I had to keep you as my attorney because I was already embedded inside JADS. I worked hard to have hands-on control over my lawyer and I couldn't lose that."

"How did you figure out I was Parky Gerald?"

"The Internet is one big cyber-archive. No one found it before because they didn't look hard enough. Parky Gerald wasn't worth the effort. Though, I have to say I'm surprised at the outpouring. I'd never heard of you."

"You're too young to remember, that's all. But isn't it interesting? You can't blackmail me anymore. My secret is out, but I'm one of the few people in the world who knows that you're the great genius Poniard."

Though I'm watching the road, I feel her body tense. I have the power.

"What are you going to do?" she says, now straining to keep her voice even.

"I'm your lawyer." I let a moment pass, long enough to let the tension subside, but not long enough to lose the conversational momentum. "What made you think Bishop was involved in Felicity's disappearance?"

"After Sam died, I found those letters between him and my mother, where he said not to trust Bishop. That's when I knew."

"But you didn't know, did you?"

"We will see."

I think for a long time about what I'm going to say next. But I'm sick of the pretending. "Brenda . . . Alicia . . . I know Sam Turner raised you, but William Bishop is your biological—"

"Don't you dare!" she says. I glance over at her. Her eyes are venomous—a woman capable of violence.

"My mother told me that my father's identity was none of my goddamned business," I say. "I still don't know who my father is."

"Well, then I envy you, Parker Stern."

Listening to her speak, I finally realize why McGrath's voice sounded so familiar when I watched her movies—Brenda sounds like her mother. And what I took for a mild speech impediment is a barely detectible French accent.

We speed past south-facing Malibu, with its stealthy, lethal riptides.

"Your damned video game," I say. "The stages with the Kreiss killings and the attack on Triggs. Melanic Oliver, or Courtney or whoever she is? Banquo?"

"Vlad would never . . ." She actually sounds indignant.

"Then what's his part in this? Does he really go around dressing up like your characters?"

"He's my right hand. He's good at winning people over, enjoys it. I don't. And it was a perfect way for him to blend in."

"Are you and he . . . ?"

"Of course not. He fell for Courtney the very moment I introduced them at school. He'd do anything for her, thinks he can rescue her . . . thought he could. And he believes in Poniard, would do anything for Poniard and The Cause."

"You know who else referred to himself in the third person? Bradley Kelly."

From the way she forces her upper teeth against her lip, she's about to tell me to fuck off, but instead she takes a deep breath and says, "I fight for a noble cause. Kelly didn't."

"The fight Banquo had with Frantz's process server," I say. "You started it, didn't you?"

"I had to get you out of JADS and focused only on my case. I thought the cosplayers hanging around there would do it, but when that didn't work, we had to take more radical action."

"Why didn't you stop Courtney?"

"I thought . . . I truly thought it was Bishop."

"Really? I think you found out she was hacking *Abduction!*, and when you told her to stop, she got violent. That's how you got that black eye."

"I never thought that she'd harm anyone else. For years, the three of us, we've . . . we've all been playing a game, she became competitive with me, and it got out of control."

I grip the steering wheel and try to squeeze the anger out through my fingers. "Some game. She hacked *Abduction!* to show the Kreiss killing and the attack on Judge Triggs, didn't she? And the last stage, the courtroom melee?"

Petulant silence.

"You knew she was violent, and you did nothing. And because of it Philip is dead, Bud and Isla Kreiss are dead." I slow the car and glance at her. "Or maybe you found out that Philip was on to you and—"

"Goddamn it, don't you lay that shit on me. I still do not know what the truth is. That fucking Bishop could've . . . damn it, Parker, she's my comrade-in-arms!"

"In your made-up war. But it's refreshing to see that you *can* show genuine emotion. By the way, nice touch to have Brenda act like a prude. I see that Alicia Turner isn't so constrained."

There's a sudden change in her demeanor, a wide-eyed, timid look—the Brenda I knew. She reaches out and squeezes my arm. "I want you to represent Courtney. She needs your help. You know I can afford—"

"Even if I wanted to, which I do not, I couldn't. I'm a witness in Philip's death and a victim of her assault."

"I just thought. . . . You're the best. I want to protect my friend."

Or maybe it's the opposite. Hiring me would ensure that Melanie Oliver would fry. Is that her goal? "She wanted to be you—to be Felicity McGrath's daughter, to be as great as Poniard. She even changed her name to take on your middle name, to be you, and you went along with it—you even still call her Courtney."

Another floppy shoulder shrug, like a teenager being asked to admit she broke curfew. "She wanted to be called Courtney. So what? People have the right to choose whatever character they want to be."

"Is everything a game with you?"

"Life is a game."

"Real life only starts when you realize it's *not* a game."

And with that, we've exhausted all words. I'm not sure that Alicia Turner, aka Poniard, has anything to say when she's not dissembling or pontificating. Fortunately, Mumford & Sons and Arcade Fire stave off the painful silence for the rest of the drive.

A little after one in the afternoon, we reach a hidden beach about forty-five minutes north of Santa Barbara. I pull off Highway 101 somewhere near Gaviota and go west until I find an unmarked private road, pitted with potholes and barely wide enough for one car to pass. The road dead ends at the beach, and I turn right onto a gravel path so narrow that if I were to veer even six inches one way or another, I'd become stuck in the sand. We stop at a locked gate with a camera mounted on top. We wait for some minutes for security to let us pass. When the gate finally opens, I drive to an isolated light-blue Cape Cod–style home, title to which is held by an offshore corporation owned by William Bishop.

Brenda gets out of the car without saying good-bye. As she walks toward the house, it's as if she's stepped into a movie screen, because she's greeted by a person who I once thought existed only on film: Paula Felicity McGrath—in her mid-fifties now, no longer a beautiful starlet, but McGrath nonetheless. The women awkwardly embrace. When they drop their arms and turn toward the house, it's as if the director has called for a long master shot, with the two figures both visible in full frame until they walk through the front door and disappear.

I circle the driveway and head back to Highway 101. Los Angeles and home lie to the south. If I were to turn north up the coast, I could disappear forever, escaping Parky Gerald and a legal career that sends me into spasms of terror whenever I go to court. I've obliterated my past before, and I could do it again in those lush coastal towns with the strange names—Pismo, Cambria, Paso Robles, Big Sur, Carmel, Mendocino, Bodega, Coos Bay, Neskowin, Willapa, Vancouver. Unfamiliar places where, like Poniard, I could walk the streets anonymous and free.

My cell phone has coverage again. Someone left a voice-mail message. I reach Highway 101 and, while stopped at the busy intersection, press *play* on my iPhone.

"Hey, Parker, it's Lovely. I was just wondering. . . . So, it seems that my son Brighton has this stupid school project where he has to interview someone who works in his future profession, and the kid says he wants to be a lawyer. I thought he was smarter than that, but. . . . Anyway, it can't be a parent, and I suggested Lou or some others at the firm, but the kid insists on you, so. . . . Maybe you could call me and the three of us could get together? If you have the time. OK, bye."

When an impatient driver behind me honks his horn, I hit the accelerator hard and turn onto the highway.

ACKNOWLEDGMENTS

Thank you: Matthew Sharpe, Les Edgerton, Robert Wolff, Lisa Doctor, Karen Karl, Suzanne Ely, Terry Hoffman, Leigh Luveen, Terri Cheney, and Natalie Karl; Jill Marr, Sandra Dijkstra, and Elise Capron of The Sandra Dijkstra Agency; Dan Mayer, Jill Maxick, Meghan Quinn, Melissa Raé Shofner, Jade Zora Scibilia, and Julia DeGraf of Seventh Street Books; and my family.

ABOUT THE AUTHOR

Robert Rotstein grew up in Culver City, California, then the location of the famed MGM Studios and so the true "Hollywood." (To this day, the city's motto is "The Heart of Screenland.") Robert's elementary school was caddy-corner to one of the studio's back lots. At an early age, he became hooked on legal dramas—not only *Perry Mason*, the archetype of the legal mystery, but also the politically charged *The Defenders* and lesser-known shows like *Judd for the Defense*, *The Young Lawyers*, and *The Trials of O'Brien*, which depicted lawyers solving crimes and doing justice. Perhaps this early combination of life in an entertainment-company town and fascination with the lawyer-as-hero made it inevitable that Robert would one day become an attorney whose practice focuses on the entertainment industry, and later a writer of legal thrillers.

He earned an undergraduate degree from UCLA and graduated with honors from the UCLA School of Law, where he was an editor of the law review. After graduation, he was a law clerk to the Honorable Anthony M. Kennedy, then Circuit Judge for the United States Court of Appeals for the Ninth Circuit and currently Associate Justice of the United States Supreme Court.

Robert then went into private practice with a Beverly Hills law firm that focused on the entertainment industry and copyright law. His first trial involved a copyright infringement lawsuit brought by a well-known science fiction writer against a major movie studio. Over the course of his career, Robert has handled lawsuits on behalf of Michael Jackson, Quincy Jones, Lionel Ritchie, John Sayles, Kenny "Babyface" Edmonds, James Cameron, and all the major motion-picture studios, among others. He authored a law review article that explores the relationship between literary theory and copyright law, and has taught as an adjunct professor at Loyola Law School, in Los Angeles, California. Robert is currently a partner in a major Los Angeles law firm, where he cochairs the firm's intellectual property department.

His first Parker Stern novel is *Corrupt Practices* (Seventh Street Books, 2013). He currently lives in Los Angeles with his family, where he's at work on the third Parker Stern novel.